THE
WITNESS

SANDRA
BROWN

HODDER

First published in the United States of America in 2001
by Warner Books

First published in Great Britain in 2008 by Hodder & Stoughton
An Hachette UK company

This paperback edition published in 2018

1

A CIP catalogue record for this title is available from the British Library

Paperback ISBN 978 0 340 96180 3

Typeset in Baskerville MT

Printed and bound in Great Britain by Clays Ltd, St Ives plc

Hodder & Stoughton policy is to use papers that are natural,
renewable and recyclable products and made from wood grown in sustainable
forests. The logging and manufacturing processes are expected to conform
to the environmental regulations of the country of origin.

Hodder & Stoughton Ltd
Carmelite House
50 Victoria Embankment
London EC4Y 0DZ

www.hodder.co.uk

Take me not off with the wicked,
with those who are workers of evil,
who speak peace with their neighbors,
while mischief is in their hearts.

PSALM 28:3

THE
WITNESS

Prologue

*T*HE INFANT'S MOUTH SUCKED AT HIS MOTHER'S breast.

"He seems like a real happy baby," the nurse observed. "Somehow you can just tell whether or not a baby's contented. I'd say that one is."

Kendall managed only a weak smile. She could barely form a coherent thought, much less engage in conversation. Her mind was still trying to absorb the fact that she and her child had survived the accident.

In the examination room of the hospital's emergency wing, a sheer yellow curtain provided patients with a minimum of privacy from the corridor. Next to the white metal cabinets that stored bandages, syringes, and splints was a stainless steel sink. Kendall sat on a padded table in the center of the cubicle cradling her baby son in her arms.

"How old is he?" the nurse asked.

"Three months."

"Only three months? He's a big one!"

"He's very healthy."

"What'd you say his name is?"

"Kevin."

The nurse smiled down at them, then shook her head in wonder and awe. "It's a miracle that you two walked away from that wreck. Must've been awful for you, honey. Weren't you scared half out of your wits?"

The accident had happened too quickly for fear to register. The car was practically on top of the felled tree before it became visible through the downpour. The passenger in the front seat had shouted a warning, and the driver had sharply cut the steering wheel and stomped on the brake, but it had been too late.

Once the tires lost traction on the wet pavement, the car went into a 180-degree spin that propelled it off the road and across the soft, narrow shoulder. It leveled the inadequate barricade. From there, it was a matter of physics and gravity.

Kendall recalled the sounds as the car plunged down the heavily vegetated ravine. Tree limbs scraped off paint, peeled away the rubber nick guards, and knocked off hubcaps. Windows shattered. The car's chassis was brutalized by boulders and tree stumps. Oddly, no one inside the car uttered a sound. She supposed resignation had rendered them silent.

Although she'd anticipated the inevitable final crash, the impact of the car hitting the massive pine tree that blocked its path was incredible.

Inertia forced the rear wheels off the ground. When the car crashed down again, it landed with the graceless, solid thud of a mortally wounded buffalo, then seemed to emit a wheezing death rattle.

In the backseat, strapped in by seat belt and shoulder harness, Kendall had survived. And even though the car was precariously perched on the steep slope, she had managed to get out of the wreckage with Kevin in her arms.

"That's rugged country out there," the nurse observed. "How in the world did you climb out of that ravine?"

It hadn't been easy.

She'd known that the climb back up to the road would

be difficult, but she'd underestimated the physical effort it required. Protecting Kevin in the process had made it doubly tough.

The terrain wasn't sympathetic; the weather was downright hostile. The ground was a mush of humus and mud. Covering it was a tangled blanket of undergrowth interspersed with jutting rocks. The wind-driven rain was falling almost horizontally, and in minutes she was soaked to the skin.

The muscles of her arms, legs, and back began to burn with fatigue and strain before she had covered a third of the distance. Her exposed skin had been gouged, scraped, cut, bruised, and lashed. At several points she had thought it was futile and longed to surrender, to stop and sleep until the elements claimed their lives.

But her survival instinct was stronger than that lulling temptation, so she kept going. Using vines and boulders for handgrips and footholds, she had pulled herself up until she finally reached the road, where she began walking to seek help.

She had been on the verge of delirium when a pair of headlights appeared through the rain. Relief and exhaustion overcame her. Rather than run toward the car, she had collapsed to her knees on the center stripe of the narrow country road, waiting for the car to reach her.

Her rescuer was a garrulous woman on her way to a Wednesday night prayer meeting. She drove Kendall to the nearest house and notified the authorities of the accident. It amazed Kendall to learn later that she had walked only a mile from the site of the accident. It had seemed like ten.

She and Kevin had been transported by ambulance to the nearest community hospital, where they were given thorough examinations. Kevin was uninjured. He had been nursing when the car plunged over the cliff. Acting on instinct, Kendall had clutched him to her breast and bent forward before the shoulder harness caught and held. Her body had protected him.

Her numerous cuts and scrapes were painful but superficial. Splinters of glass had been picked out of her arms individually, an uncomfortable and time-consuming process but insignificant when compared to what she might have suffered. Her wounds were treated with a local antiseptic; she had declined a painkiller because she was breast-feeding.

Besides, now that they had been rescued and medically treated, she had to figure out how to sneak away. Sedated, she would be unable to think straight. In order to plan another disappearance, she needed a clear head.

"Is it okay if the deputy sheriff comes in now?"

"Sheriff?" Kendall repeated. The nurse's question had jarred her from her musings.

"He's been waiting to talk to you ever since they brought you in. He's got to go over the official stuff with you."

"Oh. Of course. Ask him to come in."

Having nursed his fill, Kevin was now sleeping peacefully. Kendall pulled together the hospital tunic that she had been given after stripping off her wet, dirty, bloody clothes and taking a hot shower.

At a signal from the nurse, the local lawman stepped through the curtain and nodded in greeting. "How're you doin', ma'am? Y'all okay?" He politely removed his hat and looked at her with concern.

"We're fine, I think." She cleared her throat and tried for more conviction. "We're fine."

"I'd say y'all're real lucky to be alive and all in one piece, ma'am."

"I agree."

"Easy to see how it happened, what with that felled tree lying across the road and all. Lightning got it. Broke it clean off at ground level. Been storming 'round here for days. Seems like the rain ain't never gonna quit. Floodin' all over the region. Ain't no wonder to me that Bingham Creek sucked your car clean out of sight."

The creek had been no more than ten yards in front of the battered car. Once she had climbed out of the wreckage, she had crouched in the mud and stared at the creek with fascination and fear. The muddy water had crested far above flood level, carrying with it all manner of debris. It roiled around trees that lined its normally placid banks.

She shuddered to think what would have been their fate if the car had skidded a few more yards following its collision with the tree. She had watched in horror as the car slid down the incline and was claimed by the raging creek.

For several moments the car had remained buoyant, bobbing its way to the middle of the swift stream before flipping into a nose dive. Within seconds it had disappeared beneath the churning surface. Aside from the scars left on the trunk of the felled pine tree and the deep, parallel furrows plowed by the tires, the accident had left the landscape unscathed.

"Miracle y'all got out in time and didn't drown when it went down," the deputy was saying.

"Not all of us got out," Kendall corrected him in an emotion-husky voice. "There was a passenger in the front seat. She went down with the car."

At the mention of a fatality, the deputy's routine interrogation suddenly became anything but routine. He frowned. "What? A passenger?"

As though watching from outside herself, Kendall saw her face crumple as she began to cry, a delayed reaction to the trauma. "I'm sorry."

The nurse passed her a box of Kleenex and patted her shoulder. "It's okay, honey. After the brave thing you did, you just go right ahead and bawl all you want to."

"Didn't know there was anybody else in the car 'cept you, your baby, and the driver," the deputy said quietly, in deference to her emotional state.

Kendall blotted her nose. "She was in the passenger seat

and was already dead when the car went into the creek. She probably died instantly, upon impact."

After making certain that Kevin was unharmed, and noting how quickly the creek was rising, Kendall had approached the passenger side of the car with trepidation, almost certain of what she would find. This side had sustained the brunt of the collision. The door was caved in and the window had been broken out.

At a glance, Kendall had known the woman inside was dead. Her pleasant features were no longer recognizable from the facial bones and tissue that had been ravaged. The dashboard and a mishmash of engine parts had been driven into her chest cavity. Her head lolled against the headrest at an unnatural angle.

Ignoring the blood and gore, Kendall had reached in and pressed her fingers against the woman's neck in the vicinity of the carotid artery. She felt no pulse.

"I thought I should try and save the rest of us," she explained to the deputy after describing the scene. "I wish I could have gotten her out, too, but, knowing that she was already dead—"

"Under the circumstances you did what you had to do, little lady. You saved the living. Nobody can fault you for the choice you made." He nodded down at the sleeping infant. "You did a damn sight more than anybody could ask of you. How'd you go about getting the driver out?"

After determining that the passenger was dead, Kendall had laid Kevin on the ground and covered his face with a corner of his blanket. Although he would be uncomfortable, he would be safe for the moment. Then she stumbled around to the other side of the car. The driver's head was slumped over the steering wheel. Swallowing her dread, Kendall had called his name and pressed his shoulder.

She remembered giving it a slight shake, and how startled she'd been when this caused him to flop backward against the seat. She had recoiled as blood trickled from the corner of his slack lips. There was a deep gash on his right temple; otherwise his face was intact. His eyes were closed and still, but at that point she wasn't certain that he was dead. She reached in and placed her hand on his chest.

He had a heartbeat.

Then, without warning, the car had shifted on the uneven ground and slid several feet down the slope, dragging her along with it. Her arm, still inside the car, was nearly wrenched from its socket.

The auto came to a rocking, unsteady rest, but she'd known it was only a matter of time before it would be swallowed by the floodwaters, which were already lapping at the tires. Saturated ground was giving way beneath the weight of the car. There had been no time to contemplate the situation, or to carefully weigh her options, or to consider how badly she wanted to be rid of him.

She had every reason to fear and despise him. But she didn't wish him dead. She would never want that. A life, any life, was worth saving.

So, with a surge of adrenaline, she used her bare hands to scoop aside mud and tear at tenacious vines that prevented her from opening the driver's door.

Finally she managed to wedge it open, and when she did, his torso slumped into her waiting arms. His bloody head fell onto her shoulder. Beneath his dead weight, she collapsed to her knees.

Wrapping her arms around his chest, she pulled him from beneath the steering wheel. It was a struggle. Several times she lost her footing in the slippery mud and landed hard on her backside. But each time she clambered to her feet, dug her heels in, and put forth enormous effort into pulling him free of the wreckage. His heels had barely cleared the door when the car snapped free of its temporary moorings and slid into the creek.

Kendall related her story, omitting her private thoughts. When she finished, the deputy was practically standing at attention, looking as though he might salute her. "Lady, you'll prob'ly get a medal or something."

"I seriously doubt that," she murmured.

He removed a small spiral notebook and a ballpoint pen from the breast pocket of his shirt. "Name?"

Buying time, she pretended not to understand. "Pardon?"

"Your name?"

The small hospital staff had been kind enough to admit them without first thrusting forms and questionnaires at her. That kind of trusting, informal procedure would be unheard of in a large city hospital. But in rural Georgia, compassion superseded collecting insurance cards.

Now, however, Kendall was faced with the grim realities of her situation, and she wasn't ready to deal with them. She hadn't yet decided what to do, how much to tell, where to go from here.

She had no compunctions about stretching the truth. She had done it before. All her life. Many times. Extensively and elaborately. But lying to the police was serious business. She had never gone quite that far before.

Bowing her head, she massaged her temples and reconsidered asking for a painkiller to muffle her drumming headache. "My name?" she repeated, stalling, praying that a brilliant idea would suddenly occur to her. "Or the name of the woman who died?"

"Let's start with you."

She held her breath for a moment, then said softly, "Kendall."

"That'd be K-e-n-d-a-l-l?" he asked as he wrote it in his notebook.

She nodded.

"Okay, Mrs. Kendall. Was that also the name of the fatality?"

"No, it's Kendall—"

Before she could correct the deputy's mistake, the curtain was whisked aside with a screech of metal rings on an unoiled track. The doctor on call strode in.

Kendall's heart skipped a beat. Breathlessly, she asked, "How is he?"

The doctor grinned. "Alive, thanks to you."

"Has he regained consciousness? Has he said anything? What has he told you?"

"Want to take a look-see for yourself?"

"I . . . I suppose."

"Hey, Doc, hold on a sec. I have some questions to ask her," the deputy complained. "Lots of important paperwork, don'cha know."

"Can't that wait? She's upset, and I can't give her anything to calm her down because she's nursing."

The deputy glanced at the baby, then at Kendall's chest. His face turned the color of a ripe tomato. "Well, I reckon it'll keep for a spell. But it's got to be done."

"Sure, sure," the doctor said.

The nurse lifted Kevin from Kendall's arms. He remained asleep. "I'll find this little precious one a crib in the nursery. Don't worry about him. You go with the doctor."

The deputy fiddled with the brim of his hat while shifting his weight from one foot to the other. "I'll just sit out here. Then, whenever you're ready, ma'am, to, uh, you know, finish up here . . ."

"Have a cup of coffee, why don't you?" the doctor suggested, humoring the officer.

The doctor was young and brash and, in Kendall's estimation, very full of himself. She doubted that the ink on his medical diploma was dry yet, but he obviously enjoyed asserting his limited authority. Without a backward glance at the deputy, he ushered her down the corridor.

"He has a tibial shaft fracture, or your basic broken shinbone," he explained. "There was no displacement, so he won't require surgery, or a rod, etcetera. In that respect, he was extremely lucky. From the way you described the car—"

"The hood was pleated like a paper fan. I don't know why the steering wheel didn't crush his chest."

"Right. I was afraid he'd have busted ribs, internal bleeding, organ damage, but I see no evidence of any. His vital signs have stabilized. That's the good news.

"The bad news is that he took quite a knock on the head. X rays show only a hairline fracture on the skull, but I had to take several dozen stitches to close the wound. It isn't too pretty right now, but eventually his hair'll grow back over it. Won't spoil his good looks too much," he said, smiling down at her.

"He bled quite a lot."

"We've given him a unit of blood just to be on the safe side. He sustained a concussion, but if he's quiet for several days, he'll be okay. With his leg broken like it is, he'll be on crutches for at least a month. He won't have much choice but to lie around, be lazy, and let himself heal. Here we are." He steered her toward a room. "He just regained consciousness a few minutes ago, so he's still groggy."

The doctor went into the dimly lighted room ahead of her. She hesitated on the threshold and surveyed the room. On one wall was an atrocious paint-by-number picture of Jesus ascending into the clouds; an AIDS awareness poster hung on the opposite wall. It was a semiprivate room with two beds, but he was the only patient.

His lower leg, secured in a cast, was propped up on a pillow. He'd been dressed in a hospital gown that reached only to the middle of his thighs. They looked strong and tan against the white sheets, out of keeping with an infirmary.

A nurse was taking his blood pressure. His dark eyebrows were drawn into a frown beneath the wide gauze bandage encircling his head. His hair was matted with dried blood and an antiseptic solution. A ghastly number of bruises discolored his arms. The features of his face had been distorted by swelling, contusions, and bruises, but he was recognizable by the vertical cleft in his chin and the hard slant of his mouth, from which protruded a thermometer.

Briskly, the doctor moved to the bedside and consulted the blood pressure reading the nurse had noted on the patient's chart. "Looking better all the time." He also murmured approval when the nurse showed him the patient's current body temperature.

Although Kendall still hesitated just outside the door, the patient's eyes instantly homed in on her. They penetrated the shadowed depths of their sockets, which were sunken and dark from blood loss and pain. But his unflinching stare was as incisive as ever.

The first time she had looked directly into his eyes, she had sensed and respected their keen perception. She had even feared it a little. She still did. He seemed to possess an uncanny ability to see straight into her in a way that was most unsettling.

He had her pegged from their first meeting. He knew a liar when he saw one.

She hoped that his talent for reading her thoughts would serve now to let him know how genuinely sorry she was that he'd been injured. If not for her, the wreck never would have occurred. He had been driving, but it was she who was accountable for the pain and discomfort he was suffering. Realizing this, she was filled with remorse. She was the last person he would want hovering over his hospital bed.

Misreading the cause of her hesitation, the nurse smiled and motioned her forward. "He's decent. You can come in now."

Battling her apprehension, Kendall stepped into the room and gave the patient a faltering smile. "Hi. How do you feel?"

He fixed an unblinking stare on her that lasted for several moments. Finally, he glanced up at the doctor, then at the nurse, before his gaze moved back to Kendall. Then in a weak, hoarse voice, he asked, "Who are you?"

The doctor bent over his patient. "You mean you don't recognize her?"

"No. Am I supposed to? Where am I? *Who* am I?"

The doctor just gaped at his patient. The nurse stood dumbfounded, the hose of the blood pressure gauge dangling from her hand. Kendall appeared stunned, although she felt her emotions rioting. Her mind scurried to assimilate this shocking twist and how she might use it to her advantage.

The doctor was the first to recover. With a bravado belied by his weak smile, he said, "Well, it seems that the concussion has left our patient with amnesia. This frequently happens. It's temporary, I'm sure. Nothing to worry about. You'll laugh over it in a day or two."

He turned to Kendall. "For now, you're our only source of information. Guess you'd better tell us—and tell him—who he is."

She hesitated so long that the moment stretched taut. The doctor and nurse looked at her expectantly. The man in the hospital bed seemed both interested in and wary of her answer. His eyes narrowed suspiciously, but Kendall could tell that, miraculously, he genuinely remembered nothing. *Nothing!*

This was a blessing unforeseen, an incredibly generous gift of fate. It was almost too good, almost overwhelming, too intricate to handle without having time to prepare. But she knew one thing for certain: She would be a fool not to seize it with both hands.

With remarkable calm, she declared, "He's my husband."

Chapter One

"*B*Y THE AUTHORITY VESTED IN ME BY ALMIGHTY God and the state of South Carolina, I pronounce you husband and wife. Matthew, you may kiss your bride."

The wedding guests applauded as Matt Burnwood drew Kendall Deaton into his arms. Laughter erupted when his kiss extended beyond a chaste token. He was reluctant to stop.

"That'll have to wait," Kendall whispered against his lips. "Unfortunately."

Matt gave her a pained look, but, being a good sport, turned to face the several hundred people who had turned out in their Sunday best to attend the affair.

"Ladies and gentlemen," the minister intoned, "may I present, for the first time, Mr. and Mrs. Matthew Burnwood."

Arm in arm, Kendall and Matt faced their smiling guests. Matt's father was seated alone in the front row. He stood and opened his arms to Kendall.

"Welcome to our family," he said, embracing her. "God sent you to us. We've needed a woman in our family. If Laurelann were alive, she'd love you, Kendall. Just as I do."

Kendall kissed Gibb Burnwood's ruddy cheek. "Thank you, Gibb. That's very sweet of you."

Laurelann Burnwood had passed away when Matt was a youngster, but he and Gibb spoke of her death as though it were recent. The widower cut an impressive figure, with his white crew cut and tall, trim physique. Many widows and divorcées had set their caps for Gibb, but their affections remained unrequited. He'd had his one true love, he often said. He wasn't looking for another.

Matt placed one arm around his father's broad shoulders, the other around Kendall. "We needed each other. We're a complete family now."

"I only wish Grandmother could have been here," Kendall remarked sadly.

Matt gave her a sympathetic smile. "I wish she'd felt up to making the trip from Tennessee."

"It would have been too hard on her. She's here in spirit, though."

"Let's not get too maudlin," Gibb cut in. "These folks came to eat, drink, and be merry. This is your day. Enjoy it."

Gibb had spared no expense to guarantee that their wedding would be remembered and talked about for years to come. Kendall had been shocked by his extravagance. Shortly after accepting Matt's proposal, she had suggested that they have a private ceremony, perhaps in a pastor's study.

Gibb wouldn't hear of it.

He eschewed the tradition of the bride's family financing the wedding and insisted on hosting it himself. Kendall demurred, but Gibb, with his disarming, winning personality, had shot down all her arguments.

"Don't take offense," Matt had told her when she expressed her dismay over Gibb's elaborate plans. "Dad wants to throw a party, the likes of which Prosper has never seen. Since neither you nor your grandmother is financially able to do it, he's pleased to foot the bill. I'm his only child. This is a once-in-a-lifetime event for him. So let's give him his head and let him run."

It hadn't taken long for Kendall to be swept up in the excitement. She selected her gown, but Gibb took control of everything else, although he considerately consulted her before any major decisions were finalized.

His strict attention to detail had paid off, because today his house and lawn looked spectacular. Matt and she had exchanged vows beneath a latticed arch bedecked with gardenias, white lilies, and white roses. Inside a large tent was an elaborate buffet of salads, side dishes, and entrees to suit every palate.

The wedding cake was a breathtaking sculpture with several tiers. The creamy frosting was decorated with clusters of fresh rosebuds. There was also a chocolate groom's cake with fudge icing drizzled over strawberries nearly as large as tennis balls. Magnums of champagne were chilling in tubs of ice. The guests seemed dedicated to drinking every drop of it.

Despite such glamour, the reception was truly a family affair. Children played under the shade trees. After the bride and groom initiated the dancing with a wedding waltz, other couples crowded the floor until everyone was dancing.

It was a fairy tale wedding. Complete with an ogre.

Kendall, unaware of the menace surrounding her, couldn't have imagined being happier. Matt held her close and twirled her about the dance floor. With his tall, slender physique, he seemed made to wear a tuxedo without looking awkward. He was incredibly handsome. His evenly defined features and straight hair gave him the aristocratic bearing of a robber baron.

"You have that elegant, aloof air about you. Like Gatsby," Kendall had once told him teasingly.

She wanted to go on dancing with him for hours, but guests were vying for a dance with the bride. Among them was Judge H. W. Fargo. She all but groaned when Matt relinquished her to the judge, who demonstrated no more grace on the dance floor than he did in the courtroom.

"I had my doubts about you," Judge Fargo remarked as he swung her into a turn that almost caused her a whiplash. "When I heard they were hiring a female to be this county's public defender, I had serious misgivings that you could handle the job."

"Really?" she said coolly.

Fargo was not only a terrible dancer and a lamentable judge but a sexist to boot, Kendall thought. Since her first appearance in his courtroom, he'd made no effort to conceal his "misgivings."

"Why were you apprehensive, Judge?" she asked, struggling to keep her pleasant smile in place.

"Prosper's a conservative county and town," he said expansively. "Damn proud of it, too. Around here, folks have been doing things the same way for generations. We're slow to change and don't like it when we're forced to. A lady lawyer is a novelty."

"You think women should remain at home to cook, clean, and care for children, is that it? They shouldn't aspire to be professionals?"

He harrumphed. "I wouldn't put it like that."

"No, of course you wouldn't."

Such a candid statement might cost him votes. Everything he said in public was self-censored. Judge H. W. Fargo was a consummate politician. If only he were as effective a judge.

"All I'm saying is that Prosper is a clean little town. You don't find the problems here that other cities have. We nip corrupting influences in the bud. We—meaning myself and other public officials—intend to keep our standards high."

"Do you think I'm a corrupting influence, Judge?"

"Not at all, not at all."

"My job is to provide legal counsel for those who can't

afford their own attorney. The Constitution grants every U.S. citizen legal representation."

"I know what the Constitution grants," he said testily.

Kendall smiled to take the sting out of her mild insult. "Sometimes I must remind myself. My work brings me in close contact with an element of society we all wish weren't there. But as long as there are criminals, they will need someone to plead their cases in court. No matter how unsavory my client, I try to plead every case to the best of my ability."

"No one's questioning your ability. Despite your involvement in that nasty business back in Tennessee . . ." He broke off and smiled unctuously. "Well, why bring that up today?"

Why indeed? The judge's reminder of her past difficulties had been deliberate. Kendall resented him for thinking she was stupid enough to believe it had been a blunder.

"You're doing a fine job, a fine job," he said ingratiatingly. "I'll admit that having a woman arguing points of law with me took some getting used to." His laugh sounded like a bark. "You know, until you showed up for your interview, we thought we were hiring a man."

"My name can be misleading."

The board of directors of the Prosper County Bar Association had decided to form a public defender's office to relieve their membership of handling defense of indigents. Even on a rotating basis, these cases could be costly in time and lost revenue.

The board had been stupefied when Kendall arrived wearing three-inch heels and a dress instead of a suit and tie. Her resumé had been so impressive that they had responded promptly to her correspondence and were almost willing to hire her sight unseen. The interview should have been a mere formality.

Instead, she had been placed in the hot seat. Knowing ahead of time that she would be going up against a wall of good-ol'-boy mentality, she had carefully rehearsed her sales pitch.

The speech was worded to combat their prejudices and assuage their uncertainties without offending them.

She had desperately wanted the job. She was qualified to do it, and since her future hinged on her getting it, she had pulled out all the stops.

Obviously she had done well, because the board had offered her the job. That one blot on her professional record hadn't factored in to their decision nearly as much as her gender. Or perhaps they believed that because of her sex, she should be cut some slack. She had made a mistake, but it was forgivable because she was, after all, only a woman.

It didn't matter to Kendall what they thought or how they had reached their decision. In the eight months that she had been in Prosper, she had proven her capabilities. She had worked hard to earn the respect of her peers and the general public. Her skeptics were eating crow.

Even the publisher of the local newspaper, who, upon the announcement of her placement, had written an editorial questioning if a woman could handle such a difficult job, had undergone a change of heart.

That publisher moved up behind her now, wrapped his arms around her waist, and kissed the back of her neck. "Judge, you've monopolized the prettiest girl at the party long enough."

Fargo chuckled. "Spoken like a bridegroom."

"Thanks for rescuing me," Kendall said, sighing as Matt danced her away. She laid her cheek against the lapel of his tuxedo jacket and closed her eyes. "It's bad enough that I have to fence with that redneck-in-robes in court. It's above and beyond the call of duty to dance with him at my wedding."

"Be nice," he chided.

"I was. In fact, I was so charming I nearly made myself sick."

"The judge can be a pain, but he's an old friend of Dad's."

Matt was right. Besides, she wouldn't give Judge Fargo

the satisfaction of blighting her wedding day. She raised her head and smiled up at Matt. "I love you. How long has it been since I told you?"

"Ages. At least ten minutes."

They were nuzzling affectionately when a bellowing voice interrupted them: "Hey, kid, this is quite a bash!"

Kendall turned to see her maid of honor two-stepping past in the arms of a local pharmacist. The mousy, self-effacing man seemed bewildered to find himself in the embrace of such a vivacious, abundantly endowed woman.

"Hi, Ricki Sue," Kendall said. "Having fun?"

"Do bears shit in the woods?"

Ricki Sue Robb's tall beehive hairdo was bobbing in time to the music. Her face was shiny with sweat above the décolletage of her pale blue dress. It had been a challenge for Kendall to choose a bride's maid gown that would flatter her friend. Ricki Sue's complexion was an uneven blend of sallow skin and rusty freckles. Her hair was the color of fresh carrot juice, but, far from downplaying this distinguishing feature, Ricki Sue preferred the most elaborate styles she could devise. Her coiffures were engineering marvels worthy of architectural study.

The wide gap between her front teeth was constantly on display because she was always smiling. Her full lips glistened with fire-engine-red lipstick, an unfortunate choice considering the color of her hair.

In a voice with all the subtlety of a reveille trumpet, she blared, "You said your husband was a handsome devil, but you didn't tell me he was also rich as sin."

Kendall felt Matt stiffen with disapproval. Ricki Sue didn't mean to be offensive. In fact, she thought she was paying him a compliment. But in Prosper, personal wealth wasn't discussed in polite company. Not out loud, anyway.

After Ricki Sue and the dazed pharmacist waltzed out of

earshot, Kendall said, "It would be a polite gesture for you
to ask her to dance, Matt."

He grimaced. "I'm afraid she'd trample me."

"Matt, please."

"Sorry."

"Are you? At the rehearsal dinner last night you made it
glaringly apparent to me that you had formed an instant dislike
for Ricki Sue. I hope she didn't notice, but I certainly did."

"She's not at all the way you described her to me."

"I told you she was my best friend. That should be description enough."

Since Grandmother's declining health had prevented her
from attending the wedding, Ricki Sue was Kendall's only
guest. If for no other reason than that, she had hoped Matt
would make an effort to be friendly and cordial to her. Instead,
Ricki Sue's boisterous conversation had caused him and Gibb
to cringe. They'd been embarrassed by her unrestrained,
bawdy laugh, which seemed to originate in her massive
bosoms.

"I grant you that Ricki Sue isn't a genteel Southern lady."

Matt scoffed at the understatement. "She's coarse, Kendall.
Common. I expected her to be like you. Feminine and soft-
spoken and beautiful."

"She's very beautiful on the inside."

Ricki Sue was the receptionist at Bristol and Mathers, the
law firm where Kendall had previously been an associate.
When they'd first met, Kendall had been unable to see beyond
the redhead's brashness.

Gradually, however, she came to know and like the sensitive
woman beneath the flamboyant exterior. Ricki Sue was unpre-
tentious, practical, tolerant, and trustworthy. Especially trustworthy.

"I'm sure she has some admirable traits," Matt conceded

grudgingly. "And maybe she can't help being fat. It's just that she comes on so strong."

Kendall winced over his using the word *fat*, when other adjectives would have served just as well. Better, he could have refrained from using any derogatory adjectives.

"If you'd give her half a chance—"

He laid his finger vertically against her lips. "Are we going to quarrel at our wedding reception in front of all our guests over something so insignificant?"

She could argue that his rudeness to her friend wasn't insignificant, but his point about this not being the time to quarrel was valid. Besides, there were several of his friends she wasn't particularly fond of either.

"All right, truce," she agreed. "But if I *were* going to pick a quarrel, it would be over all the women here who've glared daggers at me. If looks could kill, I'd be dead a dozen times over."

"Who? Where?" He whipped his head around as though searching for the brokenhearted ladies.

"Not on your life," she said in a growling tone, clutching his lapels possessively. "But just out of curiosity, how many hearts did you break by marrying me?"

"Who's counting?"

"Seriously, Matt."

"Seriously?" He pulled a sober face. "Seriously, I'm one of the few bachelors in Prosper between puberty and senility. So if you see a few long faces in the crowd, that's why. The mature single women here have come one statistic closer to getting struck by lightning."

His flippancy served its purpose—she began to laugh. "Well, whatever, I'm glad you waited for matrimony until I came along."

He stopped dancing and drew her closer, tipping her head back and lowering his lips to hers. "So am I."

* * *

It wasn't easy to be inconspicuous while wearing a wedding gown and veil, but half an hour later Kendall was able to slip unnoticed into the house.

She didn't like Gibb's house, particularly the large living area where dark paneled walls provided a fitting backdrop for his hunting and fishing trophies.

To Kendall's unappreciative eye, one fish mounted on a walnut plaque looked as pathetic as another. The blind stares of deer, elk, wild boar, and other game evoked sympathy and repugnance. As Kendall moved through the living room, she cast a wary glance at the head of a ferocious razorback, preserved forever with tusks bared.

Hunting and fishing were Gibb's stock-in-trade. His sporting goods store was located on Prosper's main street. In this mountainous Blue Ridge area of northwestern South Carolina, he did a thriving business and continued to cultivate a loyal clientele. Customers traveled for miles to spend their money with him.

He was good at what he did. Hopeful hunters and fishermen valued his opinion and whipped out their Visa cards for whatever gadget, scope, or lure he suggested that might make their forays more successful. Frequently they returned with their kills or catches, dragging carcasses right into the store, to gloat over their skill with rifle or trap or rod and reel.

Gibb was generous with his praise and took no credit for the advice he gave. He was admired as an outdoorsman and as an individual. Those who couldn't claim to be his friend would have liked to.

When she reached the half-bath that served as Gibb's powder room, the door was closed. She tapped lightly.

"Be out in a sec."

"Ricki Sue?"

"That you, kid?"

Ricki Sue opened the door from the inside. She was using

a damp hand towel to mop her perspiring cleavage. "I'm sweating like a pig. Come on in."

Kendall gathered up her train and veil and joined Ricki Sue in the small bathroom, closing the door behind her. Although it was crowded, she welcomed the quiet moment alone with her friend.

"Was your room at the motel okay?" Motels were scarce in Prosper. Kendall had reserved the best room available for Ricki Sue, but it had few amenities.

"I've slept in worse. Screwed in worse, too," she said, winking at Kendall in the mirror. "Speaking of which, is that handsome stud of yours as good as he looks?"

"I never kiss and tell," Kendall retorted with a coy smile.

"Then you're shortchanging yourself, 'cause telling is half the fun."

At Bristol and Mathers, Ricki Sue had kept the associates and clerks enthralled with her sexual exploits. She added an episode to the ongoing soap opera of her life every morning at the coffee machine. Some of her tales were too farfetched to be believed. Amazingly, however, all were true.

"You worry me, Ricki Sue. It's dangerous to have multiple partners."

"I'm careful. Always have been."

"I'm sure you are, but—"

"Listen, kid, don't lecture. I do the best I can with what I've got. When you look like me, you gotta take what you can get from men. I don't know of one who's gonna fall head over heels for this." She spread her arms at her sides.

"So, rather than get my heart broken time after time, or be a perpetual wallflower and end up a bitter old maid, I made up my mind years ago to be *accommodating*.

"I give 'em what they want, and I've got a real talent for it. When the lights are out and everybody's naked, they don't care if you look like a fairy princess or a warthog so long as you've got a tight, warm place for them to put it. It all feels good in the dark, kid."

"That's such a sad and sordid philosophy."

"Works for me."

"But how do you know that one of these days Mr. Right isn't going to come sweeping into your life?"

Ricki Sue's laugh sounded like a foghorn. "I'd have a better chance of winning the lottery." Then her smile faded and she became introspective. "Don't be misled. I'd trade my life for yours in a New York minute. I'd love to have a husband, a bunch of rowdy kids, the whole package.

"But since that's not likely, I refuse to do without the fun stuff. I take whatever affection I can get and in whatever form. Behind my back, I know people say, 'How can she let men use her like that?' The truth is, I use them. Because unfortunately . . ." She paused to eye Kendall up and down with good-natured envy. "All women are *not* created equal. I look like a walrus with a good henna rinse, and you're . . . well, you."

"Don't put yourself down. Besides, I thought you loved me for my mind," Kendall teased.

"Oh, you're smart all right. So smart you frankly scare the hell out of me. And you've got more guts than anybody I ever ran across, and I've run across some pretty tough hombres."

Teasing aside, she looked at Kendall solemnly. "I'm glad things worked out for you here, kid. You took one hell of a chance. You're still taking a chance."

"To some extent, yes," Kendall agreed. "But I'm not worried. Too much time has passed. If it was going to come crashing down, it would have by now."

"I don't know," Ricki Sue said doubtfully. "I still think you're crazy as a bedbug for going through with it. And if I had it to do over again, I'd still advise you against it. Does Matt know?"

Kendall shook her head.

"Shouldn't you tell him?"

"What for?"

"Because he's your husband, for crying out loud!"

"Exactly. What difference would it make in how he feels about me?"

Ricki Sue mulled that over for a moment. "What does your grandma think?"

"The same as you," she admitted reluctantly. "She urged me to tell him."

Elvie Hancock was the only parent Kendall remembered, having been orphaned when she was five. She had reared Kendall with a firm but loving hand. On most matters of importance, Kendall agreed with her. She trusted the woman's instincts and valued the wisdom of her advanced years.

But on the issue of being totally honest with Matt, they had differing opinions. Kendall was convinced that her way was best. Quietly she said, "You and Grandmother must trust me on this, Ricki Sue."

"Okay, kid. But if a skeleton pops out of your closet and bites you on the butt, don't say I didn't warn you."

Laughing at the image Ricki Sue's words had painted, Kendall leaned forward and embraced her. "I miss you. Promise you'll come to visit often."

Ricki Sue folded the hand towel with more care than it warranted. "I don't think that'd be such a good idea."

Kendall's smile collapsed. "Why not?"

"Because your husband and his daddy have made plain their feelings for me. No, don't apologize," Ricki Sue hastened to say when she saw that Kendall was about to protest. "I don't give a rat's ass what they think of me. They remind me too much of my own self-righteous parents for me to care about their opinion. Oh, hell. I didn't mean to put them down, it's just . . ." Her heavily made up eyes pleaded for Kendall's understanding. "I don't want to be the cause of any problems."

Kendall knew exactly what her friend was trying to express, and the sentiment made her appreciate Ricki Sue all the more. "I miss you and Grandmother more than I realized I would, Ricki Sue. Tennessee seems very far away. I need a friend."

"Make one."

"I've tried, so far without success. The women here are polite, but distant. Maybe they resent me for blowing into town and stealing Matt from them. Or maybe my career puts them off. Their lives seem to have a different focus than mine. Anyway, nobody could replace you as my best friend. Please don't write me off."

"I'm not writing you off, God knows. I don't have that many friends myself. But let's be practical about this." She pressed Kendall's shoulders between her hands. "Other than me, your last remaining link to Sheridan, Tennessee, is your grandmother. When she dies, turn your back on that town forever, Kendall. Sever all ties there, including me. Don't press your luck."

Kendall nodded thoughtfully, acknowledging the merit of her friend's advice. "Grandmother won't live much longer. I wish she had moved here with me, but she refused to leave her home. This separation is breaking my heart. You know how important she is to me."

"And vice versa. She loves you. She's always wanted what's best for you. If you're happy, she'll die happy. That's the best you can wish for her."

Kendall knew that Ricki Sue was right. Her throat tightened. "Look after her for me, Ricki Sue."

"I call her every day and go see her at least twice a week, just like I promised I would." She took Kendall's hand and gave it a reassuring squeeze. "Now, I'd like to get back to the party and all that wonderful champagne and food. Maybe I can wheedle another dance out of that druggist. He's kinda cute, don't you think?"

"He's married."

"So? They're usually the ones most desperate for some of Ricki Sue's famous tender loving care." She patted her large breasts.

"Shame on you!"

"Sorry, that word's not in my vocabulary." Chuckling deeply, she scooted Kendall aside and opened the door. "I'm outta here. Much as I'd like to stick around and see how you go about it."

"Go about what?"

"Taking a leak in a wedding gown."

Chapter Two

"WILL THERE BE ANYTHING ELSE, MISS?"

The question yanked Kendall from her daydream about her wedding. She remembered even the smallest details of that day, but she felt completely removed from it, as if it had happened to someone else, or in another lifetime.

"That's all, thank you," she replied to the clerk.

Despite the inclement weather, Wal-Mart was packed with customers. The aisles were jammed with shopping carts filled with everything from roller skates to rolling pins.

"One forty-two seventy-seven. Cash, check, or charge?"

"Cash."

The young man hadn't taken any particular notice of her. She was just one of hundreds of customers to be checked out that day. If asked later, he wouldn't recall her, couldn't describe her. Anonymity was what she sought.

Last night, when she finally lay down in the bed in Stephensville Community Hospital, she had been more tired than she remembered being in her entire life. Her whole body was sore and throbbing from the accident. The ordeal of getting out of the ravine had left her with cuts and bruises that hurt worse the longer the night wore on.

She had desperately craved oblivion, but she had lain awake throughout the night.

Who are you? Who am I?

He's my husband.

The words had echoed inside her head. From her pillow, she had stared with gritty eyes at the acoustical tile ceiling, replaying those words in her mind and wondering if having spoken them would turn out to be fortune or folly. It was too late now to recall them, and even if she could she wouldn't.

His amnesia was only temporary. So, while he was locked in forgetfulness, she had to make the most of it. She hoped this would give her time to save Kevin and herself. After all, saving Kevin was the purpose behind everything she had done thus far. Protecting the baby was worth taking any chance, even one this risky.

He had caused quite a scene when informed that he had amnesia. His recovery would require rest and relaxation, the doctor had told him. He would have to take it easy in order for his leg to heal, so why not enjoy the unexpected, imposed vacation? The more pressure he placed on himself to regain his memory, the more elusive it would become. A mind under duress could be stubbornly uncooperative. He was continually urged to relax.

But he hadn't relaxed, not even when, at the doctor's suggestion, Kendall carried Kevin into his room. The sight of the child had only increased his agitation, which didn't abate until a nurse took Kevin away.

The doctor, much more subdued than he had been earlier, had tried to reassure Kendall. "I recommend that we let him rest undisturbed through the night. Amnesia's tricky. Tomorrow morning when he wakes up, he'll probably remember everything."

At first light, she had dressed in a uniform one of the nurses loaned her and anxiously returned to his room. His memory had not been restored during the night.

When she walked in, he self-consciously raised the sheet
to his waist. The nurse had just completed giving him a bed
bath, which had obviously embarrassed him. She withdrew,
taking the paraphernalia with her and leaving them alone.

Kendall gestured awkwardly. "I'm sure the bath made you
feel better."

"Some. But I hated it."

"Generally speaking, men make terrible patients." She gave
him a wavering smile and moved closer. "Is there anything
I can do to make you more comfortable?"

"No, I'm fine. Are you okay? You and the kid?"

"Miraculously, Kevin and I walked away unscathed."

He nodded. "That's good."

Kendall could tell that even this much conversation was
taxing him. "I've got some things to attend to, but if you
need anything, don't hesitate to call the nurses. They seem
competent."

Again he nodded, this time without comment.

She was about to leave, when, as an afterthought, she turned
back, leaned over him, and kissed his forehead. His eyes,
which had closed, opened suddenly. Their impact reduced
Kendall's voice to a hushed whisper. "Rest well. I'll be in to
see you later."

She hastily left his room. Shortly afterward, she approached
a nurse and said, "I need to run some errands. Is there taxi
service?"

Laughing, the nurse produced a set of car keys. "Forget
calling a taxi in this town, honey. My car is yours to use until
my shift ends at three this afternoon. Take my raincoat, too."

"Thank you so much." She had welcomed this unexpected
generosity. "Kevin needs some essentials and I can't continue
dressing in a nurse uniform. I really need to do a bit of
shopping."

The nurse gave her directions to Wal-Mart, then said hesitantly, "Forgive me for getting personal, honey. But, seeing

as how your stuff, including all your identification, went down with the car, how're you fixed for cash?"

"Fortunately I had some money zipped into a pocket of my jacket," she told the nurse, who would have been shocked at the amount of cash Kendall actually had on her. It was more than just "spending money." She had saved a lot, anticipating a catastrophe such as this. She and Kevin could survive for a long time on what she had. "It's wet, but spendable. I can afford to buy some things for Kevin and myself, and find us a place to stay."

"This one-horse town only has one shabby motor court. Don't spend your money on that. As long as you need a bed, you can stay here at the hospital."

"That's very kind of you."

"Don't mention it. Besides, when your husband recovers his memory, you'll want to be here, day or night." She touched Kendall's arm consolingly. "This is a lot for you to handle all by yourself. Are you sure there's no one you can call to help out? Family?"

"No one. We don't have an extended family. And by the way, I want to thank you and the rest of the staff for agreeing not to mention the fatality to my husband. He's already confused and upset. I see no reason to make matters worse."

The deputy too had agreed that sharing that information with the amnesiac was unnecessary at this point. The officer had returned to the hospital that morning to give Kendall an update about the car. Divers had been sent down, he told her, but had not been able to locate the wreckage. Apparently it had been washed far downstream from the site of the accident.

Shaking his head with regret, he said it was anyone's guess when and where it might turn up. "Bingham Creek runs through pure-dee wilderness for the most part. The ground is too saturated to get heavy equipment in there. Since it looks like we're in for more rain, it'll prob'ly be several days before it's safe to go exploring."

Several days.

They were without positive identification. For the time being, the wrecked car and everything inside it was lost. No one knew where they were. He had amnesia. She had time.

If she kept her cool and was very clever, she could escape with a good head start. If she failed, the consequences would be terrible. But since when had possible consequences deterred her from taking action when action was called for? She had been desperate when she moved to Prosper.

And even more desperate when she fled.

"Miss?"

Kendall shook herself alert. "I'm sorry. Did you say something?"

" 'S that it?" The Wal-Mart clerk was looking at her with puzzlement. The last thing she wanted was to call his attention to the woman in the nurse's uniform who seemed dazed and disoriented.

"Oh, yes. Thank you."

Hastily she grabbed her purchases and moved through the checkout chute toward the exit, where shoppers, reluctant to go outside, had formed a bottleneck.

Kendall didn't hesitate. She ducked her head and plunged into the downpour. She drove the borrowed car to the nearest filling station and purchased a local newspaper. She scanned it quickly, then went around to the side of the building to the pay phone mounted on the exterior wall.

"Hello? I'm calling about your ad in the newspaper. Have you sold the car yet?"

"So his physical injuries aren't that serious?"

"A broken right tibia and a gash on his head. That's it."

Kendall had waylaid the doctor in the hospital corridor. He was wearing street clothes and enough cologne to perfume a platoon. He was obviously in a hurry to end his shift and get on with his plans for Saturday night, but Kendall had questions that had to be answered. With her steady stare demanding more information, he released a heavy sigh.

"Neither of those injuries is a day in the park, but they're not catastrophic. If your husband stays off his leg, it should heal in six weeks or so. We've already had him up today, trying out the crutches. He won't win any sprints, but he can maneuver.

"His sutures can come out in a week to ten days. His scalp will be tender for a while, and there'll be some scarring, but nothing grotesque. He'll still be handsome."

"So you've said before," Kendall reminded him, ignoring his sly smile. "I'm mostly concerned about the amnesia."

"It's not that uncommon following a blow to the head and concussion."

"But usually all that's lost are the few minutes leading up to the concussion and the events that immediately follow, isn't that right?"

"*Usually* is a word that doesn't apply to medicine."

"But it's rarer for the memory to be wiped completely clean, isn't it?"

"Rarer, yes," he admitted tersely.

That afternoon, she had researched amnesia in all its various forms, reading everything on the subject in the hospital's limited library. What she had read coincided with the doctor's assessment. Still, she wasn't satisfied. She had to cover every possibility, no matter how improbable.

"What about anterograde amnesia?"

"Don't borrow trouble."

"Indulge me."

He folded his arms over his chest and assumed a "let's get this over with" stance.

Unfazed by his impatience, Kendall continued. "The way I understand anterograde amnesia, my husband may not be capable of storing information in his memory now. So, even if he recovers his memory of things that happened before the accident, he may not be able to recall events that occurred between the memory loss and the time of recovery. He would remember everything else, but this period of time would be blocked out."

"Basically, your facts are correct. But, as I said, you shouldn't worry about that until it happens. I don't think it will."

"But it *could*."

"It could. I'd rather look on the bright side, okay?"

"Will it take another blow on the head for his memory to come back?"

"That only happens in the movies," he quipped. "It's usually not that dramatic. His memory may return gradually, a little at a time. Or everything may burst through at once."

"Or it may remain lost forever."

"That's highly unlikely. Unless there's a reason why your husband wants his memory permanently blotted out." He arched his eyebrow, implying a question.

Kendall ignored his ill-concealed curiosity, but she knew she had opened up an opportunity for him to elaborate, and he couldn't resist strutting his stuff.

"See, his subconscious could be using his head injury as a valid excuse to forget something he doesn't want to remember, something he finds difficult or even impossible to cope with." He gave her a penetrating look. "Is there a reason why he'd subconsciously want to be protected by amnesia?"

"Are you licensed to practice psychology, Doctor?" Her voice remained deceptively sweet, while her eyes conveyed her true opinion of the question. He flushed with indignation. "Which brings me to my next question," she said before he could offer a comeback. "Shouldn't we consult a specialist? Perhaps a neurologist from a larger hospital?"

"I already have."

"Oh?" She was slightly taken aback by this news.

"I called a hospital in Atlanta," the doctor said. "Got the staff neurologist on the phone, faxed him your husband's charts, and described his condition and reflexes. I told him that our screening indicated no cerebral bleeding. I said that the patient shows no signs of paralysis or numbness in the extremities, no slurred speech, blurred vision, or mental incapacity—none of the symptoms that signal serious brain damage."

He finished smugly, "The neurologist said it sounded to him like the patient had taken a knock on the noggin that blew a fuse in his memory box. His prognosis matched mine to the letter."

Kendall was relieved to hear it. She intended to turn his amnesia to her advantage, but she didn't wish him permanent brain damage.

As to when he would recover his memory, that was still a giant question mark. It could be at any moment, or it could be a year from now. How much time did she have?

She must presume that it was limited and act accordingly.

She smiled at the doctor. "Thank you for taking the time to answer my questions. I'm sorry I detained you. Hot date tonight?"

Now that she had learned what she needed to know, she wanted to distract him. The best way to do that was to appeal to his ego and turn the subject to him. It was a tactic she often used on jurors to divert their attention from evidence damaging to her client.

"Dinner and dancing at the Elk's Lodge," he replied.

"Sounds like fun. Don't let me keep you any longer."

He said good night and headed toward the main exit at the front of the building. Kendall waited until he was out of sight before she slipped into the patient's room. She hesitated just inside the door.

Above the bed was a dim night-light, the metal tent directing the light away from his face and onto the ceiling. She couldn't tell that his eyes were open, so it startled her when he spoke.

"I'm awake, and I'd like to talk to you."

Chapter Three

THE SOLES OF HER NEW SNEAKERS SQUEAKED ON the vinyl tiles as she approached his bed. He lay perfectly still, silent and watchful, tracking her with his eyes.

"I thought you were asleep," she said. "Kevin's sleeping, so I thought I'd use this time to check on you. They told me you ate some soft food for supper. An appetite is an encouraging sign, isn't it?" She raised her arms to her sides and executed a neat pirouette. "Like my new outfit? Stunning, isn't it? It's all the rage."

When he failed to respond to her bright prattle, she dropped her arms and her phony grin. In his position, she would resent anyone trying to placate her with banalities and lame jokes. He was in pain, humbled by being helpless and dependent. He was probably a little afraid—afraid that he would never regain his memory, afraid of what he would learn about himself if he did.

"I'm sorry this happened to you," she said sincerely. "It must be absolutely terrifying not to remember who you are or where you came from, what you're about, what you do, what you think and feel." She paused for emphasis. "But it *will* come back."

He raised his hand to his forehead and pressed his thumb

against one temple, his middle finger against the other, as though to squeeze information from his cranium. "I can't remember a damn thing. Nothing." He lowered his hand and looked at her bleakly. "Where exactly are we?"

"The town's called Stephensville. It's in Georgia."

He repeated the names, as though trying them out on his memory. "Do we live in Georgia?"

She shook her head. "We were traveling through on our way to South Carolina."

"I was driving," he said. "To avoid hitting a felled tree blocking the road, I must've overcompensated. The road was slick. Our car swerved, plunged down into a deep ravine, crashed into a tree, then was lost in a flooded creek."

Kendall's mouth went dry. "You remember all that?"

"No, I don't remember. Those are the facts the sheriff told me."

"Sheriff?"

He was quick to catch the alarm in her voice and looked at her quizzically. "That's right. A deputy. He came by earlier today, introduced himself, and asked me some questions."

"Why?"

"I guess he wanted answers."

"I gave him answers."

After a long silence, during which he gazed at her thoughtfully, he said softly, "Apparently he thought you were lying."

"I'm not!"

"Christ." Grimacing in pain, he again raised his hand to his head.

Kendall was instantly contrite. "I'm sorry, I didn't mean to shout. Are you in pain? Should I call the nurse?"

"No." He closed his eyes tightly and gave a deep sigh. "I'll be all right."

Feeling bad about her thoughtless outburst and wanting to make amends, Kendall refilled his water glass from the sweating plastic carafe. She slipped her hand between the pillow and the back of his head and lifted it gingerly. While she held the glass to his lips, he sucked through the flexible straw several times. "Enough?" she asked when he angled his head back.

He nodded. She gently lowered his head to the pillow and replaced the glass on the wheeled bed tray. "Thanks." He sighed. "This headache is a bitch."

"It'll get better in a day or so."

"Yeah." He didn't sound convinced.

"I know it hurts, but you can be glad that no serious damage was done. The doctor here consulted a neurologist in Atlanta."

"I overheard your conversation."

"Then you should feel reassured. Your memory could come back at any moment."

"Or it could take a while. Which I think you would prefer."

She hadn't seen that remark coming and was momentarily stunned. "I don't know what . . . What do you mean?"

"Wouldn't you rather I regain my memory later than sooner?"

"Why would I want that?"

"I haven't the vaguest."

Kendall thought it best to remain silent.

After a moment, he nodded toward the corridor where she had discussed his condition with the doctor. "You've been reading up on the subject of amnesia. It sounded as though you were covering all the bases, clarifying all the possibilities. And I just wondered why you would do that."

"I wanted to learn what you—what *we*—are up against. Isn't that natural?"

"I don't know. Is it?"

"For me, yes, it is. I like to know exactly where I stand at all times. I like to be prepared for the worst so I won't be so upset if that's what happens. It comes from being orphaned at an early age. I never quite got over my fear of the unexpected."

Suddenly realizing that she was telling too much, she shut up.

"Why'd you stop?" he asked. "It was just getting inter-esting."

"I don't want to confuse you with the facts." She grinned, hoping he would take it as a joke and as a conclusion to the discussion. "Does your leg hurt?"

"Not really. It's just a damn nuisance. The bumps and bruises hurt much worse."

His right arm lay listlessly across his lap. The skin was a mottled purple from his wrist to his biceps, which curved into the wide sleeve of the hospital gown. "This looks particularly painful." She stroked the dark bruise, then left her hand resting on his muscled arm. It seemed essential, somehow, that she touch him.

His gaze dropped to her left hand. In particular, he stared at the wedding ring on her third finger, and his stare made her even more aware of the heat conducted by her fingertips from his skin into hers. She shouldn't be touching him. She certainly shouldn't be registering any sensation. Nevertheless, she couldn't bring herself to remove her hand.

He turned his head slightly and looked up at her. A heavy silence ensued while he methodically and thoroughly studied her features. His shadowed eyes moved over her face, which held his attention for what seemed a terribly long time, during which Kendall held her breath. He followed the natural waves of her tawny hair all the way down to her shoulders.

Her heart in her throat, she asked, "Any glimmers of recog-nition?"

His eyes reconnected with hers, and she wondered if he remembered that they were an unusual shade of gray, which most people found arresting and which lying witnesses found disconcerting. When his gaze lowered to her mouth, her tummy felt like she'd taken a swift elevator ride. Even more like she'd been caught doing something forbidden.

She tried to retract her hand, but he quickly reached for it and held on tightly. He turned the narrow gold band on her finger. "Not a very fancy wedding ring."

Indeed. She had bought it at Wal-Mart that day. "It's what I wanted."

"Couldn't I afford better?"

"Money wasn't a deciding factor."

He continued to rotate the ring around her finger. "I don't remember placing it on your hand." He looked quickly at her. "I don't remember you. Are you sure we're married?"

She gave a false little laugh. "That's not something I'm likely to mistake."

"No, but you might lie about it."

Her heart fluttered. Even with amnesia, his ability to read her remained intact. "Why would I lie about it?"

"I don't know. Why would you?"

"This is ridiculous." Again she tried to pull her hand away, but he held on with surprising strength.

"I'm having a real hard time buying it."

"What?"

"You. The kid. All of it." He was growing angry.

"Why do you doubt me?"

"Because I can't remember you."

"You can't remember anything!"

"Some things you don't forget," he said, raising his voice, "and I'm betting that sleeping with you would be one of them."

The overhead light came on, nearly blinding them.

"Is something wrong in here?"

"Turn off that goddamn light!" he shouted. His hand moved to shield his eyes from the blue-white glare.

"Turn it off," Kendall ordered the nurse. "Can't you see the light hurts his eyes and makes his headache worse?"

The nurse extinguished the light. No one said anything for a moment. His last words were still ringing in Kendall's head. Finally, unable to meet his eyes, she addressed the nurse. "I'm

sorry for snapping at you. And for upsetting your patient. This
memory loss is putting a strain on both of us."

"Then I'd give it a rest for the night. The doctor said not
to try to pressure him into remembering." She brandished a
tray with a syringe on it. "I've come to give him his night-
night shot."

When she turned back to him, Kendall pasted on a smile.
"The more you try to force it, the more stubborn your memory
becomes. Sleep well. I'll see you in the morning."

She touched his shoulder fleetingly, then left before his
talent for detecting the truth uncovered the lie in her eyes.

She waited a long three hours before making her move.

Kevin slept peacefully in the newborn crib, his knees tucked
beneath his chest, his diapered bottom sticking up. Every once
in a while he made a sweet, snuffling baby sound. By now
her ears were attuned to them.

She was much too wired to sleep or even to lie down on the
hospital bed. If her physical weariness overcame her mental
alertness and she accidentally fell asleep, she would miss her
chance.

She looked at her wristwatch for the umpteenth time.
Twelve forty-five. Fifteen minutes more, she decided. Not
that she was on an inflexible schedule. She was conditioned
to dealing with events as they unfolded. It was just that the
more distance she could put between herself and Stephensville
before daylight, the better.

Tiptoeing to the window, she quietly parted the blinds and
peered through the foggy glass. Rain was still coming down,
steadily and relentlessly. It would make driving more difficult,
but the bad weather had been her good fortune. If not for it,
they would never have taken a detour. If not for the detour,
there would have been no accident. If not for the accident, they
would be back in Prosper by now. The weather had turned out
to be her ally. She wouldn't pick a quarrel with it now.

From the window she could see the car where she had left it—across the street, halfway down the block in the parking lot of a twenty-four-hour laundromat.

"Tires have another few thousand miles on them," the seller had told her, kicking the front left tire with the toe of his work boot. "Ain't much to look at, but she runs good."

She didn't have time to be choosy. Besides, this was the only car for sale by a private party she had found in the Stephensville classified ads.

"I'll give you a thousand dollars."

"The asking price is twelve hunnerd."

"One thousand." Kendall had removed ten hundred-dollar bills from her pocket and extended them to him.

He spat a stringy wad of tobacco juice into the mud, scratched his whiskers thoughtfully as he gazed at the money, then reached a decision. "Wait ri'chere. I won't be a sec. The title's inside the house."

She drove the nurse's car back to the hospital and had him follow her as far as the laundromat. "I'm going to park it here for the time being," she told him as he turned over two sets of keys to her. "My husband and I will pick it up later. I'll take you back home now. Sorry for the inconvenience."

Whatever inconvenience she had caused him was alleviated by the thousand dollars lining his pocket. Naturally he was curious to know her name, where she lived, what her husband did for a living. He had asked dozens of questions. Politely and facilely, Kendall had lied.

"You're a natural-born liar," Ricki Sue had once told her. *"That's why you're such a good lawyer."*

Wistfully, Kendall smiled at the recollection. They had been making Toll House cookies in Grandmother's kitchen. Kendall envisioned their faces and voices so clearly that they could almost have been in the hospital room with her now.

Ricki Sue had intended the comment to be a chastisement, but Kendall had taken it as a compliment.

"Careful, Ricki Sue. Words to that effect only encourage her," Grandmother had said. "And Lord knows she doesn't need any encouragement to tell a fib."

"I don't fib!" Kendall had protested.

"That's the biggest fib of all." Her grandmother had admonished her by shaking a dough-covered wooden spoon at her. "When you were growing up, how many times was I called to the schoolhouse to answer to some wild tale you'd been telling your classmates? She was always making up stories," she had explained to Ricki Sue in an aside.

"I sometimes reinvented the truth to make it more interesting," Kendall had said, sniffing loftily. "But I wouldn't call it fibbing."

"Neither would I," Ricki Sue had said matter-of-factly as she tossed a handful of chocolate morsels into her mouth. "It's called lying."

Thinking of the two women she so desperately missed caused Kendall's throat to ache with emotion. If she dwelled on memories now, the heartache would be immobilizing. And she must act before any more time was lost. Before the man who seemed to read her as easily as a primer recovered his memory.

She looked at her watch—1:00 A.M. Time to go.

Tiptoeing to the door, she opened it and cautiously looked down the hallway. There were two nurses on duty. One's attention was devoted to a novel; the other was talking on the telephone.

Earlier, Kendall had slipped out unnoticed and stashed their meager belongings in the car, so that now she had only the baby to carry out.

Returning to the crib, she slid her hands beneath his tummy and gently turned him over. He made an ugly face but didn't wake up, even when she lifted him out of the crib and cradled him against her chest.

"You're such a good boy," she whispered. "You know

Mommy loves you, don't you? And that I would do any-thing—*anything*—to protect you."

She crept from the room. After being in the dark for hours, the corridor seemed unnaturally bright. She spent several precious seconds letting her eyes adjust, then began moving stealthily down the corridor.

If she could make it to the intersecting hallway without being discovered, she'd be home free. But for about thirty feet she would be exposed. If one of the nurses glimpsed her out of the corner of her eye, she had an explanation ready: Kevin had gas and was fretful. She had decided to walk him.

They would believe her without question, but her plans would be thwarted. She would have to try again tomorrow night. Each hour counted; tomorrow might be too late. She needed to disappear tonight.

She concentrated on keeping her footfalls silent and quick. Eyes trained on the two nurses, she calculated the distance to the corner. How much farther? Ten feet? Fifteen?

Kevin belched.

To Kendall's ears it sounded like a cannon being fired. She froze, her heart knocking against her ribs. But apparently no one else heard the burp. One nurse was still reading, the other was still talking, obviously warming to her topic.

"So I said that if he went bowling three nights a week anyway, why did he care if I pulled some night duty? He says, 'That's different.' And then I said, 'You're damn right. Bowling doesn't pay for shit.'"

Kendall didn't stick around to hear the outcome of the domestic dispute. As soon as she reached the corner, she sidestepped into the other hallway. She'd made it!

Flattening her spine against the wall, she closed her eyes, breathed deeply, and slowly counted to thirty. When she was certain that she hadn't roused the nurses, she opened her eyes.

He, however, had been roused.

Chapter Four

*H*E CLAMPED HIS HAND OVER HER MOUTH.

Not that it was necessary. She was too dumbfounded to scream. Nor would she have done so anyway. On the night she fled Prosper, she had been shocked by circumstances much more frightening than this, and she hadn't screamed then.

Nevertheless, she was startled. It seemed he had materialized out of the walls. How had he managed to get within inches of her without her sensing his approach?

In his weakened condition, he shouldn't have been intimidating. He leaned heavily on a pair of crutches. His complexion was ashen; his lips were practically colorless. Obviously he was in tremendous pain.

There was nothing weak about his eyes, however. They glowered at her from their sunken sockets. Kendall felt her heart in her throat.

She gave a firm, negative shake of her head, trying to make him understand that she wouldn't utter a sound that would give them away. Gradually he lowered his hand.

The nurse on the telephone had continued her litany of complaints without a glitch. The other nurse at the desk hadn't raised her eyes from the novel she was reading. There was no indication that either of them was aware that one of their patients had left his bed.

He had dressed himself in a pair of green OR scrubs. The right pants leg had been ripped apart to accommodate his cast. The tear was so ragged, it looked as though he'd chewed through the fabric. Kendall wouldn't have put it past him. He looked haggard, but his jaw was set with determination. He would have gone to whatever extremes necessary to get out of bed and clothe himself.

Kendall signaled him to follow her back toward his room. He eyed her mistrustfully, but he didn't stop her when she began to tiptoe down the hallway. As the doctor had said, he maneuvered quite well on crutches. Their rubber tips made virtually no sound as they struck the floor tiles.

Passing the room he had occupied, they continued toward the exit where the corridor came to a dead end. Red stenciled letters above the depression bar warned that this door was for emergency use only and that an alarm would sound if it was opened.

Kendall reached for the bar. In a motion too fluid and fast for a human eye to track, he raised his right crutch horizontally and placed it in front of her at chest level.

She frowned at him, mouthing, "It's okay. Trust me."

He pantomimed, "No way."

Arguing silently with hand motions and exaggerated facial expressions, she finally convinced him that nothing untoward would happen if she opened the door. He gave her a hard, threatening look, then lowered the crutch.

Kendall depressed the bar. It came unlatched with a metallic click, without setting off an alarm. Leaning forward, she pushed the door open.

She paused to listen, but the only sound that greeted her was that of hard rainfall splashing into puddles in the sparse grass of the yard and on the cement walkway from the door to the street.

Kendall held the door open while he hobbled through. She didn't let go of the closing door until she heard the click indicating that it was once again securely latched.

Only then did she speak, but in a whisper. "You're going to get soaked."

"I won't melt."

"Why don't you wait here and—"

"Not on your life."

"Do you really think I'd bolt and leave you behind?"

He shot her a retiring look. "Save it, okay? Let's go."

"All right then, this way."

"I know. The navy blue Cougar parked at the laundromat."

He struck off down the sidewalk, seeming impervious to the rain. Kendall held Kevin tightly against her and, making certain the receiving blanket covered his face, followed the man on crutches.

He was shaking from chills, pain, and weakness by the time they reached the Cougar. Kendall hurriedly unlocked the passenger door for him before running around to the driver's side. On a second trip to Wal-Mart she'd purchased an infant seat for the car. She secured Kevin in it now and replaced the damp flannel blanket with a dry one. The baby's mouth made a few sucking motions, but he didn't awaken. It was still a couple of hours before his next feeding. She had timed her getaway with his nursing schedule in mind.

She slid behind the steering wheel and fastened her seat belt, then inserted the key into the ignition. The car started instantly.

"You made a good buy. I saw you from the window of my hospital room," he explained when she looked at him inquisitively. "Who was the old codger in overalls? Friend of yours?"

"A stranger. I answered his classified ad."

"I thought it must be something like that. How'd you know the alarm wouldn't go off when you opened that exit door?"

"The maintenance man left through that door this morning. I tested it again later in the day. No alarm. I gambled on it not being on a timer or something."

"But you had a logical explanation in mind if an alarm had gone off, didn't you? Aren't you the lady who's always prepared for the worst to happen?"

"You don't have to get nasty."

"Why not? Why should I be polite to a woman who claims to be my wife but was skipping out on me."

"I wasn't leaving without you. I was on my way to your room when—"

"Look," he interrupted, his voice sounding as dry and abrasive as sandpaper. "You were sneaking out in the middle of the night and had no intention of taking me with you. You know it. I know it." He paused. "My head hurts too much to argue about it, so just . . ."

He ran short of breath. His upper body sagged with the effort of making such a long speech. With a feeble hand gesture, he motioned that she should get under way.

"Are you cold?" she asked.

"No."

"You're sopping wet."

"But I'm not cold."

"Fine."

Stephensville didn't have much of a downtown commercial district, although there were a few businesses and one bank on the four corners of the main crossroads. All the buildings were dark except for the sheriff's office. To avoid driving past it, she turned a block before she needed to.

"Do you know where you're going?" he asked.

"Why don't you try to get some sleep?"

"Because I don't trust you. If I doze off, you might push me out at the next wide spot in the road."

"If I'd wanted you dead, I wouldn't have pulled you from the wreckage. I could have left you to die."

He lapsed into a sullen silence that lasted for several miles. Kendall thought he'd taken her advice and gone to sleep, but when she turned to look at him, he was watching her with the intensity of a sniper who has his target in the crosshairs of his sight.

"You pulled me from the wreckage?"

"Yes."

"Why?"

She snickered. "Well, it seemed the humane thing to do."

"Why would you save my life, then desert me in some hillbilly hospital to fend for myself when I'm dispossessed of everything?"

"I wasn't going to desert you."

"That's a lie."

She sighed wearily. "After our conversation in your room tonight, I realized that you shared my lack of confidence in that doctor. So I thought it best to move you to another facility and get a second opinion.

"Rather than getting trapped in a mess of red tape—and I really didn't want to hurt their feelings because they've been generous and kind to Kevin and me—I planned on sneaking you out."

"What if I'd been sedated?"

"All the better. You wouldn't have given me an argument." She glanced at him. "Didn't the nurse give you the injection after I left your room?"

"She tried. I insisted on a pill instead and then didn't swallow it. I like to be prepared, too. Gut instinct told me you might do something like this. If you did, I wanted to be awake."

Kendall glanced at the green cloth clinging wetly to his skin. "You stole the scrubs from the supply closet?"

"Better that than traipsing through the countryside bare-assed. Are we on our way to South Carolina?"

"Tennessee, actually."

"Why the change in plans? What's in Tennessee?"

"If I told you, you wouldn't believe me, so why don't you just wait and see."

"What'd we do?"

"I beg your pardon?"

"We must be on the run. What crime did we commit?"

"What on earth gave you that idea?"

"It makes more sense than the crock of shit you've been feeding me."

"What part don't you believe?"

"None of it. Our being a married couple with a child, to start with. Your intention to take me along when you flew the coop. I don't believe a word of it. You're an adroit liar. Don't deny it, and don't ask me how I know. I just know. You make it up as you go along."

"That's not true."

Her protest was born of anxiety as much as affront. His gut instinct, which he seemed to trust completely, was keen. With the exception of her grandmother, no one had ever been able to see through her so clearly. Under different circumstances, she would admire such perception, but right now she knew it could prove lethal.

She needed to act the difficult part of loving wife without arousing his suspicions further. After all, this situation was temporary. Surely she could be convincing for a while longer.

They lapsed into silence. The only sounds inside the car were the hypnotic swish of the tires on the wet pavement and the rapid cadence of the windshield wipers.

Kendall envied Kevin his peaceful sleep, his freedom from responsibility. She would have given almost anything to rest, to close her eyes and let sleep claim her. But she couldn't even think of it yet. She wouldn't breathe easily until there was much more distance between them and Stephensville's inquisitive deputy sheriff.

Gathering her waning energy, she gripped the steering wheel tighter and accelerated to a lawful, safe, but mile-consuming speed.

He felt like he was lost in a dark, endless tunnel with a locomotive bearing down on him. He couldn't see it, couldn't outrun it. All he could do was brace himself for the impact. Dreading the inevitable was the worst part. He would just as soon collide with it and get it over with because the ceaseless roar in his head was trying to blast his eyeballs from his skull.

Every part of his body was uncomfortable. His limbs were cramped and stiff, but he knew even before he tried that he would be unable to stretch his aching muscles. His butt was numb from sitting so long in one position, and he'd have a stiff neck from sleeping with his head at an awkward angle. His clothes were damp. He was hungry, and he had to pee.

Most important, though, he'd had the dream again.

Shackled inside the nightmare, he couldn't escape the baby's crying, which had seemed even clearer and nearer than usual and had nudged him out of deep sleep. Now his conscious mind was coaxing him to come completely awake, but he resisted. As badly as he hated that recurring dream, he almost preferred it to full consciousness.

Why?

Then he remembered.

He remembered that he couldn't remember.

He had amnesia, which must have been caused by some weakness within himself. Even that smart-ass with a stethoscope had picked up on that psychological quirk.

It made him frustrated and angry to think that he was responsible for his intolerable malady. Surely he could remember if he really tried.

He peered into the dark recesses of his mind, straining to

see a flicker of light. Something. Anything. A clue. A hint.
An infinitesimal speck of information about himself.

But there was absolutely nothing. Not a glimmer. His life
before waking up in the hospital was as dense and absent of
light as a black hole.

To escape the nagging questions to which he had no
answers, he opened his eyes. It was day, but there was no
sunlight. Raindrops splashed against the windshield, then
merged to form crooked rivulets that trickled down the glass.

His head was resting against the passenger window. The
glass felt pleasantly cool. He dreaded moving, but did so,
tentatively raising his head. The headache wasn't as bad as
it had been yesterday, but it was still a prizewinner.

"Good morning."

He turned his head toward her voice.

What he saw scared the hell out of him.

Chapter Five

SHE WAS NURSING THE BABY.

The seat was angled back as far as it would go. Her head lay against the headrest. Her hair hadn't been combed since the rain got to it the night before, so it had dried into a tangled, blond mess. There were dark crescents of fatigue beneath her eyes. She was disheveled, but her expression was one of such unadulterated contentment that she looked beautiful.

She repeated her good-morning. Trying desperately to keep his eyes averted, and failing, he mumbled a reply.

It wasn't as though she was flaunting herself. She had draped a baby blanket over her shoulder to cover her chest. No flesh was exposed. He saw nothing of the baby except movement beneath the blanket. But she was a study of maternal bliss.

Why should that cause him to break into a cold sweat? What the hell was the matter with him?

He was nauseated. His heartbeat raced and he felt claustrophobic, as though his air passages had been stuffed with cotton and his next gasping breath might be his last.

Equally repelled and fascinated, he wanted to get as far away as he could from her and the child, as fast as he could, and yet he couldn't stop looking at them. The aura of peacefulness that surrounded her—a peace he was dead certain he had never experienced—was magnetic. The contentment so evident in her expression seemed foreign to him. He would naturally be drawn to it.

Or maybe, he thought with self-disgust, he was transfixed for a prurient reason. Which made him a perverted sicko with a thing for nursing mothers.

He squeezed his eyes shut and pinched the bridge of his nose hard enough to bring tears. Maybe he hadn't survived the accident after all. Maybe he had died, and the hospital had been his purgatory, a waystation before being zoomed into the real thing.

Because surely this was hell.

"How do you feel?"

Before he could speak, he had to swallow a mouthful of acrid saliva. "Take all the hangovers in history and multiply by ten."

"I'm sorry. I'd hoped we wouldn't wake you. You slept right through the diaper change."

"Speaking of which . . ."

"Over there."

Following the direction of her nod, he looked through the rain-streaked window. She had stopped at a roadside park; theirs was the only vehicle in sight. The picnic grounds were overgrown with weeds. Rust had eaten holes through the metal trash barrels, which were overflowing with soggy garbage. The entire area looked derelict.

"I'm afraid the facilities aren't very clean," she said. "At least the ladies' wasn't. I hated to use it, but I didn't have a choice."

"Neither do I." He reached for the door handle. "Will you still be here when I come out?"

She ignored the barb. "If you can wait until Kevin finishes, I'll give you a hand."

The baby's fist, poking out from beneath the blanket, had a grip on her blouse. The tiny fingers flexed and closed, flexed and closed. "Thanks anyway," he said gruffly. "I can make it by myself."

It was only a few yards from the car to the concrete block building. He used the stained urinal, then moved to the sink, where rusty water dripped from the faucet. He washed his hands. There was nothing with which to dry them, but it didn't matter. They'd only get wet again when he made his way back to the car. Nor was there a mirror, which was also just as well. He must look like the unlucky survivor of a long and terrible war. That's how he felt.

When he returned to the car, the baby was back in his infant seat. "There's a town about five miles ahead," she said as she started the engine. "I thought we'd stop there for coffee. Then we should make a call to the nearest neurologist."

The trip to the bathroom had sapped what little strength he had. "Coffee sounds great," he said, trying to hide his weakness from her. "But I'm not going to another doctor."

Astonished, she looked at him with wide, gray eyes. Eyes the color of fog. A fog he could get lost in if he didn't keep his head. "There's no reason to go to another doctor," he said.

"Are you nuts? You're a disaster."

"I have a concussion. As long as I don't do anything strenuous for a few days, I'll be okay. Nothing but time will heal this busted leg. So why go to another doctor and pay good money to hear the same old line?"

"You're in constant pain. At the very least, you need a prescription painkiller."

"I'll take aspirin."

"What about the amnesia? You should consult with a specialist."

"And while I'm consulting with this specialist, you'll run out on me."

"I will not."

"Look, I don't know who you are or what your story is, but until I find out, I'm not letting you out of my sight. I'm not giving you another chance to abandon me." He pointed his chin at the steering wheel. "Let's go. I need that coffee."

The next town was a small farming community, practically a clone of Stephensville. She slowed down to the speed limit on the main drag.

"Pull in there," he said, pointing to a café tucked between a dry-goods store and the post office. Several pickups were parked at the crumbling curb, although the time on all the parking meters had expired. It appeared to be the place where locals gathered early for coffee and conversation, even on rainy Sunday mornings.

"Are you hungry?" she asked.

"Yes."

"I'll get something we can take with us so you won't have to get out," she told him. "Keep an eye on the baby."

The baby. He shot an anxious glance at the backseat. Good. The kid was asleep. As long as he continued to sleep, everything would be fine.

But what if he didn't? What if he woke up and started crying? The very thought provoked an acute anxiety within, but he couldn't understand why.

He didn't breathe easily until she emerged from the café several minutes later, carrying two Styrofoam cups and a white paper sack. He removed the lid of the cup she handed him, and the tantalizing aroma of freshly brewed coffee filled the interior of the car.

"Ah." He took a sip, grimaced, then looked at her in puzzlement. "Why didn't you sweeten it?"

She drew a quick breath; her lips remained parted but she was speechless. Her eyes stayed fixed on his, then after a moment she relaxed, frowned, and tilted her head with a shame-on-you expression. "Since when did you start using sweetener in your coffee?"

Without breaking the stare, he took another sip of the straight black coffee, which he somehow knew he preferred.

He had set what he thought was a clever trap, but she was too smart to walk into it.

"You're good," he said with reluctant admiration. "You're damn good."

"I don't know what you're talking about."

He harrumphed and picked up the sack. "What's for breakfast?"

He had scarfed down two of the biscuit and pork sausage sandwiches before noticing that she had removed the meat patties from hers. "Did you poison the sausage, or what?"

"Please," she said, groaning.

"Then what's wrong with it?"

"Nothing, I guess," she said, biting into her plain biscuit. "I just don't eat pork anymore."

"Anymore? Meaning that you did at one time. Why'd you lay off pork?"

"Don't we have more urgent things to discuss?" She licked buttery crumbs from her fingertips. "You should seriously reconsider and let me take you to a doctor."

"No. *No*," he repeated with emphasis when he saw that she was about to argue. "All I need are some dry clothes and aspirin."

"Okay. Fine. It's your head."

"I'd like to know my name."

"What?" She went perfectly still, gazing at him with stricken eyes that didn't even blink.

"Everyone in the hospital was very careful not to call me by name," he said. "Even when the deputy questioned me, he didn't address me by name."

"Doctor's orders. He didn't want you to become distressed and confused."

"What's my name?"

"John."

"John," he repeated, trying on the name. It wasn't uncomfortable. But it didn't necessarily fit, either. "What's yours?"

"Kendall."

The names meant nothing to him. Zero. He gazed at her suspiciously.

Her tone was almost too innocent when she asked, "Ring any bells?"

"No. Because I'm almost certain you're lying."

She didn't even honor that with a comment. Instead, she started the car. They drove for another hour before reaching a town that had a store open on Sunday. "Give me your list," she said after she had parked.

She jotted down toiletry items as he enumerated them. "And some clothes," he added.

"Anything special?"

"Just clothes. And a newspaper, please."

"A newspaper?" She hesitated, then nodded and reached for the door. "This may take a while. I've got a shopping list, too."

Before she could get out, he asked, "How are you going to pay?"

"With cash."

"Where'd you get it?"

"I earned it," she replied curtly, opening the car door.

Again he forestalled her. "Wait. You'll need my sizes."

She reached across the car seat and squeezed his knee. "Silly. I know your sizes."

The wifely, natural, familiar gesture sent an electric shock through his system.

Watching her as she walked toward the entrance to the store, he thought for the thousandth time, *Who is this woman, and what is she to me?*

Five minutes later, the baby started fretting. At first he ignored the crying, but when it intensified, he turned and looked at the kid, who had no reason to cry that he could see.

He tried to tune him out, but the squalling increased in volume until it was earsplitting. He began to perspire. Sweat trickled from his armpits down to his ribs. It beaded on his forehead. He was burning up, but he didn't risk opening a window because the crying infant would attract attention.

Christ, where is she? What's taking so damn long?

She heard her baby crying long before she reached the car. She broke into a run and practically pulled the driver's door from its hinges.

"What's the matter with Kevin? What happened?"

She tossed the sacks of purchases into his lap and pushed forward the seat. Seconds later the baby was in her arms and she was crooning to him.

"Why didn't you do something?" she demanded. "Why'd you just let him scream like that?"

"I didn't know what to do. I don't know anything about babies."

"Well, you should, shouldn't you?" She hugged the child tighter against her and rocked him on her shoulder while patting his back. "There, there, sweetheart. It's okay. Mommy's here now." She cradled him in her left arm and, tucking him against her body, raised the hem of her shirt.

He glimpsed a milk-swollen breast and a jutting nipple a split second before it disappeared into the infant's mouth.

Because he continued to gape at the suckling infant, she shot him a defiant look. "Is something wrong?"

Something was wrong, all right, but he didn't have a clue as to what it was. He turned his head away and stared out the window. If she was his wife, as she claimed, why had he experienced a guilty thrill at seeing her breast? If she was the mother of his child—his son—why did the whole concept of maternity make him queasy?

Jesus. What kind of man was he?

The disturbing questions made his head throb painfully. He closed his eyes and tried to block out the conflicting stimuli coming from the other side of the car.

Chapter Six

*H*E PRETENDED TO DOZE EVEN AFTER THEY WERE back on the road. She drove in silence, not even consulting him before she stopped again. While she filled the gas tank, he went to the restroom. This time there was a mirror, and, as he had imagined, he looked like a Halloween mask. He considered shaving, then decided against it. It wouldn't be that much of an improvement. Besides, he didn't want to give her time to take off without him.

When he came out of the restroom, he saw that she was being hassled by a trio of teenage boys. They had cornered her at the vending machine and wouldn't let her pass. She was carrying snacks and canned drinks in both hands.

"This isn't funny, guys," she said irritably as she tried to sidestep the tallest of them.

"I think it's funny," he said. "Don't you think it's funny, Joe?"

"Real funny," Joe answered, grinning stupidly.

"We're just trying to be friendly," the third said.

"Come on, tell us your name, blondie."

"You ain't from around here, are you, cutie?"

"No," Kendall replied icily. "And from what I've seen, I'm glad of that. Now are you going to let me by, or——"

"Or what?" Joe asked, thrusting his jeering face close to hers.

"Or I'll stomp the shit out of you."

Of the four who turned around, Kendall was by far the most surprised. Ignoring the boys standing between them, she said imploringly, "Don't do anything. Please. I can handle them."

"Yeah," one of the boys said. "She can handle us." He cupped his crotch. "I'll bet she's pretty good at it, too."

Joe and the other boy thought their friend's double entendre was extremely clever. They burst into laughter.

"You can barely stand up," one chortled, pointing at him.

"Yeah. She do that to you?"

"*You're* gonna hurt *us*? I don't think so."

"Which leg you gonna stomp us with, crip?" Joe taunted.

Their laughter was abruptly halted when he swung his right crutch up and rapped Joe's shins with it. The boy's knees buckled and he went down, bellowing. The other two turned whey-faced.

"Get out of her way," he said calmly.

They moved away from Kendall. Joe continued to roll on the ground, yowling and clutching his smarting shins. Kendall stepped around him and walked swiftly to the car.

"I suggest you boys learn some manners," he said, then joined Kendall in the car.

She drove away quickly. He was feeling better now that he knew he wasn't entirely useless. So he was flabbergasted when she launched her verbal attack.

"That was brilliant. Just brilliant. Thank you very much. That's just what I needed, a knight on crutches to rescue me from some harmless flirting. I could have handled it. But no, you had to barge in and give them something to remember!"

"You're angry?"

"Yes, I'm angry. Why did you butt in? Why didn't you just mind your own business?"

"When my wife's being sexually harassed by three men, it *is* my business. Isn't it?" Her combative flare fizzled. She now looked flustered and annoyed with herself for losing her temper. "You didn't want a scene, right? Because you didn't want us to be remembered if anyone should come asking. Guess it's a good thing I didn't throw these away." He held up the OR scrubs he had been wearing. "They won't leave a trail."

She didn't take the bait. Her eyes remained on the road, but she sighed and pushed back her hair. "I'm sorry. Thank you for rushing to my defense. Do the clothes fit okay?"

"Yeah," he said, glancing down at his new shorts and T-shirt. It occurred to him then that she really had known his sizes.

They were traveling a narrow state highway that cut through dense forests. As they passed flooded fields and crossed bridges spanning swollen creeks, he was reminded of their accident.

His amnesia was her most valuable asset, because it kept him in the dark. Her word was his sole source of information. She could tell him anything, and he had no choice but to accept it because he couldn't disprove it. He had no way of finding out what the real picture was.

"You forgot to buy me a newspaper," he remarked. "Was that an oversight?"

"No, but there weren't any. I checked several dispensers. They'd sold out."

For once, she might be telling the truth, he thought. The dispensers at the gas station had been empty, too. He had made a point to check. He had hoped that a headline or even a small filler item would spark his memory.

On the other hand, he dreaded reading about a notorious character and realizing it was himself. Before the accident, had he been involved in some criminal activity?

Instinct told him that his authority was being challenged. But what authority? Professional? Marital? That couldn't be it because he didn't believe for a second that they were a married couple. He would know—somehow he would *know*—if he had slept with her.

No man alive could forget those breasts, shapely and sexy in spite of their nurturing function. The shape of her ass hadn't escaped his notice, either. She had arresting eyes and morning-after hair that seemed to have a will of its own.

She wasn't classically pretty, but even from his hospital bed he had noticed her voluptuous mouth. It was full and provocative, the kind you'd gladly pay a thousand dollars to spend the night with.

When he had watched her licking buttery biscuit crumbs from her fingers earlier, he had been convinced that his self-diagnosis was correct. He wasn't that sick.

His reactions to her were distinctly masculine, conditioned reflexes. He had responded the way any heterosexual man would to that stimuli. He would bet his life that his response was not founded on recognition and familiarity.

Made restless by the track his thoughts had taken, he switched on the radio, hoping to catch a newscast. "It's broken," she told him.

"Convenient for you," he said. "How much farther do we have to go? And where in hell are we going anyway? And don't you dare say Tennessee."

She didn't. She said, "We're going to Grandmother's house."

"Grandmother's house," he repeated caustically.

"That's right."

"Your grandmother or mine? Do I have a grandmother?"

He envisioned a stereotype—gray hair captured in a neat bun, a benign smile, admonitions to keep your jacket buttoned even when it was seventy-five degrees outside, someone who smelled of lavender soap and kitchen spices. He grasped the concept, but he couldn't imagine himself being coddled by such an individual. Or coddled by anyone, for that matter.

"It's my grandmother," she said.

"Have you notified her that we're coming?"

"She won't be there." Her voice took on a soft huskiness. "She died four months ago. Just a few weeks before Kevin was born."

He digested that. "Were you with her?"

"No. I was . . . away. And too close to term to attend her funeral."

"You two were close?"

"More than close. We shared an extraordinary relationship." His evident interest encouraged her to continue. "My mother and father were killed in an accident when I was five. Grandmother became my guardian. My grandfather had already died, so it was just the two of us. The bond between us was very strong."

"Did I know her? Have I been to her house before?"

She shook her head.

"How much farther?"

Sighing, she rolled her head around her shoulders. "Please stop asking me that. It won't get us there any sooner. I'd like to get there before dark, and the time would pass much faster for you if you would sleep. You need the rest."

He had taken three aspirins, which had dulled his headache and reduced the soreness of his muscles, but he still felt like he had been tenderized with a meat mallet. With the intention of resting his eyes for just a moment, he relaxed back against the headrest.

Hours later, when he woke, it was dusk and they had reached their destination.

The house was situated at the end of a lane that was lined with grapevines and honeysuckle bushes. The rain had abated, so as they approached the house, Kendall rolled down the car window and breathed deeply of the mingled fragrances, the sweet smells of summer. Memories of her childhood assailed her. Homesickness for her grandmother squeezed her heart like pincers with vicious teeth.

It had grown dark beneath the trees in the surrounding forest. Lightning bugs winked at her from the leafy shadows. She almost expected to hear Grandmother's voice calling her to come see this galaxy of glowworms.

The house was a frame structure with a composite roof that extended over a wide porch. It could have used a coat of paint, and the yard needed attention, but otherwise it was remarkably unchanged since her last visit.

Except that her grandmother wasn't there and never would be again.

Gravel crunched beneath the tires as she brought the car to a stop. He woke up, yawned, stretched, and peered through the gloaming to get his bearings.

Kendall opened her door and got out, for the moment leaving Kevin asleep in his infant seat. She jogged up the front steps, then stood on tiptoe to reach the key that had always been kept above the doorjamb.

She located it and inserted it into the lock. The door swung open. Hoping for the best, she reached for the light switch on the wall. When the lights came on, she breathed a sigh of relief. Ricki Sue had continued paying the utilities bills.

Swiftly she moved through the rooms. Sheets covered the furniture, and the house smelled musty from being uninhabited, but she would shortly have it livable—for only as long as she and Kevin would be there.

She returned to the living room. He had followed her inside and was standing propped on his crutches, surveying the unfamiliar surroundings.

"Like it?"

He gave a noncommittal shrug.

"I know it doesn't look like much now, but I'll fix it up." The statement evoked a memory that was so realistic, it staggered her.

Almost word for word, it echoed a statement she had made on her wedding night.

Chapter Seven

MATT SWUNG OPEN THE FRONT DOOR. "WHAT A wonderful wedding! The muscles of my face are aching from smiling so much." When he realized that Kendall hadn't followed him into the house, he looked back at her curiously. "What is it?"

"Call me a foolish romantic, but I've always dreamed of my bridegroom carrying me across the threshold."

"You *are* a foolish romantic." Smiling, he scooped her into his arms. "But that's just one of the many things I love about you."

He carried her inside. Kendall placed her hand behind his neck and drew him down for a long, meaningful kiss, one she knew she would remember for the rest of her life—their first kiss in their first home.

Gibb had presented them with the house as a wedding gift—fully furnished, mortgage-free, everything paid in full. Kendall had been astounded by his generosity, but, in keeping with his character, Gibb had dismissed her effusive thanks. He had hounded the contractor to have it ready by their wedding day, and he had accepted no excuses. It had been completed and ready for occupancy three days ago.

Now, Matt set her down in the wide entryway. "Mind if we get rid of this?" he asked, fingering her bridal veil.

"Not at all."

With some assistance from her, he lifted the veil from her head; then, holding her with a possessiveness she relished, he kissed her again. When he finally released her, she was breathless and giddy with happiness.

Flinging her arms wide, she pivoted a full 360 degrees, absorbing the beauty of her new home, from the skylight overhead to the wood grain of the floor.

It was an environmentally friendly frame house, designed to blend in to its rustic setting with the Blue Ridge Mountains as a backdrop. The interior was contemporary but warm and embracing. The rooms were spacious and bright. It smelled of new lumber and fresh paint.

This moment held special significance for Kendall. This was to be her home, she hoped for the rest of her life. She and Matt would rear their children here. In this house they would live and grow old together, a simple privilege her young parents had been denied. She wanted her happiness to be so abundant that it would make up for their loss.

She hugged herself. "I love it."

Matt had shrugged off his tuxedo jacket and was standing with his hands in his pockets, taking in the appointments of the house. The furniture still had factory tags attached. The rooms hadn't been accessorized. "It's a little stark, isn't it?"

"It's not a home yet," she said. "We'll put our stamp on it, make it more than just a house. I know it doesn't look like much now, but I'll fix it up. I can't wait to get started."

Moved by her own speech, she laid her hands on the pleats of his tuxedo shirt and leaned in to him. "Oh, Matt, I love my life here."

He slid his arms around her waist. "I'm doing okay myself," he teased. He gave her a quick, hard kiss. "But I'm starving. Dad said there'd be food in the fridge."

He released her and made his way to the kitchen. Kendall caught up with him as he was removing a bottle of champagne from the wide refrigerator. "I'll pop the cork and pour. You read the gift card. Good Lord, when Dad said there'd be food, he wasn't kidding. Most supermarkets don't have this much inventory."

He tossed the card onto the kitchen table. Kendall picked it up and read aloud: " 'You two do me proud. All my love, Dad. *P.S.* Chilled glasses in the freezer.' "

Matt laughed. "He thinks of everything, doesn't he?"

"If we'd wanted to go to Mars on our honeymoon, I think he would have tried to arrange it."

Matt stopped wrestling with the cork and looked at her with a sad smile. "I'm sorry about that, Kendall. Bad timing."

"I understand," she said softly.

Quite unexpectedly, Matt's managing editor had died recently. Mr. Gregory's passing had left a void in Matt's life, personally and professionally. He hadn't yet found a suitable replacement for the job. Until he did, he couldn't leave his newspaper, even to take a honeymoon. Naturally, Kendall sympathized with his situation.

She couldn't complain about forgoing a honeymoon, because she was enjoying such a wealth of riches. Her husband was all she had ever dreamed he would be. Her father-in-law was generous to a fault, and not only in material things. Gibb had welcomed her into their family without so much as a hint of reservation or resentment. For years he'd had Matt all to himself. Now he had to share him, and he was doing so graciously.

They chatted about the ceremony and reception while they sipped champagne and built ham sandwiches. Matt was ravenous, but Kendall was still too excited to eat.

She was picking at the crust of her bread and gazing out the windows when she said, "I want to landscape only half the yard and leave the back part of it wild, like it is now. I'd like to put bird feeders in the trees. I'll have the squirrels domesticated in no time. I hope we have raccoons, too."

"They make a mess."

"Not our raccoons. They'll be neat because they'll get regular meals and won't have to forage. And deer," she continued, her enthusiasm undimmed by his groan. "We might even get deer to come close to the house."

"Kendall, if we have deer in our yard, our friends will be over here shooting them on the first day of hunting season."

"Oh, don't say that! And don't even think of mounting a stuffed head on any of our walls."

"I don't understand your aversion to hunting. It's a sport Dad and I enjoy very much, and we're not alone."

"Well, *I* don't understand how someone can get a charge out of killing innocent animals."

"You're a softie."

"I suppose." She smiled wistfully. "One summer Grandmother and I saved a fawn's life. We found him at our favorite spot near a waterfall. It's actually not much more than a trickle, but when I was very young, I thought it was awesome. And there's this long-forgotten Confederate war memorial there. I used to play on that rusty old cannon whenever we picnicked there, which was at least once a week.

"Anyway, we came across this fawn in the woods. He had a broken leg. The two of us carried him all the way back to the car and took him home. We set his leg and nursed him until he was well enough to be returned to the forest."

"Where he was fair game the next hunting season."

"Matt!"

"I'm sorry." He reached across the table and stroked her cheek. "How can I make it up to you?"

She captured his hand and kissed the palm, then lightly worked the fleshy part of his thumb between her teeth. "Take me to bed," she whispered seductively.

The bed had already been turned down. Vases of flowers

had been placed on the nightstands and dresser. Gibb's handiwork, no doubt. But even knowing that her father-in-law had invaded the privacy of their master bedroom didn't diminish Kendall's desire.

As they faced each other, undressing each other, laughing as they fumbled with the dozens of buttons on her gown, barely containing their impatience, which only heightened their anticipation, she now was glad that this was their first time together.

Matt hadn't slept with her during their courtship and engagement. Abstinence to that degree almost deserved a banner headline. Nowadays, how many couples waited until their wedding night to make love? It was a custom on the brink of extinction.

She wasn't a virgin and neither was he, but while they were dating he had remained a gentleman, apparently adhering to a code of honor that prohibited him from sleeping with the woman he had chosen for his wife, elevating Kendall to a level above all the women with whom he had previously been involved.

It was an old-fashioned tradition that went hand in glove with the unfair double standard that women had been subjected to for centuries. But, in a way, Kendall had found his restraint sweet, endearing, and terribly romantic.

Many times, when they had said good night at the door of her apartment, sexually charged and frustrated, she had wished he would relax his stance on that principle. She had even encouraged him to. He never had.

Now as his hands moved over her skin, eagerly exploring the shape of her body, she thought there was distinct value in waiting for this moment, when their wedding attire lay at their feet and their nakedness was as new to them as their status as husband and wife.

"You're going to be exactly the wife I wanted," he murmured as he kissed her breasts. "I know it."

"I promise I will be."

* * *

For several seconds after Kendall awoke, she couldn't remember why she was suffused with such a feeling of euphoria. When she blinked her surroundings into focus, her smile turned smug. She all but purred with satisfaction.

This was the morning following her wedding night, and she was the luckiest woman in the world. Her husband was a tender and considerate lover. They'd made love until, exhausted, they'd fallen asleep.

Matt was an habitual early riser, not one to sleep late. The slant of sunlight coming through the window indicated that it was well past dawn. The thought that she must have worn him out last night brought a gamine smile to her lips.

Not wanting to disturb him, she turned cautiously. For a few moments, she wanted to watch and adore him without his being aware of it. He was sleeping on his back, his lips slightly parted, his torso rising and falling rhythmically. The sheet was pulled up to his waist.

Memories of last night's intimacy reawakened her passions. Desire curled through her, stirring her blood, shortening her breath, bringing back that dull, delicious, bittersweet ache to her lower body. Last night Matt had treated her like a cherished bride. This morning, she wanted to be treated like a woman.

Slipping her hand beneath the sheet, she whispered, "Good morning."

He grunted.

Her hand closed around his flaccid penis. "I said good morning."

He smiled, mumbled something unintelligible, then opened his eyes. "Kendall."

"Well, thank you for remembering. You sound surprised."

"I am. An alarm clock usually gets me up."

"You can throw away your alarm clock. Get used to this."

"Every morning?"

"Why not? Are we on rations?" She kneaded him while nibbling her way down the center of his chest and stomach.

"Kendall . . ."

She pulled away the sheet and took a love bite out of the skin beneath his navel.

"Kendall, it's Dad."

"Hmm?"

"Dad." Pushing her aside, he got out of bed and moved to the window. "I heard his pickup in the driveway."

Kendall had barely come out of her sexual haze when there was a knock on the front door. Matt removed a pair of jeans from the bureau. As he pulled them on he said, "You'd better get up and get dressed."

Dumbstruck, she sat up and watched him leave the room.

"Coming, Dad," he called from the hallway. Then she heard him opening the front door. "Good morning."

"Am I disturbing you?"

"Of course not. I was just about to make coffee. Come on in."

They headed for the kitchen. Kendall followed their voices until she could no longer distinguish the words, then she raised her knees and bowed her head over them, trying to quell her dismay and disappointment.

When it became obvious that Matt had no intention of returning to bed, she got up and showered.

Ten minutes later, she joined them in the kitchen. Gibb was turning bacon in a skillet. "Ah, here comes the bride!" he sang when he saw her.

He stepped around the table to give her an affectionate hug. Then, setting her away from him, he looked her straight in the eye. "You don't mind my coming over and cooking your breakfast, do you?"

Was that supposed to be a joke? Hell, yes, she minded. If this was all the honeymoon she was going to get, she wanted to enjoy it alone with Matt.

But Gibb was smiling so guilelessly that she didn't have

the heart to tell him the truth. With a feeble grin, she said, "Of course not, Gibb."

She disengaged herself from his embrace and moved to the coffeemaker. Apparently she had failed to mask her rancor, as her unenthusiastic greeting was followed by an awkward silence.

"Maybe this wasn't such a good idea." Gibb began untying the apron around his waist.

"Don't be silly, Dad," Matt objected. "Kendall's not her best in the morning. She warned me to expect some grumpiness. Right, darling?"

She smiled apologetically. "I'm afraid that's a flaw I must own up to, Gibb. I'm a bear when I first wake up."

"Hungry as a bear, too, I hope." He replaced the apron and returned to the sizzling skillet on the stove. "Do you like waffles? I make the batter from scratch and add a secret ingredient."

"What?"

He winked. "I guess I can share it with you, now that you're family. Vanilla," he whispered. "Add a teaspoon of vanilla to the batter. It makes all the difference."

"Thanks for the tip."

Matt stood up and offered her his chair. Kissing her hand in a courtly gesture, he said, "Mrs. Burnwood, please be seated. Let us wait on you."

She sat down, only then noticing the gift-wrapped packages on the table. "More gifts? There couldn't possibly be. We've received so many already."

"Dad brought them over."

"They were left at my house. Why don't you open them while your breakfast is cooking?"

She and Matt divided the presents and began unwrapping them. They received a Waterford candy dish, a pair of silver candlesticks, and a lacquered serving tray. Matt handed the last gift to her. "You may do the honors."

"Roscoe Calloway delivered that present this morning," Gibb informed them.

"Oh, how sweet of him!" Kendall exclaimed. Roscoe was the courthouse janitor. He'd been an institution there for thirty years. During her tenure as public defender, Kendall and he had formed a friendship. She opened the gift and found a picture frame inside.

" 'Best wishes,' " she read off the gift card. "It's signed Roscoe and Henrietta Calloway." Her smile turned into a puzzled frown. "Now that I think of it, I don't remember seeing them at the wedding. I wonder why they couldn't come?"

"I advised you not to invite them," Matt reminded her softly.

"But I did, because I wanted to," she insisted. "Roscoe is so nice to me. He's always leaving a fresh rose on my desk, or doing something special like that. He was so excited when we became engaged. He speaks highly of you, Matt. You, too, Gibb."

"Roscoe's a good one."

Gibb turned away from the stove to bring her a plate. The waffle was perfect—thick and golden brown with a square pad of butter melting in its center.

But Gibb's comment had ruined her appetite.

" 'A good one'?" she repeated, hoping that he wasn't implying what she feared he was.

"Roscoe knew that he and his wife would be . . . well, out of place at your wedding," her father-in-law explained.

She looked at her husband, who nodded in solemn agreement. "They would have been the only nonwhites there, Kendall."

"I'm sure Roscoe appreciated your invitation, even though he knew better than to show up. He knows the score, even if you don't." Gibb gave her shoulder an affectionate squeeze as he added, "But you'll learn."

Chapter Eight

$\mathcal{A}$FTER HOURS OF DRIVING, KENDALL WAS DEAD on her feet. But before she could even think of sleep there were things to be done, the first of which was to find Kevin a crib for the night.

In a storage closet she discovered an old playpen that had once been used as a maternity ward for a Labrador dam. Cleaning supplies were in the cupboard where Grandmother had always kept them. She scrubbed the playpen until she was satisfied that it was sanitary enough for Kevin to sleep in.

"Is there anything to eat?"

He was leaning heavily on his crutches, obviously exhausted. Soon after their arrival, she had suggested that he go to bed, but he had refused. Instead, he had tracked her through the house like a bloodhound.

"You're driving me crazy," she had snapped, having turned quickly to discover him so close behind her that she almost ran into him. "If you won't lie down, at least sit down somewhere and stop following me from room to room."

"So you can duck out the back door?"

She had sighed in exasperation. "Even if that's what I had

in mind—which it isn't—I don't have the strength to drive another mile. Relax, okay?"

He hadn't relaxed entirely, but he had let up on the stalking to some extent. In answer to his question now, she said, "I'll see what I can find to eat."

There wasn't much in the pantry—a can of string beans and a jar of peaches. "Not exactly haute cuisine," she said, referring to the meal.

"It's okay," he said. "At this point, anything is better than nothing."

"I'll buy groceries tomorrow. By then the refrigerator will be cold."

They divided the food and ate it all, including the snack crackers she had bought at the vending machine when she'd been accosted by the teenagers. His interference had made the incident memorable, especially to the boy who would wake up tomorrow with badly bruised shins. She was miffed about that.

On the other hand, his valor had surprised and pleased her. Obviously his penchant to protect was deeply ingrained and hadn't been destroyed along with his memory. She had denounced his rushing to her rescue, but she secretly conceded that it had been rather thrilling.

Even battered and bruised, he had willingly defended her. She found his force of will admirable. And he had looked quite dashing when he believed that his territory had been violated.

Kendall wasn't one to swoon over machismo. In fact, she was turned off by it. So she was almost ashamed of how much she'd enjoyed being rescued by this man whose physical power was as attractive as his inner strength.

"I can't remember, are you a good cook?" he asked, drawing her out of her disturbing musings.

"Not great, but we won't starve."

"Sounds like you're planning for us to be here awhile."

"I think we should stay until you recover your memory. It's peaceful, quiet, a good place to recuperate."

"What about my job?"

She stood up and quickly began stacking the dirty dishes. She carried some to the sink, but when she came back for more, he shocked her by thrusting his hand into the waistband of her jeans and holding on. His knuckles dug in to her stomach, and she found it wasn't altogether uncomfortable.

"I was gainfully employed, wasn't I?"

"Of course."

"What did I do?"

"If I tell you, you'll only freak out. You're a type-A personality—you think you're indispensable. You'll want to return to work immediately, which of course is impossible. Believe me, your job will be waiting for you when you recover. I've notified everyone who needs to know. They're in complete agreement."

"When did you notify them? The telephone here is disconnected."

That meant he had checked. Before the accident, he had been no mental slouch. Why had she assumed that amnesia would hinder his acuity? Trying not to show her uneasiness, she said, "I called while you were in the hospital."

"How come nobody phoned or sent a card? I find that very strange. Unbelievable, in fact."

"The doctor restricted visitors. He said since you couldn't remember anyone, you'd become frustrated if a flock of strangers descended on you, and that well-meaning friends would do you much more harm than good. We weren't there long enough for you to receive any mail."

He continued to regard her with obvious skepticism.

"It's taken care of. I promise," she stressed. "Your career is not in jeopardy."

"So it's a career, not just a job?"

"You could say so."

"Give me a hint. Doctor, lawyer, Indian chief?"

"You can remember the nursery rhyme?"

His slanted grin slipped. "I guess I do," he murmured. "How can I recall a childhood ditty, and not remember you?" His gaze lowered to her chest.

Made nervous by the close contact, Kendall pulled his hand from the front of her jeans. "I hear Kevin."

The baby's crying in the other room brought a welcome end to the interrogation. Naturally he was curious, but the less they discussed their lives before the accident, the safer she would be. A seemingly harmless, random word could trigger his memory.

The interruption had also ended the moment of awkward intimacy, which had jarred Kendall more than she wanted to admit. She must keep him believing that she was his wife, but without crossing the line herself.

After Kevin nursed, she bathed him, then lulled him to sleep in the rocking chair in the living room, singing songs her grandmother had sung to her.

He sat across the room on the sofa, his injured leg elevated on a footstool. The lamp on the end table cast deep shadows beneath his eyebrows, obscuring his eyes, although Kendall didn't need to see them to know that they were trained on her, as steady and watchful as a hawk's.

"What about my family?" he asked abruptly.

"Your mother died many years ago."

He assimilated that, then said, "I guess I can't mourn someone I can't even remember. Do I have brothers and sisters?"

She shook her head.

"What about my dad? Dead, too?"

"No. But the two of you have had something of a falling out."

"Over what?"

"Even before this happened, it upset you to talk about it. I don't think it best to go into it now."

"Does he even know about the accident?"

"I didn't think you'd want me to call him, so I didn't."

"Our estrangement is that severe? My father doesn't care if I'm dead or alive?"

"He would care if you were dead or alive, but you wouldn't want him to know about the accident. Excuse me. I need to put Kevin down." She tried to keep her exit from looking like flight.

The playpen had been set up in the smaller of the house's two bedrooms. She gently laid the baby in it. He instantly drew his knees up to his chest and stuck his bottom in the air.

"How can he sleep like that?"

She hadn't realized he'd followed her until she heard his voice just behind her shoulder. "A lot of babies sleep that way."

"Looks uncomfortable."

"I guess you have to be three months old for it to be comfortable."

"Did you have an easy pregnancy?"

"I had some difficulty the first several months. After that, it went more smoothly."

"What kind of difficulty?"

"The usual kind. Morning sickness. Fatigue. Depression."

"What were you depressed about?"

"I wasn't really depressed. Just weepy."

"What were you weepy over?"

"Please. I'm exhausted. Can't this inquisition wait?" She moved to step around him, but he lifted his crutch to block her path.

"You know," she said, fuming, "I'm getting sick and tired of you using that damn crutch like a tollgate."

"And I'm sick and tired of your evasions. Answer me: Why were you depressed and weepy while you were pregnant? Didn't you want to be pregnant?"

She didn't have the energy to remain angry. Her ire evaporated and she said wearily, "Hormonal changes in the first trimester often make women weepy. And yes, I wanted Kevin very badly."

"Did I?"

Their gazes locked for several seconds, then she calmly moved the crutch aside. "I'm going to take a bath."

She switched off the light. But no sooner was it extinguished than a pair of car lights swept the front of the house and beamed directly into the bedroom.

"Oh my God!" Kendall whirled around and stumbled toward the window, flattening herself against the wall. Her heart was pounding. She watched in fear as the car rolled to a stop.

Then it just sat there idling at the end of the lane, the headlights aimed like searchlights at the front of the house. The fog and rain lent it the properties of a leviathan, making it appear large and menacing, its motor sounding like a growl.

She heard his bump-thump approach. "Don't let them see you!" she snapped. "Get away from the window."

He froze in place. Neither of them moved. Kendall didn't even breathe, until the car backed out of the lane and drove away. She could have collapsed with relief. When she was able to speak, she forced a lightness into her voice. "Someone took a wrong turn, I guess."

When she turned around, she saw him standing in the open doorway, silhouetted against the light from the hall. He looked large and imposing. As she went past him, he moved quickly, switching on the overhead light and tilting her face up for a close examination.

"What the hell is going on?"

"Nothing."

"Nothing? You're as pale as a ghost. You practically fainted when you saw that car. What gives? Who's after us? Who's after *you*?"

Keeping her eyes averted, she said, "I just didn't expect visitors, that's all."

"Like hell. I may have lost my memory, but I'm not an imbecile, so don't treat me like one." Still cupping the lower half of her face in his palm, he forced her to look up at him. "You're running for your life, aren't you? From whom? Is someone trying to hurt you? Your baby?" He glanced toward the playpen, where Kevin was sleeping. "*Our* baby?"

"No one's going to harm us as long as we're together," she said, and she meant it. Somehow she knew that even though he didn't trust her, and despite an inexplicable aversion to Kevin, he would fight to his death protecting them. That was going to make leaving him difficult.

She knew better than to rely on anyone for protection. She could manage on her own. She *had* managed on her own for a long time. Still, she felt safer in his company, although, considering his physical condition, it was probably a false sense of security. Being lulled by it would be costly, perhaps even fatal.

She moved away from him. "I'll be in the bathroom. Let me know if Kevin needs me." This time, he didn't detain her.

She filled the claw-footed bathtub to the rim and immersed herself in the warm, soothing water. When she rejoined him in the living room fifteen minutes later, she was wearing only a towel that covered her from chest to midthigh. Her wet hair was combed back from her face, which had been scrubbed clean.

He was standing at the open front door, his back to her, staring out at the darkness and the relentless rain. Hearing the steps of her bare feet, he turned.

"I'm out now," she announced unnecessarily.

As she turned toward the bedroom, he said, "Wait." He hobbled across the room, not stopping until they stood only inches apart.

When he raised his hand to her chest, Kendall flinched. He

cocked his eyebrow quizzically, hesitated, then touched her damp skin. "Does it hurt?"

She didn't catch his meaning until she followed his gaze down and saw the ugly bruise that formed a wide, diagonal line across her chest starting at the base of her neck.

"The shoulder harness," she explained. "Not too pretty, huh? Although it's prettier than I'd look if I hadn't been wearing a seat belt."

He gave a fleeting, rueful smile. "Yeah. Then you'd look like me."

"You don't look so bad." Their eyes met and for a moment they stared at each other. Then Kendall swallowed dryly. "What I mean is, the swelling in your face has gone down considerably."

He nodded absently, because his attention had returned to the bruise across her chest. "How far down does it go?"

A rush of heat surged up through her belly and breasts. She was embarrassed, and, as his wife, she shouldn't be. Holding his eyes with hers, she raised her hands to the knot between her breasts and slowly opened the towel. Pulling it apart, she held the two ends away from her body, allowing him an unrestricted view.

She had never felt more naked, more exposed. His eyes moved over her, not just tracking the vivid bruise but drinking in every inch of skin, every contour and curve. She endured his gaze as long as she could stand it, but when she tried to reclose the towel, he stopped her.

"What's this?"

He touched her, low on her body. She sucked in a quick breath because his touch elicited such a swift and carnal reaction. Her tummy quivered, but she didn't move away as the tip of his index finger lightly traced the fine, pink scar that ran laterally through her pubic hair. He followed its entire length, and even then his hand lingered.

"That's my cesarean scar," she replied breathlessly.

"Hmm. Why are you trembling?"

"Because it's still sensitive. Especially after the accident." Indeed, the seat belt had left another wide bruise across her lap, stretching from one pelvic bone to the other. He trailed his fingers across it.

She snatched the towel closed and clutched it against her. He withdrew his hand from beneath it. She had an impulse to run from him but ordered herself to be wifely.

"The bathtub is deep," she said. "Even without a cast on your leg it's difficult to get in and out of. I suggest you let me give you a sponge bath out of the sink."

He thought it over for a moment, then brusquely shook his head. "Thanks, but I can manage."

"You're sure?"

He glanced down at her body, then quickly looked away. "Yeah. I'm sure." He thumped past her and closed the bathroom door behind him.

Kendall fell back against the doorjamb. Several minutes passed before she regained her equilibrium. This was going to be much more difficult than she had imagined. He was too perceptive, and she was too good a liar. She was so good that she had begun believing her own lies. Now her only viable means of escape had turned on her and become a snare. She had to get away from him.

But first she had to get through the night.

She found a summer-weight nightgown in the bedroom bureau, left there on a previous visit. She made up the bed for him and had just finished plumping the pillows when she heard the bathroom door open. He moved slowly down the hall.

He was wearing nothing except a pair of boxer shorts she had purchased for him that morning. The hair on his chest was damp. He smelled of soap, toothpaste, and mouthwash. He eased himself down onto the bed, every movement showing his fatigue. His motions were those of a man thirty years older. His complexion had an unhealthy grayish cast.

"Lie back," she said gently. "I'll put a pillow beneath your leg."

As she helped settle him, he let out a long sigh of relief and closed his eyes. He still looked battered. She had almost become inured to the bruises and abrasions, the sunken eyes and gaunt cheeks. But now these signs of his suffering were glaringly apparent to her and she felt a stab of compassion.

She switched off the nightstand lamp so the light wouldn't shine in his eyes. "Did you take some aspirin?"

"Several."

"I hope they help you sleep comfortably."

"I'll be all right."

"Well then, I'll see you in the morning. Good night."

His eyes sprang open. "Where are you going?"

She gestured toward the door. "I'll sleep on the living room sofa. I might accidentally bump your leg during the night."

He gave her a long, intent look.

"But if you're willing to take that chance," she heard herself say, "of course I'd rather sleep with you."

Without further discussion, he scooted to the other side of the bed. The effort cost him. His breathing was shallow and rapid, and his skin was clammy to the touch when she slipped in beside him.

"Are you all right?" she asked with concern.

"I'm fine. Tired."

"Rest well." For good measure, she leaned over and placed a soft, chaste kiss on his cheek. Rather than soothe him, the kiss seemed to spark a short fuse.

"Surely you can do better than that." Roughly he cupped the back of her head and held it in place while he kissed her mouth. Not soft, not chaste, this kiss. He used his tongue audaciously, sexily, masterfully, and possessively.

He knew exactly what he was doing, too, because, even

though she fought them, delicious sensations spiraled through her. They stunned her. And she wasn't the only one affected. When he ended the kiss, he kept her head entrapped and probed the depths of her eyes.

In his eyes she saw turbulence, indecision, and confusion. "Jesus," he said softly.

He released her suddenly, as though she were too hot to touch. He closed his eyes and went instantly to sleep. Or pretended to.

Kendall lay beside him, holding her body stiffly, afraid to stir, almost afraid to breathe for fear of upsetting some delicate balance.

My God, what had she gotten herself into? Originally, the plan to claim him as her husband had seemed clever and uncomplicated. It had worked well at the hospital. But she hadn't anticipated his slipping into the marital mode and expecting her to respond accordingly. Although she should have. He was a heterosexual male, and she was telling him that she was his wife. Based on the circumstances she had devised, he was actually behaving more normally than she.

To her further consternation, she admitted to herself that assuming the role of his wife wouldn't be altogether repugnant. His face and body had seen wear and tear, but she doubted he could walk into a room without creating a stir among the women present. He had an aloofness that somehow acted as a magnet. His personality was austere. He never wasted words. As evidenced this afternoon with the three teenagers, he possessed incredible, and justifiable, self-confidence. He wouldn't go looking for trouble, but if it found him, he could handle it.

The cleft in his chin was definitely sexy. Any woman would be attracted to him.

Before announcing that he was her husband, she had failed to consider that they might actually find each other attractive. Consequently, her strategy had backfired. She had trapped herself in an explosive situation as dangerous as a mine field. One false step and she was doomed.

She was tempted to get Kevin and make a dash for the car before the situation became worse, before she found herself wanting not to leave.

But her body demanded rest. She couldn't muster the energy to leave the bed. Besides, where else could she go that was this safe?

It was a long time before she fell asleep, lying there beside him, still tasting his kiss, and fearing that he would awaken tomorrow morning with his memory restored—in which case all her worry would be for naught.

Chapter Nine

*T*HE CHOPPER LANDING CREATED QUITE A STIR in Stephensville.

That it was marked FBI aroused even more curiosity. Nothing that exciting had happened in the small Georgia community since a gangster of marginal renown had taken refuge in his girlfriend's whorehouse on the outskirts of town and engaged in a fiery and fatal shootout with G-men. Only the old-timers remembered it.

Special Agent Jim Pepperdyne paid no heed to the gawking bystanders as he alighted from the helicopter, which had set down on the campus of the middle school. Leading a band of subordinate agents who had to jog to keep up with him, he traversed the playground, marched down the sidewalk, crossed the street, and entered the hospital where the individuals he sought had last been seen.

The staff, previously questioned at length by other agents, had been put on notice that the head honcho was on his way. They were assembled in the waiting room when Pepperdyne strode in.

After hours of grueling interrogation, his advance team had uncovered nothing of significance. They hadn't ferreted out a single clue as to what had happened to the man, the woman, and her child. Their disappearance had been so absolute. It seemed the earth had swallowed them whole.

Jim Pepperdyne didn't believe in the bogeyman. He didn't believe in aliens who beamed up hostages and took them for rides in their spaceships. What he did believe in was the evil ingeniousness of Man. Over the course of his career he had seen it evidenced time and again.

The middle-aged man who bore down on the hospital staff was not physically imposing. He was going soft around the middle, and his hair was thinning at a rate that annoyed him. Even so, he had an authoritative air that caused everyone who crossed his path to have second thoughts.

The medical personnel were on the receiving end of a nearly contemptuous once-over. Pepperdyne affected this intimidation tactic, although his anger and concern were sincere. He would remain angry and concerned until he learned the whereabouts of the three who had eluded him and every other law enforcement agency in several states.

They had been missing for thirty-six hours—thirty-six frantic hours for Pepperdyne—before a dispatcher in a sheriff's office in this out-of-the-way town linked the persons mentioned in the APB with an auto accident that had recently occurred in his county.

Until he received that call, Pepperdyne had never heard of Stephensville, Georgia, but it immediately became the geographical center of his world. He dispatched an advance team of agents, who phoned in later to say that the descriptions of the missing persons matched those of the accident victims.

More agents had been dispatched to question everyone with whom the three had come in contact. Thus far, the interrogations had turned up zilch.

The wrecked car had been recovered three miles downstream from the point of the accident. The fatality had been positively identified. Pepperdyne was awaiting the coroner's official ruling on cause of death.

Now Pepperdyne faced the silent group, feet slightly spread and firmly planted. He didn't waste time introducing himself. "Who was on duty the evening they brought them here?" Several hands were raised. He pointed to a nurse. "What happened? Tell me everything."

She gave him a concise but detailed account: "She and the baby were fine. Shaken up, but not seriously injured. Her husband needed immediate attention." She nodded toward the other agents. "We've told them this a dozen times."

Pepperdyne ignored her complaint. "Was he conscious?"

"No."

"Did he say anything? Mumble something?"

"No."

"Did he have a weapon?"

She shook her head.

"You're sure of that?"

"I had to cut off his clothes," she said stiffly. "He didn't have a gun."

"Any form of ID?"

"No. She told us later that it had gone down with the car."

"She, meaning . . . ?"

"Mrs. Kendall."

Pepperdyne glanced over his shoulder at one of the other agents, who shrugged as if to say, "I told you so."

Pepperdyne, obviously disgusted, turned back to the nurse. "Her last name is Burnwood. Kendall *Burnwood*. Did she ever mention that name?"

"No. She put John and Mary Kendall on the admission forms," the nurse replied.

"Yes, I've seen the forms." One of the other agents produced copies and slapped them into Pepperdyne's hand. He shook them at the assembled group. "She didn't leave any blank spaces, but the information is all phony. Names, addresses, phone numbers, Social Security numbers, all wrong, all invented. Didn't you folks think it was strange that she had cash with her but not a single form of identification?"

He was met with mute, defensive stares.

Finally another nurse spoke up: "I don't care what her name is, she's very sweet. And honest, too. She could have just walked out without paying us a cent. She didn't have to leave that money in her room, but she did. She left it where it was sure to be found, and the amount more than covered their bill. She's a wonderful mother, and she was very worried about her husband's memory loss."

"The reason she's worried about his memory loss is because she's afraid he'll recover it." Pepperdyne turned to the doctor. "When will that be?"

"Could be anytime. Could be never."

"Good answer," the special agent muttered in disgust. "Is he in danger from the concussion?"

"Not if he takes it easy, as I advised."

"What about his leg?"

"It was a clean break. It should be completely healed in a couple of months."

The doctor's cavalier attitude made Pepperdyne's blood pressure rise. "You let a man with a brain injury and a broken tibia waltz right out of here?"

"We had no way of knowing that she was going to sneak him out of the hospital in the middle of the night."

"Is that normal behavior? Do your patients frequently sneak out, Doctor? Didn't that strike you as a trifle suspicious? When you discovered their disappearance the following morning, why didn't you immediately report it to the sheriff?"

"The deputy had questioned them several times and appeared satisfied with their stories. He hadn't placed them under arrest or anything like that. What'd they do, anyhow? How come you've got agents crawling all over town looking for them?"

"That's classified," Pepperdyne said tightly.

If the media got its long nose into this case, things could really get messed up. He wanted these people intimidated to the point of telling him any tidbit of information they had, but not so intrigued that they would realize they were sitting on a story of national scope that any news producer would give his left nut for. So far, he had managed to keep this disappearance act under wraps. The more time he could buy before it became public knowledge, the better.

"How did they get out of town?" he asked the room at large.

He was almost certain that they were no longer in Stephensville. Having seen it from the air, Pepperdyne doubted that Mrs. Burnwood—clever and resourceful as she was—could hide an amnesiac and an infant for any length of time. There weren't that many hiding places. Furthermore, his agents had been circulating photos of them all over town. No one had seen hide nor hair.

"Any suggestions on how they left here? Did any of you see Mrs. Burnwood driving a car?"

"I lent her mine," one of the nurses volunteered. "But only for a few hours. She went to Wal-Mart and bought clothes for her and the baby."

"Did you check the mileage afterward?"

"The mileage?" she repeated, as though it were a concept foreign to her.

Another dead end. The police record had already been checked for stolen vehicles. None had been reported in Stephensville for two years. There was only one garage in town that sold used cars. Although several were rusting on the lot, one hadn't been sold in six months.

"There's no bus service out of here. No air service. No boats and no passenger trains. How the hell did they get out of town?" Pepperdyne's raised voice rattled the windowpanes, but it didn't shake loose an answer or even a suggestion.

With a sigh of defeat, he said, "Thanks for your time, people."

As they neared the waiting helicopter, one of his men asked, "Sir, how *did* they get out of here?"

Pepperdyne ducked beneath the whirling blades and angrily shouted, "We've eliminated all other possibilities, so I guess they sprouted goddamn wings and flew out!"

Chapter Ten

"WHAT'S HIS NAME? PARDON? ARE YOU SAYING 'Crook'? Common spelling?"

With the telephone receiver cradled between her shoulder and cheek, Kendall jotted down the name on a legal pad. "Caught red-handed? Uh-huh. Thanks for nothing," she muttered.

Someone tapped on her office door. When she glanced up and saw Matt, she waved him in.

"Am I disturbing you?" he mouthed.

She made a face at him for asking such a silly question. Into the phone she said, "Okay, as soon as I wrap up here, I'll go downstairs and talk to him. Right now I've got someone in my office. Goodbye."

She hung up and combed back her hair with all ten fingers. Then, giving her husband a beatific smile, she said, "You appear halfway sane. I hope so, because everyone else I've had contact with today has been out of control."

As Matt sat down on the corner of her desk, he chuckled. "It's football season. The homecoming game is Friday night. That gets everybody around here a little crazy."

"A little crazy? Try totally off the wall. Buggy. Bonkers."

"Do I sense a 'for instance' coming?"

"Let's see. There was a shouting match out in the hallway between two neighbors. One's German shepherd used the other's yard for a toilet minutes before his private pep rally started. When the cheerleaders' pyramid toppled . . . Well, you get the picture. It wasn't pretty. He's suing. Then an alleged armed robber awaiting trial asked if I could get him out of jail long enough for him to attend the game. It's his class's tenth reunion."

Matt was laughing. "Told you."

"Unrelated to football, I had a shouting match with our esteemed county prosecutor. We're arguing over the admissibility into his trial of my client's prior record for assault. I called Dabney a one-man lynch mob. He called me a bleeding heart liberal, pinko, Yankee-lover, then hung up on me, and now won't return my calls."

Matt had listened with a sympathetic ear. "Dabney's been known to sulk, but his grudges rarely last long."

Kendall and Solicitor Dabney Gorn locked horns on a regular basis. The conflict went with the territory. As Kendall saw it, if the county prosecutor wasn't upset with her, she wasn't doing her job properly.

But Gorn often took professional disagreements personally, which made things doubly difficult for her because he was a revered figure in Prosper. In the last four elections he had run uncontested, and had won by landslides in the three prior to those. Mr. Gorn was a highly regarded community leader, a symbol of law and order, upholder of truth, justice, and the American way. Therefore, anyone who disputed him was automatically considered the bad guy—or girl.

Beyond that, he was a close friend of the Burnwoods. When she referred to him around Matt and Gibb, she chose her words carefully. That's why she didn't tell Matt that she considered Dabney Gorn a pompous, self-serving manipulator of the law, more interested in maintaining his elected position than in seeing justice served.

Together with Judge Fargo, whose viewpoints unfortunately mirrored Gorn's, the prosecutor was a formidable foe. Not wanting to sound like a whiner with a persecution complex, Kendall also kept that opinion to herself.

"In summary," she said, "it's been Monday all day." Folding her hands together and placing them on the edge of her desk, she gave her husband her undivided attention. "What can I do for you, Mr. Handsome Newspaper Publisher?"

"For starters, you can give me a kiss."

"I think I can handle that."

Leaning toward each other across her desk, they kissed. When they pulled apart, she smacked her lips. "Thanks, I needed that."

"It's the season," Matt repeated. "Everybody gets hyped up over football."

"Was it this big a deal when you were playing?"

"Are you serious? Where Dad is concerned, football runs a close second to hunting. He coached me on throwing passes right along with how to handle a deer rifle."

Gibb had regaled Kendall with stories of Matt's accomplishments on the gridiron. When he spoke of them, his eyes shone like those of a new convert at a tent revival. Kendall doubted that Gibb would have been so zealous if Matt had chosen to play flute in the high school marching band.

Her father-in-law scorned everything that wasn't macho. Participation in anything artistic was reserved strictly for "the ladies," and "queers," which included any man who liked classical music, ballet, or the theater. Some of his homophobic comments were so ludicrous that Kendall wanted to burst into laughter. Or shudder.

Sometimes his ultraconservative opinions made her want to scream in frustration. Her grandmother had reared her with the belief that other people and their eccentricities should be tolerated and respected. The differences between people could even be interesting and stimulating.

Elvie Hancock's liberal leanings hadn't always been popular in Sheridan, Tennessee. Nevertheless, she had stuck by them and instilled them in her granddaughter. Kendall supposed that was one reason she had chosen to become a public defender, champion of the underdogs. That, along with the injustices she had seen take place in the hallowed corridors of Bristol and Mathers.

"Who was on the phone?" Matt asked now. "Or can't you talk about it?"

"Off the record?"

"Absolutely."

"A boy was caught shoplifting this afternoon. Get this. His last name is Crook."

"The youngest one? Billy Joe?"

"You know him?" she asked, surprised.

"I know the family. The twins, Henry and Luther, are a year older than I. There's a passel of brothers and sisters in between them and Billy Joe. Their old man ran the junk yard on the edge of town. Where that big heap of rusted metal is?"

She nodded, knowing the eyesore to which he referred. "You said 'ran,' past tense."

"He died a couple of years ago. Mrs. Crook is having a tough time trying to hold the business together."

"Why is that?"

"Old man Crook sometimes didn't wait on salvaged cars to update his inventory. Customers often bought back from him what had recently been stolen off their cars. The consensus was that the old man was operating the business like Fagin, sending the boys out to steal for him."

"Is Mrs. Crook trying to run a legitimate business?"

"Maybe, but I doubt it. It's probably a lack of cleverness, not moral conviction, that keeps her from prospering."

"Hmm. So, what you're implying is that Billy Joe comes from a long line of Crooks?"

"Ah, you're a comedienne."

"Not really. Thank you for the Crook family background, but that's probably as far as we can carry this conversation without breaching ethics."

"I understand."

He never pressed her for more information than she was willing to divulge in keeping with lawyer/client privilege. Since he published the local newspaper and wrote a biweekly editorial column, she had to be extremely careful not to discuss cases with him. Not because she didn't trust his integrity, but in order to protect her own.

"What brings you by?" she asked.

"To tell you that I won't be home for dinner tonight."

"Oh, Matt!"

He held up his hands to stave off her protests. "I'm sorry. I can't get out of it."

"This is the second time in four days. What is it this time?"

"Leonard Wiley asked Dad and me to go coon hunting tonight. He's got a new dog he's very proud of and wants to show him off. Dad accepted on my behalf."

"Tell him you can't go tonight, that we already had plans."

"We didn't."

"Tell him you promised me that we'd stay home and veg in front of the TV."

"I didn't promise."

"He won't know that!"

"But I will."

"Oh, for pity's sake!" she cried. "Haven't you ever told a fib?"

"Not to my father."

"Then tell him the truth. Tell him I've got PMS, that I'm being a real bitch about your nights away from the house, and that I'm threatening you with castration if you leave me alone tonight." She came out of her chair wielding a letter opener.

Laughing, he deflected the playful jab she made in the direction of his crotch. "I knew you would be disappointed."

"I'm not disappointed. I'm pissed."

His smile vanished. "Is that kind of language necessary?"

The reproof only made her madder. "No, it's not necessary, Matt. But saying it made me feel a hell of a lot better. My husband of three months prefers spending an evening with coon dogs instead of me. I think that entitles me to a vulgarity."

She turned her back to him and moved to the bookcase, which held her law books and tomes on South Carolina and federal law. The picture frame that Roscoe had given them for a wedding gift was on one of the shelves. She'd put a wedding snapshot in the frame and kept in it her office where the janitor couldn't help but see it every time he came in to clean.

The first time he'd seen his gift prominently displayed, his narrow chest had swelled with pride. His grin had been worth the chastening she had received from Gibb and Matt for going against their wishes and sending him a wedding invitation.

"I fail to see what's so important about a new hunting dog."

"It's not important to me," Matt said patiently. "But it's a big deal to Leonard. I can't hurt his feelings."

She turned to face him. "But you can hurt mine."

"I don't mean to."

"Well, that's what you're doing."

"What I'm doing," he said tightly, "is trying to please everyone. And, frankly, it's getting tiresome."

Apparently this topic had been eating at him. She had inadvertently opened it up for discussion, and now he had plenty to say.

"I don't know which is worse, Kendall. The wounded look I get from you when I don't do as you wish, or the ribbing I take from my friends when I do."

The words stung. "Since getting married has put a damper on your friendships, maybe you should have thought twice about getting married."

"I wanted to get married. I wanted to marry *you*. But you've got to understand that—"

"You belonged to them first. Particularly Gibb."

He closed the distance between them and took her shoulders between his hands. "That's right, I did. I was all he had after Mom died. We lived together for almost thirty years. Just the two of us. Now that I've left the house, he's lonely."

"Lonely?" she repeated incredulously. "Without even having to think hard, I could name a dozen women panting after him and competing for his company. If he accepted every invitation, he would have dinner out every night of the year. He's got more friends than he can get around to seeing. Why must you always be the chairman in charge of keeping him entertained?"

"Because he's my father and I love him. He loves me. And he loves you," he added with emphasis. "Can you honestly cite one mean or spiteful thing he's done or said to you? Hasn't he gone out of his way to bring you into the fold?"

She lowered her gaze and took a deep breath. "Yes, Matt, he has. It's just that—"

He laid his finger against her lips. "Let's not argue, Kendall. I hate it when we argue."

She hated that he always got to plead his case, then tried to make up before giving her an opportunity to plead hers. But every law student knew the value of choosing his or her arguments. This was one she could concede. It wasn't as though his outing tonight conflicted with specific plans she had made.

However, those evenings without a social obligation were the ones she loved most, when they stayed home together, sharing a television program, a bowl of popcorn. Making love. She felt excluded when he went out with his men friends, especially since she couldn't participate in, or even relate to, their outdoor activities.

But being left alone was preferable to being shunted off with the wives of their friends to pass the evenings when the men were out.

She had tried to cultivate friendships, but her attempts had met with little success. She unintentionally distanced the other women because she was so career oriented. And then there was that indefinable *something* that set her apart. She couldn't quite put her finger on it, but she felt it strongly. Call her paranoid, but she almost felt as if everyone else was in on a secret from which she was excluded. She supposed this feeling of alienation was because she didn't have deep roots in the community, as most of the others did.

The bottom line was, she'd failed to blend in. Perhaps she was taking out her sense of failure on Matt, blowing things out of proportion because he had so many friends and she had none. Perhaps she was embarrassed that she hadn't yet been accepted into these tight social circles. The shunning was making her jealous and possessive of Matt, whom everyone adored.

In any event, she was a pathetic cliché—a newlywed resentful of her husband's activities outside the marriage.

"I hope that damn dog doesn't tree a single raccoon," she said sulkily.

Taking that as the white flag of surrender it was intended to be, Matt kissed her lightly on the tip of her nose. "We shouldn't be out too late, but don't wait up."

"I'll wait up." He kissed her again, then headed for the door. "Be careful with those guns and things," she called after him.

"Always."

For a long while afterward, she sat at her desk mentally reviewing everything they'd said. Matt had made several viable points. Specifically, she had placed him in the untenable position of having to choose between his father and her, both of whom he loved and wanted to please. That was a mistake.

She could never drive a wedge between her husband and his father, nor did she want to. She loved the idea of being part of their extended family. Rather than complain about their activities that excluded her, she should cultivate an interest and join in. Matt would be delighted, and so would Gibb, who frequently remarked that he wanted her to become totally accepting of their world.

Having reached this resolve, she felt much better. If she didn't like the present situation, it was up to her to change it. Whatever was necessary, she would do.

Because she didn't want just a good marriage. She wanted a great one.

Billy Joe Crook was tall and lanky, with no discernible difference in measurement of his shoulders, waist, and hips. Sharp bones poked through his clothes. His pale, stringy hair could only be kept out of his eyes by a flicking motion of his head that was executed at such brief intervals it resembled a muscle tic.

"The police report says that at the time you were apprehended you had the CDs inside your shirt."

He snorted his sinuses clean and swallowed. "I was going to pay for them."

"Outside the store?"

"I was on the way to my car to get the money, when this asshole grabs me from behind and starts patting me down like I was a criminal or something."

"Uh-huh," Kendall said, unimpressed by his avowal of innocence. "Have you ever been caught shoplifting before?"

Colorless eyes fixed a disconcerting stare on her. Chilling as that stare was, Kendall didn't back down from it. Finally he broke eye contact, looked up at the ceiling, glanced over his shoulder at the guard at the door, and picked out several spots in the room to focus on before his cold eyes returned to her. "No."

"Don't lie to me, Billy Joe," she cautioned. "If you do, I'll find out. No matter how ugly the truth is, I'd rather hear it from you than from Mr. Gorn's office. Do you have a prior arrest record?"

"I wasn't arrested."

"But there was an incident?"

He smirked, dismissing it. "A couple years back? In the Piggly Wiggly?"

Kendall folded her arms and assumed a listening posture.

"This, uh, this checkout gal said I tried to steal a comic book." He raised his bony shoulders in an indifferent shrug. "The bitch was lying."

"You didn't take the comic book?"

"I took it off the rack, sure. I was only taking it into the bathroom with me to read while I was on the crapper. This bitch raised hell and called the manager. He ordered me out of the store and told me not to come back. As if I gave a fuck. That's the last they'll get of *my* b'iness, and I told 'em so."

"I'm sure that broke their hearts."

"Hey, bitch, whose side are you on?" he shouted, springing forward in his chair. "And how come I got a skirt for a lawyer anyway?"

Kendall shot to her feet so quickly that her chair fell over backward and clattered to the floor. The guard standing post at the door rushed over, but she staved him off with a raised hand and a shake of her head. He heeded her wishes and kept his distance, although he looked ready to pounce on Billy Joe Crook if the need arose.

Kendall glared down at her insolent client and lowered her voice to a threatening pitch. "If you ever call me that again, I'll knock your rotten teeth down your throat. Do you understand me? And if I were you, I'd prefer a female attorney.

You're so repulsive, why would a woman choose to sit beside you in a court of law and plead your case, unless she was convinced beyond a shadow of doubt that you had been wrongly accused?"

She gave him time to think it over. He fidgeted in his seat and gnawed on the nail of his index finger, which was already a nub. For all his impudence, she now detected a trace of uneasiness.

"Okay, okay," he said at last. "No need to get your panties in a wad. I didn't mean nothing by it."

"Of course you did." Calmly, she righted her chair and sat down. "I don't care what you think of me personally, Mr. Crook. I'm paid to represent you. How well or how poorly I do that is up to me. No matter the outcome of your hearing, I'll still get my paycheck next Friday. Understood?"

He understood. Tossing back his hair, he said in a subdued voice, "I don't want to go to jail."

"All right then. Let's discuss our options."

"Plead guilty? You mean, have him say he did it? You're out of your friggin' mind, lady!"

Rudeness seemed to be a Crook family trait. As did hair the color of dirty straw and eyes with practically no pigmentation. Billy Joe's older twin brothers were tall and rawboned, although their lankiness wasn't quite as pronounced as his. Maturity had eroded the sharp edges.

Henry and Luther Crook ambushed her as she tried to leave the courthouse. They, too, vociferously expressed their displeasure over having a woman represent their little brother. Ignoring their objections, she told them the avenue of defense she had advised her client to take.

"I'm not out of my mind," she said evenly. "I think Billy Joe should enter a plea of guilty."

"Plead guilty," Henry said scornfully. "Some lawyer you

are. Well, you can forget it. We'll get somebody else. Somebody who knows what the hell he's doing."

"Fine. I'll be happy to turn the case over to whomever you retain, or the court appoints. But my job is to handle this kind of case quickly. It might be weeks before another lawyer could get to it. How soon do you want it resolved?"

Luther and Henry mentally chewed on that for a moment. Henry looked forlornly at Luther and said, "It's killing Mama that her baby's in jail."

"Hear me out, and then decide," Kendall suggested. "Billy Joe is only sixteen. He's a juvenile. This is his first offense. We can forget the incident in the Piggly Wiggly. He wasn't arrested and formally charged, and even if he had been, it would be inadmissible."

"Huh?"

Henry's elbow found Luther's ribs. "Shut up and let her talk."

Since Henry was obviously the more intelligent of the pair, which wasn't saying much, she addressed her remaining comments to him.

"I believe that if Billy Joe appears before the family court judge and admits to making a *mistake* in judgment—leaving the store with the compact disks in his possession before actually paying for them, even though he had every intention of doing so—he'll probably get reprimanded and be put on probation."

"What's that mean?"

"That he won't spend any time in jail, and he won't be sent to Columbia for R&E." Reception and Evaluation was a period of forty-five days in which juvenile offenders were placed in detention and thoroughly screened by the Department of Juvenile Justice. The presiding judge then handed down his sentence on the basis of that evaluation and the department's recommendation.

"What's that probation mean?"

"It means that Billy Joe can't make another *mistake* in a specified period of time, say one year. He'll be closely monitored. During his probation, he'd better stay out of trouble."

"What if he doesn't?"

"If he doesn't, he's screwed the pooch."

As Henry mulled it over, he absently scratched his armpit. "What's the other choice?"

"The other choice is for him to plead innocent. He stands trial, which could result in a stiffer probation or an R&E. Personally, in this instance, I think a judge will respond favorably to contrition on the part of the defendant."

She was met with blank stares, so she tried again. "The judge is more likely to rule in Billy Joe's favor if he says he's sorry for what he did and promises not to do it again. I must say, the idea of probation appealed to your brother. He swore to me that if he beat this rap, he'd stay out of trouble. That's it. What's your decision?"

The twins withdrew and consulted each other in whispers. "Okay," Henry said, speaking for both of them when they rejoined her. "We'll go along with that. With what you said."

"Fine. But I want to make clear that by pleading guilty, Billy Joe is admitting to a crime. He'll have a record. And there's no guarantee that a guilty plea will soften the judge's heart. It's a gamble that could backfire on us. However, in my judgment, I think it's a safe gamble."

They agreed by eagerly bobbing their heads and saying how glad Mama was going to be to hear that little Billy Joe wouldn't be sent to jail.

" 'Course, soon as he gets out, she's gonna take a strap to his ass for causing her this worry."

Mama, Kendall thought, must be a real prize, too. "I suggest you buy Billy Joe a new suit before his court appearance," she advised. "And some toiletries." Putting it in terms they could better understand, she added, "I want him to look like he's on his way to church to get married."

Luther said, "Speaking of weddin's, you're Matt Burnwood's wife, aren't you?"

"That's right."

"Ol' Matt hitched hisself to a city girl."

"Not exactly," Kendall replied, as they moved through the
exit doors. "I grew up in eastern Tennessee, in a town even
smaller than Prosper, called Sheridan."

"You act citified, though," Luther said. "Dress like it, too,"
he observed, taking in her suit. "Funny 'bout Matt marryin'
you. Always figured he'd—"

Again, he got his brother's elbow jammed into his gut.
"Luther's always running off at the mouth," Henry apologized.
"We gotta get on home now and give Mama the good news."
He shoved his brother toward a battered car parked at a meter.

Kendall was relieved to see them drive away. They made
her feel in need of a bath.

"Tuna's on sale, three cans for a dollar."

The panhandler sitting on the courthouse steps was a familiar sight. He was reading aloud from the latest edition of
Matt's newspaper. Although his cheeks and chin were covered
with a scruffy salt-and-pepper beard, he wasn't an old man.
Probably not much older than Matt.

"Good evening, Bama," she said, smiling down at him.

"Evening, Counselor."

"How are you?"

"Can't complain."

Roscoe had told her the man's story. "He just showed up
one day, few months before you came to town. Goes by the
name of Bama, after Alabama, you know. He's out there every
day on the courthouse steps, rain or shine, hot or cold, reading
the newspaper front to back. Friendly enough fellow. Doesn't
bother anybody. Not much, anyway.

"They've tried to run him off a few times, but he always
comes back the next day. A real shame, isn't it, to waste a
life like that?" The janitor sadly shook his head over the

unknown misfortunes that had reduced Bama to living off
handouts and suffering the scorn of society.

Now Kendall took a dollar bill from her handbag and slid
it into the breast pocket of his dirty tweed jacket. "Buy some
of that tuna for yourself, Bama."

"Thank you kindly, Counselor."

"Good night."

"Night."

It had been a long day. Each minute of it had left its mark
on her like the lash of a whip. She tried to wait up for Matt,
as she had promised, but she grew so sleepy that at midnight
she finally admitted defeat and went to bed alone.

Chapter Eleven

"*Y*OUR HONOR!"

"Silence!" Judge H. W. Fargo rapped his gavel on the block. "If counsel can't control the outbursts of her client and the spectators here on his behalf, I'll hold her in contempt."

"Your Honor, if I may speak," Kendall shouted from the defense table, where she was simultaneously trying to restrain Billy Joe Crook. When he heard the judge's ruling, he started screaming obscenities.

"Your client entered a guilty plea, and I've ordered him sent to Columbia for an R&E. What further business do we have?"

"Forgive my client's outburst, Your Honor. But under the circumstances, I believe his outrage is justified."

Fargo leaned forward and smiled, but it was a nasty expression. "Oh?"

"Yes, Your Honor."

"His *honor* my ass," Billy Joe said, sneering. "You're full of shit, Judge. And so is she. And so is everybody in this goddamn court."

Kendall clamped her fingers around his skinny arm so

tightly that he yelped. "Sit down and keep your foul mouth shut. Let me do the talking."

"Why should I?" he asked, jerking his arm free. "I did what you said, and I'm going to jail for it. Same as jail, anyway. No shrink is gonna evaluate me!"

His hair, which had been slicked back with gel for his court appearance, was shaking loose. He tossed his head to keep it out of his eyes. He glared at Kendall, who glared right back. Billy Joe was the first to relent. "Shit." He dropped into his chair again. "I'll fucking escape is what I'll do. See if I don't."

Behind the rail, Henry and Luther were snarling like aggravated attack dogs on a short and fraying leash. Mrs. Crook was muttering invectives. Kendall felt trapped in a nightmare.

From the corner of her eye she noticed that Solicitor Dabney Gorn was grinning at her from the prosecution's table. He was relishing not only her defeat but her inability to control her client.

Since this was such an insignificant case, why hadn't Gorn delegated it to one of his assistants? He rarely appeared in court himself. He handed down mandates from his office, then spent the better part of each workday in the café across the street from the courthouse, drinking iced tea and shooting the breeze with anyone who wandered in.

Addressing the judge again, Kendall felt every eye in the courtroom on her, including Matt's. He had stopped by to cheer her on. She wished he hadn't. "Your Honor, ordering an R&E in this case is ridiculous. The value of the items taken is less than one hundred dollars. On what possible grounds—"

"On the grounds that your client is a thief, madam. He admitted it. If you'd like, I can ask the court reporter to read back that portion of these proceedings."

"Thank you, Your Honor, that won't be necessary. I know that my client pleaded guilty. Mr. Crook admits to making a mistake in judgment, although we do not concede that the motivation behind that mistake was thievery as the court suggests. This is my client's first offense."

"On record," Fargo said in a droll tone.

"Which should be the only consideration," Kendall retorted. "Are we to assume that this court is prejudiced against my client?"

Fargo's face turned red. "You're to assume nothing about this court." He shook his gavel in stern admonishment. "You're skating on dangerously thin ice, Counselor. Is that all?"

"No, it is not. For the record, I want to express how unfair and unjustified I believe this ruling is. Billy Joe Crook has shown remorse for his actions, and, since this is his first offense, I feel that a period of probation would be much more in keeping with accepted standards."

"Well, I'm trying to improve the accepted standards. Your client is hereby remanded into the custody of the Department of Juvenile Justice. Sentencing will be based on their report." He banged his gavel. "Case dismissed."

When the bailiffs approached Billy Joe to place him in handcuffs, he put up such a fight that they were forced to try to subdue him. That was all the encouragement his brothers needed. Both vaulted over the railing.

Kendall placed herself directly in their path, hoping to slow them down and give the bailiffs enough time to snap the handcuffs on Billy Joe's wrists.

"Please, Luther, Henry, you're not helping!"

But they weren't listening. Nor were they letting her stand in their way. One pushed her aside. She fell back, striking her hip on the corner of the table. As she pulled herself up, she saw Billy Joe being dragged, kicking and screaming, through the side door. Luther and Henry were in hot pursuit.

Suddenly, someone else ran past Kendall. It was Matt. He reached the twins before they reached the door. Grabbing Luther from behind, he slammed him into the wall. When

Henry leaped to his twin's defense, Matt assumed an attack stance. His expression was so chilling that it instantly doused Henry's bloodlust.

"You boys heard the judge's ruling," Matt said. "Case dismissed. Billy Joe's on his way to jail."

"Thanks to *her*." Luther threw Kendall a murderous glance. "Our quarrel's not with you, Matt. It's with your wife. She landed our baby brother in jail."

"Your baby brother landed himself in jail when he shoplifted those CDs. That aside, if you ever touch my wife again, I'll slit your throat."

"Matt, please." Kendall limped toward them.

The ruckus had drawn a crowd. The doorways were clogged with courthouse employees who had rushed from their offices to see what all the commotion was about. Kendall didn't want an audience witnessing her disgrace. If word got around that her husband had come to her rescue, it would damage her credibility and jeopardize the respect she had worked so hard to gain. Naysayers would have support for their argument that a woman can't handle a tough job.

She touched Matt's arm and looked at him imploringly. "This is my arena. I'll fight my own fight." She could tell he didn't like it and was about to object. "I must take care of this myself, Matt. Please."

He shot the Crook brothers a silent warning glance, then stepped aside.

Kendall approached them. "If you will recall, I cautioned you that there were risks to pleading guilty." She shook her head remorsefully. "Believe me, I'm as shocked and disappointed as you."

"Like hell you are."

Kendall turned at the sound of a new voice, which was about as soft and delicate as steel wool.

Unlike her slender offspring, Mrs. Crook was a large woman, her bulk consisting more of muscle than fat. She wore a shapeless, ill-fitting cotton print dress and had velour bedroom slippers on her wide, gnarled feet. Hard living had carved deep lines into her leathery complexion. Crevices radiated from her thin lips, as though they'd been pursed for several decades.

"I'm very sorry, Mrs. Crook," Kendall said. "It didn't go as I had expected."

"On account of you, my baby is being sent off."

"It's temporary. Billy Joe hasn't been in serious trouble before. The recommendation that comes back will surely be for probation. And although the judge doesn't have to abide by the recommendation, I'm certain he will."

"Like you were certain 'bout this?" she asked scornfully. Her eyes narrowed with malice. "You're gonna be real sorry you ever crossed us."

Looking beyond Kendall's shoulder, she signaled her sons. Obediently, they moved into place on either side of her, then without another word the three made their way up the center aisle to the exit. The onlookers parted to let them pass.

With a sinking heart, Kendall watched them go, knowing that she had made enemies this morning. People such as the Crooks rarely forgot slights.

And they never forgave.

Burnwood's Sporting Goods was twenty minutes away from closing when Dabney Gorn sauntered in. Gibb subtly raised his chin in greeting, but he stayed with the fisherman to whom he was selling a lure.

After ringing up a hefty sale, Gibb escorted his customer out, locked the door behind the man, and placed the Closed sign in the window. Turning out lights as he went through the store, he joined his visitor, who had made himself at home in the back room.

The prosecutor was thumbing through a firearms catalog as he spat tobacco into the three-gallon coffee can left in the back room for that purpose. "That one was a talker. Bent your ear long enough, didn't he?"

"It was worthwhile. He ran up quite a tab." Gibb lowered himself into the comfortably worn easy chair facing the one in which Gorn was lounging. He twisted the cap off a diet soda. "Drink?"

"Already had me one, thanks." Gorn belched, spat again, then sat forward, slowly rubbing his palms together. "Gibb, you heard what happened over to the courthouse this afternoon?"

"Matt called me, very upset. Justifiably so, if it's true that my daughter-in-law butted heads with everybody over that Crook boy."

The prosecutor gave Gibb a word-by-word, blow-by-blow account of the incident. Looking troubled, he said, "I realize she's your kin now, but she hasn't been all that long. On the other hand, you and I go way back."

The men silently acknowledged the special bond between them. It was much stronger than blood ties and longer lasting than life itself.

"What's on your mind, Dabney? You know you can speak freely."

"This girl worries me," he said.

She worried Gibb, too, but he didn't want to admit it before hearing what Gorn had to say. A great leader knows the value of holding his own counsel and listening. He doesn't reveal what he's thinking until he knows the minds of those around him.

"How so, Dabney?"

"Do you reckon she's ever going to become one of us, Gibb? *Really* one of us?" He shifted in his chair, moving closer to the edge of the cushion as if to assure confidentiality.

"Prosper needed a public defender who would . . . share our views, so to speak," Gorn continued. "We all figured a little thing like her would be a pushover. After that business in Tennessee, we didn't expect her to have a conscience. If you recall, that's the main reason she was hired."

He spat another glob into the coffee can and wiped his mouth with the back of his hand. "She's tougher than we counted on, more committed to her beliefs. She's also more scrupulous than we bargained on. She opposes us more regular than we'd like. Some of us are beginning to think we made a mistake."

Kendall's strict adherence to lofty principles had come as a surprise to Gibb, too. So had her willfulness. He had thought the girl would be much more flexible and far less outspoken. He was convinced that, after time, she would come around. It would just take longer than they had anticipated. That's what he told Gorn.

But his old friend's doubts were not assuaged. "She doesn't fit in with the other women."

"Not yet, but she will. You leave her to Matt and me. Just the other day, he told me that she's been feeling a little left out. Maybe the answer to this problem is to start including her more."

Dabney Gorn showed his astonishment. "Do you think that's wise?"

Chuckling, Gibb said, "Relax. I'm not a fool. She won't be included on anything important until we're convinced that she's in total agreement with us."

"And you really believe she will be?"

"Yes," Gibb replied without hesitation. "She's still steeped in the liberal swill she was reared with. Her grandmother can't live forever. Once she's dead, her influence over Kendall will wear off."

"What if it doesn't?"

"It will," Gibb said sharply. Then, ameliorating his tone with a broad smile, he said, "But these transitions can't be rushed, Dabney. We must move slowly. We can't hit this girl over the head with everything at once. She's too reactionary."

He squeezed his open hand into a fist, and his eyes shone in the dim room. "But think of the asset she'll be once she's entirely ours. Leave it to me. I know exactly how to handle her."

He stood and drew his friend up. "In fact, if you don't get out of here, I'm going to be late. She's invited me to supper."

At the door, Gorn faced him, still looking worried, but for a different reason. "I hope you haven't taken this the wrong way, Gibb. I—all the brothers—trust you. Always have."

"Then the brothers have nothing to worry about, do they?"

"It was a very chivalrous gesture, Matt, but I had to stand on my own." Kendall reached across the dining table and took his hand, giving it a firm squeeze.

He didn't return her peacemaking smile. "You emasculated me in front of everyone."

"Oh, please!"

"Well, didn't you? I was publicly humiliated."

She turned to Gibb and said defensively, "It was nothing like that."

"Sounds as though y'all created quite a spectacle."

"It wasn't nearly as sensational as Matt is making it sound."

"Dabney thought it was sensational."

"Dabney? You've spoken to him about this?"

Gibb nodded. "He came to the store late this afternoon and told me his version."

"Which I'm sure made me out the villainess." Kendall angrily shoved back her chair and left the table. She had hoped that inviting Gibb over for a hamburger dinner would placate Matt, whose pride had been mortally wounded because she hadn't let him defend her.

Instead, she had stacked the deck against herself. She was outnumbered. Gibb hadn't said anything critical, but she read the silent reprimand in his expression.

"It wasn't as much of a spectacle as it would have been if

Matt and the Crooks had gotten into a fistfight." Addressing her husband, she added, "I wasn't trying to embarrass you, Matt. I was trying to avoid a disaster."

He continued to pout.

Gibb said, "I can't say I was happy to hear that my son and daughter-in-law were tangling with white trash like the Crooks, for whatever reason."

"They're Kendall's friends, not mine," Matt muttered.

Kendall braced herself against the sideboard and slowly counted to ten. When she was calm enough to speak, she said, "They're not my *friends,* Matt. Billy Joe was my client. According to the Constitution of the United States, everyone, including Billy Joe Crook, is entitled to legal representation. If I'm not wrong, Prosper still abides by the Constitution. Granted, my clients are rarely the crème de la crème of our society."

"Well, I don't like it. You're rubbing elbows with lowlife day in, day out."

"I'm doing my job!"

Gibb interceded. "I think the main problem here is the matter of divided loyalties. Kendall, you took the Crooks' side against your own husband's, and everybody saw it."

She gaped at him, disbelieving that he could be serious, although it was obvious that he was. "You're blowing this way out of proportion. Both of you."

"You're probably right," Gibb said congenially. "I'd like to prevent this kind of misunderstanding from ever cropping up again. And I think I've thought of a way. Please."

He indicated Kendall's empty chair. Reluctantly she returned to it. Like Matt, Gibb didn't let her argue her position, but rather dismissed it out of hand.

"For quite a while I've been knocking around an idea," Gibb began. "Now seems like an excellent time to bring it up. Kendall, have you ever thought of going back into private practice?"

"No."

"Maybe you should."

"I don't want to join another competitive, cutthroat firm, where as much energy is expended on making rank as on practicing law."

"What if it weren't so cutthroat?" Gibb said. "What if there weren't any competition? What if I were to set you up in your own office? I'd foot the bills until you got things going."

She hadn't expected that, and for a moment she was too astonished to speak. She knew that she had to decline graciously and diplomatically, and when she was able, she said, "That's an extremely generous offer, Gibb. Thank you. But I'd never be able to repay you. I'd never have enough clients to make a living."

"I have every confidence in you."

"I don't lack confidence in myself. I lack confidence in the townsfolk. I wouldn't describe the attitudes in Prosper as progressive, would you?" she asked with a rueful smile. "The Crooks wouldn't have had me representing Billy Joe if they'd had another choice. Who around here is going to retain me, a *woman*, and entrust me with their legal problems?"

"You wouldn't have to build a large clientele," Gibb argued.

For the first time that evening, Matt showed some animation. "That's right, darling. We could direct some business your way."

"I don't want that, Matt. I would be a laughingstock— Gibb's daughter-in-law, Matt's wife, dressing up every morning and playing lawyer." She gave a firm shake of her head. "Thank you, but no."

"It's your decision, of course," Gibb said with a disappointed sigh. "Although I think your talents are wasted in public service."

He had no idea how offensive that remark was to her. "Wasted, Gibb? I don't think so. You see, the sexism and competitive spirit at Bristol and Mathers were only part of the reason I was eager to disassociate myself.

"Up to now, I haven't shared this with anyone except Ricki Sue and Grandmother, but I'll tell you because it might help you understand why I've focused my career on public defense."

She stood up and paced while she talked. "A woman came to the offices of Bristol and Mathers seeking my help. She had AIDS. Her husband had infected her with the virus, then abandoned her and their three children. Her health declined. When she could no longer work to support herself or her children, the state took custody of them and placed them in foster homes.

"After six months, she was desperate to see them, but her repeated requests to do so were denied. Her desperation led her to enter the state-agency office with a pistol, saying she would see her children or else. She was arrested. The pistol wasn't even loaded, but that was a technicality.

"She raised bail and was released. Unhappy with the lawyer assigned to her case, she came to me. I was instantly sympathetic with her plight. Yes, she had committed a crime, but the mitigating circumstances were compelling. To my mind, the law and justice were in conflict in this case. Here was a woman who wished only to see her children one last time before she died. I agreed to represent her."

She drew a deep breath to quell the anger that rose inside her each time she thought of her summons into the partners' conference room. "They were horrified. The woman had been arrested at the scene of her crime. What possible hope did I have of winning an acquittal? And did the firm really want any involvement with an AIDS patient? The implied answer was a resounding no.

"Furthermore—and this was the real deciding factor—there was no money involved. The woman had limited resources, and the firm's hourly rate was considerable. How was Bristol and Mathers to profit if it willingly handled charity cases? If the firm took one, word would get out and the associates would be besieged by freeloaders. I was summarily ordered to drop the case.

"If I'd had the gumption, I would have resigned right then. But I needed the job, and Bristol and Mathers was the most respected firm in Sheridan. So I stayed until I heard about this job in South Carolina. I thought that here, I could work toward seeing justice served without worrying about how much profit it might cost my firm. I love the law. And I hold to this outdated, outmoded belief that it was instituted for the People, not the lawyers.

"By the way, the woman died before her case was brought to trial. She died without seeing her children again. Every time I lose a case, I take it personally. It's as though I've let her down again."

After a moment of silence, Gibb said softly, "A touching story, Kendall. But you mustn't feel that you've failed because H.W. sent Billy Joe off to Columbia."

"Under the circumstances, it was unnecessary. His offense didn't warrant it."

"Well, I'm just a dumb sporting goods salesman. I wouldn't presume to know how H.W. arrived at his decision," Gibb said. "He's human just like the rest of us. Naturally you're disappointed, but his ruling isn't a poor reflection on your abilities. You did your best. That's all anyone expects of you."

She had needed to hear that. Heartened, she smiled. "Thanks for the support, Gibb."

"Dad's a wizard when it comes to putting things in perspective. He's always right."

Kendall moved up behind Matt and laid her hands on his shoulders. "I need a friend. Are we still friends?"

He angled his head back. "What do you think?"

She leaned down and kissed his forehead. "Thank you for coming to my rescue. I saw a dashing and dangerous side of you I'd never seen before. I'm sorry if I gave you the impression that I didn't appreciate your heroic gesture."

"You're forgiven." They kissed, then he folded her hands over his chest and held them there. "Dad, should we tell her the surprise in store for this weekend?"

"Surprise?" She clutched the concept with both hands.

It had been a terrible day. Tomorrow wouldn't be much better, because news of her defeat would have spread. Everyone would be talking about it. Bama, the panhandler, had already heard of it by the time she left the courthouse that afternoon.

"Too bad, Counselor," he'd said. "You'll win next time." His thumbs-up sign did little to boost her spirits. In fact, his destitution had only depressed her more.

In her heart of hearts, she knew she had done her best. Nevertheless, she didn't take defeat well. Losing always made her feel that she was disappointing those who had placed their confidence in her—her clients, their families, her grandmother, even her dead parents.

Today had been a bitter defeat, but it was behind her. She would mark the Crook case up to experience and look forward to the next. She would try harder. Work smarter. She was determined to succeed.

Filled with resolve, her mood began to lift. A relaxing weekend sounded wonderful. "What have you two got planned?" she asked.

"Matt tells me that you've been hounding him to go along on one of our outdoor excursions."

"I wouldn't use the word *hounding*," she said coyly.

"How about nagging, pestering, or harassing?"

Playfully, she socked Matt in the gut, and he gave an exaggerated grunt of pain.

Pleased that family harmony had been restored, Gibb smiled at them indulgently. "Do you want to hear this or not?"

Kendall pulled a sober face. "I want to hear it."

"This Saturday there'll be a full moon."

She envisioned a candlelight dinner at a cozy guest house in the mountains, or a moonlight boat ride on the lake.

"The full moon in November can only mean one thing," Matt said, raising her expectations even higher.

"What?" she asked breathlessly.

"Hog slaughtering."

Chapter Twelve

GIBB ARRIVED BEFORE SUNLIGHT, EAGER TO GO. Kendall was hustled out into the frosty morning air. Their breath formed clouds of vapor as they walked to Gibb's pickup truck and climbed into the cab. She shivered inside her coat and tucked her gloved hands in her armpits in an attempt to warm them.

Matt hugged her close. "Cold?"

"A little. But I'll warm up." She had asked for this; she had wanted to be included. She wouldn't be a complainer.

"Before refrigeration, it had to be near freezing before hogs could be slaughtered," Gibb told her as he steered his pickup down the lane. "Otherwise the meat could spoil."

"That makes sense."

"So slaughtering became an autumn tradition. We fatten the hogs up all summer on corn."

" 'We'?"

"Not we ourselves," Matt explained. "We have a farmer who raises them for us out at his place."

"I see."

"That ham we had on our wedding night came from one of our hogs," Matt said proudly.

She grinned sickly. "I didn't realize I'd eaten a family friend."

He and Gibb laughed. Matt said, "Did you think that meat started out in those neat vacuum-sealed packages you buy at the store?"

"I prefer to think of it that way."

"Are you sure you're not a city girl?"

His words harkened back to what the Crooks had said of her, and reminded her that Billy Joe was scheduled to be transferred to Columbia today. He was already an insolent troublemaker with a sizable chip on his shoulder. He had made it clear that he would resist analysis. In his case, she feared that the R&E would be detrimental. She was seized by a premonition of doom.

Matt hugged her tighter against him, believing that her shiver was caused by the temperature.

The clearing was in a remote, heavily forested region and could be reached only by following a bumpy, narrow dirt path off the main road. By the time they arrived, several dozen families had already gathered there.

It was a carnival atmosphere. The crisp air smelled of wood smoke, which rose from numerous campfires where huge cast iron caldrons of water were boiling.

Children were playing games of chase among the trees. The teenagers had gravitated together and were hanging out on the tailgate of a pickup. They were raucous and rowdy.

The Burnwoods were greeted by shouts of welcome as they alighted from Gibb's truck. Someone thrust a mug of coffee at Kendall. She sipped it gratefully and was just about to offer thanks for it when she spotted the carcasses.

Each hog was hanging upside down from the exposed tendons in its rear hooves, through which a slender rod had been run. The rod was suspended between two forked poles.

There were so many, she couldn't count them. Nor could she take her eyes off the grotesque sight.

"Kendall? Sweetheart?"

Matt, speaking with obvious concern, touched her cheek and turned her face to him. He had pulled on a pair of black rubber gloves, which felt cold and foreign against her skin. He'd also put on a pair of coveralls, a long rubber apron, and knee-high rubber boots.

There was very little grass on the ground beneath his boots. Even where it grew sparsely, it had been trampled down. The dirt, like her husband's overalls, looked rusty.

She pointed at the stains and asked in a faint voice, "Is that blood?"

"This is where we usually come to dress our kills."

She swallowed with difficulty.

"You look pale, Kendall. Are you all right?"

"A little queasy."

"Do I dare hope it's morning sickness?"

"Unfortunately no," she replied sadly.

His disappointment matched her own. Eager to have a child, he had promised her all the help she might need in the way of housekeepers and nannies, although she was confident that she could smoothly combine her career and motherhood.

She wasn't using any birth control, but, to their disappointment, her body continued to cycle as regularly as the moon.

Thoughts of the moon jarred her back to the present.

"I didn't expect them to look so helpless and . . . naked," she finished lamely, gesturing behind her toward the carcasses.

"They don't start out that way," Matt said, trying unsuccessfully to mask his amusement. "They're brought here and killed, usually by a bullet through the head. The jugular's pierced, and they're bled. Then the hides are soaked with hot water and the hair is scraped off. All that takes time, so we pay people to do it. Hill people mostly. For doing the dirty work, they get a few dollars, the scraps, and the heads."

Kendall's knees went weak. "The heads?"

"They cook them to make souse—head cheese."

"Matt!"

She and Matt turned and saw Gibb standing near two of the suspended carcasses. Dressed similarly to Matt, he was motioning him over.

"Coming, Dad." Matt looked at Kendall with concern. "You sure you're okay?"

"I'm fine. It's just that I've never seen . . ."

"Kendall, this isn't as scary as you're making it out to be. Even little kids get a kick out of it."

"Oh, it's awfully exciting." He and Gibb had thought this would be a treat for her. She didn't want to appear ungrateful. "I guess it just takes some getting used to."

"Matthew!"

"I'll be right there, Dad."

Matt kissed her quickly and rushed off to join his father. Kendall breathed through her mouth to stave off nausea. She inhaled each breath deeply, then let it out slowly. The air was thinner here than in town. She needed some oxygen, that's all.

Matt glanced back at her. She managed a gay little wave and a rictus of a grin for encouragement. She watched Gibb hand Matt a knife with a long, wide blade. While Gibb held one of the carcasses in place, Matt drew the knife blade around the hog's neck, sawing through the muscles and tissue of the throat, completely encircling the backbone. Then, passing the knife back to his father, he gripped the head in both hands and gave it a vicious twist.

When the head came off, Kendall fainted.

She felt the derisive stares of everyone in the congregation as she followed the usher up the aisle to the third pew, where she, Matt, and Gibb sat every Sunday morning.

As soon as she was seated, she opened her program and

pretended to read, to spare herself the embarrassment of having to meet the belittling glances of the men and the scornful eyes of the women, all of them no doubt thinking that she was a shrinking violet.

She wanted to shout at them, "I've never fainted before in my life!"

She didn't, of course, but she couldn't hide her agitation from Matt. He leaned over and whispered, "Relax, Kendall."

"I can't. Everybody knows about yesterday morning."

To her mortification, she had regained consciousness in the bed of Gibb's pickup truck with a crowd of people hovering over her, patting her cheeks, chafing her wrists, and commenting on her fragility.

"You're being paranoid," Matt said. "And even if word has gotten around that you fainted, so what?"

"I'm embarrassed!"

"There's no need to be. It was a very feminine reaction to a new experience. Besides, it gave me a chance to redeem myself. I proved myself your hero by carrying you to the truck and fussing over you." He smiled. "You're very cute when you're helpless."

She could have argued that the adjective *cute* didn't inspire much confidence in the public defender, but she didn't want to argue. His loving expression reminded her of their wedding day and made her feel warm all over. She slipped her arm through his as they were asked to stand for the invocation.

Once they got through the hymn singing, announcements, and offertory, the congregation settled in for the sermon. Kendall had tried to beg off from attending this morning, and only in part because everybody in town knew about yesterday's disgrace. Although the Burnwoods had been members of this independent Protestant church for years, she never looked forward to attending because she thoroughly disliked the minister.

Brother Bob Whitaker was a pleasant enough gentleman

and a kind and caring pastor to his extensive flock—until he
got behind the pulpit. There, he metamorphosed into a ranting,
raving preacher of hellfire and brimstone. Even that didn't
bother Kendall excessively. Television evangelists had almost
inured the public to fiery admonitions against sin.

What bothered her was the pastor's recurring message of
wrathful judgment. He quoted "an eye for an eye" so often
that she wondered if it was the only scripture he had committed
to memory. He had little to say of mercy and grace; a great
deal to say of vengeance and reparation. He depicted God
as a bloodthirsty avenger, not as the creator of love and
forgiveness.

Although she was here at Matt's urging, she couldn't be
forced to listen. Now that Brother Bob was well into his
diatribe against transgression, she tuned him out and turned
her thoughts to other matters.

She was mentally planning her week, when she happened
to lock gazes with a woman seated across the aisle and one
row back. She was positively stunning. Kendall assumed that
the man seated next to her was her husband, but he—indeed
everyone—faded into the background.

She wasn't a traditional beauty, but she was certainly
arresting. Her chestnut hair had been teased high on top and
fell in waves below her shoulders. Her eyes, nose, and mouth
were large, blending well to form a provocative, somewhat
sullen face.

Beyond her striking appearance, what held Kendall's attention was the glower the woman had fixed on her. In order to
see her, Kendall had had to turn her head at an awkward angle.
It was as though she hadn't seen the woman accidentally, but
had been drawn around by the magnetic power of her malicious stare.

Matt nudged her. "What are you looking at?"

She brought her head forward quickly. "Uh, nothing."

He reached for her hand and held it throughout the remainder of the service. Kendall wanted to turn around and see if the woman continued to stare at her, but, for some reason, she was afraid to look.

After the benediction, as they were moving up the aisle toward the exit, Kendall spotted her in the crowd. "Matt, who's that woman?" Kendall nodded in the direction of the woman. "The one in the green dress."

Before he could answer, he was distracted. "Hey, Matt." The superintendent of schools sidled up to them and shook hands with Matt. Looking across at Kendall, he winked broadly. "Y'all have ham for breakfast this morning?" He wheezed a laugh. "How 'bout coming over one night this week for supper. Me and the wife'll barbecue us some pork ribs."

Matt and Gibb had warned her that she would be ruthlessly teased about fainting at the hog slaughtering, maybe for years to come. It was the type of incident one never lived down.

Outside, at least half the congregation lingered to chat. Kendall was ambushed by a woman whose daughter was thinking of entering law school. They solicited her opinion on which university the girl should attend. While answering their questions, she kept an eye out for the woman in the green dress.

She also noticed that Gibb and Matt had joined a group of men, most of whom she recognized and could name. They had separated themselves from everyone else. Probably so that they could smoke, Kendall decided when she noticed that several had lit cigarettes.

"I just don't know if we could afford out-of-state tuition," the woman said in response to some of Kendall's recommendations. "I suppose she might—"

"Excuse me for interrupting," Kendall said. "See that couple getting into the car across the street? She's wearing a green dress. Do you know her?"

The woman shaded her eyes and looked in the direction Kendall indicated. "Oh, that's Mr. and Mrs. Lynam." She sniffed disdainfully. "They don't attend as regular as they should. And if you ask me, they need to be here every Sunday."

Kendall wasn't interested in gossip. She had only wanted to see if the woman's name rang any bells, which it hadn't. Yet it had been obvious from her glare that she held a grudge. Why?

"Excuse me, again," Kendall said. "Is Mrs. Lynam by chance related to the Crooks?"

"Land sakes, no! Whatever gave you that idea?"

Thankfully, Matt chose that moment to rejoin her. "Hello, Mrs. Gardner, Amy," he said. "Ready to go, sweetheart? Dad's buying our lunch at the country club buffet. If we don't hurry, the Baptists will get all the good tables. Right, ladies?" Flashing the woman and her daughter a disarming smile, he excused them and ushered Kendall away.

As they walked toward the parking lot, Kendall indicated the group of men from which Gibb was just now detaching himself. "That looks like a high-level conference of some kind. What's it about?"

"Why do you ask?"

She had posed the question in a harmless, almost teasing tone and was therefore puzzled by his defensive response. "No particular reason, Matt. I was just curious."

His taut expression relaxed into a smile. "Deacons. A special deacons' meeting has been called for tomorrow night to review the church budget."

"I see."

"Please don't pout."

"I won't. In fact, I've got a lot of paperwork to catch up on. I'll do it while you're out." Lately, she had made a concerted effort not to complain when he went out in the evenings. Likewise, if he had to go out, he tried to come home earlier and was especially apologetic and sweet when he returned.

To thank her for her understanding, he kissed her.

They were still nuzzling when Gibb approached, his Bible tucked under his arm. "You two keep that up and the sheriff will be along to arrest you for indecency."

He spoke in jest; he was smiling as he climbed into the backseat. "Let's go. The sermon went long and my stomach growled all the way through it."

Matt got behind the wheel and started the car. "Some news about Billy Joe Crook, huh, Dad?"

Kendall was instantly alert. "What news?"

"He was involved in an accident on the way to Columbia," Gibb told her from the backseat. She turned and looked at him. "An accident? What kind of accident? Is he all right?"

"No, Kendall. I'm afraid he's not."

Luther, gnawing on a loose cuticle, cut his eyes over to his twin. Henry's only answer to Luther's quizzical glance was a shrug that conveyed his own bewilderment.

They were jumpy. On edge. They didn't know what to make of the situation.

They had never seen their mama this still and silent. She had been like this since yesterday evening when the prison had called and told them about Billy Joe's accident.

Henry had answered the telephone. He listened, shock and outrage building inside him with each official word that came through the line. "Can we see him?"

"Not just yet," he was told. "We'll get back to you."

After hanging up, he had summoned Luther outside and told him of their little brother's fate. Luther had cursed a blue streak, picked up a hatchet and buried the blade deeply into the exterior wall of the house, then spoke the words Henry dreaded most to hear: "We gotta tell Mama."

Luther had said "we," but Henry knew he meant "you."

There was no time to call one of their sisters to do it. They lived too far away. Besides, they would only go to bawling and making a racket, and that wouldn't help the situation.

He was the oldest, the man of the family. The responsibility fell to him. So he and Luther had trudged back inside, where he broke the bad news to Mama.

But she hadn't reacted as they had expected. She hadn't gone on a rampage, hadn't started yelling or squalling or breaking stuff. She hadn't even taken a drink, not a single one. Instead, she had plopped herself down in her rocker and stared out the window, and there she still sat, almost twenty-four hours later.

It was like she had petrified, and it was beginning to get on Henry's nerves. He would rather have her carrying on than sitting there like a stump, nothing moving but her eyes when they blinked. He almost wished she would have one of her fits. He would know from experience how to deal with that.

The officials had called an hour ago and said they could see Billy Joe at five o'clock. They would have him ready by then, they said. So that presented Henry with a dilemma. He needed to see to his little brother, but he couldn't leave Mama alone. And Luther had refused to stay with her.

"By myself?" Luther's voice had gone thin and high with fear when Henry had suggested that he stay behind with Mama. "Hell no! She's spooking me out, the way she's sittin' and starin' like that. I think she's not right in the head, is what I think. This is drove her plumb out of her mind. Anyway, I ain't staying with her by myself."

Henry still hadn't resolved the problem, and time was running out. If he didn't arrive when they expected him, he might not get to see Billy Joe before—

"Henry!"

He nearly jumped out of his skin. "Here, Mama."

Making his way across the room to her rocker, he stumbled over his own large feet. When he reached her, her eyes were focused, and he could tell right off that Luther had been wrong. She wasn't out of her head.

"Your daddy'll turn over in his grave if we let 'em get by with this," she said.

"Damn right." Luther, looking relieved, knelt beside her chair. "No sir. No way in hell. We ain't gonna let 'em get by with this."

She hauled off and walloped him on the side of his head. "I ain't lost my mind. Don't ever let me hear you say such again."

Tears filled Luther's colorless eyes. He massaged his ear, which would probably still be ringing this time next year. "No, ma'am. I mean, yes, ma'am."

"What're we gonna do, Mama?" Henry asked.

As she outlined her plan, he realized that that was what she had been cooking up all the time she'd been staring out the window so strange-like.

Chapter Thirteen

"*T*HE COFFEE SMELLS GOOD."

Kendall had been so lost in thought that she hadn't heard him come into the kitchen. At the sound of his voice, she turned. Propped on his crutches in the doorway, he was dressed, but unshaven. He looked rumpled but rested. Some color had returned to his face, and the dark circles around his eyes had faded considerably.

"Good morning." Nervously she wiped her palms on the seat of her shorts. "I was just about to come check on you. How do you feel?"

"Better. Still not great."

"I hope Kevin didn't wake you."

"No. He's asleep in that square thing."

"Playpen. Sit down. I'll cook you some breakfast." She poured him a cup of coffee. "What would you like? Pancakes? Eggs? French toast? I make everything except waffles."

"What have you got against waffles?"

"We don't have a waffle iron."

"Oh. Where'd the food come from? Did fairies deliver it during the night?"

"I went shopping this morning."

He seemed surprised. "I didn't hear you leave."

"You weren't supposed to."

"How far is it to the nearest town?"

"Not far."

"Did you happen to think of a newspaper?"

"It's on the end table in the living room."

"Thanks."

She prepared the bacon and eggs he requested. He cleaned his plate quickly, leaving only one slice of bacon. "Want it?"

"Remember, I don't eat pork."

"Sticking to that story?"

"I don't have a *story*."

"I think you do. I just don't know what it is yet. Why didn't you take off this morning when you had the chance?"

Why hadn't she? That question had kept her preoccupied ever since her return. She had intended to leave for good after sneaking out at dawn. But the farther she got, the guiltier she felt.

She recalled each time he had moaned during the night. He could barely walk, and his concussion was still a major concern. She wouldn't desert an animal that was as badly injured as he. She could no more abandon him now than she could have at the scene of the accident.

This sense of responsibility for him was galling. It was a dangerous hindrance to what she had to do. But she knew she would be shackled to it until his health improved and he became more self-sufficient.

It had also occurred to her that she might be safer here than on the road. That morning on her trip to town, she had felt exposed, vulnerable. If she fled, where would she go? She had no specific destination in mind—only escape. So far she had succeeded. As long as he posed no real threat to her overall plan, why press her luck by leaving before she absolutely had to?

It also occurred to her that these arguments might be rationalizations because she loved this house. She felt safe here and didn't really want to leave it.

"I promise I won't leave you in your present condition," she said.

"Implying that you'll leave once my condition improves."

"Don't put words in my mouth."

"Well, everything you say is so damn oblique, I try and fill in the blanks."

"The blanks will fill themselves in when your mind is ready. The doctor's hypothesis was that you might be blocking your memory subconsciously. You don't want to remember."

He folded his hands around his coffee cup and looked directly into her eyes. "Is he right, Kendall?"

That was the first time he had called her by name. Hearing it on his lips unnerved her; for a moment she lost her train of thought. "Is he right?" she repeated. "Only you can answer that."

"If I can't remember anything, how would I know what I've chosen to forget?" He swore, plunging his fingers into his hair. But he had forgotten his stitches, and the impatient gesture pulled at them. "Ow!"

"Careful! Here, let me look." She moved to his side and pushed his hands out of the way. Peeling back the gauze bandage, she examined the wound. "No sign of infection. The stitches are intact. No damage has been done that I can see."

"It's beginning to itch," he said irritably.

"That means it's healing."

"I guess." She was still standing close. He glanced up at her. "Where'd you get the money for the groceries?"

"I told you, I—"

"Earned it. I know. Doing what?"

She hesitated, balancing the pros and cons of telling him, and finally deciding that he would pester her about it until she did. "I'm a lawyer."

He barked a short laugh. "Your lies are getting more elaborate."

"I'm a public defender." He looked at her as though he still didn't believe it. "It's the truth," she insisted.

"Tell me about it."

"What do you want to know?"

"Were you any good? I'll bet you were. You lie so well." She smiled. "That's what Ricki Sue said, too."

"Who's that?"

"My best friend."

"Hmm." Mindlessly, he munched on the last slice of bacon. "How good a defense lawyer were you?"

She stalled by pouring herself a cup of coffee before taking a chair across the table from him. "I believe I was fairly good. More than adequate. If nothing else, I deserved an A for effort.

"I *wanted* to be good," she said. "The people who hired me thought they were taking a huge risk by awarding the position to a woman. Consequently, I had a lot to prove. Overall, my win/loss ratio was respectable. Naturally I didn't win every case."

He assumed a listening posture that prompted her to continue. "One defeat was particularly bitter. At first the case seemed routine, but it wound up being . . . rather terrible."

"What happened?"

"I advised a sixteen-year-old boy to plead guilty to a shoplifting charge, to throw himself on the mercy of the court. Since it was his first offense, I expected the judge to be lenient. Instead, he used this boy to humiliate me." With little inflection in her voice, she recounted for him the courtroom scene.

"There's a postscript, right?"

"During the trip to Columbia, there was a terrible accident. He was handcuffed, you see, and somehow, when they stopped to take a break, the cuffs got caught on something and his arm . . ." She paused, swallowed with difficulty. "His right arm was severed at the shoulder, literally yanked off as though he had been drawn and quartered. He went into shock and almost bled to death. They were able to save his life, but he'll never fully recover, physically or psychologically."

That Sunday morning when Kendall heard about the accident, she had been assailed by dismay, guilt, and outrage. It continued to haunt her. Billy Joe was certainly no angel. But the accident had destroyed any likelihood that he would become a law-abiding, contributing member of society. Maimed and embittered, he would hold the world accountable for his misfortunes. He would blame his defense attorney in particular.

His family certainly had.

"Hell of an accident," he remarked. He had sat quietly, giving her time to reflect on the disturbing incident and its repercussions.

Was taking this discussion further a good idea? Was she telling too much? But it felt good to unload the misgivings that had burdened her for months.

"I have my own theory about it," she said.

"Which is?"

"That it wasn't an accident at all."

"Interesting." He leaned forward. "Did you have someone check into it?"

"At the time, it didn't occur to me to do so."

"Did you get the boy's account?"

"I tried to. I went to the hospital to see him, but was told he was still recovering and couldn't have visitors."

"Didn't that raise your suspicions?"

"It should have, but at the time it seemed reasonable. For weeks he was in critical condition. Then, before I even requested it, I was sent a copy of the accident report. It was a detailed account of what had happened. Everything looked official and in order. It wasn't until much later that it occurred to me that this 'accident' might have been staged. Billy Joe was a targeted victim."

She combed her fingers through her hair. Whenever she was reminded of her naïveté, it distressed her. "By the time I realized that he'd been victimized, it was too late to do anything about it. I had already—" She broke off before saying too much.

"You'd already what?"

"Nothing."

"What?"

"I think I hear Kevin crying." She jumped to her feet.

"You can't get off that easy. He's not crying. Sit down."

"I'm not a dog. I don't sit on command."

"Why don't you want to finish your story?"

"Because I . . . I . . ."

"What, Kendall? What are you running from? From me?"

"No," she replied in a gruff voice.

"You'll never admit it, but you had every intention of leaving that hospital without me. If I hadn't caught you sneaking out, you'd be gone, vamoose, whereabouts unknown. Don't bother denying it, because I know I'm right.

"Then you bring me to a place where there's no telephone, no TV, no radio that works. That's right," he said when she gave away her surprise. "I tried the one you hid in the closet. Did you break it on purpose?"

"I knew it was broken, so I put it up out of the way."

His disbelief was apparent. "We have no communication with the outside world. There aren't any nearby neighbors, at least none that I can see. You've deliberately isolated us.

"There's something you're not telling me. There's a *lot* you're not telling me—about my past, your past, our marriage. If there is a marriage."

He used the table to lever himself up. "I'm drowning in confusion and you're my only link to whatever my life was before the accident. Help me out. Enlighten me before I go crazy. Tell me what I want to know. Please."

She gripped the back of her chair so tightly that her knuckles turned white. "Okay, what do you want to know?"

"For starters, what did I do to piss you off?"

"Who says I'm pissed off?"

"It's easy enough to deduce. When you saw an unexpected but convenient way to dump me, you took it, and almost got away with it. Secondly, you claim we're married, but the signs I read clearly say that we're not. Why would you make such a claim?"

"What signs?"

"I've seen you naked. I've touched you naked. But whenever we're close, I don't get a sense of . . . of familiarity between us."

"Why do you say that?"

"Because it's too exciting."

She shifted her weight uneasily. "It might seem so. But only because you don't remember being close to me."

"Then what's your excuse?"

She dropped her gaze to the white ridge of her knuckles and said nothing. She couldn't.

He went on, "You lay beside me all night, but you were careful not to touch me, not even accidentally. I was restless and awake enough to realize how carefully you avoided making contact skin to skin."

"That's not so. We kissed good night."

"I kissed you, you didn't kiss me. And I'm positive that I've never kissed you before."

"How can you be positive?"

"Because I can't remember it."

She laughed softly. "That only means that my kisses aren't memorable."

"Hardly. Just the opposite."

The quiet raspiness of his voice drew her eyes up to meet his. Her face grew hot, as though his invasive stare were emanating heat. Since she couldn't think of a clever comeback, or a solid argument, she prudently remained silent.

After a moment he picked up where he'd left off. "Assuming for the sake of argument that we are married, were we estranged at the time of the accident?"

"I never said that."

"You didn't have to. What caused our marital rift? Did I resent the time you spent pursuing your career?"

"Not inordinately."

"Were we compatible?"

"We got along okay."

"Did we argue over the baby? I have fleeting flashbacks to arguments over having kids."

Kendall's response was unguarded. "Really?" she asked, surprised.

"Did I want a baby?"

"Of course."

He looked perplexed, troubled, and stroked his forehead. "I don't think so."

"That's a terrible thing to say!"

"I'm being brutally honest. Which makes it one out of two here."

He silently appealed to her for a truthful explanation, but, in self-defense, Kendall kept her expression remote.

"Was our fight over money?" he asked.

"No."

"Sex?"

She looked away and shook her head.

"Sex," he said, drawing his conclusion from her reaction.

"There was nothing wrong with that aspect of our relationship."

"Then come here."

"What for?"

"Come here." The repeated command was soft but no less compelling.

If she stood her ground, he might mistake her stubbornness for cowardice. And even if that was partially true, she couldn't let him know that she was afraid of him. So she moved around the table and stood directly in front of him.

"Is this a test?"

He said, "Sort of."

He covered her breast and pressed it warmly.

She gasped.

He whispered, "You fail."

It was as difficult to hold her ground now as it had been last night when he had touched her, but she knew she must or jeopardize her credibility. "It's been a long time, that's all."

"How long?" He lightly ground her nipple with his palm.

"Since before Kevin was born."

"Then it's no wonder."

"No wonder what?"

He moved closer, and when his middle made contact with hers, his meaning became obvious.

Lowering his head, he brushed her lips with his, and it caused her to tingle all over. Then he kissed her in earnest, his mouth mobile and open and sweet. He pushed his tongue against hers.

Breathless, she pulled away. "I can't."

"Why not?" His lips slid down her throat.

"I'm full."

"Full?"

"I'm lactating." She pushed his hand aside and stumbled backward several steps. Self-consciously she touched her damp, throbbing lips, her neck. Her hand made a pass over the wet spots on her T-shirt. "Under the circumstances, I don't think we should . . . do anything."

"How come?"

"It feels awkward."

"Why?"

"Because the amnesia has made us practically strangers."

"You claim that we're married."

"Yes."

"We've had a child together."

"Yes."

"But we're practically strangers? Explain that, Kendall. And while you're at it . . ." He reached behind his back and whipped something from the waistband of his shorts. "Explain this."

With a flick of his wrist, he aimed the pistol straight at her.

Chapter Fourteen

"My name is Kendall Burnwood."

She laid her briefcase on the table and extended her right hand to the woman seated alone in the interrogation room. Her hair wasn't as lustrous as before. The exotic face was distorted by swelling and bruising. Nevertheless, Kendall clearly recognized the woman she had seen only once in church.

"I know who you are. I'm Lottie Lynam."

She shook Kendall's hand with a notable lack of enthusiasm. Kendall noticed that her hand was dry, not damp with nervous perspiration. Her voice was steady, her gaze level. Under the circumstances, one would expect more emotion.

She appeared amazingly composed for a woman who had recently killed her husband.

"Can I get you something, Mrs. Lynam?"

"You can get me out of here."

"I'll go to work on that right away. What did you tell the arresting officers?"

"Nothing."

"It's essential that I know anything you said while in police custody, even if it's something you consider insignificant."

"I didn't tell them anything except that Charlie beat me up

and raped me, and that I wanted a lawyer with me before I
was questioned about how he died."

"That's good. That's very good."

"I watch a lot of TV," she said wryly.

"What time were you arrested?"

"About four A.M."

"When did the doctor see you?"

"They brought me straight here."

Kendall checked her wristwatch. It was almost seven.
"You've been sitting here three hours, in this condition? Are
you in pain?"

"A little sore. I can stand it."

"Well, I can't." Kendall scraped back her chair noisily,
crossed the room, angrily opened the door, and addressed the
squad room at large. "My client needs medical attention.
Who's going to drive us to the hospital?"

Kendall rode in the backseat of the patrol car with Mrs.
Lynam, who remained silent during the brief trip. At the
hospital, she was subjected to a pelvic examination. A rape
kit was prepared, including photographs of Mrs. Lynam's
body. Kendall was promised that she would be sent a copy
of the evidence report as soon as the police department
received its copy.

Although the bruises on Mrs. Lynam's face were unsightly,
the doctor assured her that they were "superficial" and would
fade in due time. The scratches on her shoulders, breasts, and
thighs were treated with antiseptic. Upon their return to the
courthouse, Kendall insisted that her client be given a shower
and breakfast before she was formally questioned.

"Call me when you're ready to question her," she told the
officer assigned to the case. "I'll be waiting in my office."
Before leaving, she pressed Mrs. Lynam's hand reassuringly.

Two hours later, they were back in the interrogation room.
Lottie Lynam's hair was still damp. Her face looked freshly

scrubbed—and innocent, Kendall noticed. Without makeup, she looked much younger and more vulnerable. She was dressed in a drab gray jail-issue jumpsuit and cheap faux leather slippers.

"There were three bullet holes in Char—, uh, the victim," the police detective told Kendall. "We've already got pictures of the crime scene. They're not pretty."

"May I see them please?"

He passed her a manila folder. As he'd warned her, the color prints were vividly gory.

"One bullet entered through his neck. One was fired into his forehead, 'bout here." He marked the spot on his own skull. "The other went clean through his cheek, and came out his temple on the opposite side. The gun was fired at close range. 'Bout three-thirty this morning. He died instantly in his own bed."

His eyes slid toward Lottie, who sat with her hands clasped primly in her lap. Her expression gave away nothing. Subconsciously Kendall noted how helpful her stoicism would be in the courtroom.

She thanked the policeman for the information. "Has the coroner filed the autopsy report?"

"He'll get to it this morning. He said we might have the report by the end of the day."

"I'd like a copy as soon as it's available, please."

"Sure. But it's going to back up everything I told you."

Kendall didn't respond to that. Instead she asked a simple question: "Why is my client being held on a suspicion of murder?"

The assisting officer, who thus far had been leaning against the wall with his ankles crossed, picking his teeth with a wooden toothpick, guffawed. He pointed toward the pistol lying on the table. It had been bagged and tagged. "That's the murder weapon right there. It was lying on the floor beside the bed where Charlie got his head blowed off. We've already matched her prints to it, and there were powder burns on her hands. Can't get much more conclusive than that."

"Can't you?" Kendall asked with condescension.

The other officer picked up the story. "When we got to their house, Lottie was sitting at the kitchen table sipping a straight whiskey, cool as a cucumber."

"I imagine Mrs. Lynam was in shock and deserved a drink for having been raped."

"Raped! Charlie was her husband. They were married for years," the assisting officer argued. "We got us a clear-cut case of murder here. It's plain to see what happened."

"Oh?" Kendall's inflection invited him to speculate.

"Charlie came home drunk. That didn't set too well with Lottie. She probably nagged him about it, and he knocked her around a bit. I'm not saying that was right," he added quickly. "Anyhow, Lottie was riled, so when he fell asleep, she shot and killed him."

"Have you got statements from the witnesses?" Kendall asked.

"Witnesses?"

"Anyone who was there and saw what happened," she explained innocently. "Can a neighbor substantiate that such an argument took place? Can anyone testify that Mrs. Lynam was angry with her husband and shot him with a pistol, which, incidentally, she could have handled at any time before last night?"

The two officers exchanged glances. "There aren't any neighbors," one grudgingly admitted. "Their place is out yonder in the country."

"I see. So nobody overheard this quarrel that you've alleged took place. Nobody witnessed a murder."

The officer threw his toothpick to the floor and shoved away from the wall. "Nobody witnessed any rape either."

Kendall thanked them and asked to see her client alone.

Once the policemen left the room, Lottie spoke for the first time. "It's pretty much like they said."

Kendall had feared as much, but she didn't let her discouragement show. "Based on the physical evidence they already have, it's almost certain you'll be indicted for murder. Regardless of that tap dance I did for the policemen, we know you pulled the trigger on the gun that killed your husband. You're not *innocent*—that's the fact. *Guilt*, however, is a determination. So my job is to explore and expose the circumstances of your life with Charles that will mitigate your guilt.

"Before I enter that courtroom to represent you, I'll have to know more than I'll probably need to know about you and your marriage. The courtroom is no place to spring a surprise on your own counsel. So I apologize in advance for prying into matters that deserve privacy. That's an unpleasant but necessary aspect of my job."

Lottie clearly didn't want the intrusion, but she gave Kendall a nod, indicating that she should proceed.

Kendall began by getting biographical information. She learned that Lottie had been born in Prosper, the youngest of five children. Her parents were deceased; siblings were scattered. She graduated from high school, attended one year of junior college, then took a secretarial job in an insurance office.

Charlie Lynam was a traveling salesman who sold office supplies. "He called on the insurance office," she said to Kendall. "He started flirting and asking me out. At first I said no, but finally I gave in and we dated whenever he was in town. One thing led to another."

They had been married for seven years. They had no children. "I can't have kids. I had appendicitis when I was a teenager. The resultant infection left me sterile."

Lottie Lynam hadn't led a very fulfilling life. The longer she talked, the more sympathy she evoked from Kendall, who had to remind herself to maintain a professional detachment.

She wanted very badly to help this woman, who had been forced to take desperate measures to save herself from a chronically abusive husband.

Kendall opened a file folder. "I did some research while you were showering and having breakfast. In the past three years you've called the police to the house seven times." She looked up. "Right?"

"If you say so. I lost count."

"On two of those occasions you were hospitalized. Once with several broken ribs. The other time with a burn on your back. What kind of burn, Mrs. Lynam?"

"He branded me with my curling iron," she said with remarkable composure. "I guess I was lucky. He tried to . . . get it inside me. He said he wanted to make me his once and for all."

Again Kendall had to concentrate on the facts and not let her pity show. "Was he jealous?"

"Crazy jealous. Of everybody in pants. I couldn't go anywhere, do anything, that he didn't accuse me of trying to attract other men. He wanted me to look nice, but then when I fixed up, he'd get mad if any other man so much as glanced at me. Then he'd get drunk, and beat me up."

"Did he ever threaten your life?"

"Too many times to count."

"I'd like you to think of specific times, preferably when someone might have overheard him threaten to kill you. Did you ever discuss his abusive behavior with anyone? A minister? A marriage counselor, perhaps?" Lottie shook her head. "It would be helpful if someone could corroborate how fearful you were that during one of his tantrums he might actually kill you. Wasn't there anyone you discussed this with?"

She hesitated. "No."

"Okay. What happened last night, Mrs. Lynam?"

"Charlie had been out on the road for several days. He

came home tired and cranky, and started drinking. Before long he was drunk.

"He pitched a billy fit and made a terrible mess of the dinner I'd cooked. He threw food against the wall. Broke dishes."

"Did the police see this?"

"No. I cleaned it up."

That was too bad. The evidence of a temper tantrum would have come in handy—if she could have proved that Charlie was the one who had thrown the tantrum.

"Go on," Kendall prompted.

"He stormed out of the house and was gone for hours. About midnight, he came back, drunker and meaner than when he left. I refused to have sex with him, so he did this to me," she said, indicating her battered face. "I thought it was legally rape when a woman said no."

"It is. You made it quite clear to him that you didn't choose to have sex last night, is that correct?"

She nodded. "But he forced me. He pinned me down on the bed and held his arm across my throat. He ripped off my panties and had me. It hurt. He hurt me on purpose."

"They cleaned your fingernails at the hospital. Will they find tissue beneath them, evidence that you struggled?"

"They should. I fought him like a hellcat. When he was finished, he crouched over me. He called me awful names, then threatened to kill me."

"What were his exact words?"

"He got his pistol from the bedside drawer, poked the barrel between my teeth, and said he ought to blow my goddamn head off. He might have killed me right then, except he passed out.

"For a long time I just lay there, too tired and sore and scared to move. I knew that for the hours he was asleep I'd be safe. But what about when he woke up? That's when I decided to kill him first, before he could kill me."

Looking Kendall squarely in the eye, she confessed, "I picked up the pistol and shot him in the head three times, just like they said. I'm not sorry I did it, either. Sooner or later he would have killed me. My life isn't anything to brag about, but I didn't want to die."

Back in her office, Kendall watched raindrops striking the window like metal pellets. "Uncanny," she murmured.

That morning when she arrived at the courthouse, Bama had predicted rain. "Before dark," the panhandler had said, nodding sagely.

Kendall had looked doubtfully at the clear sky overhead. "I don't see any clouds, Bama. Are you sure?"

"Storm before sunset. Mark my words."

He had been right. Thunder was echoing off the distant mountains, shrouded now in low clouds and fog. Shrugging off a vague sense of foreboding, Kendall responded to telephone messages and opened her mail.

In the mail delivered that morning was another letter from the Crooks, denouncing her and issuing veiled—and grossly misspelled—threats. It was the fifth such piece of correspondence she had received since Billy Joe's accident, but it wasn't the worst. A few days after his arm was severed, she had received a package containing a dead rat.

Word of it had spread like wildfire through the courthouse. Eventually it reached the newspaper office two blocks away. Soon, Matt was in her office, demanding to know if what he had heard was true.

When she showed him the stinking evidence, he had been ready to organize a team of vigilantes to go after the twins and anyone else by the name of Crook. Gibb, who had also heard the news, backed Matt's plan.

Kendall had prevailed upon them to do nothing. "They're upset over Billy Joe. To some extent, I sympathize with them."

"Sympathize! You did all you could for that snot-nosed little thief," Matt shouted.

"This scare tactic is way out of line, even for scum like the Crooks," Gibb said. "They're hoodlums and should be taken care of once and for all."

"They're backward people," she conceded, trying to calm them.

Matt said, "I warned that white trash that if they harmed you—"

"And they haven't. If we retaliate, we're sinking to their level. Please, Matt, Gibb. Don't do anything rash. It could ultimately prove more harmful to me than anything the Crooks might do. I must respond in a professional manner, which I believe is to ignore it."

She had managed to contain them and to win a promise that there wouldn't be any reprisals. Considering the extent of their anger, she had wisely kept silent about the other messages from the Crooks. She had told Matt that her wind-shield had been broken when a truck on the highway threw up a rock. The truth was that she had discovered it broken when she reached her car one evening after work. The rock that had broken it had a threatening, badly worded note attached.

Because they might later be used as evidence, she didn't destroy the notes sent to her office, but kept them locked in a file cabinet. She added this latest letter to the folder and returned her attention to Lottie Lynam. No doubt this case would dominate her schedule for the next several months.

As expected, she heard from Solicitor Dabney Gorn later that afternoon. He began the conversation with an expansive prediction: "Well, looks like we're going to have some excite-ment around here."

"Oh, really?" Kendall asked innocently. "Are we getting the proposed new elevator? That thing we've got is so rickety, I always take the stairs."

He chuckled in appreciation of her humor. "That dumb act

won't wash with me, Mrs. Burnwood. You've got yourself a hot case."

"True. I like sinking my teeth into something as heinous as assault and battery and rape."

"How about murder one?"

"Murder one?" she asked, sounding stunned. "Are we talking about the same case?"

"Lottie Lynam."

"You're going for murder one? I'm speechless."

"You've seen the same evidence reports that I have."

"So how could you have missed the pictures of Mrs. Lynam taken at the hospital, or the files on her previous hospital visits, or the police reports documenting the violent domestic disturbances at the Lynams' house?"

"All of which support my argument of premeditation," he said. "Lottie had a lot of reasons to do it and a long time to think about it. She'll be indicted for murder with malice aforethought. Were you hoping for manslaughter? Forget it. Your client thought it over for hours last night before finally deciding to plug Charlie."

"That can't be proved and you know it, Dabney. Right off the top of my head, I can think of a hundred ways to work in reasonable doubt."

"Okay, Counselor, let's stop beating around the bush," he said after a thoughtful moment. "Charlie Lynam isn't exactly a sympathetic victim. Everybody knows that he drank too much and routinely worked Lottie over. Let's save the taxpayers some money, and ourselves a lot of time."

"What's your best offer?" she asked, cutting to the chase.

"You get Lottie to plead guilty to voluntary manslaughter. She'll probably get twenty and serve eight at most."

"Thank you, but no thanks. My client is not guilty."

"Not guilty!" Now it was his turn to sound dismayed. "You're entering a not-guilty plea?"

"That's exactly what I'm going to do."

"What's your defense, insanity?"

"Lottie Lynam is perfectly sane. She knew what she had to do in order to save her own life. Granted, it was a desperate move, but killing her husband was an obvious act of self-defense."

Chapter Fifteen

"MR. PEPPERDYNE?"

"In here," he called.

The younger, greener agent bustled into the small kitchen. Pepperdyne glanced up from his perusal of Kendall Burnwood's household accounts, which were spread before him on the table.

"Something?"

"Yes, sir. We just found this in the bedroom. It was taped to the underside of a bureau drawer."

Pepperdyne took the bundle of papers from the excited agent and began reading them. His subordinate, too keyed up to sit still, paced the narrow space between the table and stove. "I thought that business about the preacher—that Bob Whitaker—was particularly interesting," he ventured. "Did we know that he never graduated seminary and in fact was asked to leave because his beliefs were so unorthodox?"

"No," Pepperdyne admitted tightly.

"But Mrs. Burnwood knew it. She made it her business to know. It's all documented."

"Hmm. Our Mrs. Burnwood must have been awfully busy."

"And there's a whole dossier on the D.A. in Prosper. Except that in South Carolina they're called solicitors. Have you read that yet?"

"Summarize it for me."

"Gorn was disbarred in Louisiana. That's when he moved to South Carolina. A few years later he's elected solicitor in Prosper County. Fishy, to say the least. And there's even more about the judge. Bankers, school administrators, law officers. You name a pillar of that community and she's chipped away at his foundation, exposing a crack wide enough to drive a Mack truck through. It's all in there."

In spite of himself, Pepperdyne was impressed by the extensive research, which rivaled some the department had turned out.

"It must've taken her a lot of time to do this much research," the other agent remarked. "And smarts."

"Oh, she's got plenty of smarts," Pepperdyne said. "She's also as slippery as snot on a doorknob."

"It's been almost two weeks since they left the hospital, and not a trace of them."

"I know how long it's been," Pepperdyne snapped. He shot to his feet, the sudden movement almost toppling the tiny kitchen table. His tone sent his subordinate scuttling out of the room, muttering something about continuing the search in the bedroom.

Pepperdyne moved to the kitchen sink. On the windowsill above it, a limp ivy was putting up a valiant struggle for survival despite its lack of water. It was in a ceramic pot with sunflowers on it. The window curtains had tiebacks also shaped like sunflowers. Pepperdyne caught himself fingering one, a partial smile on his lips.

These belong to a kidnapper, he reminded himself, snatching back his hand.

But at least they didn't belong to a killer. The autopsy performed on the body recovered from the auto accident in

Georgia proved that the passenger had died from the impact of the crash. Mrs. Burnwood hadn't let her drown. So she wasn't a killer. Yet.

Pepperdyne gazed out the window, ruminating over what this most recent discovery revealed about Mrs. Burnwood and the people in South Carolina with whom she'd had dealings. The more he learned, the less he knew. Every question that was answered prompted another one even more complex and alarming. The longer they were missing, the colder their trail became.

Cursing softly, he banged his fist against the windowsill. "Where are you, lady? And what have you done with *him*?"

The wall phone rang. Pepperdyne's head snapped around. He stared at the instrument. It rang a second time. There was an outside chance that someone was calling Kendall Burnwood, someone who might give them a clue to go on. If that was the case, he didn't want to scare him off.

His gut clenching, he lifted the receiver and said a cautious hello.

"Mr. Pepperdyne?"

"Speaking," he said, relaxing.

"Rawlins, sir. We've got something."

Pepperdyne's stomach quickened again when he recognized the name of one of the agents who had stayed behind in Stephensville, Georgia. "I'm listening."

"We've got a man here who says he sold a car to Kendall Burnwood. He's identified her by her picture."

"Positively identified?"

"No question."

"Where in hell has he been all this time?"

"Visiting his grandkids in Florida. He'd never flown before, so he bought a plane ticket to Miami with the money Mrs. Burnwood paid him for the car."

"She had cash?"

"That's what he said."

Bad news. She wouldn't be leaving a paper trail. Not that she would be that careless, but one could always hope.

"He was out of town when we did the door-to-door search," the agent added. "Just got back last night, he said, and was catching up on local news when he saw her picture in the paper. He read the story and called us."

"Get out an APB on that car."

"It's done, sir."

"Good. Keep tabs on him. I'm on my way."

Chapter Sixteen

"MAKE THEM STOP! I CAN'T STAND IT. STOP *their crying, stop their crying, stop their crying. Oh, Jesus! Oh, God. No!*"

His own scream woke him up. He sprang into a sitting position and glanced around wildly. Automatically he went for the weapon he had secreted beneath the mattress.

"It's not there." It was Kendall's voice. He could hear her, but he couldn't see her. "I took it and hid it where you can't find it this time."

He shook his head clear, searched the room for her, and eventually spotted her sprawled on the floor at the side of the bed. "What happened? What are you doing on the floor?"

"This is where I landed when you knocked me off the bed. You were having a nightmare and I was trying to wake you up. I got a fist in my shoulder."

"Are you hurt?"

"No," she said, pulling herself to her feet.

His heart was racing, and he was bathed in sweat. Feeling weak and disoriented, he raised the knee of his uninjured leg and rested his forehead on it.

"It must have been a doozy," she remarked. "Do you remember any of it?"

Raising his head, he looked up at her. "Luckily I don't. It scared the shit out of me."

"You're soaking wet. I'll get you a washcloth."

While she was out of the room, he got up, moved to the window, and sat in the straight chair. He raised the shade and was disappointed to see that the day was as dusty and still as it had been when he'd decided to surrender to his lethargy and take a nap. After the heavy rains two weeks ago, they were now in a dry spell. The heat was enervating.

He glanced over his bare shoulder at the twisted, sweaty sheets. "Sorry about that," he remarked to Kendall as she reentered the room.

"It won't be any trouble to change the bed." She hesitated, then added, "This isn't the first time you've had that nightmare."

"No?"

"No, but this time was by far the worst. Do you feel better now?"

He nodded and gratefully accepted the glass of lemonade she had carried in on a tray. His hand was shaking. He took several deep swallows of the icy lemonade, then rolled the cold glass against his forehead.

When he felt the cool cloth applied to his back, he was astonished. Ordinarily she went out of her way to avoid touching him.

Now, she moved the cloth across his shoulders, down his sides over his ribs, and along his spine to the small of his back, where sweat had pooled. The soft cloth felt deliciously cool, comforting. Her touch was light.

It reminded him of the way she was with her baby. For whatever else she might be, she was an excellent mother. Gentle. Giving. Attentive. Loving. She reveled in the role.

The infant prompted easy, natural smiles from her that lit up her face.

He'd observed her, usually when she wasn't aware of it, as she tended to the child. There were times when he almost envied the kid. He couldn't remember his infancy, of course, but being fussed over that way was beyond his imagination. He doubted that he had ever been loved that wholeheartedly, either as a child or as an adult.

He wondered, too, if he was capable of loving another human being so unselfishly and completely. It bothered him to think not.

"Better?" She rolled the cloth into a compress and laid it against the nape of his neck.

"Yeah. Thanks." Spontaneously he reached behind his head and covered her hand with his. He held the compress against his nape for several moments, her hand sandwiched between his palm and the cloth. "Much better."

"Good."

Eventually he removed his hand and she withdrew hers. He then used the cloth to bathe his chest and stomach, which he suddenly wished were harder, firmer, younger. When he caught Kendall watching him, she turned away quickly.

They both began speaking at once.

"I've brought—"

"What's all that for?"

"In a minute," she said, responding to his question. "Give yourself time to catch your breath."

She sat on the edge of the bed and demurely folded her hands in her lap. She wore shorts every day, so her legs had tanned. He figured she shaved them every time she bathed, because they always looked silky smooth. They *looked* smooth. He didn't know from experience, because, since that morning he had kissed her, he hadn't touched her again. For reasons as yet unknown to him, she had instituted a hands-off policy. He had tried to convince himself that the taboo was okay with him. If that's the way she wanted it, fine.

But it wasn't fine. He was suffering from a near-terminal case of lust. Living with her as her husband, while conducting himself like a stranger, was becoming more of a strain each day. He pulled his eyes away from her legs and her small, narrow feet.

Who is this woman?

What was she running from? he wondered. And she was running. She could deny it till doomsday, but he knew that something beyond the four walls of this house terrified her. Several times each night, she left the bed and tiptoed through the rooms, peering out the windows, scanning the yard. For what? He always pretended to sleep through her nocturnal patrols, but he was aware of them. Not knowing the reason for her vigilance bugged him.

Sometimes the frustration of not knowing drove him nuts. Why wouldn't she confide in him and let him help her? The only reason he could think of was that he was part of her problem. That was an upsetting possibility, but she could have dispelled it with a few simple, straightforward answers. Fat chance. He had slept beside her every night for two long weeks, but he hadn't won her confidence.

He knew the pattern of her slumbrous breathing, but she was still a stranger to him. Even blindfolded he would recognize her scent and the sound of her voice, but she didn't belong to him. He would have bet his life on that.

"How'd you find the pistol?" he asked.

"There aren't that many hiding places accessible to a man on crutches."

Their first morning there, while she had been rummaging around in the kitchen, he had rifled through her things and discovered the pistol in the kid's diaper bag, the last place one would expect to find a lethal weapon. Which confirmed what he had believed all along—she had been lying through her teeth. The situation wasn't nearly as harmless as she wanted it to appear.

Naturally, Kendall had become extremely upset when she saw him with the gun. She had accused him of snooping and meddling, to which he confessed, but when she had demanded that he return the pistol to her, he had laughed in her face.

She, however, got the last laugh because she had hidden the bullets somewhere other than the diaper bag. The gun was useless to him. Nevertheless, it had given him a false sense of power to have it in his possession. And surprisingly, he had felt comfortable with it. The weight of it in his hand had been familiar and disturbingly natural. He had handled it without awkwardness. Even though the bullets weren't available, he somehow knew the mechanics of loading and firing, and while he respected the gun, he wasn't afraid of it. Because he had felt so at ease with it, he wondered how he had acquired that familiarity. He had tried to remember if and when he had used a gun, but his memory continued to fail him. Holding that pistol had offered a glimpse into the past; he hated like hell that he no longer had it.

"I'll find it again," he said now.

"Not this time."

"I'll keep looking until I do."

"You won't."

"Who does it belong to?"

"To me."

"Nursing mothers rarely tote pistols, Kendall. What are you doing with a firearm? Did you hold someone at gunpoint and kidnap me? Are you holding me for ransom?"

She laughed at that notion. "How much do you think you're worth? Do you feel rich?"

He thought about it for a moment, then shook his head wryly. "No."

"Remember, you insisted on coming with me. I didn't take you from the hospital against your will."

That's right. She hadn't. So that shot the kidnap and ransom theory to hell. "Have you hidden the gun in the same place you hide the car key?"

"Why have you been searching for the car key?"

"Why have you hidden it?"

"If I presented the car key to you on a silver platter, what would you do with it?" she asked. "You couldn't drive with your left leg."

"I could damn sure try."

"Would you leave Kevin and me stranded here alone?"

He answered with an emphatic yes. "Just like you intend to leave me the first chance you get."

"Well, before I go," she said sarcastically, "there's something I must do first. So I'd just as well get it over and done with."

She stood up and reached for the tray she had set on the nightstand. He suspiciously regarded the plastic bottle of rubbing alcohol, the tiny scissors, and the tweezers. "Get what over and done with?"

"I'm going to remove your stitches."

"Like hell you are."

"There's nothing to it."

"Easy for you to say. They're not your stitches. Why can't we go to a doctor?"

She dampened a square of gauze with alcohol. "There's no reason to. You just have to clip them and pull them out. I've seen it done."

"I've seen open-heart surgery. That doesn't mean I can do it."

"When did you see open-heart surgery?"

"I was speaking metaphorically." He motioned toward the tray. "Put all that stuff away. You're not coming at me with those scissors. How do I know you won't jab them into my jugular?"

"If I was going to do that, I would have done it while you slept, and long before now."

She had a point. She wanted to be rid of him, but murder wasn't what she had in mind—at least he didn't think so.

"Stop being such a baby and bend your head down." She reached for him, but he grabbed her hands.

"Do you really know what you're doing?"

"Trust me."

"Not in this lifetime."

She rolled her eyes. "There are only a few stitches on the surface. Most of the sutures are beneath the skin. They've dissolved by now."

"How do you know so much?"

"The doctor told me." She gazed down at him, her expression earnest. "It won't hurt. I promise. The wound has healed."

That much was true. It hadn't hurt him for days; the headaches had disappeared. He was now able to wash his hair. The stitches had become a mild irritant, as had the circular spot surrounding them. His shaved hair was growing back, and the prickly patch on his scalp itched like mad.

Reluctantly he released her hands. "Okay. But if it starts to hurt—"

"I'll quit."

She placed her hand on his cheek and tipped his head down, then dabbed the sutured area with alcohol. "Hold still," she murmured as she laid the gauze aside and picked up the pair of manicure scissors.

She was gentle. If he hadn't heard the metallic click of the scissors, he wouldn't have known when she clipped the first suture. Of course, he was distracted by other stimuli more potent than pain—her breath in his hair, the brush of her thigh against his, her breasts so tantalizingly close to his face.

Maybe he shouldn't have goaded her into baring herself to him. It had seemed like a good idea at the time, a foolproof way of testing her "married" story. But now he feared it had

been a tactical error that had rattled him more than her.
Because now when he noticed the sway of her breasts beneath
her nightgown or her T-shirt, he had a mental picture of wet-
dream caliber.

"Are you okay?" she asked suddenly.

"Yeah, sure."

"Is your leg bothering you?"

"No."

"Then what's the matter?"

"Nothing."

"Well, stop fidgeting. I can't do this if you don't sit still."

"Just finish, okay?" he said crossly.

She returned the scissors to the tray and picked up the
tweezers. "You might feel a slight—"

"Ow!"

"Tug."

"Ow!"

She stepped back and placed her hands on her hips, stretching her T-shirt across her breasts, detailing their shape. "Do
you want to do this yourself?"

I want to do you, his mind shouted.

"Tell me and I'll stop," she said.

"You've gone this far, just get the damn things out."

When she was finished, she blotted the area again with
alcohol. It stung slightly, but he didn't complain.

Making one final dab with the moist gauze, she said, "As
soon as your hair grows out, you'll be as good as new."

"Not quite."

"You mean the amnesia? No glimmers of memory?"

"Don't pretend to be disappointed. You don't want me to
remember. Do you?"

"Of course I do."

"Then why won't you help me along? You're very stingy
when it comes to information."

"The doctor said—"

"The doctor said, the doctor said," he mimicked in a nasty tone. "You claimed not to have any confidence in that fast-talking, slick little shit, but you sure as hell quote him when it suits you."

"The doctor said I shouldn't crowd your mind with too much data."

She appeared unfazed by his querulousness and his foul language. Didn't anything fluster this woman? Her reasonable tone of voice and her unflappability didn't calm him, but only made him crankier.

"Prompting you might actually slow the recollection process," she said. "Your memory will come back when it wants to. We can't hurry it along."

"You're making that up."

Vexed, she said, "All right, shoot. What do you want to know?"

"Who fathered your baby?"

Finally! An honest, unrehearsed, uncalculated reaction. She was completely taken aback. Obviously she had expected a question about something other than her son's parentage.

"He's not my child," he said with conviction. "I know he's not mine. There's nothing there. I feel no connection to him."

"How can you tell? You never touch him. You hardly even look at him."

"I . . . I can't. He . . . Kids in general, they . . ." What could he say? That they terrified him? She would think he was crazy, and he couldn't blame her. Yet, fear was the word closest to describing how he felt each time he was close to the child.

Kendall was watching him curiously, so he had to say something. "It bothers me to hear them whining and crying."

Just thinking about crying children caused beads of perspiration to pop out on his face. He heard echoes of his recent nightmare, but instead of trying to outrun it, this time he closed his eyes and mentally reached for it, stretching the boundaries of his mind. And this time, he gained an insight that before had escaped him. In his dream, he wanted the children to stop crying. But he realized now that he feared their sudden silence as much as their crying. Because the silence signaled their death. He knew it. He also knew that somehow he was responsible. *Jesus*.

It was a long while before he opened his eyes. He felt physically drained, shaky and depleted, as though he had once again experienced the nightmare.

Kendall hadn't moved. She was watching him with a mix of concern and apprehension.

"When you tried to unload me in Stephensville, did it have something to do with your baby?" he asked. "What have I got against him?"

"Nothing."

"Don't lie to me, Kendall. I'm holding a grudge against a little baby and I don't know why. Unless I'm simply a heartless bastard, there's a reason for the way I feel toward him. What is it?"

"I don't know."

"Tell me."

"I don't know!"

Chapter Seventeen

I 'M PREGNANT!

In an effort to contain her exhilaration, Kendall gripped the steering wheel of her car. She laughed out loud and shimmied her shoulders. Anyone who happened to pass her on the street would surely think she had lost her mind, but she was too happy to care.

Did Matt suspect? She didn't think so. It wasn't unusual for her to leave the house shortly after daybreak. She frequently went to her office before the workday officially began so that she could work uninterrupted at her desk.

However, this morning she had gone to her gynecologist's office. She hadn't wanted to say anything to Matt until it had been medically confirmed that the longed-for Burnwood baby had finally been conceived.

She had prevailed upon the doctor and his office staff to keep her secret. News traveled fast in Prosper. She didn't want Matt to hear it from someone else before she had an opportunity to tell him.

At lunch, perhaps? Yes, she would call him and arrange to meet him somewhere. Or perhaps she would wait until tonight over a candlelight dinner.

It was still early when she arrived at the courthouse. Hers was the first car in the parking lot. She seemed to float above the ground as she made her way into the building and through the deserted corridors toward her office.

When she rounded a corner in the hallway, she noticed that the light was on in her office. Roscoe was working early, too. She poked her head around the open door, but instead of saying a simple good morning, she exclaimed, "Oh my God!"

The custodian nearly leaped out of his skin, but when he saw that it was Kendall, the alarm in his eyes turned to apology. "I was hoping I'd get it cleaned up before you got here, Mrs. Burnwood."

The vandalism was extensive. The windowpane in her door had been shattered, littering the floor with broken glass. File cabinets had been broken into and their contents strewn on every conceivable surface. Law books had been swept from the shelves.

Two African violets, which she had nursed with great care, had been upended onto her desk pad. Their shredded leaves and a mound of muddy potting soil were all that remained on the surface of her desk. Everything else had been thrown to the floor and either ripped, smashed, or broken. The tufted cushions of her leather desk chair had been slashed.

"Who's responsible for this?" she demanded.

"You reckon it's the handiwork of those white trash Crook twins?"

Yes, she did, but she didn't voice her suspicions. She called the city police. Shortly, two officers arrived. They went through the motions of a crime scene investigation, but Kendall could tell they were halfhearted about it. When they finished dusting for fingerprints, she followed them into the corridor, out of Roscoe's earshot.

"Did you get some usable prints?"

"Hard to say," one replied. "Yours, your secretary's, and that old nigger's are all we'll probably turn up."

The second officer hitched his chin toward the office. "How do you know he didn't do it?"

Kendall was so affronted by the racial slur that for a moment the question didn't register. "Mr. Calloway?" she asked incredulously. "What possible motivation could he have?"

The officers exchanged a glance that silently rebuked her simplemindedness.

One of them said, "We'll let you know if we turn up any significant clues, Mrs. Burnwood. You made any enemies lately?"

"Dozens," she replied tartly. "Especially in your department."

She had nothing to lose by insulting them. Her complaint would be routinely filed and then forgotten. There would be no serious investigation. She wasn't a favorite of the police. Too many of them had fallen under her attack during cross-examination.

"I'll appreciate anything you can do."

As she watched them leave, she knew that would be the end of it unless she pursued the incident herself, which she wouldn't do because of Matt. If he found out about this, he might make good his threats to do serious harm to the Crooks.

"Roscoe, will you please help me clean up this mess?" she asked as she reentered her office.

"You don't even have to ask."

"Thank you. The files must be reorganized as soon as possible." Then she added, "I would appreciate it if you would help me keep this quiet. Please don't mention it to anyone. Not even my husband."

By noon Kendall was able to move about her office without crunching glass underfoot or stumbling over a volume of law. Her secretary soon had the files in some semblance of order. Roscoe had scavenged a discarded desk chair for her to use until a new one arrived.

If she had crossed paths with either Henry or Luther Crook, she would have been tempted to shoot them herself, not only for ransacking her office but for taking the sheen off her golden day. Rather than being able to savor the secret knowledge of her pregnancy and plan a special way in which to break the news to Matt, she had been forced to deal with the Crooks' vandalism.

Naturally, the disorder in her office aroused curiosity among courthouse employees. When asked about it, she lied. She even lied to Solicitor Gorn when he strolled into her office as she was about to leave for the day.

He indicated a workman who was replacing the glass in her door. "What happened here?"

"I decided to do some redecorating." Giving him no leeway, she asked, "What's brought you over at this time of day, Dabney? Did the café across the street run out of iced tea?"

"You've got a real smart mouth, Counselor. I'm surprised that Gibb and Matt haven't taught you some better manners by now."

"Matt's my husband, not my trainer. Gibb has no authority over me at all. Besides, if I didn't have a smart mouth, I wouldn't be the thorn in your side that I am. And I'm enjoying that role more each day."

She reached for the file he had brought in with him, which she guessed was the reason behind his unannounced visit. "What have you got for me?"

"Discovery on the Lynam trial. That's everything we plan to use. You can't ever accuse my office of withholding evidence and springing it on you in court. We don't need to. We've got a clear-cut case."

He shoved his thumbs beneath the wide, red suspenders attached to his trousers. "We're ready to go to trial. I could get a conviction with one arm tied behind me."

"I don't think you really believe that, Dabney." She stood, picked up her handbag and briefcase, and headed for the door.

"If you did, you wouldn't feel compelled to remind me of it so often. Thanks for the file. Now, you'll have to excuse me. I was on my way out when you came in. I suggest you make an appointment the next time you want to see me."

Earlier in the day she had received a call from Gibb, inviting her and Matt to dinner that night. She was eager to tell Matt about the baby, but since her day had been taxing and she wasn't feeling up to cooking or to going out, she accepted her father-in-law's invitation.

It was a casual dinner. They ate off trays in his living room beneath the baleful stares of his hunting trophies. It wasn't until dessert that he broached the subject of Lottie Lynam's upcoming trial.

Never one to mince words, Gibb asked boldly, "How could you possibly plead her not guilty?"

"I can't discuss the particulars of my case, Gibb. You know that."

"I understand attorney privilege and all that. But you're among family." He smiled. "Besides, I'm not talking particulars here. I'm talking basic principles."

"Like those that Brother Whitaker expounded upon last Sunday?"

The congregation had received a tongue-lashing from the pulpit. Kendall was vexed over the nature of the sermon and decided to say so, although disagreeing with the pastor whom Matt and Gibb highly respected was like waving a red flag at them.

"What does Brother Whitaker's sermon have to do with your case?" Matt asked.

"I don't believe it was a coincidence that he chose last Sunday to remind his flock of the sanctity of marriage," she said, unable to keep the scorn out of her voice. "He preached a full hour on how blindly obedient wives should be to their husbands."

Sandra Brown

"A wife's submission is scriptural."

"Is it also scriptural that a wife should submit to a husband who tries to sodomize her with a hot curling iron?"

"That isn't very pleasant subject matter for dinnertime, is it?"

"It isn't pleasant subject matter anytime, Matt," she countered heatedly. "But getting back to Sunday's sermon, it can only be described as partisan and sexist. Prospective jurors were in that congregation. How can they help but be influenced?"

"Bob wasn't condoning wife beating, Kendall," Matt said. "Everybody knows that Charlie Lynam was a short-tempered, drunken brute."

"That didn't give her the right to kill him, son," Gibb said before turning to Kendall. "I told Dabney that you're having Lottie plead not guilty because you're unaware of her true nature."

"What do you mean *you told Dabney*? Did he discuss this case with you? He had no business—"

Gibb held up his hand to forestall her. "Dabney and I go way back, Kendall. In fact, I talked him into running for office and helped him get elected. As a *friend*, he asked me what I thought of you entering a not-guilty plea, and I explained it to him.

"You aren't from around here. Lottie has pulled the wool over your eyes. You don't know that she's been a slut ever since she became a woman. Marriage didn't change her habits. It was her whorish ways that drove Charlie to drink."

Kendall was speechless. Solicitor Gorn had grossly breached ethics by asking Gibb's opinion of a pending murder trial, but Gibb seemed not to realize that. He was too hung up on his daughter-in-law's taking the side of the town tart.

"Gibb, Mr. Gorn should never have discussed this with you. That notwithstanding, Mrs. Lynam's moral character is not on trial. You're dangerously close to saying that she deserved to be beaten and raped."

"That's another thing," he said. "I don't care what laws are on the books, how can a man *rape* his own wife?"

Matt interceded before Kendall could reply to that appalling question. "Dad, Kendall shouldn't have to argue her case to us. She's exhausted. Let's get these dishes done so I can take her home."

Kendall picked up the conversation before they were even out of Gibb's driveway. "What really frightens me is that an overwhelming percentage of the people called to jury duty will hold to Gibb's outdated beliefs about a wife's obligation to obey her husband no matter what. I may file for a change of venue. My client will never get a fair trial in Prosper."

"Dad hails from another generation, Kendall. You can't expect him and his friends to reflect the same attitudes that we do about certain social and moral issues."

"Like chronic battering and domestic rape?"

"Don't pick a fight with me," he said, responding to the testiness in her voice. "I didn't dispute your position."

"You didn't defend it, either."

"I didn't want to get caught in the middle of a meaningless quarrel."

"I don't think it's meaningless. Mrs. Lynam certainly wouldn't think it's meaningless."

"I'm not the jury," Matt said evenly. "You don't have to argue your case with me. And you shouldn't have argued it with Dad."

"He certainly had no scruples about discussing it with the prosecutor." She was equally upset and puzzled. "Tell me, Matt. Why would Dabney discuss a legal matter with Gibb?"

"Dad explained that. They're old friends and they were shooting the breeze. You're making way too much of it."

"I don't think so. It bothers me to know that Dabney ran tattling to Gibb, as though he exercised control over my performance as public defender." This was yet another troubling component to an already troubling case. She was convinced that getting an acquittal in Prosper would be just shy of a miracle.

"Would you mind if I interviewed Mrs. Lynam for an article?"

"What?" Astonished, she turned to Matt, whose offer had come out of the blue. "What kind of article?"

"Mrs. Lynam has been getting a bad rap, from the pulpit and from the man on the street. Even from my newspaper," he admitted with chagrin. "She deserves equal time."

Kendall thanked him for the offer but expressed her reservations. The matter was still under debate when they arrived home. As they walked down the hall to the bedroom, he continued to sell her on the idea.

"This is my way of making up for Dad's blunder. He's accustomed to being asked for advice, and he's used to giving it. I'm sure he didn't realize the untenable position he placed you in by airing his opinions to Dabney. Let me do this for you, Kendall. I swear the story won't be a hatchet job.

"In fact, I'll print up a list of questions beforehand. You can review them and coach Mrs. Lynam on how to answer. I won't deviate from those specific questions, and you can proofread the final draft before it goes to press. Anything you don't like, you can omit."

With the guidelines he had laid out, she could see no reason to decline. "Okay. Thanks."

He extended his arms. "You look like you need a hug."

She gladly stepped into his embrace. He held her tightly and massaged her lower back, his strong hands working out the kinks. Their dinner with Gibb had prevented her from telling him about the baby.

She had considered announcing it to them simultaneously but decided against it. Too often Gibb was a third party. This occasion was very special and deserved privacy. Selfishly, she wanted Matt all to herself when she told him.

And now they were finally alone.

His name was on the tip of her tongue, when he spoke hers first. "Kendall?" He set her away from him and stroked her cheek. "You've been awfully distracted lately. May I have your undivided attention for a while tonight?"

This was even better. After they made love, when they were relaxing in the aftermath, would be a perfect time to tell him. She slid her arms around his neck. "It will be my pleasure," she whispered.

She nuzzled and stroked his flesh, drawing comfort from his maleness and superior physical strength. She basked in the marital intimacy, which, as he had reminded her, they hadn't indulged in recently.

But the coupling wasn't as fulfilling as it could have been. When he entered her, she hadn't been quite ready to receive him. His thrusts caused her some discomfort, which detracted from the pleasure. She would have preferred more foreplay, a slow sexual awakening that would have gradually dissolved her weariness and replaced it with arousal.

Afterward, he smiled apologetically. "Was it okay?"

She lied to spare his ego.

"Your mind's too splintered, Kendall," he said, his disappointment showing. "We're no longer attuned to each other. We've lost our rhythm. Dad's right."

She propped herself up on her elbow. "Right about what?"

"You're spending too many hours on the job and not enough at home."

"You discussed my shortcomings with Gibb before even airing them with me?"

"Don't get riled. I didn't lay all the blame on you. I told him that I obviously wasn't doing something right or you wouldn't be so distant."

"Matt, be fair," she exclaimed. "Night before last, when I called to tell you I would be working late, you said that it was no problem because you were going out, too. I was at home and asleep long before you came in."

"Don't get mad."

"Why shouldn't I get mad? Your perspective is warped. When I'm late, I'm working. When you're late, you're out on a lark with your friends and Gibb."

"You're jealous."

"This isn't jealousy."

"It sounds like jealousy."

"Then I'd have to say you're jealous of my work."

"I am. I admit it. Because you're so damned obsessed by your career."

"I'm *dedicated*. I'd be thought of as a real go-getter if I were a man."

"But you're not. You're a woman. And your job keeps you from your responsibilities as my wife." Ameliorating his tone, he drew her against him and began stroking her hair. "Sweetheart, I hate quarreling."

"So do I, Matt, but sometimes quarrels are necessary. You knew when you married me that I wanted a career. I love practicing law. I want justice for—"

"I know all that," he interrupted. "I'm proud of the job you do, but must you give so much to it? Can't you be more generous with yourself? Other areas of life need your time and attention. Specifically, me. And I'd like you to become more interested in community affairs, to integrate more with other women. You know, there's a lot to be said for becoming one of a group rather than setting yourself apart."

He pressed his lips against her temple. "Dad says we need a baby. A child would give some balance to your life. I agree with him. Let's make a baby, Kendall. Tonight."

This was not the atmosphere in which Kendall had hoped to tell him that their child had already been conceived. They made love again, but his disturbing comments had doused her desire. He was too intent on making her pregnant to notice her lack of responsiveness.

Chapter Eighteen

"*W*HAT ARE YOU DOING?"

"I'm going into town with you." He was settled in the passenger seat of the car, his crutches stashed on the rear floorboard.

"No, you're not," Kendall said.

"Yes, I am."

She cautioned herself not to make an issue of it or his suspicions would be confirmed. "Take my word for it, it's not that great a town."

"I'd like to see it for myself, and I don't take your word for anything."

Damn! Why had he chosen today to accompany her? *Today!* Had the nightmare he suffered yesterday afternoon shaken loose some grains of memory? He had called out names, names that caused her blood to run cold. Because if he remembered the persons to whom those names belonged, he would remember everything. God help her then.

That's why she had decided to leave for town today and not come back.

"It's so blasted hot," she said, trying to discourage him. "You'll only get tired. Why not stay here and rest for one more day, then if you still want to go into town, I'll take you tomorrow."

"I'm touched that you're so concerned for my well-being, but . . ." He shook his head. "You'll have to wrestle me out of this car. Even with my broken leg, I'd win. Bottom line— I'm going."

A mutiny such as this had been only a matter of time, she knew. He had been gaining strength every day. The tables had gradually been turning on her. The more ambulatory he became, the more likely he was to overpower her and seize control.

He was no longer satisfied with her evasions and answers padded with just enough truth to make them plausible. Yesterday, she had parried his questions about his aversion to Kevin by saying that it was probably just a quirk of his amnesia. But she could tell that the flimsy explanation had made him more, not less, distrustful.

He was increasingly intuitive, so she was on borrowed time. She had already stayed with him longer than decency demanded. If he was strong enough to stage a rebellion, he was strong enough to fend for himself until he could summon help.

For two weeks she had been balancing her terror that he would recover his memory against her fear of leaving the safety of the house. The protection this place offered was tenuous at best, but she would be even more vulnerable on the open road, where law enforcement agencies would be looking for her. Surely by now the hubbub created by her disappearance from Stephensville would have died down. Searchers would have lost interest and become lax. All things considered, the timing was perfect to leave.

Now he had foiled her plans.

On the other hand, maybe it was better that he insisted on coming with her today. He expected her to leave and not return, but he would not expect her to bolt while he was along.

She had the drive from the house to town to figure out how she would manage to sneak away.

"If you want to go to town, fine," she said, forcing a smile. "I'll enjoy the company."

Her passenger proved to be poor company. He didn't say a word for the first ten minutes of the drive because he was too busy charting direction and picking out landmarks. He could have drawn maps for all she cared. If she was successful this morning, his crash course in navigation would be of no consequence to her.

Eventually he remarked, "You know these roads well."

"I should. This is where my grandmother taught me to drive."

"You talk about her a lot. You really loved her, didn't you?"

"Very much."

"What was she like, to inspire that kind of love?"

Kendall found that ordinary words couldn't convey the depths with which she had loved Elvie Hancock, but, working within the limitations of the language, she tried to express her feelings.

"Grandmother was creative and fun, always thinking up interesting things to do. Beyond loving her, I admired her for the human being she was. She was exceptionally tolerant, completely accepting of other people in spite of their flaws. All my life she made me feel very special. Even when I did something wrong and had to be punished, I never doubted that she loved me. That's why I loved her so much."

By now they had reached the outskirts of town. Kendall drove into the parking lot of a supermarket. He waited until after she had cut the ignition before asking, "Did you love her more than you loved me?"

Kendall was nonplussed. "What a question! They're entirely different relationships. You can't compare them."

"Love is love, isn't it?"

"Not at all. It's subjective."

"To what?"

"To the two people and the nature of their relationship."

"Did I love you? No, don't bother answering," he said. "You'd only lie about it." He stared vacantly through the windshield for a moment; then, in a reflective voice, he said, "I don't remember loving anybody. If I had loved someone, you'd think I'd remember, wouldn't you?"

He turned to face her again, and Kendall saw that his eyes were troubled. What was he thinking? she wondered. If circumstances were different . . .

But they weren't, so speculation on his emotional health was useless and self-indulgent.

She alighted quickly and removed Kevin from his car seat. "I won't be long," she lied. "You'll be fine here, won't you?"

"Sure. I'll just sit back and take in the scenery."

There was no way to retrieve the provisions she had stashed in the trunk. Maybe she could grab a few things on her way through the supermarket, although her time was limited. "Can I bring you anything?" she offered, wanting to appear as normal as possible.

"A six-pack of beer would be nice."

"What brand do you like?"

"I can't remember. But you should. Dear."

She ignored his sarcasm. "In fact, I do. Back in a jiff."

She felt his eyes like a knife blade in her back as she entered the supermarket. She forced herself to walk slowly, to appear casual and unhurried. Once inside, knowing he would be unable to see her through the reflective glass, she rushed to the pay telephone. Luckily, she had committed the number to memory.

"Hello?"

"Mrs. Williams? This is Mary Jo Smith, the woman who called you a few days ago about the car?"

"Why, I was expecting you here any minute. You didn't

change your mind, did you? Because I've been telling other callers that the car is sold."

"No, no, I didn't change my mind. It's just that . . . Remember, I told you that my car was on its last legs? Well, it died on me and won't restart. I'm stranded and can't get to your house. I've got my baby with me, and—oh, I don't know what to do!"

She let her voice crack as though she were desperate and helpless.

"Oh, dear, well . . ." Mrs. Williams sounded sympathetic but cautious. She had probably been warned about the scams inflicted on elderly widows. "I suppose I could drive the car to wherever you are."

"Oh, I couldn't possibly ask you to do that! No, no, I'll just . . . hmm. Let me think a moment."

Kendall's tactic worked. "It'll be no trouble really," Mrs. Williams said. "Where are you?"

She gave her the name of the service station she had previously spotted. It was within walking distance of the supermarket.

"That's only five minutes from my house," Mrs. Williams said, pleased. "I'll bring the car to you, we can complete our transaction, and then you can drop me back home."

"I hate to impose this way."

"Don't mention it. I'm anxious to sell the car."

"And I'm anxious to buy it. Desperate, in fact."

That much was true. By now Jim Pepperdyne might have located the man in Stephensville who had sold her his car. She needed to unload it and get another before driving on Dixie highways.

Mrs. Williams confirmed the time and place. "Okay, I'll be there. Five minutes." Kendall hung up the pay phone and headed for the exit at the opposite side of the store from which she had entered.

The automatic doors whooshed open, and Kendall was stopped dead in her tracks.

His leg already ached from the cramped ride into town, but he wasn't going to waste this opportunity to try to find out what was going on.

As soon as Kendall was out of sight, he pushed open the passenger door and reached for his crutches. He got out and looked around.

She was right. It wasn't much of a town. From his vantage point, he could see a generic filling station and service garage, a barbecue restaurant, a barber shop, and . . . a *post office!*

He set out across the asphalt parking lot, which was as hot as a griddle. In under a minute his shirt was soaked with sweat and his muscles were quivering with fatigue. God, how he despised and resented this weakness!

From the corner of his eye he saw a boy whizzing past on his bicycle. "Hey, kid!" he called.

The boy, whom he guessed to be about twelve, glanced over his shoulder, pivoted the bike on the front tire, and pedaled closer.

"What happened to your leg?"

"It got busted in a car wreck."

"Your head, too?"

"Yeah. My head, too. What town is this? Are we in Tennessee?"

The boy jerked the bike to a halt. He peered closely into his face and broke a wide grin. "Sweet. You're high, aren't you?" He formed a ring with his thumb and index finger, then placed them against his lips and sucked at them as though smoking marijuana.

"I'm not high, I just want to know where I am."

In a stage whisper, he said, "Katmandu, dude. Except ain't you a little old to be getting stoned? I mean, you gotta be at least forty."

"Yeah, I'm ancient. A relic. Now, what's the name of this fucking town?"

"Jeez, you're weird." The kid yanked the bike safely out of reach, remounted, and sped off, pedaling fast.

"Wait, come back!"

The kid shot him the finger.

He glanced around, hoping no one had witnessed the exchange. He wasn't sure he wanted the police alerted to a banged-up stranger asking strange questions. The only reason he wanted to go to the post office was to find out exactly where he was and to see if any of the wanted posters on the walls bore a picture of him.

He gauged the remaining distance and calculated that the post office was farther away than he'd thought. The exertion of crossing the parking lot, along with the heat, had sapped his strength.

How much time did he have before she returned to the car? How long would her shopping take? How many other items besides his beer did she intend to buy? She hadn't seemed to be in any particular hurry when she went into—

Suddenly he envisioned Kendall as she had looked entering the store. She had been carrying Kevin, her handbag, and the diaper bag. *The diaper bag*. If she intended to be in the store only a few minutes, why had she taken the diaper bag with her?

He turned around and began hobbling back toward the supermarket, covering the distance as rapidly as the crutches allowed. "You goddamn fool," he huffed. "Why'd you let her out of your sight?"

He'd had a hunch that she was about to split. That's why he had insisted on coming with her today. But what had made him think his presence would prevent her from doing what she was obviously determined to do? Stupidly, he had played right into her devious little hands.

Cursing his gullibility and his handicap, he forced himself to move faster.

"Oh, my God. My God." Kendall didn't realize that she had spoken aloud until she heard her whimpering voice.

Ducking her head, she backed away from the newspaper dispenser, away from the large picture of herself on the front page. She plunged headlong for the exit.

Before she was recognized, she had to get out of the store. Had five minutes elapsed? Mrs. Williams would be waiting. Kendall knew that if she wasn't there in time, the woman might leave.

Then another, more horrifying thought occurred to her: What if Mrs. Williams had read the morning newspaper and recognized her on sight?

She would have to take that chance, she decided. She had no choice. As she had feared, a manhunt was on and she was the quarry.

Outside, she squinted against the glare of the sun and kept close to the exterior wall of the building. He wouldn't be able to see her from the car, but—

"Going somewhere?"

Heart plummeting, Kendall spun around. He was leaning heavily on his crutches. His chest rose and fell with his labored breathing. His hair was literally dripping sweat.

"Why did you get out of the car?"

"Why are you coming out this door? The car's on the other side of the building."

"Oh, uh, I guess I got turned around inside."

"Uh-huh. Why didn't you buy anything?"

Why hadn't she bought anything? *Think, Kendall!* "Kevin spit up as soon as we got inside. I don't think he's feeling well. The heat or something is making him cranky and upset."

"He looks fine to me."

Kevin had, in fact, never looked healthier or happier as he

blew bubbles and batted at her earring. "Well, he isn't," she snapped. "I'll have to come back another time."

She struck off toward the car, which was in the opposite direction of the service station where a puzzled and exasperated Mrs. Williams would be waiting.

She wouldn't be buying another car today.

She wouldn't be making another escape, either.

Chapter Nineteen

"*I*s Li a Chinese name?"

In response to Kendall's question, the jail guard shrugged his broad shoulders. "Chink, Jap, who knows? I can't tell one slope from another."

Kendall's reproving glance bounced right off him. He unlocked the small room where she would confer with her new client. As she was ushered in, the accused rapist, Michael Li, came to his feet.

"I'll be right outside." The guard practically snarled the words at the young man.

Kendall closed the door on the guard, turned, and approached Li, whose posture was so rigid that she had an impulse to say, "At ease." After introducing herself and shaking hands, she indicated that he should sit down. She sat across the table from him.

"Do you need anything? Something to drink?"

"No, ma'am," he replied stoically.

Eighteen-year-old Michael Li had a virtually beardless, smooth complexion and neatly trimmed straight black hair. He was short and slight. His dark eyes were wary but curious as he watched her reach into her briefcase and remove a legal pad and pen.

"Jail is never pleasant," she said. "Even as I say that, I realize it's a gross understatement."

"Have you ever been in jail?" he asked.

"Once," she answered honestly. "I was arrested while protesting the ban of certain books in the public library."

He nodded with seeming approval.

"I'll arrange bail for you immediately."

"My family won't be able to afford it." He spoke with stiff dignity. "I don't want to burden my parents any more than this unfortunate misunderstanding already has, Mrs. Burnwood."

"I'm sure we can work out a suitable financial arrangement."

"If at all possible, I want to continue going to school," he said. "It's important that I graduate with my class."

"You're valedictorian, isn't that right?"

"That's correct."

"Your parents must be awfully proud."

"Yes, ma'am, they are. I've been offered full scholarships to several universities. I haven't decided on which to accept." He looked down at his hands and picked at a loose cuticle. "After this, having to make that decision might not be a problem."

For the time being, Kendall thought it best to steer the conversation away from Mr. Li's future. Reminders of what he stood to lose should things not go their way would be demoralizing. She continued the preliminary interview by trying to get a sense of the young man she would be defending.

"You participate in many school activities and organizations, including the National Honor Society."

"Yes, ma'am. In fact, it was on an NHS trip to Gatlinburg when Kim and I first noticed one another."

"Why don't you start there and bring me up to date."

While taking in the tourist attractions of the Tennessee

mountain town, he and his classmate Kimberly Johnson had "started hanging out together."

"After that, we went out regularly. But I never picked her up at her house. We would always meet. She didn't think her parents would approve of her dating me. They consider me a foreigner."

Suddenly his eyes came alight with fierce pride. "I'm an *American*, the same as Kim. The same as Mr. Johnson. My mother was born in America. My father's family emigrated when he was a baby. He never even learned to speak Chinese and speaks better English than Mr. Johnson."

Kendall didn't doubt that. She didn't know Herman Johnson well, but she had seen him frequently at the country club. He was usually tipsy, talking too loudly, telling off-color jokes, and generally making an ass of himself.

She didn't know Mr. Li, either, but he and his wife were to be commended for rearing such a well-mannered, over-achieving son. According to the information she had been given, they were hardworking people, worthy of their son's pride.

Over time Michael Li's relationship with Kim Johnson had intensified. "We're pretty serious," he said solemnly. He admitted that they had been having sexual relations for about two months.

"Responsibly," he added with emphasis. "I'm always pro-tected. And I swear, it was always consensual. I would never do anything to hurt Kim." Tears came to his eyes. "Never."

"I believe you," Kendall assured him. "Now tell me exactly what happened last night."

He and Kim had met at the library to study. They sat at the same table but studiously ignored each other every time they fell under the librarian's baleful gaze.

They left the building separately, but, as prearranged, he joined Kim in the parking lot and got into her car. Not quite able to meet Kendall's eyes, he admitted that they got into the backseat strictly for the purpose of having sex.

"I realize this is embarrassing for you, Michael," she said sympathetically. "But if this charge sticks and you're tried for rape, you'll have to answer much more explicit questions from the witness stand. The prosecutor will be merciless. From now on, it's mandatory that you be candid with me. Can I rely on that?"

He nodded, and she began asking him pertinent questions.

"Did Kim remove her clothing?"

"Only her underpants."

"She was wearing a skirt, then?"

"Yes."

"Blouse?"

"Yes."

"Brassiere?"

"Yes."

"None of these were removed?"

"Unfastened, but we didn't take them off."

"What about you?"

"I just unzipped my pants."

"Did you remove your shirt?"

"No."

"Unbutton it?"

"Yes."

"When you were caught, did people see you with your shirt unbuttoned?"

"I suppose so. Is that relevant?"

"It's doubtful that a rapist would take the time to unbutton his shirt. That's something a lover would do."

He relaxed; he even gave her a fleeting smile.

"Had you completed the act by the time Mr. Johnson arrived?"

"Yes."

"You had ejaculated?"

He lowered his eyes. "Into the, uh, condom."

"So the physical evidence sent to the lab is incontrovertible?"

"Yes." He raised his head. "I don't deny that Kim and I had sex, Mrs. Burnwood. But it was *not* rape, as Mr. Johnson claims. The librarian called and told him that I'd followed Kim from the building. She was concerned for Kim's safety. If you have slanted eyes, you're considered suspicious, I guess," he said scornfully.

"Anyway, since Kim wasn't home yet, Mr. Johnson panicked. He came looking for her and was already foaming at the mouth before he even found us. He pulled me from the car and started choking me. I thought he was going to kill me."

"What about Kim? What was she doing?"

"Sobbing hysterically. When the police arrived, an officer hauled her out of the backseat. She was still partially undressed."

He covered his face with his hands. "She must have been mortified. Everybody inside the library had come out to see what the commotion was about. All those people were gaping at her. There was nothing I could do to spare her that embarrassment."

Kendall set aside her pen and folded her arms on the table. "When Kim is questioned, what do you think she'll tell the police?"

"That I never raped her!" he exclaimed. "I never even coerced her. She'll tell them that, if she hasn't already. She won't let me be indicted for rape. Once the police talk to her and get the facts straight, I'll be released."

Kendall didn't share his faith in Kimberly Johnson's loyalty. Herman Johnson's violent response to finding his daughter in flagrante delicto with Michael Li might have frightened the girl so badly that she would lie to the police, the D.A., and a jury in order to escape her father's wrath.

Kendall had known witnesses with much less at stake who perjured themselves for their own protection. Kim might fear ostracism from her family if she admitted compliance, particularly if their objections to Michael Li were racially motivated.

Even if Kim admitted to her parents that she was attracted to Michael, they might force her to lie. They might not want it to become public knowledge that their daughter was having an affair with a young man of Asian descent, not even if he was valedictorian of their class and destined for greatness.

Kendall chided herself for unfairly imposing bigotry on the Johnsons, whom she hardly knew. But she feared the worst. In all likelihood, they would go to any lengths to prove that Michael Li had raped their daughter. Kim, to protect herself from scandal and reprisal, would probably go along.

Kendall didn't want her pessimism revealed to her client, however. It was crucial to put a positive spin on things. "I'm sure your classmates will testify that you and Kim are a steady couple. Your teachers will make good character witnesses. Over all, we've got a lot working in our favor."

She placed her notes in her briefcase and stood. "I hope Mr. Johnson rescinds his charge. If he doesn't, I'll try to get your arraignment set for tomorrow."

The youth insisted it wouldn't get that far. "Kim loves me as much as I love her. She'll tell them the truth. Then her father will have no choice but to withdraw the charge."

Kendall wished she could share his confidence.

She never left the courthouse without thinking of Bama. The homeless man apparently had skipped town on a freight train. At least that's what she and Roscoe had theorized.

"He's a born rambler, I guess," the custodian had replied when Kendall asked him if he, too, had noticed that Bama was missing from his usual spot on the courthouse steps. "He showed up one morning, out of nowhere. I suppose that's where he's headed to now. Nowhere. Gonna be missed 'round here," he added sadly.

More than a week had passed since Bama's disappearance. As she left the courthouse shortly after her meeting with Michael Li, she was poignantly reminded of the brief exchanges they had shared. She missed them. He had been the first to greet her when she arrived and the last to say goodbye when she left. He had become like a friend.

This afternoon, she felt friendless.

Her office was still not entirely set to rights after the Crooks' vandalism. She continued to believe they were responsible, although she had no proof and, as she had predicted, the police had made no effort to investigate.

The cluttered office had given her a bad case of claustrophobia. The session with Michael Li had depressed her. Feeling the four walls closing in, she had decided to take the discovery file on the Lynam case out to Mrs. Lynam's house. The fresh air would do her good, she decided, and the round-trip drive would give her uninterrupted time in which to think.

She felt dejected, and the reason was personal, not professional. More than twenty-four hours had passed since she learned that she was carrying Matt's child, but she still hadn't told him.

Last night he had robbed her of the opportunity by expressing viewpoints that she would never have attributed to him. She had been shocked to hear her husband professing such outmoded beliefs about marriage and the roles each partner should play.

If he had spoken in jest, or even in anger, she could have dismissed his unheralded sexist remarks. But because he had stated them with such calm conviction, she had been dwelling on them all day.

He was parroting Gibb, of course. Matt didn't really want a mousy, submissive wife. Otherwise he never would have married her. But it disturbed her that Gibb held such sway over Matt's thinking. Just as it had distressed her to find that Gibb's influence in this town extended into areas totally unrelated to him.

In order for her to recapture the euphoria she had experienced upon learning that she was pregnant, she and Matt would first have to reach a new understanding about their partnership and Gibb's meddling.

She was mildly resentful of the time, energy, and emotion such a discussion would require of her, especially at a time when all her resources needed to be channeled into defending Lottie Lynam.

Kendall and Solicitor Gorn had engaged in a bitter dispute over her bail, but Judge Fargo, to Kendall's surprise, had ruled in their favor. Mrs. Lynam had been able to raise the money by mortgaging her family's property, which had come to her by default. None of her brothers or sisters had wanted it.

The defense platform was shaky. She hoped Mrs. Lynam would spot something useful in the discovery documents she was taking to her. Perhaps she would see something in the state's evidence file that would create reasonable doubt in the minds of the jury and support an argument for self-defense.

Kendall was under no delusions. This trial was going to be tough and would require all her skills. Thinking about it caused a burning sensation between her shoulder blades. Her neck muscles were in knots.

It wouldn't be good for her client to see her anxious and uptight. On impulse, she pulled the car to a stop at the side of the narrow road. The house was only a short walk from this point. The exercise would be good for her—and for the baby.

She left her car and struck out on foot. The boughs of the trees were lined with the bright new green that announces the approach of spring. This promise of renewal, in addition to the embryo that her body was nurturing, rejuvenated Kendall's sense of purpose. She was determined to succeed, both professionally and personally. She had taken an enormous gamble when she came to Prosper. She couldn't fail.

Resolve quickened her footsteps. But they were instantly arrested when she rounded the bend and saw the car parked next to Mrs. Lynam's in front of the small, ramshackle house.

What would Matt be doing here?

Had he called her office, been told that she was on her way to Mrs. Lynam's house, and decided to meet her here to conduct the interview they had talked about last night?

No, that couldn't be it. He hadn't yet given her the list of questions as he had promised. Surely he wasn't going behind her back and interviewing Mrs. Lynam before she had an opportunity to coach her.

But if she didn't sense that his being here in the middle of the day wasn't somehow illicit, why wasn't she making her way to the door instead of ducking out of sight behind a hedge?

Her mind hadn't yet fully formulated that question when Lottie and Matt appeared. Together they came through the front door and out onto the porch. His suit jacket was slung over one shoulder, hooked by his index finger. His other arm was curled around Lottie's waist.

She was wearing only a full white slip, the old-fashioned kind with lace cups and a snug skirt that didn't quite reach her knees. One of the shoulder straps had slipped down, exposing the pale slope of her breast. Her head was resting on his chest, her body molded to his. It was impossible to tell who was supporting whom because one appeared as needful and miserable as the other.

They got only as far as the first step when Lottie stopped and turned to him. She moved against him suggestively. He let go of his jacket and it fell unheeded to the unpainted porch floor.

Her arms locked around his neck.

His hands possessively clutched her buttocks and drew her up to him.

She propped her thigh high on his hip.

He ground his pelvis against hers.

Her head fell back onto her shoulders.

He moaned her name.

Their lips sought, met, and clung with unbridled passion.

Chapter Twenty

"*W*HAT THE HELL HAPPENED TO YOUR HAIR?*"
Stepping from the bathroom into the hallway, Kendall self-consciously touched the back of her neck, now exposed after she had hacked off her hair. "It was hot, always sticking to the back of my neck. I couldn't live with it another day." She looked pointedly at the circular, semibald spot near his temple and said snidely, "Besides, you've got no room to talk about hair."

He was right; hers looked atrocious. Taking scissors to it had been a drastic but necessary move after she'd seen her face on the front page of that Nashville newspaper. The photograph was probably being shown on television, too. She hoped that the haircut would serve as a disguise.

"The baby's been crying," he said.

She stepped around him and entered the small bedroom where Kevin slept. "What's the matter, Kevin? Hmm?"

"Will he recognize you, looking like that?"

"He recognizes my voice." She lifted the infant from the playpen and carried him to the bureau that she had converted into a changing table. "Are you wet? Is that the problem?"

She heard the thump-thump of his crutches as he moved

up behind her. Still smarting over his crack about her cropped hair, she ignored him and concentrated on diapering the baby.

"He was circumcised," he remarked.

"Uh-huh."

"Religious reasons?"

"Not particularly. That's just what we agreed on."

"Why?"

"I don't know," she replied impatiently.

"Did I want him to be like me, or unlike me?"

"What do you mean?"

"Am I or aren't I?"

She made a scoffing sound. "Don't you know?"

"Yes, I know." He placed his finger beneath her chin and brought her head around. "Do *you*?"

If she had been shot with a stun gun, she couldn't have been more dumbfounded. Finally, she gave a shaky little laugh. "What a ridiculous question." She tried to return to her task, but he encircled her wrist and held on until she relented and looked up at him again.

"Which is it, Kendall?"

"I resent being tested like this."

"I resent being lied to. You claim to be my wife. If there's one thing a wife knows with certainty, it's whether or not her husband was circumcised."

He spoke with such quiet intensity that the words were barely audible. His eyes probed hers while his thumb traced lazy patterns in her palm.

"Well? Did we always make love with the lights out?"

"Of course not."

"And we showered together?"

She tried to turn away, but he gave her wrist a tug. She shot him a fierce look. "Sometimes."

"So surely you washed me. Caressed me." He raised her hand to his mouth and kissed the palm. His lips moved against it as he spoke. "I'll bet you knew how to touch me in ways that made my blood pressure rise."

Kendall felt her stomach levitate, then drop weightlessly. She tried to swallow, but her mouth was dry. Her ears echoed with the drumming of her heartbeat. "You never complained," she said faintly.

"Then this shouldn't be a difficult question."

"It's not."

"So answer."

"It's silly."

"Indulge me."

She knew her voice would be as arid and wispy as chaff, but he was waiting for an answer. It had to be the correct one.

She swallowed dryly. "You are."

He kept her suspended with a long, penetrating stare before finally releasing her wrist. She could have collapsed with relief. She was dizzy with it, giddy with the joy of being granted a reprieve.

She picked up Kevin, gave him a good-night kiss, and returned him to the playpen. She had fed him before her bath, so he was ready to go to sleep now. She draped a light receiving blanket over him.

When she straightened up and turned, he was standing alarmingly close. He took her shoulders between his hands. His eyes moved over her face, then up to her hair.

"Why'd you do it?"

"Is it so horrible?" she asked remorsefully.

"Compared to how it was before, yeah, it's pretty awful. Why'd you do that to yourself?"

"I told you—"

"You weren't telling the truth, Kendall. If your hair was hot on your neck, you could have worn it up. Instead you mutilated it. Why?" He gave her a hard, searching look. "You were going to leave today, weren't you?"

"No!"

"Stop lying to me. If you can't tell me anything except another lie, don't tell me anything." He pulled her against him. Hard. "Because I'm beginning to wish your lies were true. I want you so goddamn much, I wish you were mine. I wish . . . Oh, hell." He kissed her, hotly, hungrily.

Kendall let herself be kissed, let herself respond. Suddenly she acknowledged what her conscience had been dodging for days—she wanted him as much as he seemed to want her. Initially, she had feared and despised everything he represented. Her aversion had blinded her to the man. But having lived with him, slept beside him, his attractiveness was impossible to ignore. She had believed herself immune to his sexuality, and even to her own, but she wasn't.

And her desire wasn't strictly hormonal. Even as his injured body was healing, she had detected deep lacerations on his spirit that still needed tending. That need, which he probably wasn't even aware of or would never address, struck a chord within her. She wanted to see his eyes free of that haunted look.

With each day, each hour, they'd been moving toward this moment. It had been inevitable from the beginning. Rather than fight it any longer, she gave herself over to it.

Since his mobility was hampered, it was she who moved closer and arched into him. He groaned and pressed his hands against her breasts.

"Let me touch you," he said, his voice raspy.

He stroked her nipples and they became hard. His caresses caused damp spots to appear on her nightgown. He looked down at them, at his wet fingertips, and his features grew taut with passion.

He cupped her head between his large hands. His thumbs swept across her cheekbones, over her damp lips. He lowered his head for another kiss, but this one was surprisingly soft. His mouth barely glanced hers. Repeatedly. Each time their lips came together, they barely connected, yet the touch of his mouth against hers made Kendall hot enough to melt.

Her anticipation was finally rewarded. He kissed her deeply, using his tongue erotically to plumb her mouth. The pressure in her lower body grew unbearably sweet. She felt herself swelling, throbbing, getting wet, and she couldn't remember the last time she had experienced that sensational phenomenon. Her breasts became achy and tight, and she yearned to feel his hands, his mouth, on them. She wanted to be close to him. Closer.

"Kendall?"

"Hmm?"

"Let's go to bed."

Bed. He wanted her in bed, where they would make love. He would expect her to respond as his wife.

Unwelcome reason came crashing down on her. She could no more outrun it than she could have outdistanced an avalanche. It enveloped her, smothered her. It was inescapable.

Was she mad? Had she, too, lost her memory? She couldn't do this!

"I'm sorry. I can't."

She pulled away from him so abruptly that both of them almost lost their balance. She braced herself against the bureau and held out her arm to stave him off. "Please, don't touch me like that again."

His face was dark and filled with arousal. He cursed in a raw, ragged voice. "This doesn't make any sense, Kendall. Why can't you?"

"Plainly and simply, I said no. That puts an end to it."

"Not from my side, it doesn't. I'm entitled to an explanation."

"I've already explained it."

"In riddles that would stump a wizard." He shouted, which caused Kevin to mew in disapproval. Once the baby had resettled into slumber, he pressed his temples with the heels of his hands and expelled a deep breath. "I don't get it. If we're husband and wife as you claim, if we both want it—"

"*I* no longer want it. I haven't for a long time."

"Why not?"

"Because of the pain."

"Pain?" His face went pale. "I hurt you?"

She shook her head. "Not physically. Emotionally." Tears filled her eyes. "I remember it all too well, and it still hurts."

All the pain and betrayal she had experienced that afternoon at Lottie Lynam's house surged to the front of her consciousness. She crossed her arms over her middle as though her insides were twisting in agony.

"Oh, shit." His lips, which moments before had been so erotically insistent against hers, turned thin with bitterness and regret. "It was another woman, wasn't it?"

Chapter Twenty-one

S EATED IN THE ADIRONDACK CHAIR ON THE PORCH, Kendall stared sightlessly into near space. She was unaware of the squirrels that chased one another from tree to tree, although she usually enjoyed watching their antics. She didn't hear the grating drone of the chainsaw that a distant neighbor was using, or the scolding she received from a territorial bluejay.

Her senses had gone numb when she saw her husband making love to Lottie Lynam with more passion than he had ever brought to their marriage bed.

Kendall berated herself for not confronting them. She had caught them in the act. They couldn't have denied it. Why hadn't she admonished them with the contempt they well deserved?

Because at the time, she hadn't had the wherewithal to do anything except slink away to lick her wounds. For several moments after she first saw them, she had stared in utter disbelief, halfway expecting them to turn to her, laughing and saying, "Gotcha!" making her the butt of a cruel practical joke.

But it hadn't been a joke. It had been tragically real. She

had watched the entwined lovers with fascinated horror. When she couldn't take any more, she had retreated unseen down the dusty road. Before reaching her car, she had been seized with an attack of nausea and had vomited into the grapevines that grew in the ditch. Somehow she had managed to drive herself home, although she didn't remember the trip.

Several hours had elapsed since then. Anger had elbowed its way in and blunted some of the pain. She was now ready to confront her husband with his betrayal, although she was uncertain what approach to take. This wasn't something that could be planned or rehearsed.

In any event, she was out of time. He was home.

She watched his car turn off the main road and enter their long driveway. He honked the horn twice when he saw her sitting on the porch. He got out, smiling and happy to see her.

"Hi! I called your office, but your secretary said you'd left early. Where'd you go?"

"I had some errands to run."

He jogged up the steps, set his briefcase on the porch, draped his jacket over the arm of the chair, and bent down to kiss her forehead. It took every ounce of self-control she possessed not to turn away from him. At least he hadn't kissed her on the lips. She couldn't have stood that.

He noticed her lack of enthusiasm and asked sympathetically, "Hard day?"

"Average."

Average? On the contrary, it couldn't have been much more tumultuous. She had been betrayed by her life partner and a client whose future rested with her.

Matt loosened his necktie and sat in the chair next to hers. "I spent most of the day on the phone, trying to get somebody in the capitol building to talk to a lowly newspaperman like me about the new public school budget. Everybody in Columbia is too busy for an interview unless you're from a big city newspaper."

He had removed his shoes and socks. With one ankle propped on his opposite knee, he was giving himself a foot rub. "Did you talk to Dad today?"

"No."

"I didn't hear from him either. Wonder what he's up to. Think I'll go in and call him."

She stopped him before he reached the door. "Matt, when can I expect that list of questions?"

"What list of questions?"

"For the interview with Mrs. Lynam."

He snapped his fingers. "Oh, right. Then you agree to the idea? Do I get a green light?"

"To interview her or to fuck her?"

It wasn't exactly a graceful segue, but it packed a punch and it certainly served its purpose. His expression went perfectly blank.

In a voice much calmer that she could have hoped for, she said, "Don't embarrass yourself or insult me by playing dumb. This isn't a nasty rumor I picked up in the hair salon. I went out to the Lynam house this afternoon and saw you together in broad daylight. There was only one conclusion to draw. Nothing was left to speculation."

He moved to the porch railing and gazed out over the yard, his back to her. With shrinking patience, Kendall waited for him to respond. She was on the brink of verbally lashing out at him when he finally turned to face her. Casually he folded his arms across his chest.

"What you saw has nothing to do with you."

The statement was spoken rationally and calmly. Conversely, it rocked Kendall with the force of a tidal wave. "Nothing to do with me!" she cried. "Nothing to do with me? I'm your wife!"

"Exactly, Kendall. I chose you for my wife."

"And Lottie Lynam for your lover!"

"That's right. Years ago. Before I ever heard of you."

"Years ago?"

He turned his back to her again, but she vaulted from the chair, closed the distance between them, caught hold of his sleeve, and forced him around. "How long have you been sleeping with her, Matt? I want to know."

His temper snapped, and he slung off her grip. "Since I was fourteen."

Aghast, Kendall fell back a step.

"There. Are you better off knowing that, Kendall? Does it make you feel better? Of course not. You should have left it alone."

He didn't, however. He didn't stop with that startling piece of information. Now that the affair had been exposed, he held nothing back.

"From the time we were curious kids, there was something between Lottie and me," he began. "Chemistry, karma, whatever you want to call it. I was always attracted to her and she to me. When we were fourteen, we satisfied our curiosity. That's how it started."

Kendall pressed her fingers against her lips to keep them from trembling. The situation was worse than she had thought. Much worse. This wasn't a casual fling, an error in judgment that he would correct and then look back on with remorse and regret. He and Lottie Lynam had more than an affair together. They had a relationship that had lasted longer than most marriages.

Kendall had prepared herself for a fight. She had anticipated hearing first a denial, then a confession, followed by a plea for understanding and forgiveness. She wasn't prepared for this.

"After that first time, Lottie and I met in secret every chance we got. I dated other girls. She went out with other boys. But that was only so nobody would suspect what we had going.

Lottie bought the rubbers so the druggist wouldn't tell Dad how many I was using. As a result, Lottie earned a reputation for being promiscuous. Nobody realized she only had one lover.

"Of course, it eventually got out that we were seeing each other on the sly. Dad got wind of it. He asked me if the rumor was true; I denied it. Then he left me alone for a weekend, ostensibly to attend a sporting goods trade show in Memphis. Lottie was in bed with me when he barged in on us.

"He called her daddy to come get her. Dad gave me a thrashing and a lecture on feminine wiles, on how girls of Lottie's rank trapped boys like me. Then he gave me the name and address of a madam over in Georgia. He said that whenever I needed to be with a woman, he'd gladly pay for it. But I was to stay away from trash like Lottie. Nothing good could come of messing with her, he said.

"For a while, I was afraid to see her, afraid he'd find out. Then I went away to college. Years passed, and the memory of her faded. I graduated, came back to Prosper, and started putting together the deal to buy the newspaper. Once it was mine, I went into the insurance office to check on insuring the building and equipment. There sat Lottie."

He was quiet for a moment, as though envisioning her sitting at her desk in the insurance office.

"A look passed between us. That's all it took. We picked up where we left off. For a few years everything was great. Then she started issuing ultimatums. She said I either had to marry her or get out of her life altogether. I called her bluff and stopped seeing her. Three months later she married Charlie Lynam."

"To spite you."

He nodded. "She's been miserable every day since."

"Except for the time she spends with my husband."

Impatiently he shoved his fingers through his hair. "Today was an exception, Kendall. I hadn't been with Lottie since you and I got married. Imagine how I felt when I heard you were representing her in this murder trial. I wasn't at all pleased, but there wasn't anything I could do about it."

"Why did you go see her today?"

"I don't know," he replied testily. "What difference does it make?"

"It makes a difference to me. You've been unfaithful to our marriage vows. I want an explanation. At the very least, I deserve that."

Obviously feeling backed into a corner, he glared at her while gnawing his inner cheek. "It can't be explained, okay?"

"No. It's not okay." It cost her a tremendous amount of pride, but she had to ask. "Do you love her, Matt?"

He denied it with a shake of his head and a firm no. "But Lottie's always been able to . . ."

"To what?" she prompted. "What does she do for you?"

"She fulfills a particular need!" he shouted.

"A need that I don't fulfill?"

He clamped his lips together tightly and remained mute, although the answer was readily apparent and came as a hard blow to Kendall's self-esteem. After today, would she ever have confidence in her desirability?

As though reading her thoughts, he said, "I never wanted to hurt you."

"Well, it's a little late for that, Mr. Burnwood, because you've hurt me terribly. I'm also angry, but mostly confused. If Lottie fulfills your needs so well, why in hell didn't you marry her?"

He gave a short, humorless laugh of incredulity. "Marry her? That would have been out of the question. Dad would never have permitted it."

"What do you mean he wouldn't have permitted it? Was it Gibb's choice to make? Did he choose me, or did you?"

"Don't put words in my mouth, Kendall."

"And don't use that superior tone of voice with me."

"You're getting hysterical."

"I'm not hysterical. I'm mad. Damn good and mad. You duped me. You've made a fool of me."

He raised his hands at his sides, a gesture of dismay and innocence. "How did I dupe you?"

"By courting me and pretending to love me."

"I do love you. I waited years for the perfect wife to come along, and you are she. I chose you because you possess all the qualities I wanted."

"Like options on a new car. You waited for the right model before you bought."

"You're being unreasonable, Kendall."

"I think my unreasonableness is justified."

"Because I slipped up once? Because I spent one afternoon with an old flame? I can't imagine why you're so shocked and upset."

She couldn't believe her ears. Who was this man? Did she really know him? Did he know her? Didn't he realize how important faithfulness was to her? They had never discussed it per se, but surely it had been tacitly understood that she expected fidelity.

"What if I'd been the one to slip up?" she asked. "What if you'd caught me making love with an old flame?"

"Hardly the same thing."

"How is it different?"

"It's different," he said curtly.

"There aren't two sets of rules, Matt, one for the little boys and one for the little girls."

"This conversation has sunk to an absurd level. I'd like to lay it to rest, go into the house, and change." He tried to move past her, but she blocked his path.

"This conversation is not absurd, and it's far from being laid to rest. I saw you with her, Matt. I saw how the two of you clung together, and, frankly, I think you're fooling yourself where your feelings for Lottie are concerned. It didn't look nearly as casual as you claim. Quite the opposite, in fact. I can't pretend it didn't happen. I can't easily dismiss that you committed adultery."

Her voice cracked. She took a deep breath to ward off an outburst of tears. Any sign of weakness would jeopardize her position.

Once her voice was under control, she said, "I want you to move in with Gibb. I need time alone to sort this out. Until I do, I don't want to live in the same house with you."

He gave her a rueful smile, as though her naïveté evoked his sympathy. "That will never happen, Kendall," he said softly. "This is *my* house. You are *my* wife. I didn't go to Lottie with the intention of hurting you. I'm sorry you saw me with her, but what you will do now is forget about it."

He brushed her aside and reached for the door. Speaking pleasantly, as though the confrontation had never taken place, he said, "Dad and I are going to do some work at our deer lease. I probably won't be home until very late."

Chapter Twenty-two

*I*N LESS THAN TEN MINUTES, MATT HAD CHANGED into outdoor clothes and boots, packed a canvas bag with hunting gear, and left the house. He seemed amused by her sullen lack of response to his goodbye kiss.

Long after his departure, Kendall remained in her chair on the porch, immobilized by despair. She didn't know which had affected her worse, Matt's unfaithfulness or his cavalier dismissal of it.

Was she expected to overlook it because this was the first time he had cheated? Was he to be commended for resisting temptation this long? How dare he treat her fury with such casual disregard and not the seriousness it deserved!

It would serve him right if she packed her things and left while he was out. That would get his attention!

But that was an angry impulse, not a wise, well-thought-out course of action. If she was committed to making a good marriage, she mustn't react rashly. His infidelity had devastated her; she would never fully recover from it. Yet she knew that anger and pride could be equally as destructive.

The most difficult fact to accept was that Matt had been

in love with Lottie for years and would have married her if Gibb had approved.

Lottie wasn't the type of woman Gibb had in mind for his son. She didn't meet the Burnwood standards. But Gibb had approved of Kendall Deaton, who was cultured, educated, articulate, and poised.

Her only shortcoming was that she didn't fulfill all her husband's needs, she thought bitterly.

Had she been Matt's choice or Gibb's? she wondered. It frightened her to think that Gibb exercised that much control over Matt's decisions. As long as she remained in Gibb's favor, everything would be fine. But if she crossed her father-in-law, he would become a powerful enemy.

For the time being, she shelved that troublesome thought. Right now she had to resolve what she would do about her marriage.

Did she want to preserve it? Yes, she did. So, how was she to go about it?

She had two distinct advantages over Lottie Lynam. First, Gibb didn't approve of her, and Gibb's opinion went a long way with Matt. Second, Lottie couldn't have children. Kendall was pregnant with Matt's child.

But rather than drawing comfort from that secret weapon, it only increased her heartache. She and Matt should be celebrating tonight. They should be marveling over this miracle of nature brought about by their loving. They should be designing the nursery, discussing names, mapping out a bright future for their child.

Instead, he had walked out, leaving her miserable, alone, and contemplating lingering images of him and Lottie. He was going about his business unfazed.

"Damn him!" she said. How could he just walk away and pretend that nothing had happened? He hadn't even honored her with a good fight.

Suddenly she shot from her porch chair and ran into the

Sandra Brown

house. She stayed only long enough to grab her purse. Within seconds of her decision, she was in her car, speeding down the lane.

She wanted to remain married to Matt. She wanted to create a family. She wanted to *belong* to a family.

But not if it meant sacrificing her self-respect. She would not be ignored. She would not become a doormat. She would not allow Matt to reduce her outrage to a mere fit of pique.

If he wanted their marriage to remain intact, he must admit his culpability. She must have his word that there would be no recurrence of his affair with Lottie or with anyone else. Fidelity was not a negotiable point. If he was willing to concede that what he had done was wrong, she would forgive him.

But the offer was good for tonight only.

She wouldn't wait at home like an obedient, obsequious, good little wife until he returned. He had walked out on a fight, so she would take the fight to him. If Gibb was with him, fine. Let him explain his sordid, extramarital affair with Lottie Lynam to his disapproving father.

Kendall knew that in this respect she would have Gibb's unswerving support.

It had grown dark by the time she reached the outskirts of town. Soon it became apparent that finding Matt was not going to be as easy as she had thought. Now that the lights of Prosper were in the distance, there were no landmarks to guide her.

She had been to the deer lease with Matt only once. On it was a small, rustic cabin that he and Gibb had built themselves. He had proudly shown it off to her. She now wished she had paid more attention to how he had gotten there.

The roads that wound through the rolling, forested hills surrounding Prosper were unpaved, narrow, and dark. Few were marked with road signs. Only a native of the area could distinguish one from the other. To an outsider, they all looked alike.

Determined that she would eventually come across something recognizable, she kept going. But when she passed the same derelict barn she had driven past ten minutes earlier, she had to acknowledge that she was hopelessly lost.

She stopped the car in the middle of the road. "Dammit!" Tears of frustration filled her eyes. She was desperate to find Matt. The sooner they thrashed this out, the sooner they could put it behind them and get on with their lives.

Exasperated, she got out of the car and looked in every direction, trying to spot a familiar landmark. On all sides there was nothing but deep, foreboding forest.

She climbed back into her car and started out again, knowing that sooner or later she would find a road leading back to Prosper. She would have to give up trying to find the deer lease at this hour.

Now she realized that getting lost had served a good purpose. She had had time to calm down before confronting Matt. Now she would have an opportunity to look at the problem from all angles. Maybe she could discover what had driven Matt to seek the company of his former lover in the first place. Was she somehow to blame?

Eager to get on with the business of reconciliation, she sped up. As the car topped an incline, she noticed a reddish glow above the treetops about half a mile ahead. Her first panicked thought was that it was a forest fire. But she soon dismissed that alarming possibility because it appeared that the fire was confined to one area and not widespread.

Then, as she drew nearer to the blaze, the landscape began to look familiar. She realized where she was. She had been here last November on the morning of the hog slaughtering. At least from here she knew her way home. And maybe by the time she got there Matt would have had second thoughts and would be waiting for her.

Nevertheless, she removed her foot from the gas pedal and applied it to the brake. What was burning?

Maybe her first thought had been correct. Someone could

have left a campfire smoldering. There were no cars in sight, so it was easy to conclude that the fire was unattended. It could be a hazard to the entire forest.

She stopped her car but left the engine to idle. After taking a cautious look around, she unlocked her door and got out. There was a strong but not unpleasant smell of wood smoke in the warm, spring air.

Apprehensively, she regarded the dark woods. Maybe she should return to town as quickly as possible and report this to the fire marshal.

But what if it was a group of teenagers having a wiener roast, or a family enjoying a cookout? She would have raised a ruckus over nothing. It would be another incident she would have to live down, just like fainting when the hogs were butchered.

One thing was certain—she couldn't walk away if there was the slightest possibility of a forest fire. Garnering her courage, she set out on foot.

Still wearing the business suit and high heels she had put on that morning, she was hardly dressed for a hike through the wilderness. Her pantyhose didn't have a prayer. Brambles and vines, burgeoning after months of winter dormancy, snagged her hair and clothing, leaving scratches on her arms and legs. Something rustled in the underbrush only yards away from her, but she hastened on without pausing to investigate and identify.

A scream rent the air.

Kendall froze. Fear clutched her throat. What in heaven's name was that? An animal? A wild cat of some kind? Didn't panthers sound like that?

No, it had been a human sound—frighteningly, terrifyingly human. What in God's name had she stumbled upon?

That first high-pitched shriek was followed by several choppy outbursts of sheer agony.

Galvanized by someone's obvious need for help, and forgetting her apprehension, she plunged headlong into the darkness, losing the beaten path as she sought the quickest route. She had to claw her way through the dense foliage, ignoring the stabs of pain when her skin was ripped by branches and pricked by nettles and thorns.

Then, ahead of her, she saw the familiar clearing. Through the trees she caught glimpses of flickering firelight and human forms silhouetted against it.

There were two dozen people or more. They were shouting. But their shouting didn't appear to be from alarm or pain.

Relieved, she stopped to catch her breath, concerned that the frightful hike through the forest had been too much exertion for the first trimester. Propping her hand against a tree trunk, she bent at the waist and breathed deeply.

A sudden burst of laughter brought her head back up. Curiosity prompted her to find out what this odd gathering was about. But she felt she should proceed covertly. Until she knew who had screamed and why, caution was the best approach.

She soon discerned that the group was comprised exclusively of men. Was she witnessing a fraternity initiation? She had almost decided that that was it, when she spotted a familiar face that caused her to gasp.

Dabney Gorn. What was the county solicitor doing out here in the middle of nowhere? And there was Judge Fargo, too. Was it some sort of club meeting?

She also spotted the president of the school board, Prosper's postmaster, Herman Johnson, and Bob Whitaker, the pastor.

To a man, their attention was focused on something lying on the ground. They had formed a tight circle around it, so Kendall couldn't see it clearly enough to identify it.

She nearly jumped out of her skin when another shout went up. Herman Johnson threw his head back and released a warbling, bloodcurdling yell as several of his cohorts hoisted up the object that had been lying on the ground.

It was a Christian cross.

And nailed to it was Michael Li.

Chapter Twenty-three

T HE YOUNG MAN WAS NAKED.

Where his genitals should have been was a fountain pumping dark, red blood. His head dangled lifelessly over his thin chest. He was either dead or unconscious.

Kendall was too transfixed by horror to scream. She watched in mute terror as one of the men cupped his hands for Mr. Johnson's right foot and gave him a boost up. On eye level with Michael Li, he grabbed a handful of the boy's hair and pulled his head up, then forced open his mouth and stuffed something inside. Kendall could easily guess what it was.

As Johnson dropped back to the ground, everyone else cheered. When the cheering stopped, the group fell eerily silent. Moments later, they began singing a hymn.

Nausea rose in the back of Kendall's throat. She swallowed the bile to keep from retching, and began stealthily backing away, fearful now that she would be discovered. She had witnessed the vigilante-style execution of an innocent boy. If they knew she had seen them, they would show her no more mercy than they had Michael Li.

As soon as she was certain she couldn't be seen, she turned and fled, tearing through the trees more madly than she had before, heedless of the noise she made. They wouldn't hear her. They were still singing a hymn, making a travesty of the composer's holy words.

A vine tripped her and she nearly fell. Reflexively she laid a protective hand over her tummy. She knew that she had to be careful for the baby's sake. She must go slower. But she must hurry. If the authorities were alerted immediately, they could come and arrest them all at the scene of their vile crime.

"My God," she gasped, thinking of the shockwaves this would send throughout the community. How had Herman Johnson, considered by most an obnoxious lout, talked these pillars of the community into participating in such an atrocity?

Moving quickly but no longer at a dead run, Kendall tried to retrace the path she had made earlier, but in the darkness that was impossible. Darkness also concealed the depression in the ground until it was too late.

Losing her footing, she pitched forward, falling facedown and landing hard. The fall knocked the wind out of her, and for several moments she could only lie there and suck in deep breaths.

That's when she was assailed by an overwhelming odor so ghastly that it made her gag. In the same instant, she realized that she was sprawled not on dirt but on cloth. Bracing herself on the heels of her hands, she pushed herself up. When she did, she came face to face with Bama.

Half of his face was missing, and the half that remained was badly decomposed. One of his eye sockets was empty, save for the teeming insects that were still making a meal of it.

"Ohmygodmygodmygod." Whimpering in fright, Kendall scrambled backward and vomited onto the ground.

Then, still on hands and knees, she stared down at the rotting corpse, which had obviously been buried in a grave too shallow to protect it from scavengers. Flesh had been torn from the skeleton, but animals hadn't killed him. He had died from a gunshot. There was a black, flyblown hole in the center of his forehead.

Suicide? Doubtful. Was it a coincidence that Bama's body had been left so near the scene of an execution? There was little doubt in Kendall's mind who had killed him.

Her knees were almost too shaky to support her, but she forced herself to her feet. She stepped over Bama's desecrated remains and continued to stagger blindly in the general direction of the road until she reached it. She had veered several degrees off course, but her car was in sight. She loped toward it and was glad she had left the engine running. It would save time. Besides, she didn't think her trembling hands could have handled an ignition key.

As she sped away, she planned her strategy. In order to reach the center of town, she would have to go past her house. Why not stop there and call the sheriff? Maybe—please, God—Matt would be home. She needed him. His infidelity with Lottie Lynam receded to insignificance when measured against what she had just witnessed.

She focused her eyes on the road, gripped the steering wheel, and tried to concentrate on what she must do, but her mind projected images of Michael Li on that hideous cross. She heard again the men cheering when his genitals were stuffed into his mouth.

And Bama. Sweet, harmless Bama, who had a kind word for everyone, who predicted the weather with remarkable accuracy. He had no doubt been executed because he was a blight to the city's attractiveness. He was a nuisance, an unproductive citizen, a bad role model for Prosper's children.

My God, how many other undesirables had been disposed of or punished in this savage, barbaric fashion?

Billy Joe Crook? Surely! He was a thief, so they had severed his arm. Who would dispute the seemingly innocent, albeit tragic, story about an accident? Certainly not Billy Joe, whose life would be in jeopardy if he revealed that his misfortune had in fact been the brainchild of a group of self-appointed judges.

"An eye for an eye" was their credo. Michael Li had stepped over the line with a white girl. Castration and death were his sentence.

Kendall actually gave a glad cry when she saw Matt's car parked in front of their house. Racing up the front steps, she shouted his name. As she ran down the hall, he stepped from the bedroom, obviously fresh from the shower. His hair was still damp. A towel was wrapped around his waist.

"Kendall, where have you been? I came back to find the house empty. After our quarrel—"

"Matt, thank God you're here." She threw herself into his arms and sobbed against his bare chest.

He hugged her tightly. "Darling! Can you forgive me? Can we begin again?"

"Yes, of course, but listen, listen to me!"

When she pulled herself away from him, he realized that her enthusiasm over seeing him wasn't passion-driven. "What in the world happened? You're as pale as a sheet. What's this in your hair?" He plucked a twig from it and looked at it curiously.

"Matt, it was horrible." She sobbed. "I never would have believed it if I hadn't seen it. They had Michael Li. You probably don't know him. He's . . . Never mind, I can fill you in later. You'd better get dressed. I'm going to call the police right now. They can meet us here because it's on the way. I'll lead them to—"

"Kendall, get a grip. What in heaven's name are you talking about?" Now that he'd had time to look her over, he was becoming nearly as alarmed as she. He touched her cheek, and his finger came away red. "You're bleeding. How did you get scratched up like this?"

"I'm fine. Really. Just scared."

"Who hurt you?" he demanded angrily. "The Crook twins? If those bastards—"

"No, no!" she shouted over him. "Listen, Matt. They killed Michael Li. At least I think he was dead. They had castrated him and there was blood everywhere. On him, on the ground." She worked free of him and stepped over his pile of dirty clothes to reach the telephone. She punched out 911.

"You're not making any sense, Kendall. Who are you talking about?"

"Michael Li," she repeated impatiently. "A boy falsely accused of raping Kim Johnson. They killed Bama, too. I found his body out there when I was running— Hello? Yes? This is— No, don't put me on hold!" she screamed into the receiver, her voice cracking.

Matt moved quickly to her side. "Kendall, you're hysterical."

"No, I'm not. I swear I'm not." She swallowed, forcibly repressing the rising hysteria she had denied. Her teeth were chattering uncontrollably. "By the time the police get here, I'll be calm. I can take them straight to it."

"Straight to what?"

"Where the hogs are slaughtered. They probably do their killing there so the blood won't be noticed," she added, the thought having suddenly occurred to her. "They're smart. And there are so many of them. People we know and would never suspect."

"What were you doing out in the woods alone at night?"

"I was coming to find you." Hot, salty tears spilled over her eyelids and rolled down her cheeks. "I wanted to see you. I didn't want this thing with Lottie to fester and become irreparable. I couldn't wait until you got home to make everything right between us. I was trying to find the deer lease, but I got lost."

"Emergency services. How can I help you?"

"Yes, hello?" She signaled Matt that someone had finally

returned to the line. "I need the police or the sheriff's office immediately. My name is—"

Matt snatched the receiver from her and hung it up. She gaped at him, dumbfounded. "Why'd you do that? I've got to report this! I can take them there. If they can get out there soon enough—"

"You're not going anywhere except to the shower, then to bed." He stroked her hair. "The forest can be spooky at night if you're not used to it. You got lost and panicked, darling. You're having an anxiety attack. After a hot shower and a cold glass of wine, you'll forget all about it."

"This isn't an anxiety attack!" Realizing that her screeching tone only supported his theory, she took a deep breath. "I'm in full control of my faculties, I assure you. I'm terrified, but I'm not crazy."

"I'm not suggesting you're crazy. But you've been under an enormous amount of stress lately, and—"

She pushed him aside. "Stop patronizing me and *listen*. Matt, they—"

"First of all, who is this 'they' you keep referring to?"

"Just about everyone with some authority around here. I could name a dozen prominent men."

She was ticking off a list when he interrupted her again. "And you're saying these men are connected to a castration and crucifixion? Not to mention the murder of a panhandler?" He cocked his eyebrows skeptically. "Kendall, be reasonable. How do you expect me to believe such a tale?"

"You believe it."

He tilted his head in puzzlement.

A shudder passed through her. "I never mentioned a crucifixion."

Her eyes dropped to the pile of discarded clothes on the floor. The soles of his boots were caked with mud, studded with twigs and pine needles. She detected a faint smell of wood smoke.

Slowly her eyes moved back up to his. He was watching her calmly, his expression bland. "You were there, weren't you?" she whispered gruffly. "You're one of them. And Gibb, too."

"Kendall." He reached for her.

She turned and ran, but had taken no more than a few steps before he grabbed the back of her jacket and jerked her to a halt. "Let go of me!" Reaching behind her, she tried to scratch his face with her nails and derived some satisfaction when she heard him grunt in pain.

"You just couldn't leave well enough alone, could you, Miss Buttinsky?"

She elbowed him in the stomach. He released her and grabbed his gut. Kendall made a dash for the door, but he caught her again.

They struggled, and finally he managed to pin her arms to her sides. His face was contorted with rage. Spittle flew from his mouth as he bent low and shouted directly into her face.

"You want to talk to the sheriff? Or the police chief? Fine. You'll find them out there with the rest of us."

"Who are you?"

"The Brotherhood. We mete out justice because so-called democracy and the legal system have turned against us. It's all on the side of the riffraff now. To even the odds, we're forced to take matters into our own hands."

"You kill people?"

"Sometimes."

"How many? How long has this been going on?"

"For decades."

Her knees buckled and she would have collapsed if he hadn't held her up. "We had hoped you would join us, Kendall. You certainly can't fight us."

"Wanna bet?"

She drove her knee into his groin. He swore as he bent double. Without even thinking about it, Kendall whirled, grabbed a vase of roses from the dresser, and swung it with all her might at his head. He went down like a felled tree and lay motionless.

For several moments she stared at his still form, not quite believing what she had done. Her breathing was loud and harsh. She thought of her baby. Would it survive this night? Would she?

Only if she fled.

She removed her wedding ring and threw it down at Matt. Then she headed for the front door at a run.

But car headlights were approaching the house. The vehicle stopped. Gibb got out of his pickup truck, came up the steps, and knocked.

On impulse, Kendall raced back into the bedroom, but only long enough to snatch a robe from the closet.

"Coming!" she called. Rushing to the front door, she shoved her arms into the robe and pulled it tightly around her to cover her dirty clothes and scratched arms. At the last moment, she remembered to kick off her shoes. Then she opened the door a crack and peered out.

"Oh, hi, Gibb." She hoped he would attribute her breathlessness to something besides fear. He was wearing outdoor clothes. His boots were as muddy as Matt's, and he, too, smelled of smoke. He had come straight from a bloody execution, but no one would ever have guessed that from his benign smile.

"You two still up?"

She glanced over her shoulder, almost expecting to see Matt staggering from the bedroom massaging the bloody lump on his head.

If he wasn't dead.

She formed what she hoped was a demure smile and turned back to her father-in-law. "Actually no. I mean . . . well, we weren't asleep yet. Just . . . you know." She simpered, southern belle style. "I can get Matt for you if it's really important that you see him right now."

He chuckled. "I doubt it's as important as what he's doing."

"Well," she said coyly, "we're in the middle of making up. We had a squabble earlier." Playing a hunch, she added, "Didn't he mention it?"

"Matter of fact, he did, although he didn't tell me what the quarrel was about. I came over to see if I could help smooth things over." Grinning broadly, he winked at her. "I see that my peacekeeping services aren't necessary. So I'm going to mosey on home and leave you two to your business." When he reached out and squeezed her arm, she feared she might vomit again. "You get back to your husband. Good night, now."

"Good night."

He turned and tromped down the steps.

For good measure, Kendall called after him, "Come back for breakfast, why don't you? I'm hungry for your famous waffles."

"I'll be here by eight."

She watched until his taillights disappeared, then she dashed back into the bedroom. Matt was just as she had left him. She couldn't bring herself to touch him, even to check for a pulse. What difference did it make?

Whether he was dead or alive, her life as she had known it was over.

Chapter Twenty-four

"MY NAME IS KENDALL DEATON BURNWOOD. What I'm going to tell you will sound beyond belief. You'll think I'm insane. I assure you I'm not." She paused to take a sip of the Coke she'd bought at the motel vending machine.

"I'm listening."

Agent Braddock of the FBI sounded sleepy and put out. Too damn bad. What she had to tell him would jar him awake. To lend plausibility to her implausible story, she had introduced herself as a public defender. Otherwise, he might have thought he was talking to an absolute kook.

"For almost two years I've been living and working in Prosper. Tonight I discovered a secret vigilante group that is committing unspeakable crimes, including murder. The group is comprised of some of the town's most prominent men. They call themselves the Brotherhood. My . . . my husband is one of them.

"By his own admission, they mete out punishment to anyone they feel deserves it, but who has somehow slipped through the cracks of the legal system.

"I can't guess how many people they've eliminated over the years, but I witnessed a murder tonight." She then told him about Michael Li's execution and finding Bama's remains. "He wasn't a criminal, but I suspect them of killing him, too."

She told the agent what she had seen in the woods, keeping her account factual and precise, her voice composed. Too much emotion would jeopardize her credibility. "This clearing is deep in the woods in a remote area. They slaughter hogs there. And, I guess," she added shakily, "not only hogs."

She paused, realizing that he had remained silent throughout the telling. "Are you still there?"

"I'm still here. It's just ... Well, ma'am, this is quite a tale. Did you report this alleged murder to the local police?"

"They're in on it."

"The police, too? I see."

Clearly, he didn't see at all. She was being humored. What could she say to convince him that she wasn't a mental case? She pushed back her hair and took another sip of her drink. Tension had brought on a stabbing pain between her shoulder blades. She had driven 150 miles before she felt it was safe to stop. For each of those miles, she had kept one eye on the road ahead, and one on the rearview mirror.

When would Matt regain consciousness and alert the other members of the Brotherhood that she was on to them? Or if she had killed him with that vase, when would his body be discovered? She hoped it wouldn't be before eight o'clock that morning, when Gibb would come to the house to cook waffles. She looked at her watch. It was already past two. Time was running short.

"Agent Braddock, I warned you that this would sound unbelievable."

"You must admit it is a bit farfetched. What I know of Prosper is that it's a neat little community."

"That's how it appears, but the innocence is camouflage. Look, I know you get outrageous stories from wackos every day, but I swear to you I'm telling the truth. I saw that boy nailed to a cross."

"Calm down, Mrs. Burnwood. We won't get anywhere if you get hysterical."

"We won't get anywhere if you ignore me, either."

"I'm not ignoring—"

"Then what are you going to do about this?"

"You've named some pretty important people," he said, hedging. "Men with authority."

"Don't you think I realize that? At first I couldn't believe who was involved. But the more I think about it, the more sense it makes."

"Why do you say that?"

"There's a pervasive attitude in that town. I can't exactly describe it, but I've *felt* it since I moved there. The people aren't as flagrant as skinheads. They're not aggressive like some of the better known neo-Nazi groups. But their philosophies are similar."

"That's disturbing."

"All the more so because they operate so subversively. You can't spot them. You don't recognize them immediately for what they are. They're men who hold positions of trust and authority, not rabble-rousers with shaved heads and swastikas carved on their foreheads. They don't wear robes and peaked caps. They don't hold rallies where they scream racial slurs and preach white supremacy. Come to think of it, being Anglo isn't even good enough for them. Billy Joe Crook is white. So was Bama."

"Billy Joe Crook?"

She told him about the juvenile offender and his "accident." "I suppose that in the eyes of the Brotherhood, one must be white and *chosen*," she said with ill-disguised disgust.

The FBI agent exhaled a deep breath. "You sound like a reasonable person, Mrs. Burnwood. I don't think you could have fabricated all this. I'll file a report and see what I can do."

"Thank you, but filing a bureaucratic report won't cut it. I won't be safe until they're all behind bars."

"I agree, but before we start rounding up suspects, I'm going to dispatch an agent to take a look at this clearing you've told me about. If we brought someone in for questioning, your husband for instance, that would alert the rest of them. They could scatter. Go underground. We need some physical evidence before we make any arrests, and then it must be done in an organized and covert manner."

He was right, of course. That was the best strategy. But she wouldn't take an easy breath until her husband, Gibb, and the others were in custody. "When will you begin?"

"If you'll give me directions to the site now, I'll send somebody out there at first light."

She told him where he could find Bama's body. She was almost certain that when Michael Li was found, he would be a corpse, too. It would be interesting to hear how his disappearance from the Prosper jail was explained.

In recounting her struggle with Matt, she had told Braddock only that she had knocked him unconscious. She didn't tell him that she feared she might have killed him. She would cross that bridge only if and when she had to.

"Where are you?" he asked. "If we find evidence that backs up your story, you'll be a key witness and will need the government's protection."

She didn't argue with that. "I'm in a town called Kingwood." She gave him the number of the state highway that ran through the center of town. "I'm at the Pleasant View Motel. You can't miss it. It's on the highway. Room 103. What time will you be here?"

"Nine o'clock."

Seven hours. Could she stand to be alone that long? She

had no choice. She had called in the cavalry; she would have to wait for it to arrive.

"Stay put," the agent told her. "Don't get stupid and mistake it for bravery. If what you've told me is true—and I'm beginning to believe it is—these are extremely dangerous men we're dealing with."

"Believe me, I know. If they find me, they'll kill me without a qualm."

"I'm glad you understand that. Don't venture out for any reason. Could you have been followed?"

"I would swear I wasn't."

"No one else knows where you are?"

"No. I drove in circles and didn't stop until I thought it was safe. I called you first."

"Good. I'll be driving an unmarked government car. It's a plain gray sedan."

"I'll watch for you."

"I'll be there at nine o'clock to drive you straight to our main office in Columbia."

"Thank you, Mr. Braddock."

Kendall hung up but kept her hand on the receiver. Should she call her grandmother? A call of any sort at this hour would alarm the elderly lady. This particular call would terrify her.

She picked up the phone and dialed.

"This had better be damned important."

"Ricki Sue, it's me."

Her friend went from disgruntled to surprised in an instant. "Kendall, what—"

"Is someone with you?"

"Does the Pope wear a beanie?"

"I'm sorry, truly. I wouldn't ask this favor unless it was vitally important."

"What's going on? Is something wrong?"

"Yes, but it will take too long to explain it now. Can you

please go out to Grandmother's house and stay the rest of the night with her?"

"Like . . . now?" Ricki Sue asked unenthusiastically.

"Like immediately."

"Kendall, what the hell—"

"Please, Ricki Sue. You know I wouldn't ask unless the situation was critical. Stay with Grandmother until I call you back. Lock the doors and don't open them to anyone, not even Matt or Gibb."

"What—"

"Don't answer the phone unless it rings twice first. That'll mean it's me. Okay, Ricki Sue? Give Grandmother my love and assure her that for the moment I'm safe. I'll call as soon as I can. Thanks."

She hung up before Ricki Sue had time to object or ask further questions. *If* Matt had survived, and *if* he and Gibb started hunting for her, they would look for her first in Tennessee. Grandmother's life was in as much danger as hers. So was her child's.

Kendall was suddenly struck by the far-reaching effects of her predicament. In the best-case scenario, all members of the Brotherhood would be apprehended to face trial for their crimes. She would be a material witness for at least one murder. She would be under the government's protection for months, possibly years, while prosecutors hashed through the evidence and constructed their case. The investigation itself could take years. Then there would be postponements, delays, appeals, a hopeless snarl of legal machinations that could drag out indefinitely. She and her child would be at the center of the tangle.

Until the case was closed, her life would belong to the government. Everything she did would be monitored. She would need the government's permission for every move she made. She would have no more decision-making authority over her own life than would a puppet.

She covered her face with her hands and groaned. Was this to be her penance? Was this how she was to atone for what she had done to get that job in Prosper?

When the feds began poking around in the dim corners of their prime witness's life, would they ever receive a big surprise. They were bound to uncover everything about Kendall Deaton. How much credibility would she have when her secret came to light?

She was caught in a trap of her own making and had no one to blame but herself. She longed to cry, but she feared that if she started she would be unable to stop. If Agent Braddock found her weeping uncontrollably when he arrived, he would dismiss her as a woman who'd had a spat with her husband and had dreamed up a fable guaranteed to embarrass him.

To calm herself and ease her aching, tense body, she took a hot shower, but kept the shower curtain open so that she could see through the bedroom to the door. She had fled with only the clothes on her back. Her suit was stained and torn, but she put it back on and lay on the bed.

As exhausted as she was, she couldn't sleep. She dozed, waking to every sound no matter how slight. With annoying frequency she checked the time.

It was a long night.

"Want a sweet roll to go with that? We've got some good honey buns this morning."

"No, thanks, just the coffee."

It was only eight-twenty. Kendall had been up since six o'clock, pacing the orange shag carpet in her motel room, counting each minute that crawled by. Deciding she couldn't stand the room a moment longer, and craving a cup of coffee, she had disobeyed Braddock's order not to venture outside. Constantly looking over her shoulder for vigilantes in hot pursuit, she had crossed the street to the diner.

Kendall paid the friendly cashier and left with her carryout coffee. She spotted a telephone booth at the corner of the building. One more quick call to Sheridan, just to make certain they were all right? She could always use the telephone in her motel room, but the fewer charges she had on that bill, the better.

It was an old-fashioned phone booth with a hinged, folding door. She pulled it closed and placed her call, using coins. She let the phone ring twice, hung up, then dialed again.

Ricki Sue answered on the first ring. "What's up? Did they find out? Are you in trouble?"

"I'm in trouble," Kendall replied. "But not for the reason you think. How's Grandmother?"

"Okay. Worried naturally. We'd both appreciate knowing what the hell is going on."

"Did anyone call there asking for me?"

"No. Where are you, Kendall?"

"I can't talk long. I—"

"Speak up, kid. I can barely hear you. You sound like you're in a well."

A gray sedan pulled off the highway and into the motel parking lot across the street. Agent Braddock was thirty minutes early.

"Kendall? You still there?"

"Yes, I'm here. Hold on." Her eyes stayed on the car as it slowly rolled past the numbered doors. There were two men in the front seat. Braddock hadn't mentioned bringing anyone with him, but didn't federal agents usually work in pairs?

"Kendall, your grandmother wants to talk to you."

"No, wait. Stay on the line, Ricki Sue. Get something to write with. Hurry."

The sedan stopped in front of room 103. A tall, slender, gray-haired man got out. He had on sunglasses and wore a dark suit with a white shirt, a typical federal officer's uniform. He glanced around, then walked to the door of room 103. He knocked, waited, knocked again. Turning toward the car, he shrugged his shoulders.

"*Kendall!* Speak to me. What is all this about?"

The second man alighted from the passenger side of the car. It was Gibb Burnwood.

"Ricki Sue, you must listen. Don't ask questions, please. There's no time for them." She spoke rapidly, reeling off instructions in clipped words and phrases while keeping her eyes fixed on the two men across the busy two-lane highway. "Have you got all that?"

"I took it down in shorthand. But can't you tell me—"

"Not now."

Kendall hung up. Her heart was in her throat. Agent Braddock and Gibb were conferring outside the motel room. They hadn't seen her yet, but they hadn't looked. If they glanced toward the diner, there was a good chance they would spot her.

The agent slipped something from his coat pocket and bent over the doorknob. Within seconds, the door to room 103 swung open. They went inside.

Kendall pushed open the door, dashed out of the phone booth, and slipped into the alley between the diner and a feed store. As she ran between the buildings, she disturbed a cat foraging for breakfast in a Dumpster, but no one else saw her.

The far end of the alley opened into a narrow parking lot behind a row of single-story commercial buildings. That's where she had left her car the night before. At the time, taking that precautionary measure had seemed melodramatic. Now she thanked God she'd had the foresight.

She chose a street at random, driving neither too fast nor too slowly. She followed the street through a residential neighborhood, past the Fighting Trojans football stadium, then beyond the city limits until the street became a rural route that would lead somewhere.

Or nowhere.

Chapter Twenty-five

THEY MET IN CHATTANOOGA AT THE MOTEL that Kendall had specified during her brief telephone conversation with Ricki Sue that morning. Her grandmother held her against her thin body and stroked her hair. "My dear girl, you've had me worried sick. What mischief have you got yourself into now?"

"You naturally assume that I'm the perpetrator."

"Experience is a good teacher."

Kendall laughed and hugged her grandmother tightly. She was delighted to see her, but shocked by how the older woman had aged since their last visit. Her eyes, however, were as bright and lively as ever.

Ricki Sue nearly squeezed the life from Kendall when they hugged. "Now," she said, sounding cross, "you pulled me away from a real stud last night. This morning, you were spitting out instructions as fast as a machine gun shoots bullets. I've driven so far my buns are numb. I'd like to know what the hell is going on."

"I don't blame you for being exasperated. I apologize for the inconvenience and thank you from the bottom of my heart for everything you've done. I think you'll understand the need for urgency when I explain everything. It's a long story. Before I begin, are you sure you weren't followed?"

"We drove around this city so many times we got dizzy. I'm positive we weren't followed."

The three of them sat on one bed while Kendall told her spellbinding story. The two women listened with rapt attention, except that every once in a while Ricki Sue muttered swear words of incredulity.

"So this morning, when I saw Gibb with Agent Braddock, I realized that either, one, he didn't believe me and had called in the nearest relative to rescue a woman on the brink of a nervous breakdown. Or, two—and this is the really scary possibility—the Brotherhood has members in the regional office of the FBI."

"Good God!" Ricki Sue exclaimed. "Either way, you're screwed."

"Right. So I can't risk calling the federal authorities again until I'm far away. In the meantime, I'm the only nonmember who knows about the Brotherhood and its nefarious pastimes. I can blow the whistle on them, so they'll be after me. I intend to go underground until the bastards have been arrested, charged, and held without bail."

Her grandmother squeezed her hand. Concern made the creases in her face more noticeable. "Until then, your life's in danger. Where will you go?" Grandmother asked.

"I don't know. But I want you to come with me. Please, Grandmother," Kendall implored when she saw that the older woman was about to protest. "I might be away for months. I want you with me, not only for my sake but for yours. They might try to reach me through you. You must come."

For over an hour she tried to persuade the older woman, but to no avail. Grandmother remained steadfast. "You'll be safer without me in tow."

Kendall called upon Ricki Sue to make her grandmother see reason, but Ricki Sue took the opposing side. "You're the

one who's not thinking straight, kid. Your grandma's right.
You can change your hair color, put on a pair of glasses, dress
differently, alter your appearance any number of ways. A
woman your grandma's age would be hard to disguise."

"Besides," her grandmother said, "you know I want to die
at home and be buried beside your grandfather and your
parents. When my time comes, I couldn't stand being in an
alien place and interred among strangers."

Kendall had no argument for that, although she chastened
her grandmother for talking about her death as though it were
imminent.

She and her grandmother slept in the same bed that night,
while Ricki Sue snored from the other. Throughout the night,
Kendall held her grandmother close. They whispered of days
gone by. Giggling, they relived good times they had shared.
They spoke poignantly of Kendall's parents and grandfather,
none of whom she remembered. She knew them only from her
grandmother's descriptions, which had been communicated so
frequently and so well that Kendall's images of them were
vivid.

"Considering the strikes against us, we've done all right,
haven't we?" the old woman asked, patting Kendall's hand.

"Much better than all right, Grandmother. I was exceptionally blessed to have you in my life. You loved me more than
most natural parents love their children."

"I wish my love had been sufficient."

"It was!" Kendall exclaimed in a whisper.

"No. Like any child, you wanted your mommy and daddy's
love and approval, and they weren't there to give it." She
turned to Kendall and pressed her cool, dry, age-spotted hand
against her cheek.

"You don't need to prove yourself to anyone, dear. Especially not to them. You're everything they would have wanted
their living legacy to be, and more. Don't be so hard on
yourself. Enjoy your life."

"After this, I doubt there'll be much enjoyment."

Her grandmother smiled with the complacency of a fortune-teller who has seen something prodigious in her crystal ball. "You'll survive this. You've always been curious and courageous, and both traits have served you well. The first time I saw you in the hospital nursery, you were peering about, not sleeping peacefully in your crib like all the other babies. I told your mother then that you were special, and I haven't changed my mind."

Her eyes twinkled. "You are unique. Wonderful things are being held in store for you. Wait and see if I'm not right."

Morning found them a subdued and somber trio.

Kendall's grandmother pressed an envelope stuffed with cash into her hand. It cost her some pride to accept it, but she had no choice. "I'll pay you back as soon as I get somewhere and find a job."

"You know that what's mine is yours. And don't worry about a large withdrawal showing up at the bank. That cash has been hidden in various parts of the house for years."

"Hey! You're a clever old broad," Ricki Sue said, patting her on the back. "I like your style, Granny."

Kendall took comfort in the friendship that had developed between them. She felt confident in placing her grandmother under Ricki Sue's care.

"I'll call you when I can," she promised them. "But I probably won't be able to talk for very long at a time. They might put tracers on your telephones." In response to their shocked expressions, she said, "I don't put anything past them. Be extremely careful."

She longed to tell them about the baby she was carrying but decided against it. Knowing about the child would only double their worry. Besides, she didn't trust her own strength. They might prevail upon her not to leave for parts unknown, and she might be tempted to stay.

The inevitable time of parting came. Kendall hugged her grandmother fiercely, memorizing her smell and the feel of her frail body. "I love you, Grandmother. I'll see you as soon as it's possible."

The older woman set her away and gazed into her face for a long time. "I love you, too. Very, very much. Be happy, child." Kendall read in her wistful expression a final goodbye.

Knowing that this was probably the last time she would see her grandmother alive, she wanted to cling to her and never let go. But she followed her grandmother's dignified example and managed a brave, though wavering, smile.

Ricki Sue, who was crying noisily and unabashedly, announced that she for one didn't want any murdering rednecks or traitorous feebs on her ass, and whisked Grandmother out the door.

Kendall watched from the window as they drove away, then sobbed until her throat was raw. What did she have to fear from the Brotherhood? Before they tracked her down, she was sure to die of heartache.

She deserted her car in the parking lot of the Chattanooga motel and, using some of the cash Grandmother had given her, bought a clunker from an individual who had advertised in the classified ads.

The car got her as far as Denver, where it coughed one final time and died. She left it on the busy freeway, walked to the nearest McDonald's, and, over a Big Mac, perused the rental ads for a place to live.

She found exactly what she was looking for in an older neighborhood. Her landlady was a widow who supplemented her Social Security by leasing a garage apartment. The house was within walking distance of a branch of the public library, where Kendall obtained a job.

She worked long hours. She made no friends. She didn't even have a telephone installed. When her pregnancy became

evident, she responded to polite questions with a reticence
that discouraged further prying.

As far as she could tell, none of her calls to the FBI had
sparked any interest, much less investigations. Every few
weeks she phoned a different office and reported what she
had witnessed in Prosper.

Apparently they wrote her off as a nut case. She faithfully
watched national news reports and read periodicals, hoping
to see a story about the exposure of a vigilante organization
in South Carolina. No such story appeared.

The men of the Brotherhood were getting away with murder, and there was nothing she could do about it without
risking her life. But she couldn't sit idle and do nothing.

She spent her off-duty hours at the library gleaning information. A wide range of computer sources were at her fingertips,
so she used them. Gradually, she built her own library. It
was comprised of the records of public officials in Prosper,
unsolved murders, missing-persons reports, anything that
might one day help bring the vigilantes to justice.

For their own safety, Kendall didn't let Grandmother or
Ricki Sue know her whereabouts. So she didn't learn of her
grandmother's death until she placed a routine call.

"I'm so sorry, Kendall." Ricki Sue wept as she imparted
the news. "It breaks my heart to have to tell you like this."

"Was she alone?"

"Yes. I went over that morning to check on her, but she
didn't answer the door. I found her in bed."

"Then she died in her sleep. That's a blessing."

"What do you want me to do about the house?"

"Give her clothes away to anyone who can use them. Put
all her personal belongings and valuables in a safe deposit
box. Leave everything else as it is and lock up the house. Pay
the bills out of the account at the bank." She had authorized
Ricki Sue to sign her grandmother's checks when she had
moved to Prosper.

There was no one with whom Kendall could share her grief, so she suffered through it alone.

She worked until the last two weeks of her term, during which she prepared the tiny apartment for the baby's arrival. She went into labor early one morning and used her landlady's telephone to call a cab to take her to the hospital.

Her baby was born that afternoon. He was a healthy, happy boy who weighed eight pounds three ounces. She named him Kevin Grant, after her father and grandfather. Her joy was so encompassing that she couldn't contain all of it. It had to be shared.

"A baby!" Ricki Sue shrieked. As delighted as she was to hear about the birth of Kendall's son, she was angry that Kendall hadn't told her of the pregnancy.

"Can't you come back now? My God, how long are you going to remain a fugitive? You've done nothing wrong, for crissake!"

To Kendall's dismay, no one in Prosper had tried to contact her through either Ricki Sue or her grandmother. Obviously Gibb had provided an explanation for her sudden disappearance; but why wasn't he seeking retribution? She was more suspicious of their failure to come after her than she would have been if they had tried terrorizing the people close to her.

Or maybe they knew where she was and were only biding their time before they struck.

Because they could conceivably be around the next corner at any given time, she did nothing to call attention to herself. She was resigned to living the rest of her life in obscurity, under a false name, sacrificing her career in law, and working at low-profile odd jobs to support herself and Kevin.

She could never pursue a meaningful career. She could never marry. Ricki Sue had offered to make inquiries into whether Matt had died from the blow to his head, but Kendall didn't want to know. If he had died, she could conceivably face charges of manslaughter. If he had survived, she was still married. Either way, she was permanently shackled.

Kevin was three months old that afternoon she sat with him on a quilt on the lawn of the widow's house. Denver was enjoying a gloriously warm spring day. The sky was clear, but Kendall sensed the approach of the government car as one senses when the sun is about to slip behind a cloud. She suddenly experienced a chill and realized that her days in exile were over.

The navy blue sedan pulled to a stop at the curb. Two men got out and started up the sidewalk toward her. The shorter, stockier one smiled pleasantly. The tall one didn't.

The first one addressed her. "Mrs. Burnwood?"

Her landlady came out onto the stoop. She didn't know Kendall by that name and looked bewildered when Kendall replied in the affirmative.

He removed a leather billfold from the breast pocket of his jacket and flipped it open to show her his ID. "I'm Agent Jim Pepperdyne. FBI." He nodded to the man with the stern mouth and opaque sunglasses. "This is U.S. Marshal John McGrath."

Chapter Twenty-six

*J*OHN MCGRATH WOKE UP WITH HIS MEMORY FULLY restored.

He awoke suddenly and experienced no lingering drowsiness or disorientation. With stark clarity, he instantly remembered everything about his recent and distant past.

He knew his name, recalled his childhood in Raleigh, North Carolina, and remembered the number on his high school football jersey.

He remembered his stint with the FBI and the life-shattering event that had caused him to abandon the bureau two years ago. He remembered his present job. He recalled being sent to Denver, and why.

The car crash would probably be blocked from his memory forever, but he remembered driving over the rain-slick highway and coming upon the felled tree. He remembered feeling helpless in the face of certain disaster and resigning himself to die when the car plunged over the cliff. He remembered regaining consciousness in the hospital, hurting all over. Surrounded by strangers, he had been a stranger even to himself.

Most vividly, he remembered Kendall looking him straight in the eye and saying, *"He's my husband."* John laid his arm across his forehead and swore beneath his breath, because he also remembered everything that had happened since that moment.

Especially last night.

Last night had him in shit up to his eyebrows.

Last night he had had carnal knowledge of Kendall Burnwood.

The pillow beside his was empty now, but it hadn't been for long. It still bore the imprint of Kendall's head. Recalling every sigh, murmur, sensation, and taste, he groaned and dragged his hands down his face.

Good God, was it any wonder his memory had been jostled? Everything that made John McGrath who he was had been shaken loose by what he'd done.

He covered his eyes again, this time rubbing the heels of his hands against his eye sockets. How could he account for this to Pepperdyne? How could he account for it to himself? At least he hadn't been unfaithful to another woman. He and Lisa—

Lisa. Lisa Frank. Like everything else, all recollection of her had been gone until this moment. Now memories of her came rushing back. And how fitting that the first thing he remembered of their relationship wasn't one of their good times, but a quarrel.

John had arrived home after a trip to France to escort an escaped felon back to the States. He was exhausted, grimy, and gritty-eyed. He had jetlag and wanted to sleep for about thirty hours undisturbed. As he inserted the key into the lock, he hoped that Lisa was away.

But she was in the apartment. Wired. Spoiling for a fight because some first-class passenger on her flight that afternoon had acted like a jerk.

"I'm sorry you had a rough flight," he said, trying to sound convincingly sympathetic. "Mine wasn't exactly a lark, either.

I'm going to shower. Then let's go to bed and sleep it off, okay?"

But compliance simply wasn't among Lisa's character traits. She was there with a towel when he stepped from the shower stall, and when he entered the bedroom, she was waiting for him between the sheets, smiling seductively.

From the time he had discovered the delightful differences between boys and girls, the sight of a naked woman had never failed to evoke a response. Nevertheless, that night he performed sloppily and selfishly, and Lisa missed his usual finesse.

She snapped on the nightstand lamp. "John, we need to talk."

"Not now, please, Lisa. I'm exhausted." He knew by her tone that it was going to be the "our relationship is going nowhere" talk, and he was too tired for it tonight. Even on good nights he resisted relationship analyses.

Disregarding his fatigue and foul mood, she launched into a familiar litany on the aspects of their relationship that were unsatisfactory, which, coincidentally, were the very aspects he liked about it.

They didn't see each other often enough, she said. As a flight attendant for a major airline, she had an irregular schedule and was away much of the time. His work involved extensive travel. They were in the apartment together often enough to keep their libidos well tuned, but not so often as to become dependent on each other. John preferred it that way. Lisa wanted more.

"You won't make a commitment," she complained.

He said that wasn't true, while silently acknowledging that it was. He liked their arrangement—he didn't even think of it in terms of a "relationship"—the way it was. It required very little time, effort, and attention from him. That's the way he wanted to keep it.

But that night Lisa continued to harp on his shortcomings

until he got angry. "I'm not going to talk about this tonight, Lisa." He switched off the lamp and buried his head in the pillow.

She muttered, "You son of a bitch," but he ignored it.

The following morning, he woke before her. Lying there looking at her while she slept, he realized that Lisa Frank was as much a stranger to him as she'd been the day they had exchanged telephone numbers following a flight during which she'd been his attendant.

He had been intimate with her body many times, but he didn't know her. She didn't know him. No one got inside John McGrath's skin. He supposed he should have played more fairly and warned her of that. Instead, he had let them drift along until the final showdown and breakup.

His reverie was interrupted when he heard Kendall singing a lullaby to Kevin in the other room. She had probably just nursed him for the first time that day. John pictured her cradling the baby in her arms, smiling down at him, running her fingertips over the small features of his face, showering him with maternal love.

That's what she had been doing the first time he saw her, sitting on a quilt in the yard of that house in Denver. When Jim Pepperdyne identified himself to her, she had almost looked relieved, as though she had anticipated being found and no longer had to dread it.

They gave her time to gather her and the baby's things before walking her to the car. As she was about to get in, she hesitated. Her eyes darted anxiously between him and Jim. "Are you taking me back to South Carolina?"

"Yes, ma'am," Jim had replied. "You've got to go back."

In the course of his career, John had witnessed nearly every emotional response that a human being could experience. He was a student of reflex, both conditioned and involuntary. He was an expert at reading inflections of speech and expressions. He could distinguish truth from lies with amazing accuracy.

It had been his vocation to do so. Others relied on his expertise in human behavior.

So when Jim told her that their intention was to return her to the state from which she had fled, and her eyes filled with tears and she clutched her baby protectively to her chest, John was absolutely certain that Kendall Deaton Burnwood believed with all her heart precisely what she said: "If you take me back, they will kill me."

John had previously worked with Jim Pepperdyne on a Hostage Rescue Team. Pepperdyne was an excellent agent; John considered him one of his few real friends. Even though John was no longer with the Bureau, Pepperdyne had invited him to sit in while he questioned Mrs. Burnwood.

"Just as an observer," he had said casually as they made their way down the hall toward an office where Kendall was waiting. "You might find it very interesting. Besides, I need a read on her trustworthiness. Is she telling the truth, or a pack of lies?"

"You already know she's telling the truth."

"But her testimony has to be strong enough to convince a jury of something they'll think is preposterous. You're a coldhearted bastard," Pepperdyne had said amicably. "You're tougher and more cynical than most jurors will be. If she convinces you, we're home free."

"This isn't my line of work anymore," John had reminded him when they reached the office door.

Pepperdyne placed his hand on the doorknob, shot John a retiring look, and said, "Bullshit."

Chapter Twenty-seven

S HE WAS ALONE INSIDE THE OFFICE, HAVING DECLINED
counsel and saying that she would act on her own behalf. Her
son was being baby-sat by another agent. She gave no outward
appearance of anxiety, even when Pepperdyne served her the
warrant.

She skimmed it, then looked up at them, perplexed. "This
is a material-witness warrant."

"What did you expect?" Pepperdyne said. "A murder warrant, maybe?"

"Is he dead?"

"Matt Burnwood? No."

She rolled her lips inward, but John couldn't tell whether
the reaction was one of relief or consternation. "I thought I'd
killed him."

"If Mr. Burnwood is convicted of the charges filed against
him, he'll probably wish he were dead."

She touched her forehead, her misapprehension plain to
see. "Wait. I don't understand. Are you telling me that Matt
has been arrested and charged?"

"Him, his father, assorted others whom you tagged as being
members of this vigilante group." Pepperdyne passed her a

list of names. "The charges range from conspiracy to commit
murder all the way up to capital murder. Since the district
judge and the district attorney have been indicted, appointees
are now serving in those positions. They're all in custody,
Mrs. Burnwood. All have been denied bail."

"I can't believe it," she said in a small voice. "Someone
finally took my calls seriously."

"They would have been taken seriously from the beginning
if they'd been channeled to the right office." Pepperdyne sat
on the corner of the desk. "Somebody in Justice had already
picked up the odor of something fishy going on down there.
Too many prisoners turned up either dead or injured while in
Prosper's jail. Sentences were extraordinarily stiff."

"They were already under investigation?"

"Even before you were hired to be the public defender,"
Jim replied. "We had a man down there working undercover.
Before he could obtain incontrovertible evidence against any
of the suspects, he disappeared without a trace."

He opened a file folder and handed her a photograph. "I
think you'll recognize him."

"Bama! Oh, my God!"

Pepperdyne glanced at John. John nodded. Her surprise
was genuine.

"The night I saw them kill Michael Li, I discovered his
body," she said. "He'd been missing for about a week."

"He's still missing as far as we're concerned. We've
searched the area but can't find a trace of the grave you
mentioned in your phone calls. Do you think you could find
it again?"

"I doubt it. It's been over a year. It was dark that night. I
was lost, disoriented, terrified. I literally stumbled across his
body and then ran for my life. Even if I could take you to
the exact spot, the elements would have eroded any physical
evidence."

"We might be able to turn up something."

She pressed her lips with her fingers in an attempt to hide their trembling. "I can't believe that Bama was an FBI agent."

"Agent Robert McCoy. He must've blown his cover and paid for it with his life."

"Not necessarily. The Brotherhood might have been doing some spring cleaning and decided that the steps of the courthouse needed to be swept. That would have been ample motivation for them to kill him."

She stood up and walked to the window. Her arms were folded over her middle, her shoulders hunched forward self-protectively. John thought she looked very vulnerable and afraid.

Her voice was barely above a whisper. "You can't imagine what they're capable of."

"We have a pretty good idea," Pepperdyne said. "Remember the managing editor of your husband's newspaper?"

"I only met the gentleman once. He died suddenly while Matt and I were engaged."

"We don't believe he died of 'natural causes' like the death certificate said. He had gone on record as disagreeing with your husband's politics. We're exhuming his body for a forensic investigation." Pepperdyne looked at her grimly. "No, ma'am. We haven't underestimated this bunch.

"I'm afraid your own office has been infiltrated. An Agent Braddock—"

"Is in jail with the rest of them. That's taken care of."

"Is it? How do you know it stops with Braddock? How many members of the Brotherhood are there? Do you know?" she asked, raising her voice in agitation. "If I testify against them, they'll have me killed. They'll find a way."

"You'll be under our protection." Pepperdyne had gestured toward John, and she gave him a glance that clearly dismissed his adequacy.

"You can't protect me. No matter what measures you take, they won't be enough."

"Your testimony is vital to our case, Mrs. Burnwood."

"Who else is testifying against them?" When Pepperdyne couldn't produce the name of another witness, she laughed scornfully. "I'm it, right? And you think you'll win a conviction on my testimony alone? Their defense attorney will rip me to shreds. He'll say I invented this outlandish tale to get even with my enemies in Prosper."

"What about Matt Burnwood? Is he an enemy, too?"

John was glad that Jim had asked. According to the report, she had tried to brain the guy with a crystal vase. John was curious to know why.

"Are you willing to testify against him, Mrs. Burnwood?"

"I'm willing, all right. The problem is that I didn't actually see Matt at the site of Michael Li's execution. Nor my father-in-law. But they were there. I know it."

"We know it, too." Pepperdyne opened another file and referred to the documents inside. "The Brotherhood wouldn't have carried out a ritual killing without Gibbons Burnwood there because he's its founder and high priest."

She sucked in a quick little breath, then said gruffly, "I should have realized."

"How much do you know about your father-in-law's past?"

She enumerated a few facts, then said, "That's not much, is it?"

Pepperdyne began to summarize from the thick dossier he had on Gibb Burnwood. "His father was a Marine during World War II, serving in the South Pacific. He and a handful of other men volunteered for a special detail. The others were killed during the first week, but he survived for eight months on a Japanese-occupied flyspeck of an island, living off raw fish he caught with his hands. He managed to take out fifty of the enemy without being caught. When the Marines recaptured the island, he was shipped home and hailed as a hero.

"It pissed him off that the war ended before he could return to it. One day in October 1947, he meticulously cleaned his rifle, then put the barrel in his mouth and pulled the trigger with his big toe.

"Despite the suicide, young Gibb idolized his father and wanted to follow in his footsteps. He joined the Marines, and saw some action in Korea, but that war was over too soon to suit him. By the time Vietnam came around, he was too old to serve. He had missed all the good wars, so he started waging his own, coaching Matt every step of the way.

"Like his father, Gibb was a member of the Klan, but in the early sixties he had a falling out with them. Apparently their methods were too tame for Gibb Burnwood. He decided to form his own group, a closed group limited to members so carefully handpicked that he wouldn't have to answer to anybody. We figure he organized the Brotherhood sometime around the midsixties. Naturally, he's grooming Matt to take over for him when he dies.

"We've been on to him for about thirty months, but we have no concrete evidence. It's all circumstantial. You're our best shot at getting this guy, Mrs. Burnwood. If he topples, the others will fall like dominoes."

During Pepperdyne's long recitation, Kendall had listened without uttering a sound. When she laid aside the file on Burnwood, she said, "You still can't prove that he and Matt participated in Michael Li's execution. They've had a year to destroy any physical evidence. A good defense attorney—and Matt and Gibb will hire the best—will say my testimony is nothing but revenge for Matt's having an affair with one of my clients."

"He was having an affair with one of your clients?"

"Yes."

Pepperdyne winced, scratched his head, and looked to John for consultation.

"I'm afraid she's right, Jim," he said. "If that comes out in court, it'll make her look like a woman scorned and could weaken her testimony."

"Jeez."

"It doesn't matter, Mr. Pepperdyne," she said in an angry outburst. "This whole discussion is pointless. I'll be dead before they ever go to trial. The Brotherhood couldn't have endured for thirty years without absolute loyalty from its members and their families. Do you think they're going to let me survive?

"I saw them castrate and crucify a wonderful young man simply because he was Asian and dared to love one of their daughters. To them, my crime is a thousand times worse than that. Even if I refused to testify, they would kill me for betraying them. They would murder me without remorse and feel that they were justified, because what is really frightening about all this is that they *believe* they're right, that God is on *their* side. They've been anointed. Everything they do, they do in his name. They sang hymns while Michael Li bled to death. In their regard, I'm a heretic. Killing me would be a holy mission.

"And suppose I live long enough to testify, but they're acquitted? Suppose that the evidence you present, coupled with the weakened testimony of a scorned wife, isn't enough to convict, and they walk? If Matt didn't have me assassinated, he would accuse me of desertion and try and get custody of Kevin."

Pepperdyne harrumphed uncomfortably. "Perhaps you should know, Mrs. Burnwood, that he has already obtained a divorce. He claimed physical abuse."

"Because I was defending myself when I struck him?"

Pepperdyne shrugged. "He filed. You didn't respond within the required time, so the court granted the divorce by default."

"Judge Fargo?"

"Exactly."

John watched her as she digested the fact that she was legally free of Matt Burnwood. He could tell she wasn't emotionally upset over the divorce, but her brow was puckered.

Her next question explained her concern. "Does my ex-husband know about Kevin?"

"Not through us," Pepperdyne said. "We didn't know you'd had a baby until we found you. Of course, there's a possibility that word has reached him by another source."

She sank back into her chair, hugged her elbows, and rocked back and forth. "He will stop at nothing to have me killed and turn Kevin over to some secret member of the Brotherhood. No," she said emphatically. "I can't go back. I won't."

Pepperdyne said, "You know as well as I that you have no choice, Mrs. Burnwood. You fled the district where several state and federal crimes were committed. Unlawful flight to avoid the giving of testimony is a federal offense.

"You're scheduled to appear before a magistrate judge in half an hour. He'll issue an order directing that you be detained as a material witness and returned, in custody, to the prosecuting district. You, of course, can retain counsel now if you wish."

"I'm fully aware of the law, Mr. Pepperdyne," she said coolly. "And I'll continue to serve as my own counsel."

"We're willing to drop the charges against you if you'll help us convict them." He gave her an opportunity to speak, but she said nothing. "You came in here thinking you were being arrested for murder. I figured you would be relieved."

She shook her head sadly. "You don't understand. They'll see to it that I'm killed."

"We leave tonight," Pepperdyne said briskly.

John knew that his friend wasn't entirely unsympathetic to her predicament. But Jim was a company man. He toed the company line. He had a job to do, and he would do it.

"Our flight is at three," he said. "You'll be transferred to Columbia, where you'll stay in a safe house until the first trial. I'll be going with you as far as Dallas, then a female marshal and Marshal McGrath will accompany you the rest of the way."

John felt like the rug had been yanked out from under him. He followed Pepperdyne out into the corridor and confronted him. "What did you mean by that?"

"By what?"

"*I'm* escorting her to Columbia? Me?"

Pepperdyne's expression was too innocent to be convincing. "That's the gig, John."

"It's not my gig. Stewart was supposed to be here, not me. He called in sick at the last minute, and I was sent in his place."

"Guess it's just your unlucky draw, then."

"Jim," he said, grabbing his friend by the sleeve and forcing him to stand still and listen. "I didn't know she had a kid."

"That surprised us all, John."

"I can't accept the assignment. It'll . . . it'll drive me crazy. You know that."

"You're scared?"

"Damn right."

"Of an infant?"

It had sounded ludicrous even to his own ears. Nevertheless, it was true. "You know what I went through after that fiasco in New Mexico. It still gives me nightmares."

Pepperdyne could have laughed at his irrational fear. John would always appreciate him for not doing so. Instead, he tried to reason with him.

"John, I've seen you bargain with the meanest bastards God ever created. You've talked terrorists into laying down their weapons even though they believed that surrendering would keep them out of heaven. Such are your powers of persuasion."

"Once, maybe. Not anymore."

"You had one bad day and things went south."

"One bad day? You can reduce what happened to *one* bad day?"

"I didn't mean to minimize it. But no one held you responsible. No one, John. You couldn't have known that the kook was going to carry out his threats."

"I should have known, though, shouldn't I? That's what all my schooling and training was about. That's what the Ph.D. behind my name was for. I was supposed to know how far to push and when to pull back."

"You're the best in the business, John. We still need you, and sooner or later I hope you'll forgive yourself for New Mexico and come back." Pepperdyne laid a hand on his shoulder. "You've got nerves of steel. Now, realistically, how much damage can a teeny-weeny, toothless infant inflict?"

Chapter Twenty-eight

$\mathcal{A}$S THEY BOARDED THE AIRPLANE IN DENVER, John had a prescience of disaster. He was gripped by a powerful premonition that this trip was doomed.

Now, weeks later, as he lay in the bed he had shared with his prisoner, his leg broken, a fresh scar on his head, and recently cured of amnesia, he asked himself what, if anything, he could have done to alter the chain of events.

He couldn't have prevented them from boarding that aircraft. Pepperdyne would have thought him certifiably nuts if he had pulled him aside and told him that this wasn't a good idea, that his gut instinct was urging him to rethink the situation and come up with another plan.

Pepperdyne was to remain in Dallas while John and his partner, Ruthie Fordham, a pleasant, soft-spoken Hispanic woman, were to fly with Mrs. Burnwood and her child on to Raleigh–Durham, then catch a connecting flight to Columbia.

That was the itinerary.

Fate intervened.

Shortly after takeoff from Denver, Kendall's ears began troubling her. Marshal Fordham called her discomfort to the attention of the flight attendant, who assured her that once the plane reached its cruising altitude, the pain would abate. It didn't.

For the duration of the hour-and-forty-minute flight, she was in agony. Sensing his mother's distress, the baby fretted and cried. Seated across the aisle from them, John gripped the arms of his seat and prayed that the kid would stop squalling. But the harder John prayed, the louder the baby wailed.

"Maybe you should order a drink," Pepperdyne suggested when he noticed the beads of perspiration on John's forehead.

"I'm on duty."

"Screw the rules. You're turning green."

"I'm okay." He wasn't, but he focused on one of the rivets in the ceiling of the cabin and tried to block out the baby's crying.

Taxiing to the gate seemed to take almost as long as the flight. When the plane finally stopped, John elbowed aside other passengers in his haste to get off the aircraft. As soon as they came through the jetway, Marshal Fordham hustled Kendall into the nearest ladies' room. Pepperdyne had been left to carry the baby and was looking ill at ease in his new role as nanny. At any other time, John would have laughed at his bachelor friend's awkwardness. Now he couldn't muster a smile or a quip.

"This husband of hers, what's he like?" he asked. He didn't care, he was just talking to ignore the baby in Pepperdyne's arms.

"I haven't yet had the pleasure of meeting him." The baby had stopped crying. Pepperdyne gingerly bounced him up and down. "From what I understand, Matt Burnwood is your basic white supremacist in a classy three-piece suit. He's handsome, articulate, educated, and cultured. But he's also a weapons expert, a gung-ho survivalist, and fanatical as hell. He believes his daddy has God in his hip pocket. Gibb says jump and he asks how high." He paused before adding, "Anyone who crosses them is as good as dead."

John looked at him sharply.

"She's right, John," Pepperdyne said, guessing his friend's thought. "Her ass is dust if they or any of their cronies get close to her."

"So this isn't just a baby-sitting job."

"Far from it. The Burnwoods might be behind bars, but they've got long tentacles. Some—maybe even most—we might not know about yet."

"Jesus."

"You can't let her out of your sight. Suspect everybody."

A few minutes later the women rejoined them. Kendall took the baby from Pepperdyne. Marshal Fordham broke the news that changed the course of events. "Mrs. Burnwood cannot get on another airplane until her ears have been checked by a doctor."

"I've recently had problems with allergies," Kendall explained. "An infection must have settled in my ears. The pressure in the cabin caused excruciating pain."

Pepperdyne dumped it on John: "It's your call."

McGrath turned to her, the first time they looked each other straight in the eye. He couldn't say why he had avoided looking at her closely before. Maybe for fear of what he might see and how it would affect him.

Lisa had split. While he was away on assignment, she had moved out, taking with her all her belongings and a number of his. She left no note, no phone number, no forwarding address. Nothing. Zip. He hadn't cared, except he wished he could let her know just how little she was missed. Since her departure, he had been enjoying his solitude. He had sworn off women for a while.

But there was something about this one . . .

She had looked directly at him, without flinching. That's when he first suspected that she was an accomplished liar. Her gaze was too steady to be entirely honest. Candor to that extent could only be achieved with many hours of practice.

He guessed that this alleged earache was a ruse to delay their trip. She might even try to escape, to elude them in the swarm of travelers at the Dallas–Fort Worth airport.

However, on the outside chance that her discomfort was genuine, he had to take her to a medical facility and schedule them on a later flight.

Outside the terminal, Pepperdyne abandoned him. As he said goodbye, he slapped John on the back. "Have fun, pal."

"Fuck you," John muttered. His friend merely laughed and hailed the next taxi in line.

John was then crammed into a taxi with a non–English-speaking driver, two women, and a crying baby. Relying on a few key words and hand gestures, he communicated to the confused driver that they needed to be taken to the nearest emergency hospital.

When they arrived, Marshal Fordham stayed in the waiting lounge with the baby. John accompanied Kendall into the examination room. A nurse took her blood pressure and temperature, asked a few pertinent questions, then left them alone.

She sat on the padded examination table, her feet dangling over the side. John shoved his hands into his pants pockets and, keeping his back to her, studied a color diagram of the human circulatory system that was taped to the wall.

"Are you afraid I'll bolt?"

He came around. "Sorry?"

"Did you come in here with me because you think I might escape through the back door?" He said nothing, but he didn't have to. She laughed softly. "Do you think I would abandon my baby?"

"I don't know. Would you?"

Her pleasant expression turned wooden. "No," she said curtly.

"It's my job to protect you, Mrs. Burnwood."

"And then to deliver me to the authorities in South Carolina."

"That's right."

"Where I'll probably be killed. Don't you see the irony in that? You'll guard my life while returning me to the place where I'll be in the greatest danger?"

Actually, he could see the irony in that. But, hell, he was only doing his job. He wasn't paid to question the pros and cons of it. "While you're in my custody, I can't let you out of my sight," he said stiffly.

When the doctor came in, he looked at John curiously. "You Mr. Burnwood?" he asked, referring to the form Kendall had filled out upon being admitted.

He showed the doctor his ID.

"U.S. marshal? Really? Is she your prisoner? What'd she do?"

"She got an earache on an airplane," John said with a distinct edge in his voice. "Are you going to examine her or what?"

The doctor listened to her chest, fingered the glands in her throat, and remarked that they were slightly swollen, then checked her ears, after which he confirmed that she had a nasty infection behind both eardrums.

"Can she fly?" John asked.

"Out of the question. Unless you want to risk having her eardrums burst."

He waited in the hall while a nurse administered an injection of antibiotics. Kendall emerged and, as they walked down the corridor to the waiting area, she surprised him by saying, "You thought I was lying, didn't you?"

"It crossed my mind."

"I wouldn't waste a lie on something that could be so easily disproved."

"Meaning that you'd save lying for when you were likely to get away with it."

She stopped and turned to him. "Exactly, Mr. McGrath."

* * *

"It shouldn't be too bad."

"That's easy for you to say." John was in a foul mood and found Pepperdyne's banalities irritating. "You don't have to make the thousand-mile road trip."

After securing a motel room for the two women and the baby, he had gone to report directly to Pepperdyne, who was coordinating Mrs. Burnwood's transfer with the U.S. Marshal's office in Columbia.

"There's no help for it, John," Pepperdyne said patiently. "According to the doctor, she shouldn't fly for at least a month. We can't wait that long. This trip will only take three days' travel, two nights on the road."

"I could make it in two days, easy."

"Alone. Not with passengers. Especially an infant. You'll cover approximately three hundred miles a day. It won't be a picnic, but it won't last forever."

Ignoring John's pained expression, Pepperdyne handed him an itinerary and a road map. "You'll leave in the morning and spend the first night in Monroe, Louisiana. Second night in Birmingham. Next day, you'll go on to Columbia."

Would he live to see it? he wondered. "At least Ruthie Fordham is along," he said, trying to look on the bright side, if there was one. "She seems to get along well with both of them."

"She'll stay with Mrs. Burnwood and the baby. We've arranged for you to have the connecting room at each of the motels."

John glanced over the itinerary. "I dread every mile of it. Do you think we can trust her not to try something crazy?"

"Like escape, you mean?"

"She's scared, Jim."

Pepperdyne grinned. "Couldn't help it, could you? You've analyzed her in spite of yourself."

"I didn't have to analyze her. A blind fool could see that she's terrified."

"She won't go anywhere without her baby. It would be awfully difficult for her to overpower you and Ms. Fordham, and make a run for it while toting a child."

"You're probably right, but the lady has moxie. And there's something else you should know. She's a liar."

"A liar?" Pepperdyne repeated with a laugh. "What do you mean?"

"I mean," John said drolly, "that she tells stories."

"You don't believe she's making up this—"

"No. She's telling the truth about the Brotherhood. The evidence you've got so far bears that out. But Mrs. Burnwood holds her cards very close to her chest. There's something she's holding back. She has a devious streak."

"She's a lawyer."

Pepperdyne's offhand comment prompted a snicker from an agent who was manning a computer printer across the room. Pepperdyne turned to him. "Got anything yet?"

"Nope."

Pepperdyne said to John, "We're running a routine background check on her, although she seems to be on the up and up. According to her win/loss record, she was a shrewd public defender and gave the good-ol'-boy legal system in Prosper a run for its money. Knowing what we do now about the people in key positions there, she'd have to be tough to have survived as long as she did."

"So what's the problem?" John asked, nodding toward the computer, which he knew was linked to numerous national and international information networks.

"Apparently there's a bug in our system. The data we received made no sense. He's trying to straighten it out."

"Let me know when you get something."

Jim chuckled. "Dr. McGrath is curious to see what makes her tick, huh?"

"It's nothing for you to get a hard-on about, Jim," John said as he turned to leave. "Old habits are hard to break, that's all."

"You can have your job back whenever you want it. I'd love for you to work out of my division."

Pepperdyne was serious, and John was grateful for his former colleague's vote of confidence, but his answer was still no. "Too much pressure. My present occupation is less stressful."

Then he glanced at the road map marking their route from Texas to South Carolina and added grimly, "Up till now."

John's recollections brought him to the morning of the accident. When they left Birmingham, he was grumpy and eager to relinquish Mrs. Burnwood and her baby. He estimated that they would reach the South Carolina capital around sundown. As soon as they had eaten breakfast in the motel coffeeshop, he hustled them through a light rain to the car.

The farther east they drove, the heavier the rainfall became. By noon his nerves were shot. His shoulders ached from keeping such a tight grip on the wheel. Silently he cursed the trailer trucks that passed at speeds he considered unsafe even on an interstate highway. Sure enough, one of the teamsters made an error in judgment.

John immediately noticed when traffic began slowing down in all lanes. Eventually it was reduced to a crawl. He turned up the volume on the police radio, with which the car was equipped, and listened with mounting impatience as officers discussed the major accident that was causing the bottleneck.

The wreck involving several vehicles was another consequence of a stalled weather system that continued to dump rain on the whole southeastern region of the country, causing local flooding and other hazards.

According to John's rough calculations, the accident was miles ahead of them. Other traffic was being halted so that emergency vehicles could reach the scene. While he was sympathetic toward the people involved, he was irritated by the delay.

Ruthie Fordham had been sharing the front seat with him. He handed her the map and asked her if she saw an alternate route they could take. There was one, she told him, but it would take them out of their way. He decided that driving a few extra miles was preferable to sitting still. He took the next exit.

That's how they came to be on that rural road where fate had placed a felled tree. His decision to divert from the prearranged route had cost Ruthie Fordham her life. They hadn't been in a cellular area, so he couldn't call the office in Columbia on the car phone. The police radio was jammed with calls relating to the accident, so he had decided not to add to the confusion on those channels.

Once they left the interstate, he intended to stop and use a pay phone. But there were no pay phones on the country roads. Consequently, no one knew exactly where he was.

How long had they waited for them in Columbia before putting out a bulletin? Surely by now Jim's men had tracked them as far as that hospital in Stephensville. He assumed that Ruthie Fordham was dead. Did she have a family? John wondered. Because of his poor judgment, his colleague had died needlessly. Chalk up another one to John McGrath.

Of course the doctor would have apprised Jim of his injuries, but that was all he would know.

Damn, Kendall Burnwood was clever. Thinking back on it, John could see now that she hadn't left a single clue. There would be no trail to follow. To anyone investigating their disappearance, it would seem that he, Kendall, and the baby had vanished into thin air.

He realized now that she was no longer singing a lullaby. He heard the water pipes knocking inside the walls and knew that she had turned on the faucet in the shower. He had a few more minutes to think before she discovered that he was awake.

It had been a stroke of genius for her to claim him as her husband. That had given her authority to speak for him while he was incapacitated. But once she had told that lie, she was trapped into perpetuating it. That, too, had been handled cleverly.

All her answers to his questions had been based on truth. So had her accounts of their wedding day, their wedding night, his affair. Everything had been factual. Except that she had been recounting her married life with Matt Burnwood. By sticking to the truth, rather than inventing another story, she couldn't be tripped up as easily. Smart. She had also used his own name, just in case she made a slip. She was very good.

So good that John began to wonder if last night had been just another lie.

Chapter Twenty-nine

ANOTHER NIGHTMARE HAD AWAKENED HIM LAST night. It hadn't been as severe as previous ones, but it had disturbed him enough to jolt him awake. Restless and hot, he had worked himself free of the damp, clinging sheet and had sat up.

Kendall's side of the bed had been vacant, but that hadn't alarmed him. She frequently got up during the night to check on the baby. She possessed that instinctual, maternal sensory system that immediately alerted her to the child's needs. Sometimes she even anticipated them, which never failed to amaze him.

Propping the crutches under his arms, he hobbled across the hall to the second bedroom. The crib was empty. So was the room. He experienced an unmanly pang of anxiety and regret. Had she sneaked out? She had been noticeably quiet and subdued all day. Had she been planning another departure?

He wheeled around and did what passed for running on crutches until he reached the living room, where he came to a halt so abruptly that he nearly sent himself sprawling.

The room was dark except for the moonlight streaming through the sheer curtains on the open windows. They billowed into the room, filled like sails with a cool breeze, which was probably what Kendall had been seeking.

She was sitting in the rocking chair, holding Kevin in her arms. The shoulder strap of her nightgown had been lowered so she could nurse him. His tiny mouth was fastened to her nipple. Every few seconds he made suckling motions, his plump cheeks working like a bellows, then his mouth would relax again.

Both were asleep.

Now, in retrospect, John conceded that his ogling had been totally inappropriate, a gross invasion of her privacy, but damned if he could force himself to silently retreat and return to the bedroom. He had been transfixed by lust.

Even the wretched haircut didn't detract from the beautiful picture she made, her head resting against the back of the chair. Illuminated by moonlight was the intriguing arch of her throat and the shallow depression at the base of her neck. The cleavage between her breasts was shadowed and mysterious. He wanted to explore that entrancing valley. He imagined nuzzling her there, and the fantasy caused a surge of sexual desire so strong he involuntarily groaned.

He instantly muted it, afraid that he might awaken her. He was too old to be sneaking peeks at a woman's bared breast. Getting secretly turned on from a room's width away was silly, immature, and as one-sided as masturbating.

Disgusted with himself, he had wanted to turn away, but hadn't been able to. Focusing on her lips, those full, pouty lips that had driven him to distraction, he'd had an intense desire to devour them. He had wanted to sample the lushness of her breasts, explore the exotic terrain of her lap, and collect her taste on his tongue. He had wanted—

Suddenly a shrill whistle had pierced the silence.

She was startled awake.

He nearly jumped out of his skin; one of his crutches clattered to the floor.

For several seconds they remained frozen in that tableau. He was aroused, and embarrassed and angry that she had caught him.

"What the hell is that?"

"The teakettle," she answered breathlessly. Hastily she replaced the shoulder strap of her nightgown. The baby winced and made a fretful sound as she removed him from her breast and raised him to her shoulder. "I put the kettle on before I sat down to feed Kevin. What are you doing up?"

"It's too damn hot to sleep."

"I noticed that you were restless tonight. Would you like some tea?" The kettle was still whistling furiously. "Herbal tea. No caffeine."

"No thanks."

She came toward him. "Then hold Kevin for me while I brew myself a cup."

As she moved past, she thrust the kid at him, then sashayed down the hallway and disappeared into the kitchen. For several moments he did nothing. He forced his mind into neutral, refusing to let it register any sensations. Then, gradually, he allowed a few sensory impulses to seep through the dual barriers of aversion and terror.

Kevin was a plump baby. Consequently, it came as a surprise that he was incredibly light. Also amazing was the softness of his skin. Or maybe it had just seemed soft in contrast to his hairy chest.

He had finally worked up enough nerve to look down at the child. Disconcertingly, the baby's eyes were focused on him. He held his breath. The kid was sure to start squalling when he failed to recognize the person holding him.

Instead, Kevin's pink mouth stretched open in a wide yawn, exposing his toothless gums and small tongue. Then he released three little farts, a trio of tiny expulsions that could be felt through his diaper.

In spite of himself, he chuckled.

"I had a hunch the two of you would get along well if you ever let down your guard."

He hadn't noticed Kendall's return until she spoke. He looked up and saw her watching him over a steaming cup of tea that smelled like oranges.

"He's okay, I guess."

"He's wonderful and you know it. He likes you."

"How do you know?"

"He's blowing bubbles. Whenever he's happy, he blows bubbles."

The baby was in fact sputtering drool all over his chin and happily waving his arms. He appeared content, but John was still unsure. "You'd better take him now."

She seemed amused but said nothing as she set her cup of tea on the end table, took the baby, and carried him into his bedroom. "He dropped right off to sleep again," she remarked when she came back. "Why can't adults be so lucky?"

"We have too much on our minds."

"Have you got something on your mind?"

He listened for underlying mockery in her tone but heard none. She had posed the question seriously, so he answered in kind. "Yes, I've got something on my mind. In fact, it stays on my mind."

He didn't need to elaborate. Her eyes grew misty and her voice husky. "It's never far from my mind either."

He didn't think he could survive another rejection, but after she said that, there was no way he could keep from reaching for her. She landed softly against his chest. Her fingers curled through his chest hair as she tilted her face up to his. He let go of his crutch. As it fell, he dug his fingers into her cropped hair and held her head tightly.

Her lips were waiting and pliant. Because of the tea, the inside of her mouth was hot. He dipped his tongue into it, again and again, kissing her with such total possession that when he finally stopped, she rested her cheek against his chest.

"Slower, John. I can hardly breathe."

"Fine," he said in a growling voice. "Breathing's optional."

Laughing softly, she ran her hands across his shoulders. "I can't believe I'm touching you. I've wanted to so badly, so many times."

"Touch your fill."

The most he had hoped for was one long, uninterrupted kiss to slake his hunger. One taste of her to get him through the night. So her responses, verbal and physical, had surpassed his expectations. The reality was more mind-blowing than any fantasies he had entertained. She felt so damn good—as cool as alabaster on the surface, but raging hot within.

As his mouth continued to sip at hers, her arms went around his neck. He cupped her armpits in his palms, then slid his hands down her rib cage, pressing the sides of her breasts. They made firm impressions against his chest, and the contact inflamed him.

He lowered his head and rubbed his scratchy cheek against the pale slope of her breasts. He kissed them through the soft cloth of her nightgown, then impatiently pulled at it until she was beneath his lips, inside his mouth, against his tongue.

Milky and musky, the taste of her infused and intoxicated him. He held her nipple secure against the roof of his mouth and tugged strongly.

"Oh, God." The catch in her throat and her sigh were the sexiest sounds he could imagine. He kissed her neck. With his teeth he affectionately nipped the back of her neck beneath the jagged hairline.

She continued to turn, moving against the wall until she was facing it, her forehead grinding into the rose-patterned wallpaper. He positioned her arms slightly above her head, flattening her forearms against the wall from elbows to finger-tips.

Taking a handful of her nightgown, he began gathering up the fabric, bunching it into his fist. He pushed his hands into the waistband of her panties and kneaded her buttocks. Then one hand reached around her and cupped her breast, while the other slid down her belly, over her pubic hair, and between her thighs.

She was very wet. The discovery made him dizzy with desire. He fondled her with two fingers, gently working them between the folds of her sex, then into her.

And he knew that as long as he lived, he would never forget the sensation of being sheathed so snugly and intimately.

He tilted his hips forward and nestled his erection in the cleft of her bottom. He feathered her taut nipple, teased it, while his fingers gently moved inside her. Soon she began pushing her hips forward against his hand, until he could keep it entirely still and all the movements came from the eager motion of her hips. Against the rose-patterned wallpaper, her hands closed into small, drumming fists.

She came silently but violently. As soon as the shudders subsided, he withdrew his hand and, turning her to face him, enveloped her in his arms. She rested against him weakly, damply, her breath raspy as she moaned through his chest hair.

After a while, he placed his finger beneath her chin and tilted her head up. "I'd carry you to bed if I could."

She understood. She picked up his crutches and handed them to him, then led him down the hall to the bedroom. He slipped off his underwear and got into bed.

Then suddenly she had hesitated. Even after the incredibly sensual experience they had just shared, she had looked virginal and unsure standing beside the bed.

This morning, he understood why she had hesitated. For the last couple of weeks they had spent nearly every waking hour in each other's company, but essentially they were strangers. He wasn't her husband. He was a first-time lover.

Somewhere deep within himself, he had known that.

But he had ignored that nagging inner voice. He had turned a deaf ear to his affronted conscience. Disregarding the intuition that had told him this was very wrong, he had taken her hand and pulled her down onto the bed beside him.

"Lie down."

"Can you ... with your cast ... ?"

"No problem."

He eased her onto her back. He removed her nightgown and tossed it to the floor, then his hands caressed her breasts and abdomen, which were still flushed from her orgasm.

Watching her face for reaction, John guided her hand to his crotch. For an infinitesimal speck of time, she hesitated. Then she stroked him from root to tip. And again.

Swearing beneath his breath, he parted her thighs and lowered himself between them. He noticed the faint pink cesarean scar running laterally beneath her light pubic hair. Frowning, he traced it with the tip of his finger, as he had that first night in this house. "Are you sure it's okay if we ... ?"

She smiled and laid her hands on his chest. "It's okay."

Because of the cast on his leg, he had to support himself entirely on his arms. His eyes were locked with hers when he entered her with deliberate slowness.

He sank into her until it was impossible to go any deeper. Holding her head between his hands, he kissed her mouth. When at last they pulled apart, he whispered, "You've lied to me, Kendall."

She gave him a quick, startled look.

He began to move, thrusting and withdrawing in perfect rhythm with the undulation of her hips. "I've never been with you this way before." He spoke rapidly, trying to hold on to his slipping control. "I couldn't have forgotten this."

She hugged him tighter, shifted beneath him. "Just don't stop."

"I would remember you. I would remember this. Who the hell are you?" he grated through clenched teeth.

Her back arched. "Please, don't stop."

He couldn't have anyway. They rocked each other toward a tumultuous orgasm, their bodies communing in a way he knew he had never experienced before.

When he rolled off her, she reversed their positions and flung herself across his chest. "Hold me," she whispered. "Tightly."

He had done so gladly. For weeks he had fantasized touching what he could see.

Replete, her voice drowsy, she had murmured, "John, why wasn't I shy with you?"

"You weren't supposed to be shy with me. I'm your husband."

She had said nothing in response because she had fallen asleep. He wondered now if she realized she had spoken aloud her thoughts. She had given vent to her sensuality with a man she had never been with before, and she had wanted to know why.

John wanted to know that himself.

But he couldn't allow himself to dwell on personal considerations. He had to think only of the overwhelming fact that he'd had sex with a material witness placed in his charge. Traumatic amnesia was no excuse. He had known. Dammit, he had *known* that she was lying to him all along.

But he'd slept with her anyway. And it had been bloody great, so electrically charged that it had jump-started his memory. He now remembered that he was a federal officer. Federal officers weren't supposed to have carnal knowledge of the women in their custody. Everybody from Uncle Sam on down frowned on that.

So what the hell was he going to do?

None of his training as a psychologist, an FBI agent, or as a U.S. marshal had prepared him for this kind of situation.

He had no identification or credentials to prove who he was. And who was around to prove it to? He didn't even know exactly where they were.

On top of all that, he had a broken leg. How far could he expect to get on a pair of crutches? She wasn't about to let him get his hands on the car key. If he managed to sneak it away from her and take the car, he had no doubt that she would be gone by the time he returned. She certainly had enough motivation to want to disappear again, and she was incredibly resourceful. She would find a way for her and Kevin to vanish.

Where the hell was his revolver? She had said he wouldn't find the hiding place this time, and so far she had been right. While she wasn't around, he had looked everywhere for it.

She was very proud of herself for leaving nothing to chance and always planning ahead. Until now, she'd had a fairly easy time of it because of his confusion. Well, he told himself, Marshal John McGrath may have been helplessly out of his mind and flat on his back the last couple of weeks, but as of now he was back in commission.

He got out of bed and hobbled to the dresser for a fresh pair of underwear. She had his shorts nicely folded in the drawer, separate from his socks. *How wifely*, he thought with a sneer, angrily slamming the drawer.

The sudden noise sounded like a cannon blast in the still house, causing him to grimace. He paused to listen and was relieved when he heard the water in the shower still running. He had a few more minutes to search for his pistol.

She was too smart to have disposed of it. If she didn't intend to use it on him—although that was still a possibility, he thought grimly—she would have kept it for protection. There could be vigilantes on the loose, beating the bushes in search of her. She wouldn't have wasted the weapon.

John looked through her drawers, trying not to upset the neat arrangements of her panties and bras. Finding nothing in the bureau, he returned to the bed and ran his hands between the mattress and box spring, although he didn't expect to find it there since that had been his original, unimaginative hiding place.

He searched the shelf at the top of the closet. He crawled along the floor, looking for loose planks under which she might have stashed his gun. The nightstand drawers were empty.

The water in the shower went off.

John plowed his hands through his hair in frustration and self-incrimination. What was he going to do? He had to make a decision. Quickly. Immediately.

His impression of Kendall Deaton Burnwood had proved correct—she was a skilled liar. She had the gall and intelligence to carry out even the most audacious scheme, even if it meant consummating her bogus marriage to a man who was, in effect, her jailer.

Furthermore, she was a mother, afraid for her child's life as well as her own. To protect her child, she would go to extremes.

But even motherhood didn't justify her kidnapping a federal officer. She had broken more laws than he could think of right now. His duty was to deliver her to the proper authorities. That's what he would do. By whatever means necessary.

He stepped into the hall. The bathroom door was slightly ajar. Trying not to make a sound, he slowly made his way to it and gave it a slight push. It silently swung open.

Kendall was standing at the basin. Her hair, recently towel dried, was radiating from her head in damp spikes. She was wearing only panties. One arm was raised above her head; she was applying dusting powder to her underarm.

She was humming, tunelessly and endearingly off-key.

He didn't allow himself a smile. He didn't allow himself a tender thought.

Jesus, could he go through with this?

It was smart. It was necessary. But it was going to be damn difficult, perhaps the most difficult duty of his career. Of *both* careers.

Although a thousand instincts tried to hold him back, he forced himself forward. He was afraid that she might catch a glimpse of him in the mirror, but she didn't, even when he was within a foot of her. Gradually he eased the crutch from beneath his arm and got a good grip on it. Then with his other hand he grasped her upper arm and spun her around.

Chapter Thirty

"*W*HAT DO YOU MEAN SHE'S VANISHED?" GIBB Burnwood wasn't taking the news well. His voice was as murderous as his glare.

The Burnwoods' attorney remained unruffled. Seated with his spindly legs crossed at the knees and his long, narrow hands folded in his lap, Quincy Lamar was a study of southern elegance and composure.

He looked as though he had never broken a sweat in his life. His suit was impeccably tailored. The French cuffs of his shirt were speared with diamond-studded cuff links. His hair was oiled, his nails buffed.

His effeminate affectations turned Gibb's stomach. He would have had no tolerance for Lamar except that he was reputed to be a crackerjack trial lawyer, the cagiest, most corruptible criminal attorney money could buy. Some of the South's most crooked crooks owed their freedom to Quincy Lamar.

"How did she get away? When?" Gibb asked.

"As I understand it, she's been missing for more than two weeks."

"Two weeks!" Gibb thundered. "And word is just now reaching us? Why weren't we told before?"

"I see no call for you to shout at me, Mr. Burnwood. I've told you everything I know, as soon as I learned it myself."

Lamar's voice was as smooth as sipping whiskey. Like the intoxicant, his mellifluous voice seemed harmless. But it could sneak up on a jury or legal opponent and deliver a sound wallop.

"Mrs. Burnwood was taken into custody in Denver. She was being escorted back to South Carolina to appear as a material witness at your trial."

Matt spoke for the first time. "Too bad I divorced her. Then she couldn't be forced to testify against me."

"I'm sure she's not being forced," Lamar countered smoothly. He paused to flick an imaginary piece of lint off his sleeve. "Somewhere along the way Mrs. Burnwood eluded them and—"

"Them? She overpowered and escaped from two U.S. marshals?"

Lamar glanced at Matt. "Do you wish me to continue? Or will you persist in interrupting?"

"I'm sorry," Matt said tightly.

The lawyer took his time before resuming. He shot Gibb a disparaging look that conveyed that he should have taught his son better manners. Gibb could easily have throttled the attorney, but he was as anxious as Matt to hear how Kendall had disappeared.

"One of the marshals was a woman," Lamar explained. He told them about Kendall's ear infection, which had necessitated taking the trip by car and spending several nights on the road.

He added an afterthought: "I suppose a female marshal was required to assure Mrs. Burnwood's protection and privacy while she attended to the baby."

Gibb and Matt looked at each other, then both shot from

their chairs simultaneously. Gibb took pleasure in the lawyer's look of alarm when he grabbed him by his lavender necktie and hauled him out of his chair. "What did you say?"

The jail guard barged in, already reaching for the pistol in his hip holster. "Let him go!" he shouted at Gibb.

Gibb released Lamar, whose bony butt landed hard on the seat of the wooden chair. He stretched his neck as though to make certain that his head was still attached.

"Everything is fine," he told the guard as he patted his hair back into place. "My client just became a little overwrought. It won't happen again."

The guard waited to make certain that the lawyer had the situation under control, then he backed out of the room and closed the door.

"Kendall has a baby?"

"Boy or girl? How old?"

Ignoring their questions, Lamar regarded Gibb with the unblinking menace of a reptile. "If you ever lay a hand on me again, I'll walk out of here, and you'll fry along with your fascist redneck friends. Do we have an understanding, Mr. Burnwood?"

His sibilant voice would have raised goosebumps on an ordinary man, but Gibb had always considered himself many notches above ordinary. He leaned across the table so far that his face came within inches of the lawyer's narrow nose.

"Don't threaten me, you cocksucking queer. I'm not impressed with your fancy suits and your slick hair and your silk neckties. And I hate this damn thing." He yanked the fresh carnation from Lamar's lapel and crushed it in his fist.

"I'd just as soon squash you as look at you. And right now you'd better tell me what I want to know about the baby my daughter-in-law has with her, or I'll tear your throat out with my bare hands and use it for fish bait. Do *we* have an understanding?"

Quincy Lamar, famous for reducing hostile witnesses to

quivering blobs of jelly, was speechless. His eyes darted toward Matt, whose stony stare only underscored his father's threat. The lawyer's prominent Adam's apple slid up and down to accommodate a dry swallow.

Finally, he continued his story. "Mrs. Burnwood has a baby boy." From his attaché case he removed a copy of the child's birth certificate and passed it to them. "I presume the baby is—"

"Mine," Matt said unequivocally after checking the date of birth. "He's mine!"

Gibb flung his arms around Matt and thumped him on the back. "I'm so proud for you, son. Lord have mercy, I finally have a grandson!" Their joyous celebration was short-lived, however. Gibb struck the table with his fist. "That *bitch*."

Matt turned to Lamar. "Listen here, I want my son. Do whatever's necessary for me to get him and keep him. I obtained a divorce not knowing she was pregnant. On top of trying to kill me, and deserting me, she has concealed the fact that I have a son. So it shouldn't be too difficult for me to get awarded exclusive custody."

Lamar cast a nervous glance at Gibb. "Be reasonable, Mr. Burnwood. You've been indicted on several felony charges. Shouldn't we concentrate on having you acquitted of these crimes before we undertake any other litigious action?"

"They can't prove that Dad and I were involved with killing that Li boy. Or with this newly trumped-up charge involving that Bama character."

" 'That Bama character' happened to be an FBI agent," the lawyer solemnly reminded him.

"Whatever he was, we had nothing to do with shooting him in the head and burying him somewhere out there in the woods. No one has produced a body, so they're not even sure he's dead. The bum wandered out of town, same as he wandered in."

"What of Michael Li's disappearance from the jail?"

"Obviously he escaped. His body hasn't materialized either,

and it won't. He's not about to resurface—if he did, he'd have to face rape charges. So he's lying low, while Dad and I are being accused of two murders that never took place."

"Then how do you account for the story Mrs. Burnwood has told the authorities?" Lamar asked.

"She got lost in the woods, became hysterical, and hallucinated. At the same time, she seized an opportunity to get vengeance on me for my affair with Lottie Lynam."

Gibb clenched his jaw. It was a conditioned reflex every time Matt mentioned Lottie's name. Almost to the day that Matt had resumed his affair with her, Gibb had known about it. He found it incomprehensible that his son, who was so obedient and tractable in every other area of his life, had such a weakness for that red-haired tramp.

Gibb hadn't liked it, but, to keep peace in the family, he had turned a blind eye to the affair. Lottie was married, after all. Nothing too disastrous could come of the affair—such as an accidental baby. Years ago he had seen to it that there would be no unwanted pregnancy.

When Gibb had gotten wind of sixteen-year-old Matt's secret infatuation with Lottie, he had paid a call on her father. He had agreed with Gibb that it was up to them to see that those crazy kids didn't get into trouble. For seventy-five dollars, the old man had promised to slip a pill into Lottie's milk. It was a safe narcotic, Gibb had assured him; it had come straight from the doctor himself.

The pill had produced Lottie's cramps, which the same doctor diagnosed as appendicitis. The doctor's bribe had cost Gibb another two hundred dollars, plus the cost of the operation to remove Lottie's perfectly healthy appendix—and ligate her fallopian tubes. For under a thousand dollars, Gibb had guaranteed that Lottie wouldn't produce a bastard Burnwood. To this day, he believed it was the best money he'd ever spent.

As long as the affair didn't interfere with Matt's marrying and producing a legitimate son and heir, Gibb had figured there was no real harm in his seeing Lottie when her drunkard husband was out of town.

But he did not want their affair to become public knowledge. Matt Burnwood, heir apparent to the leadership of the Brotherhood, had no business carrying a torch for a white-trash slut. It would be bad for their image. If Matt was allowed leeway with the strict code of the Brotherhood, others would begin asking for exceptions to the rules. Consanguinity with lowlifes or other races was the primary, number-one taboo.

That's why Gibb hated knowing that his son's affair would be exposed during the trial. Keeping it under wraps was out of the question. Quincy Lamar had even suggested that Matt use Lottie as an alibi for the night Michael Li mysteriously disappeared from the county jail, never to be seen or heard from again.

If Mrs. Lynam swore under oath that Matt was with her that night, it might help sway a teetering jury. Lamar advised Matt to confess to the lesser of the two crimes. Adultery was a sin, but it wasn't punishable by death. Not in America, anyway.

Matt and Gibb had discussed this option but hadn't yet reached a decision. Gibb wanted to hold out for as long as possible before formally linking Matt to the woman. Their affair wasn't his son's greatest achievement, but if it became public, that's what people would remember most about him.

The flip side to that argument was that the sum total of their defense consisted of denials. Gibb knew that it would be foolish not to exploit every avenue of defense, no matter how unsavory. Learning that he had a grandson added a new dimension to the situation. Priorities had shifted. The focus had changed. Perhaps the hard line he had taken against using Lottie Lynam should be reevaluated.

Although his thoughts had been sidetracked, Gibb had been following the argument between Matt and their attorney. Their verbal volleys were getting them nowhere. Finally, Gibb spoke up, his voice overriding theirs.

"What my son is telling you, Mr. Lamar, is that we want the baby returned to us. He's rightfully ours. And we want him."

"Precisely," Matt agreed.

Lamar held up both hands, palms forward, as though to ward off an attack. "I tell you this for your own good, gentlemen. You're clinging to an unrealistic hope."

The lawyer's words did nothing to weaken Matt's resolve. "I'll do whatever it takes to get my son away from his mother. Kendall is wholly unfit to rear a Burnwood. She won't make a good mother, because she wasn't even a good wife.

"I gave her total freedom to pursue her career, which she jeopardized by making enemies of her colleagues. I was generous with money. I treated her kindly and never shunned my responsibilities as a husband. Ask anyone. You'll hear that we had a perfect marriage.

"This is how she repays me. By telling vicious lies about me and my father. She attacked me physically in our home and left me for dead. She abandoned me. And now, more than a year later, I learn that I have a son. He's three months old and I didn't even know that he existed! What a monster she is, to withhold my son from me."

Quincy Lamar, having listened patiently to his client, calmly latched his attaché and rose to his feet. "That's an excellent speech, Mr. Burnwood. Potent content. Persuasive delivery. Very passionate. You've convinced me not only that you're innocent of the crimes of which you've been accused, but that you're also a victim of Mrs. Burnwood's unspeakable treachery. See that you do that well under cross-examination."

He tapped on the door to signal the conclusion of the meeting. While waiting for the guard to unlock the door, he added, "As long as Mrs. Burnwood is unavailable for comment, no one can dispute your heartrending story. When she's found—and you can bet that the feds are turning over every rock in Dixie looking for her—a few adjustments might be required."

After he left, Gibb and Matt had only a few moments alone before being escorted to their respective jail cells.

"Dad, I have a son! A boy."

Gibb grasped Matt's shoulders. "It's wonderful news, son. I'm thrilled. But we'll have to celebrate later. Unfortunately, we don't have time for it now. I don't trust that pansy-assed lawyer as far as I can throw him."

"I don't like him either. Do you want to fire him and get someone else?"

Gibb shook his head. "All lawyers are incompetent in one way or another. They can be devious and disloyal, even if they're a member of your own family," he added dryly. "We should never have relied on him, or anyone else, to do our thinking and acting for us."

Matt looked puzzled. "What are you leading to, Dad?"

"It's time we took matters into our own hands."

Lottie read the letter a second time. Then a third. The message was brash, bold, and to the point.

She crumpled the single sheet of paper and tossed it to the floor. Swearing, she moved to the window and looked out over her untended yard. As plain as a lettered sign, it said, *Trash lives here.* Charlie had been not only a sorry husband but a sorry provider. She had never been able to afford to spruce up the place and make it pretty.

Well, what had she expected? That matrimony would work a miracle in her life?

She had come from trash and would always be trash. She knew it. So did Charlie. And so did Matt. In fact, that's what he had called her the first time he ever spoke to her.

They were in the fourth grade when he had waylaid her one afternoon on her walk home from school. He dropped from the low branches of a tree, scaring her half to death and blocking her path.

"You think you're hot snot, don't you, red?" he challenged.

"Well, you're not. My daddy says your folks are poor white trash and that I should have nothing to do with the likes of you."

"And I say you and your daddy are chicken shit. I'll be more than happy to have nothing to do with you, Matt Burnwood. Now get out of my way."

She had tried to go around him, but he executed a deft sidestep and grabbed her by the shoulders. "What's your hurry?" He tried to kiss her. She kneed him in the groin and ran away.

It was another few years before he worked up his courage to try again to kiss her. That time, she allowed it. From that day forward they were ever aware of each other, just as they were aware that anything meaningful between them was impossible. Even as children they had understood the nuances that distinguished their castes. They came from opposite sides of the tracks, figuratively and literally. The breach could not be crossed.

Nevertheless, they had flirted, waving red flags of allure at their burgeoning sexuality, which went unappeased until one sweltering summer afternoon when they met at a stream in the hills. Stripping to their underwear, they frolicked in the water. Matt suggested a contest to see who could stay beneath the surface the longest.

He won, of course. As his prize, he demanded that she take off her brassiere and let him see her breasts. Behind his arrogance, she had detected a vulnerability she found very sweet.

Off came the brassiere.

He looked.

Then looking advanced to touching. His touch had been tentative and gentle. That's why she had granted him liberties that she withheld from other boys. Soon she was touching him, too.

That first time had been awkward and uncomfortable. Matt

had been clumsy and anxious; she, eager to please. But she remembered the feverish heat of their skin, the rush of their mingling breath, the thudding of their hearts, and their sighs of joyous discovery. Their lust had been honest and unabashed, brimming, bursting. And, in many ways, innocent.

Now, as Lottie leaned her head against the grimy windowpane, tears rolled down her cheeks. She had loved Matt Burnwood to distraction then. As now. And for always.

That's why she let him use her. She recognized and responded to the desperation behind his desire for her. She filled a need in him, and she suspected it wasn't entirely sexual.

She was Matthew Burnwood's private rebellion for being Matthew Burnwood. He had achieved all the goals his father had set for him. He lived up to the expectations other people imposed on him. He always performed as he was expected to. His affair with her was the one failing he allowed himself.

That it must be kept secret was part of its attraction for him. She was the antithesis of the kind of woman he was expected to have. If she had been even moderately acceptable in the social circles to which the Burnwoods belonged, Matt probably would have lost interest in her years ago. It was because she was so blatantly unsuitable that he had continued to come to her all these years.

Yet, she knew that in his own way Matt loved her. He would never love anyone as much as he loved his father. No one would ever receive from him the blind loyalty and devotion he reserved for Gibb.

For that reason, Lottie sympathized with Kendall Deaton, who had married Matt with such misplaced optimism. When it came to her husband's affections, Kendall had resented running a distant second to her father-in-law and apparently had made her feelings known. Even before divorcing her, Matt had often complained that Kendall was too outspoken for her own good.

So what did that make Lottie? A doormat? An obedient, uncomplaining, obliging mistress?

The answer was evident in the letter she had received from Matt today. She bent down, picked it up off the floor, and spread it open on the table, smoothing out the creases she'd made when she balled it up.

Matt needed her now, more desperately than ever before, and more than he would ever need her again.

She gazed around the room at the tired, faded furnishings, the water-stained ceiling, the scuffed hardwood floor that creaked beneath each step.

This is as good as my life is ever going to get, she thought sadly.

When Kendall left town, Lottie's murder trial had been postponed until new counsel could be arranged. A lawyer had been appointed; his first course of action had been to request an extension to allow him time to review the case and prepare his strategy. The court had granted his request. In view of the high-profile cases now pending, it might be months before another trial date was scheduled.

But Lottie wanted to get it over with as soon as possible. Regardless of the outcome of the trial, until she was judged for killing Charlie, her life would remain in a state of limbo. She wasn't in jail, but she certainly wasn't free.

She had no husband, no children, no family who would claim her. She had a house, but it was shelter, not a home. She had no status in the community.

The only happiness she had known in her whole life had been found in Matt Burnwood's arms. Even knowing his weaknesses and his prejudice, she loved him.

Again she read the letter he had written her from his jail cell. He was asking an enormous favor. If she granted it, she would be gambling with her life.

On the other hand, after taking inventory of her life, it was clear that she had absolutely nothing to lose.

Chapter Thirty-one

"*T*HEY'VE ESCAPED!"

The bearer of this shocking news was a deputy sheriff whose only responsibility was to give directions and be of assistance to anyone who had business in the Prosper County Courthouse.

His genetic pool had more than its share of stagnant genes, particularly in those that involved acuity. He had barely passed the application exam required for the job. But he *had* passed, and he proudly wore the khaki uniform and badge of his office. The stiff shirt collar was far too large for his scrawny neck, which formed a wobbling pedestal for his small, pointed head.

His name was Lee Simon Crook. He was a cousin of Billy Joe and the twins.

Luther Crook had a perfect shot lined up when Lee Simon burst through the door of the pool hall and blurted out the news that had sent him running the two blocks from the courthouse. Cursing because he had missed the shot that would have won back the ten dollars he'd lost earlier, Luther swung around, fists doubled up and ready to fight.

"Lee Simon, you little pissant! I ought to stamp you to mush. I had a perfect—"

"Shut up, Luther," Henry ordered from his barstool. "Wha'd you say about somebody escaping, Lee Simon?"

"They escaped. From the jailhouse."

Luther grabbed his cousin by the sleeve of his uniform and spun him around. "Who escaped, shithead?"

"The B-B-Burnwoods."

"What the hell you sayin'?"

"Swear to God." He drew an X over the center of his concave chest. " 'Bout ten minutes ago, it was. All hell's broke loose over there. In all the confusion, I snuck out and hightailed it over here quick as I could."

Even during the middle of the day there was always a small crowd of men in the billiards hall, loafers who spent their time drinking beer and grumbling about the mail service, which was consistently late in delivering their welfare checks.

Scowling, Henry dragged his cousin to one of the dim, smoky corners of the saloon, signaling Luther to join them in the back booth.

"You gonna forfeit?" Luther's competitor asked him.

Luther tossed another ten-dollar bill on the felt, racked his cue stick, and slid into the booth beside his brother, so that they sat facing the cousin whom they had tormented all his life. The ornery twins had made every family gathering pure hell for the physically inferior child of their father's brother out of his third wife.

Their chronic abuse had worked conversely to earn them Lee Simon's undying affection, admiration, and loyalty. That his cousins were often on the opposite side of the law seemed only to enamor him more.

"Y'all told me to keep an eye on things over yonder," he began, hitching his thumb in the general direction of the courthouse. "Well, that's what I done. Sure as hell didn't figure on anything this excitin' happenin'."

"What did happen?"

"They busted out. Matt and his old man. In broad daylight."

"How? They get a guard down?"

"Got him up, you mean," Lee Simon chortled.

"Huh?"

"Miss Lottie Lynam . . . ?"

"Yeah," the twins chorused.

"Well, the last few days, she's been coming to see Matt regular like. Brings him cheeseburgers and coconut cream pie from the café. Magazines and books, stuff like that."

He leaned across the table and assumed a man-to-man inflection. "You know how good she's put together? Well, she sashays into that jail like she was the Queen of Sheba. Gets everybody in there all worked up, don'cha know. Including the guards. Me, even. Hell, we might be in uniform, but we're men underneath, right?"

"Yeah, she's got a set of tits that'll knock out headlights," Luther said impatiently. "Get on with it, will ya?"

Lee Simon licked away the spittle that often formed in the corners of his lips. "So Lottie comes a-prancin' in there today, wearing a real tight-fittin' dress. And she makes damn sure she's got everybody's undivided attention, including ol' Wiley Jones."

Getting into his story, he scooted forward on the seat of the booth. More spittle was collecting. "Wiley lets her into the visitin' area, where she trips and spills her purse. She went down on all fours to pick up her stuff, and I heard tell that ol' Wiley's eyes nearly popped right outta his head. Also heard tell that she didn't have no underwear on, but that might be a rumor. Or wishful thinkin'."

"If you don't get to the point—"

"Okay, okay. I don't want to leave nothin' out." He drew a quick breath. "You know how everybody makes a big to-do over Gibb Burnwood? Thinks he's a great guy and all. Well, most of the guards think he's getting a bad rap, so the security 'round him and Matt has been relaxed, you might say.

"When Miss Lottie drops her purse, Wiley leaves his post and rushes to help her. While he's scooping up lipsticks and chewing gum, Matt and Gibb, who'd been waiting to see Lottie, pass through the door, slick as owl shit.

"Lottie thanks Wiley for helping her, then says all breathless like, 'Goodness me, I can't see my friends lookin' like this!' She's smoothing her hair, runnin' her hands down her dress, s'posed to be straightening it and all, you see.

"Then she takes off for the nearest ladies' room, where Matt and Gibb are waitin'. She locks the door, they change into clothes she'd stashed there earlier, then the three of them walk out the front door, get into her car, and drive away, pretty as you please.

"Several people saw them leavin' the courthouse. They smiled, shook hands, said they'd just been granted bail, and wasn't that great. Justice had prevailed. The system works. Stuff like that. Brass balls is what them Burnwoods've got.

"Wiley, poor ol' cuss, didn't even realize what happened. When the shit hit the fan, he was reared back in his chair, passin' the time till Miss Lottie returned from refreshin' herself in the ladies' room by daydreamin' 'bout the view he'd had up her dress. He was still so dazed, he didn't even know his prisoners were out!"

"Where are they now?"

"How long have they been gone?"

"Hold on, cousins. I'll get around to it all. Could sure use something to wet my whistle, though," Lee Simon said, eyeing the bar.

Henry signaled the bartender, who brought the deputy a beer. "Ain't s'posed to drink while in uniform, but nobody's gonna be noticing my beer breath, what with all that hullabaloo going on over there today." He slurped the head off his draft.

"I ain't seed him for myself, but they say this FBI agent, Pepperdyne—hell of a name, huh?—they say that when word of the breakout reached him, he pitched a conniption fit. He

wants to know how come an old man with his head up his
ass is guardin' federal prisoners. Asked who left ol' Wiley in
charge. They said if words could kill, everybody over there,
includin' men on Pepperdyne's own team, would be deader
'n doornails. He's on the warpath."

"How'd Lottie get them out of town?" Henry asked.

"The way they figure it, she had another car waiting. Just
before I tore off for here, I heard tell they'd found hers under
a bridge out on the highway. Nobody saw them make the
switch. All the Burnwoods' vehicles are accounted for. She
musta got hold of a car somewhere, but nobody knows what
it is. They're long gone, is my guess."

"To where?"

Lee Simon shrugged his knobby shoulders. "It's anybody's
guess, I reckon."

"No ideas?" Luther asked.

"Well, there's talk around the courthouse. Gossip, mostly."
He took another noisy sip of beer. "Everybody thinks they'll
go after Matt's ex-wife to shut her up. That's why this Pepperdyne throwed such a shit fit. She's the one who's saying they
killed that chink that disappeared from the jailhouse. Get
this—she said they cut off his pecker and crucified him," he
whispered.

Henry and Luther exchanged a look of disgust over the
lawmen's ineptitude. Henry said, "We heard she gave the slip
to the marshals who were bringing her back to testify."

"It's true. Nobody knows where she's at." Lee Simon lowered his voice. "Bet y'all wish ya did."

"Right you are, Lee Simon. You're not near as stupid as
you are ugly."

Lee Simon beamed at the praise of his older, tougher,
meaner cousins. "My ma says y'all blame Mrs. Burnwood
for landing Billy Joe in prison. She says your mama ain't got
over it yet."

Billy Joe had eventually recovered from his wound and

was sent to a rehabilitation hospital, where he was fitted with a prosthesis. He hadn't yet mastered it when he attacked one of his therapists. Using the mechanical arm as a weapon, he inflicted serious damage to the man's head.

This time, he was tried as an adult, convicted, and was currently serving time in the Central Corrections Institute. Billy Joe's misfortunes could be directly traced back to the public defender in Prosper, who had double-crossed the family.

"We should never have trusted her," Henry said with a mean, bitter slant to his mouth. "What do quiffs know about lawyering?"

"Not a damn thing," Luther replied. "Or our little brother wouldn't be in prison."

"And he'd still have his right arm."

Lee Simon drained his mug and belched rudely in an attempt to impress his cousins. "I better get back. Knew y'all'd want to know the latest."

The brothers absently muttered goodbye. Luther got up and assumed Lee Simon's place so that he could face his brother. They stared at each other across the table until after a while, Luther asked, "What're you thinking, Henry?"

"What're you thinking?"

"I asked you first."

Henry tapped his chin like a scholar contemplating a tricky law of physics. "It'd be a crying shame if somebody—even Gibb and Matt—killed Mrs. Burnwood before we got a chance."

"A damn crying shame."

"I couldn't look myself in the mirror no more."

"It's a matter of family pride."

"Honor."

"We swore to Ma we'd get even with Kendall Burnwood for everything that happened to Billy Joe."

"She oughtn't to have crossed us Crooks."

"If we're gonna keep our vow to Ma——"

"We got to find her before they do." Henry slid from the booth and motioned for his brother to follow. "Let's go see what Mama thinks."

Mama thought it was a splendid idea. She even added an incentive that the twins hadn't thought of but that was quite compatible with their own reasons for wanting to get Kendall Burnwood.

With a wicked twinkle in her eyes, Mama posed a question to the twins: "Who's to say what old man Burnwood might do if we take care of his problem for him? Huh? He's got plenty of money, don't he?"

Henry was the first to catch Mama's drift. He winked at his brother. "Bet he'd be willing to part with some cash, if he was spared having to account for hisself in court."

When the story of the Brotherhood broke and the Crooks learned that there was a group of vigilantes operating in their midst, they'd been incensed—but only because they hadn't been invited to join. Striving to keep Prosper racially pure and free of foreigners sounded like a great idea to them, and they couldn't comprehend men being punished for it.

Of course, they never guessed that it was Judge Fargo who had ordered Billy Joe's arm to be severed to teach both him and Kendall Burnwood a hard lesson on respect. Nor did they know that they, too, had been targeted for special punishment for daring to threaten a Burnwood, specifically Kendall. However, because of more pressing matters, the Brotherhood had been forced to sideline their cases.

Erroneously, the Crook clan held Kendall responsible for their calamities. From the day Billy Joe was taken from them, they had been planning their revenge. Breaking her windshield, the threatening letters, and the dead rat had been only warm-ups.

In order to vandalize her office, they had enlisted Lee Simon's help. He had slipped them into the building after hours. In return, the twins had procured a woman who, for twenty dollars, agreed to spend a whole night with Lee Simon. The twins had considered this a bargain; their cousin had been beside himself with glee.

Their plan, as outlined by Mama, was to continue harassing Mrs. Burnwood until she had a fatal "accident." Only she would know, moments before dying, that the Crooks had gotten their vengeance.

Unfortunately, before the grand finale could be staged, Mrs. Burnwood had left town for parts unknown. Angry and frustrated over the setback, Henry and Luther had gotten roaring drunk and burned down a hay barn just to make themselves feel better.

Their vows of revenge had not been forgotten, however. Their hatred of Kendall Burnwood had not abated in the year since her disappearance. When they heard that she had been located in Colorado and was being transported back to South Carolina, they had celebrated with another drinking binge and the deflowering of a twelve-year-old niece.

They had barely recovered from their hangovers when they learned that their nemesis had eluded the U.S. marshals and was presently at large. The twins had sunk into deep despair once again.

But now Lee Simon's news had revived their determination to get revenge. Mama had figured a way to line their pockets while they were at it. They gathered around the kitchen table with a bottle of rye to toast their promised prosperity and to formalize their plans.

"But I heard she's got a kid," Luther noted, his brow puckering. "After we kill her, what'll we do with the baby?"

Mama clouted him on the jaw. "Numb-nuts! You bring it back to old man Burnwood, of course. He'll probably pay double to have his grandbaby."

The twins grinned at each other. When it came to doing business, Mama was a whiz, wasn't she?

Chapter Thirty-two

"*I*S THAT THE BABY?"

Kendall stirred. "Hmm?"

"I hear Kevin crying."

"He slept longer than I expected, so I can't complain." She got up and slipped on a robe. "Do you mind if I bring him in here?"

"Uh . . . no."

What had caused John's aversion to children? she wondered as she went into Kevin's room. In his nightmare, he had screamed for Pepperdyne to make them stop crying. Did he hear children crying in his dream? And how did children relate to his work? What incident continued to torment him?

That was just one of the million questions she would have asked him had circumstances been different. How ironic, that his amnesia was her fragile and tenuous protection against discovery, while it was also the impenetrable barrier that kept her from learning anything personal about John McGrath. She knew nothing of his background. She didn't know his birthday or his middle name.

He was a stranger to her. Yet so very familiar.

She knew every nuance of his voice, its range and timbre,

but she didn't know anything about his beliefs or his morals. She knew every nick and scar on his body, but not how he'd acquired them. Her fingertips had explored every inch of his skin, but she had no idea how many other women had caressed it.

He might even be married.

She hastily pushed aside that disturbing thought. She wouldn't allow herself to think about whom he might love, whom he might be betraying by sleeping with her. He couldn't be held responsible for his actions while suffering from amnesia, she reasoned.

The blame would belong solely to her, and she accepted that. She had claimed him as her husband on a whim, thinking it an ingenious way to buy time until she could escape. She hadn't planned on kidnapping and living in close contact with him for weeks. She hadn't planned on the changes in him that had come about by his being with her and Kevin, the softening in his character that had made him less forbidding and more endearing.

She certainly hadn't planned on falling in love with him.

The morning after they first made love, she'd had a moment of panic. He had sneaked up behind her while she was standing at the bathroom sink. When he grabbed her roughly and spun her around, his eyes had been so fiercely aglow that she was certain he had regained his memory.

But the gleam she had mistaken for anger was instead one of passion. He had kissed her hard, laying her anxiety to rest. John wouldn't shirk his duty as a federal officer. She knew that when his memory returned, he would be outraged. He would do everything within his power to return her to South Carolina. It was a certainty she didn't want to think about.

After diapering Kevin, she returned to bed carrying the baby with her. John propped himself up on one elbow and watched as she cradled the infant beneath her breast. Kevin's tiny fist pummeled her while his mouth blindly sought her nipple. She guided it toward him and he latched on to it eagerly.

"Greedy little cuss," John remarked.

"He has a healthy appetite."

"Why was he born cesarean?"

She smoothed down the peach fuzz on Kevin's head. "He was asserting his independence even before he was born," she replied with a smile. "He refused to get into the correct position in the birth canal. My OB tried turning him, but Kevin would have none of it. It was vanity, I think. He didn't want to spoil the perfect shape of his head."

Hesitantly, John extended his hand and touched Kevin's temple, where a strong pulse beat beneath the translucent skin. Then he gingerly covered the baby's head with his hand, being careful of the soft spot. "He is a handsome kid."

"Thank you."

"He resembles you."

"Really?"

"Really. And you're beautiful."

Their eyes connected. "Do you think so?"

"Yes."

"Especially my hair, huh?"

His eyes took in the blunt, cropped strands. "You might start a new fashion trend."

"Coiffure by John Deere."

"Who's that?"

"It doesn't matter," she said, laughing softly.

"That's right. It doesn't matter. You're still beautiful."

She knew he meant it. And in her opinion, he was beautiful, too. Not classically handsome, certainly. But his features were arresting and wholly masculine, from his expressive eyebrows to the square angles of his chin.

Actually it was odd that she found him so appealing, because physically he was a direct opposite of Matt, whom she had thought was the most handsome man she'd ever seen.

Matt had a tall, lean physique. John was just as tall, but his body was more solid. Matt was blond; John's hair was dark with a sprinkling of gray. Matt had refined, patrician features, but they were almost too symmetrical to be interesting. John's face had seen wear and tear, but it had a tremendous amount of character.

And she loved his eyes, which were an intriguing mix of green and brown. Depending on his mood, they changed patterns like the crystals in a kaleidoscope.

He could be downright dour, but that only made his rare smiles and wry jokes more special. He had a mean streak that she attributed to an unhappy childhood. She guessed that he hadn't been shown much tenderness when he was growing up. He hadn't learned how to express emotions and affection and therefore was awkward in interpersonal relationships. But he was capable of deep feelings and didn't hesitate to act on them. Remembering how he had dealt with the teenage boys who had pestered her, she knew he would go to the mat to protect her and Kevin.

He was tough, but he could also be incredibly gentle, as he had been earlier that night, when his eyes had seemed to drift across the features of her face like a soft forest mist.

In a voice as rough as sandpaper, he had asked, "Have you ever done that before?"

"What?"

"Gone down on me."

She had blushed hotly, turned her face into his shoulder, and shook her head.

"Why not?"

Raising her head, she met his gaze directly. "I've never wanted to before."

For the longest time he had continued to stare into her eyes in that incisive way of his; then, muttering a curse, he had drawn her into a tight hug and tucked her head beneath his chin.

After a while, she had asked shyly, "Didn't I do it right?"

His answer had been a soft groan. "Oh, yeah. You did it just fine."

He had continued to hold her, caressing her back and hips, stoking her desire. Finally he had lifted her to straddle his lap and sheathe his erection.

"I've never done it this way either," she had admitted.

"You don't have to do anything. Just be you."

He had cupped her chin in his hand, his thumb tracing the shape of her lips, separating them, skimming her front teeth, touching her tongue. Then his hands had moved down her chest and covered her breasts. As he had pressed and stroked and reshaped them, she had ridden him with escalating passion.

"Christ," he'd whispered, encircling her waist with his hands to hold and guide her.

Then he had slipped one hand between their bodies. His middle finger deftly massaged that slight protrusion, and Kendall had been speared with such intense pleasure that she thought she would die of it.

Now she was experiencing pleasure of another kind, but it was just as intense and perhaps more meaningful. While Kevin nursed and John looked on, she could almost fool herself into believing that they really were a family.

This was what she had always wanted but had never had—a man who loved her, a child, a family. It seemed that destiny was bent on denying her that simple dream, so she was forced to playact it. Temporarily.

It couldn't last much longer. At any moment the fantasy could shatter. John could suddenly recover his memory. Or federal officers could locate them and come barging through the door to arrest her for kidnapping. Or—and this possibility was the one she feared most—the Burnwoods would somehow find her.

They were hunters. They knew how to track prey. The

trophies of their successful forays were stuffed and mounted on the walls of Gibb's house. She could identify with those poor animals who had been caught in the crosshairs of their sights. She feared that she would be their next kill, and that Kevin would fall into their evil hands.

In any event, there would be no happily-ever-after ending to this story. The best she could hope for was to escape from John, never see him again, and remain a fugitive for the rest of her life.

That meant leaving him now, before he regained his memory and recalled that she was his prisoner. When he realized that she had made him an unwitting player in a short-lived fairy tale, he would hate her. She had done the unforgivable: She had made him care for her and Kevin, knowing that she was going to vanish, leaving him alone to face the consequences of her duplicity. He would despise her on a professional level, and even more so on a personal one.

She hoped she would have disappeared by then and would never have to experience his contempt face-to-face. She could stand anything but that. God forbid that he ever think, even for a single instant, that her lovemaking had been just another devious manipulation.

But how could she bring herself to leave him, when he was looking at her as he was now? How, when he laid his hand against her cheek and took her mouth in a long, deep kiss?

To cover a sob, Kendall clutched his hair and kissed him with all the fervor of her love and her fear. He pulled her and Kevin into the circle of his arms and held them close while the baby continued to suckle. She wanted this sweet intimacy to last forever.

It couldn't. She had to leave him.

But not tonight.

Chapter Thirty-three

"*W*HAT DO YOU THINK WILL HAPPEN TO US, MATT? How will this end?"

He ran his hand over the curve of Lottie's hip. "Don't worry about it. Dad will take care of everything."

She rolled away from him and sat up. "Of course I worry about it, Matt. I broke the law. I'm a fugitive."

"Dad's got it all figured out."

She raked her hand through her russet hair, and laughed without mirth. "Your daddy is a maniac, Matt. Can't you see that?"

"Shh! He'll hear you."

He glanced nervously toward the wall that separated Gibb's motel room from the one that he and Lottie occupied. It was a wretched place, a row of shabby rooms with thin walls and threadbare carpeting, a place where illicit lovers might rendezvous if finances were a factor.

Matt didn't consider himself and Lottie illicit lovers. This was the fulfillment of a love affair that had begun when his hormones were still in chaos. Back then he hadn't guessed that the girl he lusted after would become the woman he loved.

Two days earlier he had added jailbreak to the list of crimes he had been accused of and was guilty of committing, but Matt Burnwood had never been happier in his life. He was with Lottie. Out in the open. With the approval of his father.

He realized that he appeared naïve to her, and probably to everyone else, for trusting his father so wholeheartedly. But he did trust Gibb to work things out. He had said he would take care of the situation, and Gibb's word was gold. He was never wrong. As far back as Matt could remember, his father had been right about everything. He was the embodiment of a true American hero.

Just like Grandpa Burnwood had been. Matt hadn't known his grandfather, but he knew everything about him. Gibb had told him about Grandpa's unparalleled soldiering skills. In fact, Gibb knew every detail of his father's ordeal in the South Pacific and how he had survived against overwhelming odds.

Just as Gibb had believed that his father was above reproach, Matt trusted Gibb implicitly. He had never steered him wrong.

Well, maybe he had misjudged Kendall.

Gibb had urged him to marry her. He'd said that Kendall would be a perfect screen for the activities of the Brotherhood. Through her, they would have even greater access to those individuals who, unless they were exterminated, could erode the foundation on which America had been built.

In theory, marrying the public defender, whom they had mistakenly thought was corruptible, was a terrific idea. Unfortunately, they had underestimated Kendall's independence. She hadn't been as malleable as they had expected or wished, but that was her failing, not Gibb's.

Matt acknowledged that his father could easily be misunderstood. He was obsessive about control. When it came to being slighted, he had the memory of an elephant; he never forgot or forgave an affront. Once someone had crossed him, they were enemies for life. He could be dogmatic and inflexible when he thought he was right. And when he set his mind on something, he persisted with a doggedness that went far beyond determination.

In Matt's eyes, these traits were virtues, not flaws. It was a matter of perspective. Where others might see Gibb as radical, Matt admired him for being dedicated, courageous, and consistent. Gibb never backed down from what he believed. Matt wished he were a fraction as strong as his father and grandfather.

Although, if he were as strong as they, he might not have been able to love Lottie as much as he did. If loving her was a weakness, it was one he would never try to overcome.

"Please don't be upset," he whispered as he reached for her again. At first she resisted, then finally allowed him to pull her back into his arms.

He kissed the back of her neck, thinking how much he loved the taste of her skin. He loved everything about her. As many times as he had explored her body, he'd never found a single flaw. She was perfect.

Except for that one thing—her barrenness. If it hadn't been for that, he probably would have put his foot down, told his father that this was the woman he wanted, and married her years ago.

She smiled sadly. "You just can't see it, can you, Matt?"

"See that you're beautiful? Of course I see that. Everybody thinks you're beautiful."

"You've been brainwashed, my darling, and you don't even realize it." She hesitated, then asked, "Matt, is it true what they're saying about you, and your daddy and the others? Did you ritualistically kill those people? Did you mutilate and crucify that Li boy?"

He kissed her. "Those are matters that have nothing to do with us, Lottie."

"But *did* you?"

"Whatever we did was done with God's blessing."

"Then it is true," she said, groaning. "Jesus, Matt. Don't you realize that we're on a one-way trip to disaster?"

He kissed her lightly on the tip of her nose. "You're a pessimist."

"And you're a fool."

"If you truly think that, then why did you help us escape? Why did you come along?"

She sank her fingers into his hair and clenched them so tightly it hurt. "You idiot. You poor, stupid, beautiful idiot." Matt was startled to see tears in her eyes. "I love you," she vowed in a fierce whisper. "The only joy I've known in my rotten life has been in loving you. For as long as it can last, I'll continue to love you."

She lay back on the mattress and carried him down with her.

Lottie turned off the faucets and stepped out of the shower stall. She reached for the thin, dingy towel, but then suddenly she sensed a presence behind her, turned, and uttered a startled cry.

"Good morning, Lottie," Gibb said. "Sleep well?"

"What are you doing in here?"

"Of course you slept well. You exhausted yourself fornicating with my son."

Lottie clutched the meager towel to the front of her body. Her teeth began to chatter. "Get out of here. If Matt finds you—"

"He won't. As you know, he went out for coffee and doughnuts. He called my room before he left to ask what I'd like. He's always been such a thoughtful, obedient son. Except for you."

Gibb had congratulated her for the daring role she had played in their escape and praised her for having the grit and composure to execute their bold plan.

But his accolades rang hollow. There was no warmth in

his eyes when he spoke to her. And now, her shivering was due only in part to being wet and naked. She was terrified of him.

Gibb Burnwood had always made her skin crawl. Even when she was a little girl and went into his store with her daddy, she had felt uneasy in Gibb's presence. Her aversion was instinctual, animalistic. Like pets who take an instant dislike to a family member for no apparent reason, she sensed something repugnant in Gibb Burnwood, but as far as she knew, no one else felt as she did.

Now, after her conversation with Matt last night, she knew why she so disliked Gibb. He was an evil man who had indoctrinated his son to his own twisted credo based on bigotry and violence.

"I'd like to dress, please." She tried to keep her voice level, knowing that his hunting instincts would detect her fear.

"Why? You've always been proud of your body. At least you've flaunted it in front of my son for decades, keeping him miserable with lust. Why should you pretend to be modest now?"

"Look, I don't know what you think you're doing, but I don't like it. And I assure you Matt won't either."

"I know what's best for Matt."

"Turning him into a vigilante killer? You call that doing what's best for your son? You call that love?"

He backhanded her hard across the face. She reeled against the basin and clutched the cool porcelain to keep from falling. The walls seemed to tilt as bright sparks of yellow exploded against a field of black. The pain was delayed for several seconds. When it registered in her brain, it had the force of a rocket blast.

"You whore. Who are you to act sanctimonious with me!" He gripped her shoulder and shoved her down to her knees.

"Please," she whispered. "Don't. Whatever . . ."

She knew it would do no good to beg, so she closed her

eyes and prayed for the first time in her life. She prayed for unconsciousness.

But he gripped a handful of her wet hair and jerked her head up. The pain and humiliation he inflicted were so severe that there was no chance that she would faint.

Following Gibb's instructions, Matt had gone into a crowded convenience store where the clerks and customers were too busy to pay attention to one another.

He filled three Styrofoam cups with hot coffee at a self-service bar and bought a half-dozen doughnuts at the cash register. No one gave him a second glance.

Dad's always right.

He used his key to open the door to his motel room. "Dad, hi!" he said when he noticed Gibb sitting in the room's only chair. "I didn't expect you to be in here. Just as you said—"

He screamed and dropped the carry out sack. The lids on the Styrofoam cups popped off. Scalding coffee splashed onto his pants legs, but he was unmindful of the burns.

"Shut the door, Matt."

Matt stared in horror at the bed where Lottie lay—naked, spread-eagled, and unquestionably dead. Her eyes were frozen open in terror. Her throat had been cut. Recently. The wound was still sluggishly pumping blood; the sheets were bright red with it. A severed artery had spurted blood onto the wall behind the bed, spoiling a bad painting of a dogwood tree in bloom.

Gibb got up, stepped around his horror-stricken son, and calmly closed the door. One of the coffee cups had remained intact. Gibb picked it up off the floor, removed the lid, and took a sip.

Matt stumbled forward and would have thrown himself across Lottie's body if Gibb hadn't grabbed him from behind and pulled him back.

"There was no other way, son," he said in a smooth and reasonable tone. "You know that. She killed her husband in cold blood. She accused him of raping her, then shot him while he slept. What kind of example is that for young women? Do we want our women to start believing that if their husbands exercise their God-given dominion over them and claim their conjugal rights, they can murder them?

"The Brotherhood had already marked her for extermination. It was out of respect for you that they granted your petition for a postponement, but her execution was only a matter of time. I did her a favor, actually. I was merciful and quick. She died doing what she loved best."

Matt looked at his father with eyes as dead as Lottie's.

"That's right, son. She died with me on her. I tested her, just as Satan tested our Lord in the wilderness. Unlike Jesus, she failed." He glanced at the corpse.

Matt said nothing. He hadn't uttered a sound after the first shock of seeing Lottie dead.

"Writhing and begging like a wanton," Gibb said, "she opened her legs to me. She weakened me and made me sin, just as she's weakened you all these years. You can still see my seed there, mingling with yours. Only a slut would commit such an abomination."

Matt gazed without blinking at the obscenely positioned body. Gibb laid his hand on his son's shoulder. "She was the Devil's spawn, Matthew. A harlot of hell. If I hadn't stopped her, she would have continued fanning men's lust and corrupting you. I couldn't have that."

Matt swallowed. "But—"

"Think of your son. He'll soon be with us. We couldn't have her tainting him, too."

"She . . . she wouldn't have. Lottie was good."

"Ah, Matt, you're wrong. I know how hard it is to understand now, but eventually you'll come to see that I'm right.

Remember how difficult it was for us to eliminate your mother?"

Matt nodded dumbly.

"I loved that woman, son. I loved Laurelann dearly, but she overstepped her bounds. She discovered the truth behind the Brotherhood and planned to expose us to those who wouldn't understand our mission. She had to be silenced, Matt. I cried. You cried, too. Remember?"

"Yes, sir."

"It was painful but necessary. You were only a boy, but even then you understood the necessity of it, didn't you, son?"

"Yes, sir."

"Eventually the pain eased, just as I told you it would. Your spirit healed. You learned not to miss your mother so much. Believe me, son, you're much better off without this contaminating influence in your life. It's even possible that your marriage to Kendall would have remained intact, that we wouldn't be in this awkward fix, if it hadn't been for this Lynam whore.

"I believe that in time, once she understood our goals, Kendall would have accepted the Brotherhood. But her pride would never have let her accept Lottie. And rightfully so. You were committing adultery, son. It wasn't your fault. I know that." He pointed to the corpse. "Her body was designed by the Devil to make you burn with lust. All the blame belongs to her. She tempted you beyond what you were able to resist. So don't weep for her."

He clapped Matt on the back. "Now, let's get our things into the car. We can't let this interfere with what we must do—find your son."

Chapter Thirty-four

*T*HE HOUSE WAS A FAIR DISTANCE FROM THE ROAD and could be reached only via a narrow gravel lane that was lined with dense foliage. Tree branches extended over the road, forming an almost solid canopy that blocked out the moonlight.

For their purposes, the house couldn't have been better situated.

It was long past midnight. For more than an hour, there hadn't been a single car on the road. Cutting the headlights, they had cruised past the entrance to the lane several times before finally pulling the car to the edge of a ditch and turning off the engine. Then they had sat quietly waiting for any indication that their arrival had been noticed. For more than sixty minutes, nothing.

"Do you think she's in there?"

"We won't know until we get inside. She's not going to advertise it."

Darkness concealed them as they left the car and crept along the lane, wending their way through the foliage, two tall shadows blending with myriad others. Thirty yards from the porch, they crouched behind the shrubbery and studied the house previously owned by Elvie Hancock, Kendall's grandmother.

Using hand signals to communicate, they split up. One swung out wide to the left, the other to the right. Avoiding the clearing, they kept to the shadows of the woods that encircled the property. They approached the rear of the house from different directions and reunited behind a storage shed.

"Hear or see anything?"

"It's as still as a tomb."

"That doesn't mean she's not in there with the baby."

"And McGrath?"

"Who knows?"

They gazed at each other with indecision. Finally one asked the other, "You ready?"

"Let's go."

They were prepared to pick the lock on the back door, but they found it unlocked. The door made only a slight squeak when pulled open. They slipped into the utility room and soundlessly entered the kitchen through the connecting door.

From what they could tell, it was as neat as a pin. There were dishes stacked in the sink, no clutter on the counter. One opened the refrigerator to investigate, but when the light came on and the motor began to hum, he quickly closed it.

Kendall sat up. "What was that?"

"What?"

Something had awakened her and she was unaccountably frightened. "Did you hear something?" she whispered.

John raised his head and listened, but the house was silent. "I don't hear anything. What did it sound like?"

"I don't know. I'm sorry I woke you. I guess it was a dream."

"Scary?"

"Must have been."

He resettled his head on the pillow and nuzzled her bare shoulder. "Baby okay?"

"He's fine."

They had kept Kevin in bed with them after his last feeding. He was cradled against Kendall's chest. She was lying in the curve of John's body, her bottom to his belly, her thighs nestled against his. He hugged her and Kevin closer to him. She forced herself to relax. With John holding her so closely, she felt safe and secure.

All the same, she was glad that she still had the pistol hidden where John couldn't find it. She despised guns. Bama's death mask was a grim reminder of the devastation they could inflict. Although Matt had repeatedly offered to teach her how to shoot, she had never fired a weapon.

But if it came to saving Kevin's life, or John's, she wouldn't hesitate to shoot to kill.

They had been tiptoeing around inside the house for five minutes but still hadn't learned whether their quarry had taken refuge there.

As they moved stealthily through the living areas, it was impossible to tell if the rooms had been occupied recently. In order to look for telltale personal items they needed a flashlight, but they didn't dare, for fear of revealing themselves.

After several minutes of futile groping, one turned to face the other and gave an exaggerated shrug. The other signaled that they should proceed to the bedrooms, where anyone inside the house was likely to be at this time of night.

Single file, they entered the hallway. Three doors opened off it. They were about to enter the first room when the leader nearly stumbled over something, avoiding it just in time. He knelt and picked up the object.

It was a teddy bear.

He held it up for his partner to see. They smiled at each other. The leader pointed to the room across the hall and received a nod of agreement. The door was slightly ajar. They gave it a gentle push. Slowly, soundlessly, it swung open.

Facing each other from either side of the opening, they silently counted to three, then rushed into the room.

Kendall dropped the correct number of coins into the slot. The long-distance call was put through and the telephone on the other end began to ring. She gripped the receiver with sweating hands.

Ricki Sue answered on the second ring. "Bristol and Mathers."

"It's me. Don't say anything. Can you talk?"

"Holy Christ, you're alive! I've been sick, *sick* with worry. You're the best diet I've ever been on."

"I knew you'd be worried, but I couldn't risk calling before. I shouldn't be calling now."

"Did you really kidnap a U.S. marshal?" Ricki Sue asked in a low, urgent tone.

"In a manner of speaking."

"What does that mean? Did you or didn't you? Where the devil are you?"

"For your own sake, I can't tell you, and we can't talk long. They probably have the phones tapped."

"I wouldn't doubt it. Sheridan's crawling with federal agents, and they're all looking for you, kid."

Kendall wasn't surprised. But hearing her fears verbalized caused her already sinking spirits to plummet.

"Agents have been here at the law firm several times," Ricki Sue said. "They've pored over everything pertaining to Kendall Deaton."

"Oh, God."

"They even stationed guys inside your grandmother's house."

"Inside?" Kendall felt nauseated. Her grandmother would have hated that intrusion into her privacy. "That's so stupid and unnecessary. Knowing that's the first place they would look for me, I wouldn't go near Grandmother's house."

"The feds weren't the only ones to think you might. Last night, two men broke in, obviously expecting to find you there."

"Two men? Who were they?"

"The FBI had laid a trap, but it didn't work. The intruders got away before they were identified. They ran for their car in a hail of bullets that could have raised the dead, but the authorities don't think they were even wounded."

"But who—"

"Don't panic, kid, but it might have been your husband and his daddy."

"They're in jail," Kendall protested weakly.

"Not anymore. They escaped three days ago."

Kendall hung up immediately, but she kept both hands on the receiver, clinging to it like a lifeline. She dreaded turning around, fearing that she would see Matt and Gibb watching her, smiling complacently now that they had her in their sights.

"Are you through with the phone, lady?"

Kendall jumped reflexively, then glanced hastily over her shoulder. A man in a baseball uniform and cleats was waiting impatiently to use the pay phone.

"Oh, sorry."

She moved away, keeping her head low. There seemed nothing sinister afoot at the service station. One customer was pumping gas into his RV. Another was feeding coins into a cigarette vending machine. Two mechanics were standing beneath a car on the hydraulic lift, conferring with its owner.

No one was paying the least bit of attention to the tomboy in jeans and sneakers who bore virtually no similarity to the published photos of Kendall Burnwood, the missing public defender.

State police all over the South would be on the lookout for the car she had driven from Stephensville. It was a moving target, and she took an enormous risk each time she drove it.

But she'd needed to learn how the manhunt was proceeding and how close she was to being recaptured.

She hurried back to the car. As soon as possible she would at least switch the license plates on it. Inside the car, the heat was breath-stealing, but Kendall was shivering when she pulled onto the highway and started for home.

Home?

Yes. That house had seemed as much a home to her as her grandmother's house in Sheridan. The farmhouse had been a legacy to her grandfather from an uncle. Her grandfather had died before having many opportunities to enjoy it, but Kendall and her grandmother had put the property to good use every summer.

As soon as school was dismissed for the season, they headed for the country, where they spent lazy, halcyon days. Sometimes they fished, sometimes they canned the fresh fruit they bought at roadside stands, and sometimes they did nothing at all except enjoy each other's company. They read stories aloud to each other in the evenings, braided daisy chains on the front porch, and went on frequent picnics at their favorite spot near the waterfall.

They had never entertained guests at the farmhouse. No one was ever invited to join them during their summer hiatus. Friends knew that every year they left Sheridan in early June and didn't return until after Labor Day, but none knew the location of their retreat. That's why Kendall had known it would be a safe place to hide.

But how safe was she anywhere, now that Matt and Gibb were at large?

Pepperdyne must be frantic. He had lost his material witness, his friend John McGrath, and now his prime suspects. He had impressed Kendall as a basically kind man with a gruff exterior. She couldn't hate him for doing what he was paid to do. But she would do whatever she could to prevent him from capturing her.

However, she preferred to be arrested again rather than have Matt and Gibb find her. And they would find her. Her only possible chance of survival was to stay ahead of them until they were recaptured and returned to jail. She knew that she should take Kevin and leave tonight.

But what about John?

Although he still walked with one crutch, he was almost completely healed. She could leave him now with a clear conscience. The hitch was, she didn't want to.

But if she loved him, wasn't that all the more reason to leave? As long as he was near her, his life, too, was in danger. He wouldn't allow the Burnwoods to lay a hand on her or Kevin, with whom he bonded closer each day. He could lose his life protecting them, and he would die not knowing what it had all been about.

She couldn't let that happen. They had no future together, but, even if she lived the rest of her life without him, she wanted to know that he was alive.

What should she do? Turn herself in?

She immediately dismissed that thought. Ricki Sue had said that the FBI had been to the law office, asking questions, delving into her background. If they found out everything about her, her credibility would be reduced to shreds.

She would be deemed an unreliable witness, so what good would she be to them? Either they would prosecute her for kidnapping John and she would be sent to prison, or the authorities would release her, leaving her without any protection against Matt, his father, and their disciples.

Her only viable choice was to disappear again. She berated herself for having left Kevin with John this afternoon. If she had the baby with her now, she could just keep driving. It would have been heart-wrenching not to see John and tell him a silent goodbye, but leaving after seeing him again would be even harder.

But she knew she must.

* * *

"Who fucked up?"

The agents under Pepperdyne's unmerciful gaze didn't say a word. They were afraid to breathe. "Well?" His bellow rattled the window glass in the Sheridan, Tennessee, police station, where he had set up his command post after moving it from Prosper.

One of the two agents involved in the snafu the night before finally worked up enough courage to speak. "We'd been staking out the house ever since her disappearance, sir, and nothing had happened."

"So?"

"So, we . . . uh . . . fucked up," the agent finished lamely.

"Sir?" the other agent ventured timorously. "We were afraid to shoot for fear it might be Mrs. Burnwood. Or Marshal McGrath."

"That's right, sir," his partner chimed in, grateful for this granule of defense. "What if it had been them, and they'd had the baby with them?"

"Well, for all we know it *was* them. Or maybe it was Little Red Riding Hood and the Big Bad Wolf. We don't know who it was, do we? Because you didn't identify the intruders or get a make on their car."

"It wasn't Mrs. Burnwood," one agent stated adamantly. "It was definitely two men."

"Oh, definitely two men. Well, that narrows it down. Maybe it was Batman and Robin." Pepperdyne exhaled, letting several obscenities float out on the stream of air. "You guys are going to spend an hour today on a firing range I've set up in the sunniest, hottest spot in this county. You're gonna shoot till your hands are on fire. Because last night you couldn't hit a bull in the butt with a bass fiddle." One of the agents unwisely cracked a smile. "You think that's funny?" Pepperdyne roared. "You can stay *two* hours on the range. Now get out of my sight before I get really pissed."

They filed out, closing the door behind them. Alone, Pepperdyne sank into the desk chair and dragged his hands down his face. The optimism he had felt upon returning to Stephensville and getting a description of the car had long since fizzled.

He hadn't had a single break in this case from the very beginning, when they'd mistakenly thought they had a computer glitch. If the computer technician hadn't dismissed the data he had received, Ruthie Fordham would still be alive, and Mrs. Burnwood wouldn't be missing again with John right along with her. By the time they had realized their error and unraveled the data puzzle, John was driving toward disaster. Efforts to reach him on his cellular phone had failed. Then he'd had a run-in with a felled tree and his memory had been wiped clean.

Jesus. What a bizarre chain of events.

The Burnwoods' jailbreak in Prosper had been another major setback. Now, he not only had to find Mrs. Burnwood and John, he had to find them before those maniacs did. It wasn't going to be easy. She had managed to lose herself in Denver for a whole year before they had tracked her there.

She wasn't dumb enough to return to her hometown, but obviously someone else thought she might. They had gone looking for her in her grandmother's house last night.

Pepperdyne's reaction to the debacle was founded as much on fear as anger and embarrassment. He feared he knew the intruders' identities—Gibb and Matt Burnwood.

He gazed down at the photograph of Mrs. Burnwood that had been sent to law enforcement agencies across the country. Then he looked at the crime scene photos that had been brought to him less than an hour ago. The pictures of Lottie Lynam's bloody, nude corpse turned his stomach.

Addressing the photo of Matt Burnwood's wife, Pepperdyne muttered, "Lady, you'd better hope I find you before he and his daddy do."

And what the hell was John doing all this time?

Chapter Thirty-five

JOHN WATCHED FROM THE FRONT DOOR AS Kendall drove out of sight, then he hobbled into the bedroom where Kevin lay on his back in the playpen.

"Look, uh, I'm on a tight schedule. So I need your full cooperation, okay? You'll be all right here by yourself. I won't be gone long. I *can't* be gone long. Just, you know, chill out until I get back."

He hesitated, as though he might get an argument from the baby. Kevin blew bubbles and waved his fists, giving no indication that he was upset over being left alone.

"Okay then," John said, backing away.

He left the house and was halfway across the clearing when he halted, thinking he'd heard a noise. Was it a choking sound? A whimper? He considered all the horrendous possibilities. Fire. Wild animals. Insects. Asphyxiation.

"Shit."

He retraced his crutch-assisted steps. "Okay, sport. I hope you're up to this." Then he added beneath his breath, "I hope *I'm* up to this."

He slipped on the sling that Kendall sometimes used to carry the baby against her chest. Propping his crutches against the playpen, he balanced on one leg and bent down to lift Kevin out.

"Yeah, yeah, this is lots of fun," he muttered when Kevin gurgled happily. Once Kevin was comfortably positioned, he retrieved his crutches and set out again.

"Not a word of this to your mother, understand? She's a clever lady, your mother. She's got my weapon again, so I can't hold her at gunpoint and demand that she drive us out of here. I could drive myself, but she would be gone by the time I returned."

He glanced down at the child. "I don't suppose you know where she hid my weapon, do you? She's too smart to have thrown it away, but damned ... excuse me, *darned* if I can find it. I've turned the freaking house upside down."

He quickly covered the distance to the main road, where he paused to catch his breath. Sweat was already pouring from him. It trickled down his forehead and ran into his eyes, stinging them. Wiping them with his sleeve was difficult when he needed both hands to maneuver the crutches. He had known this expedition was going to be physically exerting, and he hadn't counted on carrying Kevin's extra fifteen pounds.

He struck out for the house he had spotted the day he'd gone to town with Kendall. "Frankly, I think your mother is too smart for her own good," he said, huffing. "She should return my pistol to me. I'd know better how to use it if the need arose."

He talked to keep from thinking about what a long shot it was that this expedition would meet with success. He wasn't in condition for this much exercise, so his breathing was labored. It was a hot, sultry afternoon. Although he took advantage of every patch of shade along the road, even they provided little relief.

He was working under a deadline. He had to return to the house before Kendall did, and he had no idea how long today's errand would take her. The day he rode with her to town, he

The Witness   323

had mentally clocked the distance. One way it was twelve miles, give or take a few. On the curving roads, and factoring in time spent on errands, she couldn't possibly make the trip in under half an hour. He'd given himself only that long to try to get help.

But his pace was slow, and he was out of shape. If luck was with him, a car would come along and give him a ride to the nearest telephone. That's all he needed—sixty seconds on a telephone.

He glanced at his wristwatch. Seven minutes had elapsed since she'd left. The muscles in his back and arms were burning with the strain, but he pushed himself to move faster.

His efforts were rewarded when he topped a rise in the road and spotted the house he had made note of. It was a quarter of a mile away, maybe less. Distance was hard to gauge because of the heat waves rising from the pavement and distorting the landscape.

"If I push myself to the limit, I might make it there in four minutes," he said to Kevin. "Five, max. In any event, I'm crazy for talking to someone who can't possibly understand me. Maybe I'm still in a coma and having one hell of a dream. That's it. You're only a dream. You—"

Suddenly John began to laugh. "You're peeing on me, aren't you?" The scalding stream trickled down his chest. "Well, that's one way of convincing me that you're real."

The one-sided conversation had helped keep his mind off his protesting muscles, the blistering heat, and the distance he had yet to cover. He was enormously grateful when he reached the driveway to the house. The incline nearly killed him. When he got to the porch, he collapsed.

Leaning against a support post, he called out, "Hello?" To his surprise, the word came out as a dry croak. He took several deep breaths, swallowed all the saliva he could work up, and tried again. "Hello!"

Kevin began to cry. "Shh. I'm not shouting at you." He

patted the baby's butt reassuringly. Kevin stopped crying, but
his mood was tenuous. The corners of his mouth were turned
down, and tears hovered in his eyes.

"I know how you feel, buddy. I might start crying myself."

Now that he had taken a closer look at the house, it became
apparent that no one was at home and hadn't been in a long
time. The potted plants on the porch had turned to brown,
leafless stalks. All the window shades were lowered. Spiders
had set up housekeeping in the corners of the doorjamb.

Now what? His clothes were soaked with perspiration. He
might well dehydrate before he got back to Kendall's house.
And the baby—

Christ! If he was this hot and dry, Kevin had to be, too.
He remembered having heard something about babies having
a higher body temperature than adults. He pressed his palm
against Kevin's forehead. His skin was hot; he was burning
up.

Galvanized, John slipped one of his crutches beneath his
arm and leaned on it heavily as he stood up. Using one of
the terra-cotta flower pots, he broke out a windowpane in the
front door, reached inside and undid the lock, then opened
the door.

He didn't care if a silent alarm alerted the local police.
Now that he knew he wasn't a fugitive guilty of a crime, he
wanted to be caught. In the meantime, he had to get some
fluid into him and the baby.

It wasn't a large house. The rooms hadn't been occupied
in a while and showed obvious signs of neglect. But John
moved through them so quickly, he scarcely took in the
appointments. He located the kitchen within seconds, moved
to the sink, and turned on the cold water tap. Nothing.

"Dammit!"

But then there was a knock, a rattle and a ping, and water
gushed from the faucet. It was rusty at first, but after several
seconds it ran clear. John scooped handfuls of it into his

mouth and swallowed greedily. He ladled water over the back of his neck.

Then, wetting his hand again, he smoothed it over Kevin's head. "Feel better? Cooler?" He bathed the baby's red cheeks.

But Kevin needed fluids inside him, and it suddenly occurred to John that he didn't have a means of conveying water into the child. Kendall sometimes gave him a drink of juice or water from a baby bottle, but of course John hadn't thought to bring one along. There was glassware in the cabinets, but if he tried pouring water down Kevin's throat, he might choke. The kid only knew how to suck, so how—

He didn't even think about it before thrusting his index finger beneath the faucet. He carried it, dripping, to Kevin's mouth and tapped it against the baby's lips. Kevin immediately began to suck.

The sensation was foreign and unsettling, yet oddly gratifying. "Not exactly your mother's milk, is it, boy?" he murmured as he wet his finger again and let Kevin suck the water from it.

John wondered what his friends and colleagues would think if they could see this bizarre scene. They wouldn't believe their eyes.

And Lisa? Forget it. Lisa had called him a selfish son of a bitch because he refused to give her a baby. He had refused even to discuss having a child. That was the disagreement that had caused their split.

"My biological clock is running out," she announced one evening.

"So wind it," he said from behind his newspaper.

She threw a pillow at him. He lowered the newspaper, sensing that they were gearing up for the battle royal, the Waterloo of their relationship. She had raised the topic before, but he'd always skirted it. That night she took the direct approach.

"I'd like to have a baby, John. And I'd like you to be the father."

"I'm flattered, but no thanks. I don't want a baby. Never have. Never will."

"Why not?"

"The reasons are too many to name."

She nestled her bottom more comfortably in her chair, the way a soldier burrows into a foxhole and psyches himself up for hand-to-hand combat. "I'm in no hurry. Let's hear your objections."

"For starters," he said, "it's an unworkable idea. We both travel and are rarely here."

"I'd take a leave of absence from the airline. Next obstacle?" she said with an irritating flippancy.

"I don't—"

He'd been about to say that he didn't love her. At the very least, he believed a kid deserved to be brought into the world by two people who loved each other.

A victim of divorce when he was less than two years old, John didn't remember living with a complete family. Until he was old enough to be independent, he had been shuttled back and forth between two distracted individuals to whom he was an afterthought, an inconvenience, and a reminder of their failed attempt at marriage.

His parents had diligently pursued their respective careers and had been successful. His father had attained tenure in the humanities department of an Ivy League university. His mother held a vice presidency in an architectural firm.

But as parents they had been abysmal failures. Beyond obligatory calls on holidays, he had little contact with them now. They certainly didn't exercise any influence over his life, nor did they care to. Their infrequent conversations were polite but distant. From birth, he had been treated as an intrusion into their busy lives. That self-perception hadn't changed in forty-three years.

Consequently, he had developed a jaundiced regard for hearth and home. His dysfunctional family hadn't prepared him for long-term relationships, nor had it instilled in him a desire to be a father. Quite the contrary.

He had nothing against children. In fact, he felt compassion for them. More often than not, defenseless kids were stuck with rotten parents. So, if you knew from the start that you were likely to be a lousy parent, why have a baby?

Through his studies in psychology, he had learned what a handicap parents could be to a child's emotional development. They could turn a perfectly good baby into a maladjusted adult at best, or into a serial killer at worst. To err this grossly, parents didn't necessarily have to be abusive or malicious, just selfish.

That's why he had refused to have a baby with Lisa—he wasn't that selfish. He seriously doubted that he and Lisa would grow old together. It was irresponsible to have a child when you knew with a measurable degree of certainty that you would make his or her life miserable.

Added to that was the fiasco that had prompted him to resign from the FBI. As though reading his thoughts, Lisa touched on that sore spot: "Does this have anything to do with what happened out in New Mexico?"

"No."

"I think it does."

"It *doesn't*."

"If you would only talk to me about it, John, you'd feel better."

"I don't want to talk about it, and I don't want a baby. Period. End of discussion."

"You selfish son of a bitch!"

She pouted for several days before deigning to speak to him again. He didn't trust her not to get pregnant without his consent, so he scheduled a vasectomy and used condoms in the meantime.

Before he could have the surgery, Lisa got pissed over the condoms and exited his life forever. Shortly after that, he had been called to Denver to escort a witness back to South Carolina.

And now here he was, giving a baby a drink of water by letting him suck the tip of his finger. Three weeks ago, under threat of death, he wouldn't have gone near a baby. He wouldn't have touched one or even talked to one. What he was doing now wouldn't have been within the realm of possibility.

"Life's a bitch, huh, Kevin?"

The baby now seemed content and satisfied. John checked his watch. Shit. Twenty-three minutes had passed since Kendall had left. He couldn't let her get back before he did. As long as she believed that he still had amnesia, he held the advantage. If she found out that he'd left the house in search of a—

Telephone!

In his rush to give the baby a drink, he had forgotten the reason why he was here. He turned off the water and rushed back to the living room. There it was, sitting on an end table, an old-fashioned black rotary-dial telephone.

John laughed out loud as he picked up the receiver. Then he realized that the line was dead. He jiggled the button, hoping that, like the water pipes, the telephone needed to be primed. But it was no use, and now he was wasting time.

With Kevin tucked into the sling, John closed the front door securely behind him. "Sorry about the window glass," he muttered to the absent owners as he eased himself down the steps and picked up the crutch he'd left on the porch.

At least the return trip was downhill, but the heat was brutal, and his muscles, normally toned by two or three strenuous workouts a week, felt like jelly being spiked with nails.

When he reached the mailbox at the end of the drive, he leaned against it and sucked air into his burning lungs. The metal box was hot, and after a few seconds it felt like a brand against his arm.

Leave a note in the mailbox, you dumb jerk!

The discomfort was worth that burst of inspiration. He could write a note tonight, then sneak out and place it in the mailbox. He would address the note to the postman and tell him to summon the local authorities. He would also write down the telephone number of his office, and Pepperdyne's, in case the postman thought it was a prank and wanted to check him out. Then he would raise the red flag on the mailbox. With any luck, the postman would notice it tomorrow and stop. Even better, he might catch the postman on his route.

Now that he had another plan in mind, he felt energized. He covered the distance back to the house in half the time. Even so, as he reached the porch he heard her car turning into the lane.

He dropped one of his crutches in the living room and limped down the hallway and into the bathroom. He locked the door behind him and pressed his head against it. His muscles were screaming in protest. His breathing was as loud as a thrashing machine. His clothes were sopping wet. And he stank.

If Kendall saw him like this, she would know he was up to something.

Although he was trembling with fatigue, he lifted Kevin out of the sling and laid him on the bath mat on the floor. "We're in this together, right?" He pushed the stopper into the tub drain and turned on the water.

He heard her footsteps on the porch.

"John?"

Working frantically, he stripped to the skin and stuffed his sweaty clothes into the hamper, then he went to work on Kevin.

"John?"

"Yeah?" He had Kevin stripped down to his diaper.

"Where are you?"

"Kendall?" Off came Kevin's diaper. "Are you back already?"

John lowered himself into the tub, keeping his cast out of the water. It took some maneuvering, but he managed to bend forward far enough to duck his head beneath the faucet and thoroughly wet his hair, then he reached for the naked baby lying on the bath mat.

"You're a real sport," he whispered as he leaned back and laid Kevin on his chest. "I won't forget this, pal."

"John, what are you doing? Where's Kevin?"

"What? I can't hear you, Kendall. The water's running."

"Where's Kevin?"

"He's in here with me." He splashed water over the baby, who cooed in delight and happily slapped his palms against John's chest.

"He's with you?"

"Of course. Where'd you think he was?"

She tried the doorknob. "You locked the door."

"Oh. Sorry," he lied.

"Open the door."

"I'm already in the tub. And it's a hell of a feat to get in and out of it with this cast on."

"I'm coming in."

He had guessed she would. He'd heard the panic in her voice, and it made clear to him that even though they were lovers, she didn't entirely trust him.

And she was smart not to.

Given an opportunity today he would have turned her in. If the house had been occupied, if the telephone had been working, if he had been able to flag down a car, federal officers would be on their way now to take her back into custody.

He had failed today, but he would try again tomorrow, and the next day, and for as long as it took. Without his weapon, and with his busted leg, he could offer her little protection if any members of the Brotherhood came looking for her.

The government needed her testimony to put the Burnwoods away. Moreover, she didn't stand a chance against the secret society of vigilantes unless she had the government's protection. He planned to get it for her, although she would hate him for it.

The flimsy lock opened with a hairpin. Kendall burst through the door, then drew up short when she saw the two of them reclining in the tub. They made quite a sight—he with one leg dangling over the side of the tub and Kevin looking small and smooth and pink against his chest.

"You're just in time to join us," he said, smiling up at her guilelessly. "Although it might be a tight squeeze. Can you turn off those faucets for me? I think the water's deep enough."

"What are you doing?" Her voice was shrill with anxiety, as though she hadn't heard a word of his glib greeting.

Looking puzzled, he stated the obvious: "Taking a bath."

"With Kevin?"

"Why not? I thought he would enjoy cooling off, too."

"I came in and the house looked deserted. I didn't know where you were. Kevin wasn't in his crib. I thought . . . I don't know what I thought."

She sat down heavily on the commode lid. On the verge of tears, her face was pale and her lips had lost their color. Bending her head down, she massaged her temples. She was very upset, and John didn't think it was solely because he and Kevin had been momentarily out of her sight.

Something had happened in town.

What? She was even more shaken now than she'd been a few days ago when she had butchered her hair in an attempt to disguise herself. He needed to know the latest update. How had she obtained the information? What had she learned to make her so upset?

She dropped her hand into her lap and raised her head. "Please don't scare me like that again, John."

The way she was looking at him, and her tremulous tone of voice, made him feel like an A-1 bastard. "I didn't mean to scare you."

Before he went entirely soft, he reminded himself that, pathetic as she looked with her stricken expression and ragged hair, this woman had committed two federal offenses—kidnapping, and fleeing to avoid giving testimony.

It was his sworn duty to use whatever means necessary to bring her in unharmed. Granted, his methods weren't exactly orthodox, but the training manual hadn't covered these particular circumstances. He was doing the best he could.

He hadn't asked for this assignment. It had been thrust on him first by Jim, then by Kendall. So if he had to make up the game plan as he went along, that was just too damn bad. Keeping his recovered memory a secret, bonding with the baby, and making love with Kendall were, in this instance, job requirements.

Good speech, McGrath. If he recited it often enough, he might even believe it himself.

Chapter Thirty-six

RICKI SUE IMPATIENTLY PICKED AT THE LOOSE cuticle on her thumb. When old man Bristol himself had approached her desk and discreetly asked her to follow him, she had pretended that a summons from a senior partner was a daily occurrence.

Ignoring the curious stares of clerks and paralegals, she held her shoulders straight and her head high as she followed Bristol's waddling gait down the carpeted hallway to the conference room, where he held open the massive door for her.

"Wait in here, please, Miss Robb. They'll be with you shortly."

Yeah, right, she thought.

She had been in here for over half an hour and "they" hadn't yet appeared. The conference room was seldom used and had all the gaiety of a mausoleum. It was cold enough to store meat. From gilded frames, austere portraits of partners long deceased stared down at her, their forbidding expressions lofty and judgmental.

She had a fleeting impulse to flash the sour pusses, then thought better of it. She wouldn't put it past the partners of

Bristol and Mathers to keep hidden cameras on their employees. They had caught Kendall, hadn't they?

Ricki Sue wouldn't have admitted it even under torture, but she was nervous. FBI agents had already questioned her several times, more than anyone else in the firm, because obviously they knew that she was Mrs. Burnwood's special friend.

She had told them nothing, of course. And she would continue to play dumb even if they rammed bamboo shoots underneath her fingernails.

Suddenly the door whooshed open and a man strode in, trailed by two others. All were dressed in dark suits and white shirts, but there was no question as to which one was in charge. His demeanor as well as his walk were straightforward and purposeful.

"Miss Robb? I'm Special Agent Pepperdyne."

He introduced the agents accompanying him, but Ricki Sue was so taken by Pepperdyne's air of authority that she paid scant attention to his cohorts. Besides, she had already met them. They were the ones who had questioned her before.

Apparently she rated the top gun this time. Pepperdyne. He was kinda cute, and he certainly knew how to make an entrance. She wished old man Bristol had given her time to check her hair and put on fresh lipstick.

Without preamble, Pepperdyne said, "I'm running out of time, Miss Robb, so let's cut to the chase."

He sat on the corner of the conference table and tossed a heavy file folder onto its glossy surface. Several documents spilled out, but Ricki Sue didn't need to read them to know what they were.

"When we first began running a computer check into Kendall Deaton's background, we turned up some confusing data. It took us a while to straighten it out. Now we know everything."

"Is that so?"

"Yes, that's so." He scanned several of the documents, although she guessed he knew their contents as well as she did. "Tampering with evidence is a pretty serious charge for a lawyer."

"The allegation was never proved," Ricki Sue retorted. "And in America isn't someone presumed innocent until proven guilty?"

He slammed his hand down on the table, and she shivered with prurient excitement. She would love to get this guy in bed and see him really riled.

"This file is chock-full of reports of lies and deceit and mismanagement of confidential information. But then I don't need to itemize the contents for you, because you know it all, right?"

"Then why'd you ask to see me privately?" Lowering her voice, she asked with a seductive undertone, "Or isn't this meeting business related?"

The two other agents snickered, but Pepperdyne remained impassive. He shot his subordinates a warning glance, then fixed an intimidating stare on Ricki Sue.

"You sure are taking this lightly, Miss Robb. Mrs. Burnwood's life is in peril, while you're cracking jokes and making sexual innuendos. A federal officer is missing, and it appears that she's the only person on the planet who might know where he is. I want them both found, and you're going to help me."

"Why should I?" She flicked her hand at the file. "Now that you think you know everything, why should I help you?"

"Because you've professed to be Mrs. Burnwood's friend and I have every reason to fear that she might not live much longer."

Addressing the other two agents, she said, "Feel free to start playing 'good cop' at any time." Then she said to Pepperdyne, "You're the bad cop, right? You're using scare tactics to get me to talk. Well, I'm not falling for that bullshit. Do you think I was born yesterday? Actually it was April 14, 1962. Okay, 1960, but who's counting?"

Pepperdyne's eyes narrowed. "You still think this is a joke? I assure you, it's not. Your friend kidnapped a U.S. marshal. For all we know, she has killed John McGrath and disposed of his body."

"She wouldn't do that!" Ricki Sue exclaimed.

"She left Marshal Fordham's body in a sinking car," he shouted.

"That woman was already dead," Ricki Sue shouted back. "The newspaper said so. I read the coroner's report the same as you did, so stop trying to bully me. My friend wouldn't harm a fly. Especially a guy with a broken leg and amnesia, for crissake. In fact, I'm sure she's counting on him for protection."

"Then she's in even greater danger than you can possibly imagine." Pepperdyne's voice turned surprisingly quiet, but it was filled with such foreboding that it raised gooseflesh on her freckled arms. "Because if there's one man Mrs. Burnwood shouldn't be messing with, it's John McGrath."

Ricki Sue divided a wary glance between the other agents, but they remained stoically silent and deferential to their superior.

"Two years ago," he began, "in some shithole town in New Mexico, the name of which I can't even recall, a man barged into a federal bank one morning, wielding two automatic weapons and hundreds of rounds of ammunition. He demanded to speak to his ex-wife, whom he hoped to persuade to come back to him and patch things up.

"Ordinarily his wife worked as a teller in the bank, but, unknown to him, she had called in sick that day. When the nutcase learned of his mistake, he went even nuttier and decided, What the hell? Since he was already there, armed to the teeth, he'd just as well start shooting until he'd killed everybody in the building, or until his ex-wife promised to reconcile, whichever came first."

Ricki Sue assumed a bored air. She shifted in her seat and sighed. "This is a really fascinating story, Mr. Pepperdyne, but—"

"Shut up and listen."

"Okay, I'm listening." She folded her arms over her massive breasts. "But this time away from my desk better not count as my break or I'm gonna be pissed."

Ignoring her, Pepperdyne continued. "As the day stretched out, the hostage situation inside that bank got real sticky. Local police tried to reason with the gunman, but he grew more antsy and trigger-happy by the hour.

"Just to let them know he meant business, he shot a bank guard and threw his body out a second-story window. That's when I was called in. I flew down there and took with me the best negotiator the bureau had, Dr. John McGrath."

Ricki Sue's eyes opened wide.

"Yes, *Dr.* John McGrath. He holds Ph.D.s in psychology and criminology. Anyway, by the time we got there, a communication system had already been set up. John politely asked the nutcase to talk to him over the phone. He made all the promises we make in standoff situations like that, and he did it so well, he had me believing we'd deliver.

"John talked to him about his wife. Did he really expect her to be enamored by this behavior? Would she want him back if he continued to kill? Stuff like that. The gunman's resolve began to waver. John was getting through. We were hopeful that it would end without somebody else getting killed.

"One of the hostages had her two kids with her, an infant and a toddler around two years old. To make a long story short, the baby started crying. Then the toddler tuned up. The racket made the gunman nervous. He ordered their mother to keep them quiet.

"She did her best, but the kids were tired and hungry. They were too young to understand the danger they were in, and they continued to whine and cry. The gunman threatened to shoot them if they didn't shut up. I can't describe to you what it was like for us to listen to those little kids crying and to hear their mother pleading for their lives to be spared.

"I honestly don't know how John managed to sound so calm. The rest of us were cussing and pacing, but John kept his cool. He pulled out all the stops. He promised the nutcase the goddamn moon if he would release that mother and her kids unharmed. His voice sounded as composed and unruffled as a hypnotist's, but he was as anxious as the rest of us. Before or since, I've never seen a man sweat like that. He nearly tore his hair out during that negotiation. He wanted like hell to save those babies."

He stopped talking, and Ricki Sue knew that he was looking inward, remembering. She swallowed noisily. "What happened?"

Pepperdyne's eyes pinned her to the tufted leather chair. "The guy shot them at point-blank range. In cold blood, Miss Robb. Mother. Baby. Little boy. He took them out in three clean shots. Luckily, a SWAT team rushed in and blew the guy apart, but he'd already executed that pretty young woman and her babies.

"We all took it hard, but no one took it harder than John. I watched my colleague and friend come apart at the seams. A few months after the incident, he quit the Bureau and went to work for the U.S. Marshal's office.

"To this day he blames himself. He believes he failed, and that his failure cost a young man his whole family. There was nothing more John could have done, nothing he could have said that he didn't say. His powers of persuasion had never been more effective, but none of his efforts paid off. He couldn't spare those three lives, and he's been sick with guilt over it ever since."

A heavy silence ensued. Ricki Sue wilted beneath Pepperdyne's smoldering stare. Finally she asked, "Why are you telling me this?"

"To let you know that your friend might think she's done something really smart by taking John, but she's walking a tightrope and doesn't even know it. He's emotionally unstable, especially around babies."

He leaned down until his nose was almost touching hers. "Are you getting my drift, Ricki Sue?" he asked softly, dropping all formality. "Mrs. Burnwood and her baby are in danger."

Ricki Sue had become so entranced by the sexy intensity in Pepperdyne's eyes that at first she didn't respond. Finally she blinked and angled her head back, away from him. "You're bullshitting me again, and it won't work."

He consulted the other two agents: "Am I bullshitting her?"

Solemnly they shook their heads. Pepperdyne turned back to her. "Even though John lost his memory in that car wreck, trust me, that phobia about kids is still buried deep in his subconscious. He goes nuts every time he's around a kid. You should have seen him during that flight we all took together from Denver to Dallas. He hears a baby cry, he freaks."

"If he's as unstable as you say, why did you entrust them to him in the first place?" she asked.

"Because I didn't know they were going to have a wreck, or that Deputy Fordham was going to die. I'll have to take full responsibility if John cracks up and does something harmful. My intentions were good. I thought that protecting Mrs. Burnwood and her baby would be good therapy for him. Of course, I had no idea she would do something this foolhardy. And criminal.

"As it is," he said, spreading his hands innocently, "I can't guarantee that John hasn't already snapped and done them in."

"He hasn't. They're okay." Then, realizing that she had slipped, Ricki Sue swore beneath her breath.

Pepperdyne pounced on it. "So you have heard from her?"

"No. No, I haven't."

"Where is she?"

"I don't know."

"Ricki Sue, you aren't doing her any favors by keeping her whereabouts a secret."

"I swear I don't know where she is." She realized she was blinking too rapidly, a telltale sign that she was lying. "Okay, I have talked to her. This morning. She called here at the office, knowing that I would answer the phone. She told me that she and Kevin were all right, then she hung up. She only talked for a few seconds because she was afraid y'all might be tracing incoming calls."

She waited for him to deny it. He merely gazed back at her. "You have tapped the phones here, haven't you? And probably mine at home, too!" She shot to her feet. "You goddamn son of a bitch! If you already knew that I'd talked to her, why'd you hound me about it?"

"Sit down."

"Go fuck yourself."

"Sit down." Pepperdyne pushed her back into the chair. Ricki Sue was mad enough to chew nails, but she was also excited. He really was attractive when he got angry.

"You're her oldest friend, Ricki Sue. You must have some idea where she is."

"You've been eavesdropping. You heard me ask her where she is. She refused to tell me."

"But you must have an idea."

"I don't."

"If I find out you're lying to me, I'll have you charged with aiding and abetting."

"Oooh, I'm scared." She hugged her elbows and shuddered.

"Cute."

"Think so?" Grinning, she winked at the two other agents. Pepperdyne looked ready to strangle her—which she thought might be a lot of fun.

"Look, I didn't even know where she was the whole year she spent in Denver," she said. "I swear that's the truth. She didn't tell me or her grandmother where she was living. It was for our own protection, she said. She didn't want us to have to lie if someone came searching for her." Ricki Sue gave him a cheeky grin. "She's very clever that way."

"Much more clever than you." Pepperdyne placed his hands on the arms of her chair and leaned over her. "She's in the company of a man who comes unglued every time he hears a baby crying. Mrs. Burnwood has a baby."

Ricki Sue made a noise like the buzzer on a quiz show when a contestant gives the wrong answer. "Try again. McGrath couldn't be that unstable or he wouldn't be working at all. That fed-cum-shrink isn't going to hurt Kevin or her."

Pepperdyne's level stare lasted for what seemed an eternity. Finally he said, "Maybe not. But John's mental stability is just one of her problems."

He extended his hand to one of the other agents, who slapped a manila envelope into his palm with the efficiency of an OR nurse with a scalpel. Pepperdyne's eyes never left Ricki Sue's as he opened the envelope and removed a photograph. Without saying a word, he handed it to her.

Ricki Sue looked at it and gave a sharp cry. Bile rose in her throat. She clapped her hand over her mouth. Her freckles stood out in sharp contrast to her sudden paleness.

"That's what Gibb and Matt Burnwood did to Matt's lover, Lottie Lynam, the one who helped him escape jail. The cut was so deep, it almost severed her head."

"Please!" Ricki Sue gasped, holding up a trembling hand.

"Please? Please stop? Please don't say any more?" He raised his voice. "Hell yes I'll say more, if it'll jar some information out of you."

"I've told you," she whimpered, "I don't know where Kendall is."

"You're missing the big picture, Ricki Sue. Jailbreak is a serious crime. Not to mention rape and murder. Yes, we believe that Mrs. Lynam was raped before her throat was cut. These are madmen we're dealing with. It's obvious the Burnwoods will stop at nothing. At this point there's no going back for them. The lives they previously led are over, and they know it. They've got nothing to lose.

"But even madmen don't go to these extremes unless they're on a mission." He leaned closer to her and whispered, "Now, what do you suppose that mission is?"

"To find . . . find her."

"Precisely," he said, nodding grimly.

"Was it them who broke into her grandma's house?"

"We presume so. Scary, isn't it?"

"They're that close?"

"They're that determined. At least Gibb is, and apparently Matt goes along with anything his father says or does."

Ricki Sue nodded. That had been her first impression, and every confidence Kendall had shared regarding her marriage confirmed it.

"It's all or nothing now," Pepperdyne said. "The Burnwoods don't even care if they're caught, so long as they silence the person who blew the whistle on them in the first place. They feel that she betrayed them. In their opinion, she's a heretic. They're righteously indignant that she dared question their methods and turn against them.

"And keep in mind that until a few days ago, Matt Burnwood didn't even know he had a son. I don't think he's too happy with his ex-wife for keeping that boy a secret from him."

He smiled faintly. "You haven't seen the baby yet, have you, Ricki Sue? I've seen him. I've held him. He's a cute little guy. Looks a lot like his mother, your best friend."

"Stop."

He added in a bland, matter-of-fact tone, "In the course of my career, I've investigated a lot of unspeakable crimes. But I have to tell you that what I've learned about the Burnwoods and the Brotherhood over the last few days has made my blood run cold, and we've barely skimmed the surface."

He leaned down again, bringing his face close to hers. "I can envision these fanatics performing some kind of ritualistic killing on the baby, just to prove that they're chosen. Holy. Above the laws of man; even above the laws of God. Do you want little Kevin to wind up looking like this?" He held the photo of Lottie Lynam up to her face.

"Stop it!" Ricki Sue knocked the picture out of his hand and tried to stand.

Pepperdyne pressed her shoulder, keeping her in the chair. "If you know where Mrs. Burnwood is hiding, you'll be saving her life by telling me."

"I swear I don't know," Ricki Sue said, sobbing.

"*Think!* Where would she go?"

"I don't know!"

Pepperdyne straightened up and gave a deep sigh. "Very well, Ricki Sue. Don't trust me. Don't tell me. But by keeping silent you're placing two lives in grave danger, not to mention Marshal McGrath's."

He laid his business card on the table. "On the back I've written the local number where I can be reached. We've set up an office in the Sheridan Police Department. Someone there will know where I am twenty-four hours a day. If Mrs. Burnwood calls, tell her to come in. Beg her to come in. I swear we'll protect her."

Ricki Sue wiped her running nose with the back of her hand. "You'll protect her? Like you did before?"

She derived some satisfaction from getting in that parting shot. Pepperdyne was frowning when he stormed from the room.

Chapter Thirty-seven

"**M**AMA'S MADDER THAN A WET HEN." LOOKING glum, Henry hung up the pay telephone and turned to his brother.

Luther was eating a bean burrito and drinking a Big Red. Absently, he offered a bite of the burrito to Henry. His attention had been drawn to the three teenage girls who were pumping gas into a Mustang convertible in one of the self-service bays at the convenience store.

"They ought not to run around half-nekkid like that," Luther observed, taking a swig of his soda. "Their britches are so short their butt cheeks are showing. And look how skimpy those tops are. But if a guy like me was to try and take some of what they're showin' off, there'd be hell to pay. Jailbait," he grumbled.

Henry glanced at the girls but was too crestfallen to appreciate the view. He had just received a tongue-lashing from Mama, which was almost as painful as the whippings his daddy used to give him with a strop. Mama's harsh criticism could almost raise welts. "Did you hear what I said, Luther? Mama's pissed at us."

Luther finished the burrito in one huge bite, wadded up the wrapping, and dropped it on the ground. "How come?"

"On account of what happened last night."

"How were we supposed to know the feds would be inside that old lady's house? I thought it was damn clever of us to trace Mrs. Burnwood to that house. Did you tell Mama that?"

"I tried. But I don't think she got it all. She was yellin' too loud. You know how she gets. When she's on a tear, she ain't interested in listenin'."

Luther nodded. The girls passed him on their way inside to pay for the gas. They were so involved in their giggling conversation that they didn't give him a second glance. Rich girls like that, who drove shiny new cars their daddies gave them when they turned sixteen, were worlds above him. They looked through him as if he were invisible, like he was trash. Luther resented that.

"There ought to be a law against them letting their tits jiggle like that," he muttered. "I mean, Jesus! They know damn well what it does to a guy."

"Will you stop jerking off and pay attention," Henry shouted.

Henry was only a few minutes older than his twin, but he took the role of elder sibling seriously. He was the planner, the worrier. It had never been cause for conflict between them. Luther submitted to his brother's leadership qualities. He preferred to be free of the responsibility. He did what he was told to do. He could be counted on to do his part in any undertaking, legal or not, but his participation was physical, not mental.

Henry was still despondent over Mama's lecture. "She said that even if our brains were combined, we'd come up short. She said even a damn fool could figure out Mrs. Burnwood wouldn't go back to her granny's house, that it was the first place everybody'd be looking for her."

"Can I tell you something, Henry?" Luther asked. "Swear to God you'll never repeat it, especially to Mama?"

"What?"

"I peed my pants when those feds came running after us, shooting. I ain't never been that scared."

"Me neither. We got lucky, is all, or our asses would be in jail right now."

The mention of jail immediately reminded them of Billy Joe and the hardships he continued to suffer because of the woman they sought. Occasionally their zeal would diminish, as they became tired, or discouraged, or bored with this difficult undertaking.

But each reminder of their little brother, locked behind bars with queers and weirdos of every color, having to live the rest of his life as a freak with only one arm, fanned the fires of hatred and rekindled their vows of vengeance.

"Well, we're wasting time standin' around here," Henry said. "Every minute that passes, her trail grows colder."

"I'll be right back." Luther headed for the entrance. "I want me another burrito."

Henry grabbed the back of Luther's shirt and hauled him to the car. "Burrito, my ass. You want another gander at those girls."

"Nothing wrong with looking, is there?"

For an hour they cruised the streets of Sheridan, hoping that something in Kendall Burnwood's hometown would spark an idea, hoping that they would absorb by osmosis a clue that would lead them to Kendall's hiding place, which they'd learned the hard way wasn't inside her late grandmother's house in a sparsely populated area on the outskirts of town.

They hadn't figured it would be so hard to find her. They were discouraged and homesick. Back in Prosper, Mama was furious over their failure. If they didn't produce something quick, she would have their hides for sure.

After an hour of aimless driving, Henry pulled into the parking lot of the courthouse. "What the hell are you doing here, Henry?" Luther glanced around nervously. "Cops are thicker than flies on a dead possum."

"They didn't get a good look at us or our car. The papers said we were 'unidentified intruders.' For all they know, we were thieving kids looking for a stereo to fence for dope money."

The explanation did nothing to calm Luther's jitters. "I still don't get it. What're we doing here?"

"Watching."

"Watching what?"

"Just watching to see what we can see. We might pick up something. I don't figure we're going to find that bitch by ourselves. Somebody's gonna have to lead us to her."

Luther slouched down in his seat, leaned his head back, and closed his eyes. He whistled tunelessly through his teeth and entertained lewd fantasies in which the three teenage girls in short shorts and crop-tops were enthusiastically granting his every wish. He must have dozed, because he jumped when Henry poked him in the ribs.

"Come on, let's go."

He sat up and yawned. "Where to?"

"See those men crossing the street yonder?"

Luther followed Henry's pointing finger. "In the dark suits?"

"They just came out of the courthouse. What do they look like to you?"

"Feebs, as I live and breathe."

"Uh-huh."

"Ain't that the building where Mrs. Burnwood used to work? They're in a hurry to get there."

"That's why I think this might be important," Henry said.

They left their car and hastened across the street, following the FBI agents into the building that housed the Bristol and Mathers offices. They had already done some amateur sleuthing around the building, but it hadn't brought them any closer to finding their prey.

"They're up there all right," Henry remarked as they entered the lobby. "See where the elevator stopped? Fifth floor."

They loitered in the lobby, trying not to look conspicuous, although they were so remarkably alike that nearly everyone who came into the building did a double take when they saw them.

Luther soon grew bored with the stakeout and began complaining, but Henry refused to leave. It was half an hour later when their diligence paid off. The elevator emptied the three men into the lobby. They were obviously agitated. One was talking as briskly as he walked.

"I still say she's holding back. She's much more afraid of betraying her friend than she is of us."

That was all the Crooks heard before the three men went through the revolving glass door. The twins looked at each other. "What do you reckon that was all about?" Luther asked.

As though in answer, the elevator doors opened again and a large, busty woman with a totem pole of red hair marched out. Her face was blotchy and her eyes were puffy and red, making it obvious that she'd been crying.

Even as Luther and Henry watched, she put a tissue to her nose and honked loudly. She didn't notice the twins because she was focused on the trio of federal agents who were now making their way across the street to the courthouse. As soon as she got outside, she shot them the bird. Although the agents missed the gesture, it seemed to give her immense satisfaction.

"Who's the fat gal?"

"I don't know," Henry replied thoughtfully. "But there's no love lost between her and the feebs, is there? And who else could they have in common except Kendall Burnwood?"

"She's disgusting."

Gibb swept the stack of *Playgirl* magazines off Ricki Sue's coffee table. "Filth. Rubbish. Just what you'd expect to find in the house of a whore."

Matt stared down at the magazines on the floor, but if he found them as repulsive as his father did, he didn't show it. He had been virtually unresponsive since leaving the motel where they had killed Lottie and left her body.

"This woman is loud and obnoxious. Always making lewd innuendos. Remember how she embarrassed us at your wedding, son?"

"Yes, sir."

"Not at all a proper friend for the wife of a Burnwood."

"No, sir."

"But then, as it turns out, you were married to a traitor."

"Yes, sir."

For several hours they had been in Ricki Sue's house, searching for a clue to Kendall's whereabouts. They had emptied every drawer and read every sheet of paper in the house, whether it was a tax return, a diary, or a Post-it with a handwritten reminder.

So far they had turned up nothing about Kendall, but they had a clear insight into Ricki Sue's lifestyle. Besides having the largest supply of beauty products outside a drugstore, she had an extensive collection of erotic books and videos.

They had discovered a supply of condoms in her nightstand drawer that would rival a pharmacist's inventory. There was a full range of designs, colors, and sizes.

She liked overly sweet floral perfumes and bath gels. She owned a vast amount of lingerie, including one floor-length plaid flannel nightgown and two pairs of crotchless panties.

Her kitchen cupboards were stocked with cookies, potato chips, and diet sodas. In her refrigerator they found only a quart of milk, four six-packs of beer, and a cloudy jar of olives.

Ricki Sue was not a meticulous housekeeper, but by the time Matt and Gibb finished their search, it didn't matter. They had thoroughly ransacked the place. They were now making one last walk-through to make certain they hadn't overlooked anything.

"Did you look under the bed?" Gibb asked.

"No, sir."

They had stripped off the covers when they searched beneath the mattress, but neither remembered looking beneath the bed. Matt knelt. "There's a box down here, Dad."

Gibb was instantly alert. "What kind of box?"

Matt retrieved the ordinary shoe box and raised the dusty lid. When he saw that it contained a stack of personal letters and postcards, he showed it to Gibb. "There might be something in there from Kendall," Gibb said excitedly. "Let's get started."

They went to the living room, where there was more room to spread out the pieces of correspondence. Before they started sorting through them, Gibb held up his hand for quiet. He crept to the front window and peered out. "She's here. Her car just pulled into the driveway."

He gave the collection of pornographic books a glance of unmitigated disgust, then slowly moved his eyes to Matt. "We must take advantage of this opportunity, Matthew. We were sent here to do this, son. It was meant to be. Why else would she come home unexpectedly, hours before her normal work-day ends? Do you understand what I'm saying?"

Without a word of contradiction or misgiving, Matt nodded. "Yes, sir."

Gibb signaled for him to hide behind the door. Gibb stepped into the dining alcove, which kept him partially hidden while affording him a view of the front door. Both men's eyes were on the doorknob as Ricki Sue inserted her key.

"Hey, Red!"

The shout came from the street.

At this unexpected turn, Matt looked to Gibb for further instruction. Gibb was peeping between the slats of the blinds, trying to see who had distracted Ricki Sue.

"Hey, what?" She left her key in the lock and turned from the door to see who had shouted at her.

"We're looking for Sunset Street. Do you know where it's at?"

"Maybe I do, and maybe I don't," she answered saucily.

"Care to come over here and discuss it with us?"

Gibb's features turned rigid with outrage. He jabbed the air with his index finger, indicating that Matt should look outside. An old Camaro was parked at the curb. Inside it were Henry and Luther Crook.

"What are they doing here?" Gibb whispered.

Ricki Sue had sauntered over to the car and was leaning into the driver's window to give directions to Sunset Street. She was flirting, and the twins were obviously dazzled by her abundant figure.

"They must be doing the same thing we are," Gibb said after a moment. "They're trying to locate Kendall because of Billy Joe. They blame her for his unfortunate accident." He snickered.

"They want vengeance, so they've got to find her before the authorities do." He looked at Matt. "The same as us, son. Except they don't have the Higher Power on their side like we do. It was probably them who walked into that FBI trap at her grandmother's house. The newspapers have speculated that it was us. As though we'd be that stupid."

Matt listened, continually nodding in agreement.

Ricki Sue was gesturing broadly, telling the twins how to reach their destination.

Gibb moved behind Matt and laid a hand on his shoulder. "Let's go. Obviously the Lord changed his mind. The time isn't right. When it is, he'll let us know. Bring the box."

Gibb headed for the bedroom and the back window through which they had let themselves in. Wordlessly, Matt followed.

Chapter Thirty-eight

THE SHERIDAN POLICEMAN STEPPED INTO PEPPER-dyne's temporary office. "Somebody wants to speak to you, sir. She refused to talk to anyone else. Line three."

"She"? Mrs. Burnwood? With a surge of hope, Pepperdyne snatched up the telephone receiver and depressed the blinking button. "Pepperdyne speaking."

"You son of a bitch."

"Pardon?"

"You heard me. You're a scum-sucking son of a bitch! And that's just for starters. When I run out of all the dirty names I know in English, I'm going to start on foreign languages until you get the general idea of how loathsome I think you are."

Pepperdyne sighed. "I get the general idea, Ms. Robb. Want to tell me what prompted this obscene call?"

"You know why I'm calling, you lowlife prick!"

Her shout was so loud that other agents in the room could hear her through the receiver. They stopped what they were doing and looked askance at Pepperdyne. Most of them proba-bly wished they had Ricki Sue Robb's nerve.

"Those lousy bastards tore up my house," she yelled.

"What lousy bastards?"

"*Your* lousy bastards. They pawed through my drawers. And I mean that literally. My undies are scattered all over the floor—"

"Wait a minute." Pepperdyne sprang forward in the reclining chair. "Your house has been ransacked?"

"No shit, Sherlock."

"And you think my men did it?"

"Don't play dumb with me. They—"

"I'm on my way." He hung up on her. Barking orders for two of his men to come with him, he yanked his suit jacket from the coat tree and jogged to the nearest exit.

Five minutes later, he was facing Ricki Sue at her front door. She was trembling with indignation so intense that her hair sculpture was beginning to crack.

"The FBI needs to give you a crash course in manners, Special Agent Pepperdyne. First you send a couple of perverts over here to trash my place, then you hang up on me. I'm not paying another red cent in taxes if this is the best the fucking federal—"

"My 'perverts' didn't trash your place." He moved her aside, went in, and began firing questions. "Is this exactly the way you found it? What time did you discover the break-in? Have you noticed anything missing? Have you touched anything?"

While the two other agents milled around, assessing the extent of the damage without disturbing anything that might later become evidence, Ricki Sue took root in the middle of her living room, her fists planted solidly on her wide hips.

"Are you jerking me around, Pepperdyne?"

"No," he replied. "For an authorized search, you would have been served a warrant. We're playing strictly by the book on this one, just in case a judge with more compassion than brains, or ethics, chooses to dismiss the case later on a technicality. Anyway, I assure you that whoever did this isn't from my office, the U.S. Marshal's office, or the Sheridan police."

"Then who the hell was it?"

"I don't know. But I intend to find out," he added tersely. "Is anything missing?"

"I haven't noticed anything, but I haven't really looked. I came in, saw the mess, and was so angry I didn't take inventory before calling you."

"Check around."

She did as he asked while his men got on the phone and requested that a crime lab unit be dispatched immediately. Ricki Sue stood by and watched helplessly as her house was pillaged for the second time that day, this time by professionals looking for clues as to who might have initially vandalized it.

"Look, this isn't an ordinary B&E," Pepperdyne said when her vocal protests turned vituperative. "We're working on a federal case, and because of your close personal relationship with Mrs. Burnwood, you've become an important element in this case."

"This was probably a random burglary and had nothing to do with that."

"You don't believe that any more than I do," he said, guessing that her angry outbursts were bluffs to hide her increasing apprehension. Her complaints had lost some of their previous bluster, which was good. If he couldn't bully her into helping them locate her friend, maybe fear would motivate her to reveal a few secrets.

"Whoever did this wasn't out to steal," he explained. "He didn't take the normal stuff—TVs, cameras, stereos. He was looking for something altogether different."

"Like what?"

"Like a clue into Mrs. Burnwood's whereabouts."

"Then they're s.o.l.—shit out of luck."

Pepperdyne ignored the vulgarity as he picked up on something else. "I'm betting that one man didn't do all this. Subconsciously, so are you. Every reference you've made to the burglars has been plural."

"Don't get all excited, Pepperdyne. I only said what popped into my head."

"It popped into your head for a reason, Ricki Sue. You have someone in mind, don't you? Just as I do."

Suddenly nervous, she wet her lips. "You mean, maybe it was Matt Burnwood and his father?"

"It's a possibility."

"Oh, shit!" She groaned. "I want nothing to do with those goons."

"When I arrived, you referred to the burglars as 'perverts.' Why?" Pepperdyne asked. "Beyond the obvious. They emptied your lingerie drawers, but that's common to all thieves looking for treasure troves."

"It wasn't that." She took his arm and dragged him across the living room to the coffee table. "Look at these magazines."

A naked, muscle-bound hunk smiled enticingly at Pepperdyne from the centerfold of a *Playgirl*. "Quite a schlong. So what?"

"Quite a schlong is right. So why would I grind my heel against it and ruin it?"

In the center of the photo, the paper was pleated, the folds radiating from a central point in a whorl. It did appear that someone had ground his heel on it. "Could have been unintentional."

Ricki Sue shook her collapsing monument of hair. "I don't think so, because there's another one over here. This really pisses me off, too. I paid fifty bucks for this book. It was the one souvenir I brought back from San Francisco when I vacationed there two summers ago."

She directed him around the sofa. Books and videos had been swept from the shelves and left where they'd fallen. Pepperdyne knelt to take a closer look at the book to which she referred. The volume of erotica was opened to a full page color photograph of a couple engaged in a sexual act. Across the photograph were scuff marks, as though someone had cleaned his shoes on it.

"Not exactly the missionary position," Pepperdyne remarked.

"That's why this was the ultimate turn-on picture in the whole book. Jack-be-nimble, the man of my dreams. This pic alone was worth the fifty bucks."

"I'll buy you another copy," Pepperdyne said as he came to his feet. "I'll buy you a whole goddamn library of dirty books if you'll tell me where Mrs. Burnwood is."

"You don't listen very good, do you? Read my lips, asshole. *I don't know.*" She spread her arms wide to encompass the disarray inside the house. "Whoever came here and trashed my place searching for a 'clue' is barking up the same wrong tree as you."

"Sir, it was them all right. The prints match."

Pepperdyne thanked the officer who had brought him the report as soon as it was available, then he spun around and addressed the police captain.

"You heard him. Gibb and Matt Burnwood vandalized Ms. Robb's house this afternoon. They are in this town. Call in every man on your force. My men are at your disposal, and more are on the way. I want these bastards found. Tonight. Now."

The policeman charged off to do Pepperdyne's bidding, but the FBI man called him back for one final word: "They're mean sons of bitches. Tell your men not to be deceived by their good looks and pleasant mannerisms. They're fanatics, believing that they're ordained to carry out a godly mission. They'll kill anyone who stands in their way. Tell your officers to proceed with extreme caution if they sight them."

"Yes, sir."

Pepperdyne flopped back in the desk chair and rubbed his tired eyes with the heels of his palms. Surrendering to his fatigue was a luxury he couldn't afford. Since John had been reported missing, he'd only napped now and then, catching a few minutes of sleep whenever he could. He wouldn't sleep through a whole night until his friend and Mrs. Burnwood were found and Matt and Gibb Burnwood were either dead or behind bars under armed guard.

What he had told that redheaded virago had been a personal confession—he *did* feel responsible for getting John into this mess.

It had begun as a joke, albeit a rather cruel one. He had thought it would be therapeutic for John. Spending time with Mrs. Burnwood's baby might undo the damage done to his psyche in New Mexico.

This had been Pepperdyne's thinking when he entrusted them into John's care. Never in his wildest imagination had he thought his friend would wind up a key player in one of the most bizarre crimes of the decade.

The more the Bureau uncovered on the Brotherhood, the more Pepperdyne feared for John and Mrs. Burnwood. Ritualistic executions and disfigurements, chants and secret passwords, enough torture and bloodshed to make the Marquis de Sade seem an amateur—these were the Brotherhood's stock-in-trade.

Dejectedly, Pepperdyne rose to his feet and stretched his aching lower back. He walked to the window and gazed out over the town of Sheridan. Darkness had fallen. Nighttime would provide the Burnwoods more places to hide and more opportunities to avoid recapture. They were somewhere out there. But where?

Also somewhere out there were Mrs. Burnwood and his friend, John McGrath. No one, not even someone as clever as Mrs. Burnwood, could disappear completely. Somebody had noticed them. They were somewhere.

"But where, dammit?" Pepperdyne said out loud.

He didn't even know where to start looking for them.

The only thing Special Agent Jim Pepperdyne knew with absolute certainty was that if Matt Burnwood found his former wife before the authorities did, she wouldn't have to worry about being prosecuted for her crimes.

She would be dead.

Chapter Thirty-nine

"

    ... AND THE WOMAN DIED BEFORE HER CASE was brought to trial. She died of AIDS, without dignity and in pain. Yet all she cared about was saying goodbye to her children. A request that was denied."

Kendall was recounting for John the story she had told Matt and Gibb in what seemed another lifetime. It had been another lifetime, far removed from this small bedroom in her grandmother's farmhouse in southeastern Tennessee.

"Every time I lose a case, I take it personally. It's as though I've let her down again."

"So that's why you chose one of the toughest jobs available in your profession."

"I suppose."

"It was certainly an impelling incident, but I think there's more. I think you were achievement oriented long before you became a lawyer and got involved with this AIDS patient's case."

She raised her head from his shoulder and looked into his face. "Why do you want to talk about my personal history? Is it important?"

"I know nothing about you except what's happened since I regained consciousness. Yes, it's important to me."

Sighing, she returned her head to his shoulder. Actually, she wasn't as disinclined to talk as she pretended. His quiet manner inspired personal confessions, and she wanted him to remember her. Afterward.

"Why are you so driven, Kendall?"

"Who says I am?"

"Hey," he chided, "talk to me. What happened to your parents?"

"They died in a private-plane crash on their way to a ski vacation in Colorado."

"What were they like?"

"Vital. Energetic. Funny. Affectionate with each other and with me. I thought they were the most wonderful two people on the face of the earth. I loved them with all my heart."

"They were killed years ahead of their prime. So you feel that you must live life for them and get from it what they were denied. That's what drives you."

Her head popped up again. "What are you, a shrink?" She was teasing, but he remained unsmiling.

"What made you the determined, headstrong woman you are, Kendall?"

"I told you—"

"Dig deeper."

"All right, if you want to play doctor, I'll humor you." Resigned, she took a deep breath. "The morning they left for Colorado, while we were saying our goodbyes and hugging all around, my dad said, 'Before we come back, see if you can straighten up your room and make us proud.' Well, they never came back. So I guess I'm still trying to make them proud."

"That's the condensed version, but it's very insightful."

"Thank you. Now, can we move on to something more

recreational? There are more fun ways to play doctor, you know."

"You can't win the approval of someone who's dead, Kendall. You don't have to be the best at everything."

"So I've been told."

"By whom?"

"My husband."

He gave her a sharp look, and Kendall's heart almost stopped. Panic seized her, but she knew she had to keep talking, had to offer a hasty explanation. "I mean, you're so different now, that I think of *that* husband, the one who betrayed me, as someone else."

"I am someone else. Aren't I?"

"Yes, you are," she replied huskily. "You've changed even since we've been here. And you don't even resemble the man I married. He belongs in a bad dream that happened a long time ago, in another place."

He held her gaze for a long time before resuming the discussion. "You began lying when your parents were killed, right?"

"I don't lie."

"That's not even a debatable point, Kendall. You're very good at it."

"If I were that good, you wouldn't suspect that everything I tell you is a lie."

"Not everything. But a lot. You must have had years of practice."

"I always wanted to make things better than they were. When I was a child, I would . . . rearrange reality, make it more palatable. Rather than having parents who were dead, I invented two fascinating parents with fabulous careers that prevented them from living with me.

"One year they were film stars who wanted to protect me from Hollywood's corruption. One year, explorers to the North Pole. Then they were missionaries to an Iron Curtain country who converted the lost on Sundays and ran dangerous errands for the CIA during the week."

"Quite an imagination."

Smiling reminiscently, she added, "My imagination didn't go over so well with school counselors and teachers. I stayed in trouble for what they called lying, but what I considered readjusting the facts to improve an otherwise intolerable situation."

"What about later, in adulthood? If an intolerable situation cropped up, did you readjust the facts?"

"For instance?" she asked cautiously.

"For instance, if your husband was stricken with amnesia, and couldn't remember you or anything about your relationship, would you fake how you really felt about him?"

Tears formed in her eyes. She shook her head. "You're right, I've told too many lies to count. Usually to put a more positive spin on a situation. Sometimes, I admit, to get my way."

She touched his hair, his eyelashes, his lips. "But some things can't be faked. And one of them is love. If I didn't love you, I couldn't pretend to. Even with amnesia, you would know the truth, wouldn't you? You would *feel* it."

She guided his hand to her heart and held it pressed there. "When you regain your memory, you might suffer another kind of amnesia that will block out everything that occurred after the accident. You will have forgotten this time we've spent together, here in this house."

She framed his face between her hands. "But if you don't remember anything else, remember that I loved you while we were here." She kissed him softly to seal the vow.

He kissed her in return. Soon their mouths melded. His hands began to explore the soft contours of her body. Her bent knee provocatively nudged his groin.

"Again," he whispered.

She lightly ground her knee against the firm fuzziness of

his lap until his erection became distinct. She took it between her hands and massaged its hard, smooth length.

He kissed his way down her center, leaning into her until she was lying on her back. He nipped her tummy with his teeth and nuzzled her mound. He stroked her thighs, gradually separating them.

Then his mouth was intimate with her.

Kendall gave herself over to the breathtaking sensations. Without shame or modesty she allowed them to undulate up through her belly and breasts. Delicately his tongue probed and flicked and stroked and laved until she shattered like a fine piece of crystal.

He rose above her, but not until he was kissing her mouth did he enter her. When she adjusted her hips to take in all of him, he closed his eyes and swore softly.

Kendall sank her fingers in his hair and clasped his head. "Open your eyes, John. Look at me," she said in a soft, urgent voice. "Look at my face. Remember me."

He did as she asked, but he didn't cease the firm, fluid thrusts that sent him deep inside her. When he came, he called her name in a hoarse, choppy voice, then surrendered to the spasms that rocked his body, his world.

When it was over, he gathered her beneath him, enfolding her, his face buried in her neck. Kendall held him for a long time, occasionally stroking his head and whispering, "Remember me, John. Remember me."

Chapter Forty

$\mathcal{A}$ MAN SLID INTO THE BOOTH ACROSS FROM RICKI Sue. "Hi."

"Fuck off."

"That ain't very neighborly. Don't you remember me? My brother and me asked you for directions today."

For the past half hour Ricki Sue had been sitting alone, drinking steadily, trying to dull the cutting edge of Pepperdyne's sharp warnings.

If something terrible happened to Mrs. Burnwood and her baby, it would be Ricki Sue's fault, he had said.

If she wanted to see her best friend alive, she had better play straight with him and tell him everything she knew.

If they died, she would forever after have their deaths on her conscience. Their lives were in her hands.

He had gone on and on, spouting so many dire predictions that she had felt the need to escape his voice. After he'd left, the house made her claustrophobic. It was still a mess. Pepperdyne had promised to send over a cleaning crew tomorrow to help with the black dusting powder, but she couldn't stand looking at the damage a moment longer.

The constant reminder that someone had invaded her

privacy and handled her personal things had left her with a rare sense of vulnerability. Besides—and she would never admit this to Pepperdyne—she was frightened to be there alone.

She'd had to get out. So she had come to this bar. It wasn't a place she visited often. Not wanting company tonight, she had avoided the clubs where she was well known and likely to run into friends wanting to party.

She wanted to get stinko tonight. Alone. Already a few men had regarded her speculatively, but she'd shot down their come-ons with hostile glares. No one had dared approach her until now.

When she raised her head and looked more closely at the man who had joined her, she recognized him instantly. Her heart gave a little skip. Her standard, scathing brush-off died on her lips. Her scowl reversed into a smile.

"Did you find Sunset Street?"

"Yeah, thanks to you. But the friend we were looking for had moved. Somewhere out of town." Henry Crook shrugged indifferently. "Don't matter none. We were just knocking around and thought we'd look him up."

"Where's your brother?"

"Luther's his name. Mine's Henry."

"I'm Ricki Sue. Ricki Sue Robb."

"Fancy running into you twice in one day. Must be destiny or something."

"Must be," Ricki Sue simpered.

His eyes were an exceptional color of blue. Nice blond hair, too. No mental giant, but so what? Pepperdyne was smart, and he was a royal pain in the ass.

Besides, supersmart men made her feel inferior. She preferred men who were her intellectual equals. Ordinarily she was turned off by bad grammar, but Henry and his twin had a tough, rawboned appeal that aroused her.

She fluttered her eyelashes. "I'm almost finished with my drink."

"Can I buy you another one?"

"That would be lovely. Whiskey and soda, please."

He went to the bar and ordered. Looking back at her, he smiled in a boyishly shy way that caused a catch in her throat. Shy men never failed to turn her on. There was so much she could teach them!

He returned with their drinks. After the first few sips, she asked, "Where're y'all from?"

"Uh, West Virginia."

"Hmm. You sound more southern than that."

"We were raised in South Carolina, but the family moved when me and Luther were in high school."

"What do you do?"

"We're in the automotive business."

"How interesting!" she exclaimed breathlessly. "I'm fascinated with cars and engines and stuff."

She wasn't in the least, but her phony fascination gave her an opportunity to lean forward and provide Henry a stunning view of her deep cleavage. She was wearing a black, open-weave top over a black bra, which was meant to reveal.

Transfixed by the display, Henry sloshed his draft beer as he raised the mug to his mouth. "My brother and me came back to see you, you know."

"You did? When?"

"After we found out our friend didn't live here no more. Looked to us like cops were all over your place."

Ricki Sue frowned. "They were. Somebody had broken in to my house."

"No shit? Wha'd he steal?"

She leaned farther forward. "Henry, honey, do you mind if we don't talk about it? I just get so upset."

She reached for his hand and he clasped it tightly. "Ain't

surprising. Me and Luther figured something was awful wrong when we spotted those private dicks watching your house from down the block."

Her reactions were somewhat dulled by the alcohol she had consumed, but Ricki Sue was instantly brought to attention. She jerked her hand free of his. "What private dicks? What are you talking about?"

"Whoa. I didn't mean to get you all worked up. Me and Luther figured your ex probably put them on you."

"I don't have an ex."

"Oh." He frowned with perplexity. "Well, whoever wants you watched is doing it up right. They followed you here."

The Burnwoods! They were here! They had her in their sights! The back of her head was in the crosshairs of one of their ghastly hunting rifles that Kendall had told her about!

"Where?" she croaked.

"Right over yonder by the cigarette machine." He nodded toward a spot behind her. "You can turn around. They ain't looking right now."

She gave the vending machine a quick glance. One of the men belonged to Pepperdyne. The second was new to her, but she was sure that he, too, was an FBI agent. They looked ridiculous in the clean, new dozer caps that were meant to make them blend in with the locals.

"That asshole!" she hissed. "I can't believe him. He's having me tailed, like *I* was the criminal."

"Who? What's the matter? What's this asshole's name? Want me and Luther to hurt him for you?"

"No, no. It's nothing, really, just—"

"Listen, if you're in some kind of trouble—"

"I'm not, but a friend of mine is. Those guys are from the FBI. They think I know something that I'm not telling."

"Do you?"

"If I did, I wouldn't tell."

It was risky to let a potential date know that she was

involved in something serious enough to include the feds. But instead of appearing wary, Henry seemed impressed.

"Whew! You lead an exciting life, lady."

Ricki Sue hid her relief and flashed him a naughty smile. "You don't know the half of it, honey."

"But I'd sure like to."

"Then let's get out of here," she said, making a spontaneous decision. If ever she'd been in need of some R&R, tonight was the night. "I know some places that are much more suited for private conversation."

She finished her drink in one swallow and was about to leave the booth when she remembered Pepperdyne's surveillance team. "Damn! I don't want them tagging along."

Henry pondered the problem for a moment. "I have an idea. My brother's in the back room playing pool. What say me and you walk back there. I'll stay awhile, then come back in here, making out like we hadn't got on, you know? Luther and you can sneak out the back. Eventually I'll leave by the front door. By the time they get curious and go into the back room looking for you, you'll be long gone."

"Brilliant!" She swayed when she tried to stand. "Oops. Already on my way to wasted." She giggled.

Henry placed an arm around her waist to steady her. "Hell, you ain't wasted. You just know how to have a good time, is all."

She leaned against him. "Y'all are gonna be a riot. I can tell."

Henry's plan to trick the agents worked. In less than half an hour he rejoined her and Luther at the appointed street corner. He arrived on foot and jumped into the front seat of the Camaro the second it pulled to a stop. Luther floorboarded the accelerator, and they sped off with a squeal of tires.

Ricki Sue thought Luther was just as cute and charming as his twin. With all of them crammed into the front seat, she had to straddle the console, which generated a round of double entendres and lewd comments. The car jounced over potholes, tossing her toward the ceiling and causing a great deal of hilarity.

She had a bottle of Jack Daniel's tilted toward her mouth when they crossed the railroad tracks. She spilled the liquor down her front. "Now look what you made me do!" She gasped, laughing so hard that she could barely draw breath.

"Hey, Luther," Henry said, "on account of your reckless drivin', the lady got all wet."

"The least we can do is help her wipe it up."

"The very least."

Ricki Sue slapped each of them on the thigh. "Y'all are so naughty! I know what you're thinking."

Henry leaned over and began licking her neck. " 'S that so? What are we thinking?"

Ricki Sue's head lolled back and she began to moan and squirm.

"No fair, you two," Luther whined. "I gotta drive." But he managed to steer with one hand while the other groped between her thighs.

Later, Ricki Sue couldn't actually remember who had first suggested stopping at the motor court. Perhaps she had. It certainly wasn't the first time she had been to that particular motel. The desk clerk was a dopehead. He was always stoned and couldn't care less who signed the register, or even if it was signed, as long as a twenty was laid on the counter.

However, it was the first time she had been there, or anywhere, with twins. The novelty of it heightened her excitement as she stumbled drunkenly into the rented room.

Luther, or maybe it was Henry—the more she drank, the less distinguishable they became—said something hysterically funny. In the throes of laughter, she fell across the bed.

Luther lay down on one side of her, Henry on the other.

One kissed her. Then the other. Then the first again. And so it went, until she couldn't tell one mouth from the other.

With good-natured protests, she shoved them away. "Stop. Listen. Wait a minute. Hey, y'all, hold it!"

She staved them off and struggled to a sitting position. The room reeled, and she raised a hand to the side of her head to help regain her balance. Assuming the solemnity that only the extremely inebriated are capable of, she said, "Patience, boys. From here on, nothing happens without rubbers."

As the twins grappled with the foil packets she produced from her handbag, Ricki Sue languished against the bed's flimsy headboard, anticipating the attention she would get tomorrow morning at the coffee machine. Would she ever have some wild stories to tell!

Chapter Forty-one

MATT DROVE UNTIL GIBB INSTRUCTED HIM TO stop at a roadside park. Staying within the speed limit, and observing all traffic laws, he had put what Gibb believed was a safe distance between them and the town of Sheridan.

Gibb was eager to learn what the contents of the shoe box found underneath Ricki Sue's bed might reveal. He emptied the cards and letters between them on the seat of the car. They divided them and began reading.

It soon became apparent that Ricki Sue had saved every piece of correspondence she had ever received from a male. The task became tiresome. Matt grew bored.

"There's nothing here."

"We can't dismiss a single one," his father said stubbornly. "It might be just the one that could tell us something."

Among the lurid letters from former lovers was a badly printed note from a grade school classmate named Jeff, asking if Ricki Sue would show him her panties. Another long, rambling letter had been signed by her cousin Joe, who had served his country aboard the USS *John F. Kennedy* and who had promised to pass along her address to his lonely shipmates. There was a postcard from her Sunday school teacher, Mr.

Howard, telling her that she had been missed the preceding
Sunday.

Then Matt picked up a postcard and immediately recognized the handwriting. "This one's from Kendall."

He couldn't work up any enthusiasm for the find. He was
on automatic pilot, and he seemed incapable of resuming
control. It was easier just to do as he was told. The automation
was a buffer that shielded him from the pain of feeling.

He had been like this since Lottie's murder.

It was as though he had died, too. He couldn't see himself
writing another editorial, putting out another issue of his newspaper. He couldn't imagine having a zest for anything—food,
drink, hunting, the Brotherhood, life in general. Lottie's death
had left an emptiness inside him that would never be filled.
Dad had told him that he would feel differently when they
found his son, but Matt had his doubts.

As wrenching as his heartache had been when he and Lottie
were youngsters and his father had forbidden him to see her,
there had always been a glimmer of hope that one day they
would be together. He had clung to that hope. It had gotten
him through days when he thought he would die from wanting
her.

Now that she was lost to him forever, there was nothing
to look forward to. In an attempt to console him, his father
had reminded him that their real reward was waiting for them
in Heaven, but Matt had found his own heaven with Lottie.
He wasn't certain he wanted life everlasting if it meant living
through eternity without her.

Kendall was responsible for Lottie's death. His father had
awakened him to that fact. If Kendall hadn't butted in to
things beyond her understanding, if she had been the meek
and obedient wife she should have been, none of this would
have happened. Lottie would still be alive, greeting him with
the smiles and kisses and embraces that he had lived for.

Each time he thought of his loss, he nearly choked on his

hatred for Kendall. She would pay. He would see to it. Just like all the others who had been punished by the Brotherhood, it was Kendall herself who had brought on their judgment.

He stared down at the postcard, hating it because it had come from her. "I recognize her handwriting."

"When was it written?"

Matt held it up to the dome light. "The postmark is smeared, but it looks old. It's yellowed around the edges."

"Read it anyway."

" 'Having a wonderful time, except for heat and mosquitoes. Almost carried me off yesterday when G and I went to favorite spot for picnic.' "

"*G* must refer to her grandmother," Gibb said. "Anything else?"

"She was running out of room. The writing is cramped." Matt squinted to read the smaller letters. " 'I've told you about the place, CSA cannon, waterfall, etc. See ya soon.' That's all. She drew a little heart instead of signing her name."

"CSA? Confederate States? There's a Confederate cannon in her favorite spot. Did she ever mention this place to you?"

Matt searched his memory, but it was hard to see past the mental picture of Lottie's lifeless eyes. "She might have. I think so. She told me she and her grandmother spent their summers at an old farmhouse."

"An old farmhouse located near a Confederate cannon and a waterfall." His excitement growing, Gibb opened the glove compartment, removed the Tennessee road map, and eagerly spread it open in his lap.

"What do you know about wildlife, Matthew?" he asked. "When an animal has been wounded, or when it's frightened, what does it do? Where does it go?"

"To its lair."

"In other words, home," Gibb said. "Kendall didn't return home. She couldn't. So she might have gone to the next best place. We need to find a Civil War memorial near a waterfall."

His eyes twinkling, he added, "Think of it, son. By dawn you could be holding your baby boy."

Matt tried to work up some enthusiasm. He tried to envision bouncing his son on his knee. He tried to imagine himself laughing, feeling happy and free. *Free?* Yes, he realized. In his whole life, he had never felt free.

And never more shackled than now.

Kendall eased out of John's embrace. He mumbled an unintelligible question.

"I'm going to the bathroom," she whispered. "I'll be right back."

He drifted back to sleep. She leaned over and kissed his forehead, then paused and gazed at his face, memorizing every nuance of it.

If everything went according to plan, this would be the last time she saw him.

She felt a sob rising. Quelling it, she slipped out of bed and dressed silently and quickly in the darkness.

From the moment Ricki Sue had told her of Matt and Gibb's escape from jail, Kendall had known she must flee. There was no more time to spare. She had already waited too long. In spite of the time it had cost her, she had given herself one last night with John.

Matt and Gibb would track her and find her. She knew they would. She had far more confidence in their hunting instincts than she did in the FBI's fancy computers and network of investigators.

If it were only her life involved, she would risk staying with John. But she had Kevin to think of. If the Burnwoods found her, they would kill her and take him. It was too horrifying to contemplate. Even if they were recaptured, Kevin would become a ward of the state, and his future would be determined by a committee of strangers.

She had to protect her child, even though it meant leaving

behind the man she loved. She would leave without explanation, without saying goodbye. In the morning, when he discovered that she was gone, he would be confused, probably angry. But it wouldn't last long.

She was writing him a note, promising that help was on the way. Before leaving town that afternoon, she had sent a postcard to the local authorities telling them where they could find John McGrath, the missing U.S. marshal.

As soon as they got mail, they would dispatch someone to the farmhouse. John's friend Jim Pepperdyne would see that he got the best neurological care. In time, his memory would return. It broke her heart to know that he might not remember this idyll they had shared.

As much as the thought saddened her, she knew it would be for the best if he didn't remember. He couldn't be held accountable for all that had happened between them, either to his supervisors or to himself.

Moving soundlessly into Kevin's room, she retrieved the bag that was already packed with his clothing, diapers, and several days' supply of everything else she considered essential. She planned to travel as light as possible.

For the time being she left Kevin in his crib. Peeping into the bedroom, she saw that John was still sleeping soundly. She made her way through the house and let herself out the back door.

Dawn was still hours away, but every minute counted now. She placed the bag in the car. Earlier she had found some paint in the shed behind the house and used it to make 8s of the two 3s on the license plate. The alteration wouldn't stand up to close inspection, but it might keep her from being stopped until she could unload the car and buy another.

Returning to the house, she went to the pantry, where she had sacks already loaded with nonperishables and bottled water. She could eat and drink while driving, stopping only when she had to feed Kevin or use a restroom. Of course, they'd have to stop to sleep. She would choose out-of-the-way motels where paying with cash wouldn't arouse suspicion.

When she needed money, she would make arrangements with Ricki Sue, as they had done before. She trusted Ricki Sue implicitly, but, for her friend's protection, Kendall wanted to postpone contacting her until it was absolutely necessary.

After placing the sacks of food in the car, she returned one last time to the house and went into the living room. Kneeling in front of the fireplace, she reached up into the chimney and withdrew the pistol.

The gun was the only real protection she would have against Matt and Gibb if they found her, but she was still loath to touch it. Handling it with the utmost care, she placed it in her skirt pocket.

Then a disturbing possibility occurred to her. What if the Burnwoods tracked her here before John could be rescued? They would know that he was the marshal she had "kidnapped" from the hospital in Stephensville. They would murder him without a qualm.

She removed the pistol from her pocket and carried it to the kitchen. She lay the envelope containing her note on the table and anchored it there with the revolver. It seemed fitting somehow, that the last thing she returned to John was the first thing she had taken from him while he lay unconscious on the rain-soaked ground.

How far they had come together since then.

Feeling the onset of tears, she tiptoed quickly into Kevin's room and lifted him from the crib. He mewed an objection, but she settled him against her shoulder and he immediately went back to sleep.

Glancing one final time into the dim bedroom, she saw that John hadn't moved. She went swiftly down the hallway and through the kitchen. Regardless of her determination not to cry, a tear slid down her cheek.

These were the last few moments she would spend in this

house that held so many precious memories for her. Once discovered, she could never use it as a refuge again. She could never return to these rooms that echoed with Grandmother's laughter. Here she had known love, first from Grandmother, then from John.

Must she always say goodbye to everything and everyone she loved?

Kevin squirmed against her. "Not everyone," she whispered. She kissed his head, then moved purposefully toward the door. She had just raised her hand to it when the overhead light came on.

She spun around, but, blinded by the sudden brightness, she could only make out the silhouette of a man bearing down on her and Kevin.

Chapter Forty-two

THE CROOK TWINS WERE IN THE MOTEL BATHROOM, holding a little conference about their dilemma. They needed to ply the fat redhead with enough liquor to loosen her tongue without letting her drink herself unconscious.

"Hey, boys," she called from the bed in a high, singsong voice. "Whach'y'all doin' in there, huh?"

"I don't think I can get it up again." Luther gazed forlornly at his flaccid penis. "I ain't never seen a woman who could take so much. You figure she's a freak of nature or somethin'?"

"Stop whining. We gotta get her to talking about Kendall."

Luther massaged his testicles with a sympathetic hand. "How do you plan on doing that, Henry? She's already polished off nearly a whole bottle of Jack Daniels, and it ain't fazed her, 'cept to make her hornier."

Henry mulled it over. Ricki Sue summoned them again from the bedroom. "We'd better be gettin' back to her before she gets suspicious. I'll think of something. Whatever I say, just play along."

Ricki Sue was still sprawled across the bed. She was pouting. "I was beginnin' to think y'all were partyin' without me."

Henry noticed that her speech was more slurred than before.

He gave Luther a surreptitious thumbs-up as he stretched out beside Ricki Sue. "Naw. We couldn't have no fun without our party girl, could we, Luther?"

"No sir. No fun at all. In fact, I believe it's time for another round of drinks."

He pretended to take a long swallow from the bottle before passing it to Ricki Sue. She divided a suspicious look between them. "Are you boys tryin' to get me drunk, or what?"

Before either could answer, she belted out a gutsy laugh and raised the bottle to her mouth. Henry winked at his brother across the mound of pale, freckled, female flesh.

"Swear to God, Ricki Sue, you're a drinker like nobody I've ever seen. Right, Luther?"

"Right."

"In fact, you impress me on all counts. For instance, the way you outsmarted those feds. Now that was something to see. Serves 'em right, too, for butting in to everybody's bi'ness the way they do."

She snorted with contempt. "That Pepperdyne thinks his shit don't stink. 'You know where Mrs. Burnwood is,' he says. You know this, you know that," she mimicked. "How does he know what I know, when only I know what I know?"

"Yeah," Luther said. "Where does he get off asking you personal questions about your best friend?"

Henry shot his brother a venomous look. Why couldn't Luther just keep his mouth shut? Mama was right—his twin was so ignorant, he was dangerous. With that single comment, he could have tipped off Ricki Sue that they weren't after her strictly for fun and games.

But she was too far gone to notice Luther's giveaway. "I wanna protec' Kendall," she said sobbing. "She's my frien'. Wouldn't tell Pepperdyne where she was, even if I knew, which I don't."

She took another drink and almost strangled on it when she began to laugh. Raising her finger to make her point, she said, "But I have a pret-ty good i-de-a." She separated the syllables, pronouncing each one distinctly.

"Aw, you don't have to bluff us, Ricki Sue. We aren't laws, are we, Luther?"

"Hell no."

Henry began smooching her neck. "Forget that Pepperdyne character. Let's get back to partying."

Ricki Sue pushed him away. "I wasn't bluffin'. I *do* know where she might be at. I'm the only one in the whole world who knows."

"Sure, sure, honey. We believe you. Don't we, Luther?" He winked at his brother conspiratorially, but Luther wasn't following. The reverse psychology was lost on him.

"Uh . . . uh, yeah. That's right. What Henry said."

"It's the truf," Ricki Sue averred as she made an effort to sit up. "I bet she's at the place where she used to go in the summers with her grandma."

"Okay, baby, okay." Henry gave her thigh a patronizing pat. "If you say so."

She thumped the mattress with her fist. "I know where she is. Well, not 'xactly. But it's somewhere near Morton. And there's a . . ."

"A what?"

"A waterfaw."

"Waterfall?"

She tilted her head to a condescending angle and looked down her nose at Henry. "Isn't that what I just said?"

"Sure, honey. Didn't mean to make you mad."

"And there's a . . . big gun. Whaddaya call it? On wheels. They used 'em in old-timey days."

"A cannon?"

She dug the nail of her index finger into Henry's chest. "Tha's right! You win! You get first prize!" She spread her arms away from her body, offering it as the trophy. Then her eyes rolled back into her head, and she fell back on the bed, unconscious.

"Hot damn!" Henry cried. "It worked. We'll drive to Morton."

"Where's that?"

"Don't know. But it's gotta be on a map. Hurry up, Luther, get dressed."

"What about her?"

"You know what Mama said."

Gazing down at Ricki Sue, Luther smacked his lips with regret. "It's a damn shame, having to destroy such a novelty. I ain't never had snatch that fiery red before."

"Excuse me?" Teeth grinding, Pepperdyne clutched the telephone receiver so tightly that his knuckles turned white. "Would you kindly repeat what you just said?"

"We, uh, lost her, sir. She went into this bar, a dive, really. She was sitting by herself in a booth, knocking back whiskeys like a seasoned drinker."

"Get on with it."

"Yes, sir. This guy—"

"What guy?"

"Some guy. A tall, lanky man with straw-colored hair and weird-looking eyes. He joins her in the booth. He buys her a drink. They sit and chat."

"Did you ask anyone this man's name?"

"Of course, sir. Nobody in the place knew him."

"Car?"

"We asked about that, too. Nobody remembered seeing him and his brother arrive, so we couldn't get a make on the car."

"Did you say 'brother'? He had a brother?"

"Yes, sir. A twin."

"Christ."

Pepperdyne tossed two aspirins into his mouth and washed them down with a swig of Maalox. Why must everything be so goddamn complicated? Not just a brother, which would have been difficult enough. But twins.

"Identical twins?"

"That's what we were told. That you couldn't tell one from the other."

"Naturally."

"We never saw the second one. He stayed in the billiards room in the back." The agent explained how Ricki Sue and her companions had given them the slip.

"How'd he pay for the drinks?"

"Cash."

"I figured as much," Pepperdyne muttered. "And no one there knew who these men were?"

"No, sir. No name. Nothing. Apparently they weren't locals." Pepperdyne's subordinate paused, as though bracing for the dressing-down he knew was coming. When his boss said nothing, he offered an opinion: "What I think, sir, is that she met up with these guys and left with them."

"That's apparent, isn't it?"

"What I mean, sir, is that I don't think the twins are connected to the break-in this afternoon. They sure as hell weren't Matt and Gibb Burnwood. It looked like a random pickup to me. Witnesses said that Miss Robb got real chummy with these guys real fast, know what I mean?

"In fact, one of them volunteered to give us the lowdown on her. He said—and several others corroborated—that she's a well-known swinger. Hot to trot. It isn't unusual for her to leave a bar with a stranger, he said."

Pepperdyne's temper snapped. "Listen to me. I don't give a rat's ass if Miss Robb screws a hundred men at high noon in the town square every Saturday. She's a citizen, and even if she is withholding valuable information from us, it's our duty to protect her.

"You were ordered not to let her out of your sight, and you fucked up. So now she's missing. We don't know who she's with, or where she is, and there are two maniacs who think they're God's right-hand men out assassinating anybody who crosses them, and that includes Miss Robb because it's her best friend and confidante that they're ultimately after!" He stopped shouting and paused for breath. His softer voice conveyed even more of a threat. "Am I getting through to you?"

"Yes, sir. I think so, sir."

"Just so there's no misunderstanding, let me spell it out for you. If anything bad happens to Ricki Sue Robb, I'm gonna nail your balls to the floor, then set it on fire."

"Yes, sir."

"Get on it."

"Yes, sir."

Pepperdyne slammed down the receiver. He dispatched more men to the tavern to try to pick up the trail of the unidentified twins. He gave them a thumbnail description. "Tall, lanky, straw-colored hair. Something weird about their eyes. They're identical. The woman is a plump redhead. Nobody who's seen her could possibly forget her, so talk to everybody."

Pepperdyne sipped from the bottle of Maalox as he paced the office, thinking. Was it a coincidence that on the day Ricki Sue's house was ransacked by the Burnwoods, she was picked up in a honky-tonk by nameless twins?

How could the two incidents be related? Were these twins members of the Brotherhood, the Burnwoods' lieutenants carrying out orders? Or was it as the agent had speculated: One event had no bearing on the other?

Pepperdyne's gut instinct told him to assume the worst. If these twins were in cahoots with the Burnwoods or otherwise connected to the case, he now had four lives to worry about: John; Mrs. Burnwood and her baby; and Ricki Sue Robb.

If the Burnwoods located any of them before his men did . . .

He couldn't let that happen. It was as simple as that.

* * *

Getting Ricki Sue from the motel bed to the Camaro was no easy feat, but they managed to do it without rousing her. They weren't as lucky when they tried hauling her out of the car.

The moment she came to, she began struggling to be released. "Hey, what's going on?" she asked querulously, trying to get her bearings. The car was parked on the edge of a ditch beside a dark, narrow road. "Where the hell are we? What are we doing out here? Where're my clothes?"

Luther's answer to her question was his standard slack-jawed stare.

Henry said, "We, uh, thought you might want to go swimming."

Luther gaped at his brother, then turned to Ricki Sue, bobbing his head eagerly. "Skinny-dipping, ya know?"

"Swimming?" She gave the surroundings an apprehensive glance. "We're out in the middle of nowhere, aren't we?"

"We know where we're at," Henry boasted. "Me and Luther were here earlier today. There's a pretty little stream 'bout fifty yards there through the woods."

Ricki Sue followed his pointing finger, but wasn't heartened by what she saw, which was a deep, dark, scary-looking forest. Traipsing around buck naked through the woods in the middle of the night wasn't her idea of a good time. She was all for adventure, but she preferred to conduct her escapades in places that had walls and ceilings.

She had never liked the great outdoors. The sun was a curse to her fair skin, which either freckled or blistered. She was allergic to poison ivy and mosquito bites, which resulted in ugly red bumps that usually festered and had to be treated with antibiotics.

On the other hand, she had developed a real lust for the twins' lean, rangy bodies. Being sandwiched between them had been a turn-on to end all turn-ons. Naked, under water, they would be as sleek as eels, sliding up against her full curves.

She shivered with anticipation. "Lead the way."

"Let's play Indian and go single file," Henry suggested. "Luther, you lead. I'll bring up the rear," he said, sliding his hands beneath her bare buttocks and giving each cheek a squeeze.

Ricki Sue squealed in delight and took her place between them. Henry crowded up behind her. She hugged Luther around the waist as they marched through the forest.

When they reached the creek and she heard the gently flowing water, she sighed. "This is gonna be so romantic. Or am I just drunk?"

Henry had had the foresight to bring along a fresh bottle. "You're not drunk. After that hike, I figure we could all use another drink."

The bottle went around once, each of them taking a drink. But the liquor seemed to have little effect on the twins' jitters. Ricki Sue began noticing that they seemed nervous, especially when she took each of them by the hand and pulled them toward the creek.

"What's the matter, boys? Having second thoughts? Think I'm too much woman to handle, even for both of you?"

"We, uh, we had a baby brother who drowned," Henry blurted. "We were just kids, but we remember it. So we're neither one crazy for the water."

If her head had been clearer, she would have wondered why they had suggested an orgy in the water if they had an aversion to it. Instead, she reacted with compassion. "Oh, you poor babies. Come to Ricki Sue."

Henry had stumbled upon Ricki Sue's dearest desire, which she kept a secret, chiefly because the chances of its ever being fulfilled were nil. She longed to nurture, to be a source of comfort and solace, to a husband, a child, or even to a parent who regarded her with pride rather than scorn. She had a huge capacity for love, but her love had never been asked for. A surplus of it was stored in her heart.

So Henry's lie about the drowned brother evoked a deeply emotional response. Tears came to her eyes. She drew each of them to her and stroked their heads while murmuring condolences. "Let me make it better. Don't think about your brother. His little soul is in heaven."

Soon, however, their closeness began to have the programmed effect—it became erotic. She hugged them tighter. "Don't worry, sweethearts," she whispered. "Before this night is over, you'll have a whole new outlook on water sports. Just leave everything to Ricki Sue."

She waded into the water, but when they started to follow, she held up a halting hand. "How come I'm the only one of this trio who's naked?"

Luther looked at Henry, who shrugged and began stripping, dropping his clothing on the muddy creek bank. Luther did likewise. Henry waded in first and joined Ricki Sue where she stood in water about knee deep.

"Sweet baby." She reached for him and fondled his sex, but it was unresponsive.

"Sorry," he said. "Guess you wore it plumb out back there at the motel. A little encouragement of a different sort would prob'ly do the trick."

She laughed huskily and sank to her knees. "Say no more. If that's what it takes . . ." The silt on the bottom of the creek was slippery and cool. The water felt delicious lapping against her skin. She smiled up at Henry and rubbed her breasts against his thighs.

She actually sensed the movement of air near her head and heard the sickening, melon-splitting sound before the pain reached her. Then it shot through her skull. She gasped. Whiskey surged up from her stomach and filled her mouth. It dribbled over her chin when she cried out. She fell heavily to her side, creating a splash.

Dazed and on the verge of blacking out, she looked up and saw Luther standing over her. In his hands was a short, stout club. As she watched, he raised it above his head, then put all his strength behind it as he swung it down again.

There wasn't time for Ricki Sue to experience any fear, only a fleeting bewilderment.

Chapter Forty-three

THE SCREAM DIED IN KENDALL'S THROAT.

"John!"

"Yes, John. How clever of you to use my real name. It was easier that way, right?"

Realization rendered her pale. "You remember."

"Yes. I woke up remembering."

They stared at each other across the space separating them, and it seemed much wider than it actually was. Until this moment, all the advantages had been on her side. But now the balance had shifted.

"I . . . I thought you were asleep."

"That's what I wanted you to think."

"You knew I was going to leave?"

"Running away is second nature to you, isn't it?"

Beneath the glare of the kitchen light, her face was as white as chalk. She clutched Kevin to her chest protectively. Or maybe she was using the baby as a shield to protect herself from John in case he decided to do her bodily harm. He was so angry that he felt tempted.

Instead, he reached for the revolver she had left on the table and shoved it into the waistband of the shorts he'd pulled on before leaving the bedroom. "What made you decide to leave me the weapon?"

"I thought you might need it for protection."

"How kind of you." Propping himself on one crutch, he yanked a chair from beneath the table and shoved it toward her. "Sit down."

"John, if you'll only listen to—"

"Sit down!" he thundered.

Watching him warily, she approached the chair and gingerly lowered herself into it. "Do you remember everything?"

"Everything," he said. "My life before I got amnesia, and everything that's happened since. John McGrath. Middle name, Leland, which happens to be my mother's maiden name. Born the twenty-third of May, 1952, in Raleigh, North Carolina. Went to school there and graduated eighteen years later. In 1979, I earned a doctorate in psychology."

"Psychology? You're a psychologist?"

For the meantime he bypassed that. "My dissertation was on Delayed Stress Syndrome, and I did a lot of clinical work at Bethesda. That's what brought me to the attention of the FBI, specifically Agent Jim Pepperdyne, who recruited me for his Hostage Rescue Team. We worked together frequently.

"Two years ago I left the Bureau and went to work for the U.S. Marshal's office." After a significant pause, he added, "I was kidnapped on the twelfth of July, 1994. But then you know that date, don't you?"

"John, I can explain."

"You sure as hell can, and you will. But you'd better take care of Kevin first."

The baby had begun to fret. John didn't want any distractions during this conversation. But even more than that, he didn't want the baby to be uncomfortable.

"He's wet. I'll go change him."

She stood and attempted to move past John, but he caught her arm. "Nice try, but no way. Change him here."

"On the kitchen table?"

"We won't be eating off it anymore. Change him here."

She spread Kevin's blanket on the table and removed the wet diaper. "The fresh ones are in the car."

"Go get them."

"Aren't you afraid I'll make a run for it?" she asked snidely.

"Not without Kevin. He stays with me. Hurry up." She glanced down at her child, then back at him. "Either you go get the diapers out of the car," he said, "or Kevin goes au naturel. I don't think it matters to him, and it sure as hell doesn't make any difference to me."

She let the kitchen door slam behind her this time.

He had been awake from the moment she'd left their bed. He'd expected her to take off and implement stage two of her plan, whatever the hell that stage might be.

Her attempt to sneak out didn't surprise him. What did surprise him was the painful effect her clandestine leave-taking had on him. He was angry, but he also felt wounded.

Naturally, he wouldn't allow any personal considerations to cloud his judgment. The situation called for a pragmatic, unemotional, detached professionalism. That was his duty, and God knows he had shirked it over the last few weeks, beginning with taking an unreported detour and ending with making love to his prisoner no more than two hours ago.

Kendall returned with a bag of Huggies and rapidly put one on Kevin. Lifting him to her shoulder, she returned to the chair and sat down. "Well, Marshal McGrath, will I be confined to quarters and given only bread and water?"

"Don't smart-mouth me, Kendall. This isn't fun and games. If you hadn't stolen my handcuffs, I'd use them to keep you in that chair. You must have taken the cuffs from me at the same time you relieved me of my weapon."

"I couldn't have you arriving at the hospital toting a pistol, could I?"

"No, I guess you couldn't. It would have prompted questions that you couldn't answer. So you kept the story simple."

"I tried."

"When did you decide to tell them I was your husband? In the ambulance?"

"Actually no. I didn't know what I was going to tell them. When the doctor asked me who you were, the answer just popped out. It was plausible. I had a newborn. We were traveling together. Our ages are compatible." She looked at him and shrugged, as if the lie's advantages were obvious.

"And I couldn't dispute it."

"That's right. You couldn't dispute it."

"As my wife you exercised a lot of control."

"That was the general idea."

"What did you tell them about Marshal Fordham?"

"That she was your sister."

"How'd you convince them of that?"

"They just took my word for it."

"She was Hispanic."

"They didn't know that at the time."

"Oh. Right. They couldn't recover the car because of the flood."

"Which also worked to my advantage."

"Yeah, everything was going your way. Good thing Ms. Fordham was dead, huh?"

"That's a horrible thing to say!" she cried.

"*Was* she dead?"

"What?"

"Was she already dead when the car went into the creek?"

She turned her head away and stared at the far wall for a long moment. He could tell that she was furious. Her jaw was working, and there were angry tears in her eyes when she turned back to face him. "Fuck you."

"You have," he replied with matching contempt. "Many

times." They glared at each other. "Did you let Ruthie Fordham drown?"

She was silent.

"Answer me, dammit!" he shouted. "Was she already dead when—"

"Yes! *Yes*. She died on impact. I'm certain the coroner's report will confirm that."

He wanted to believe her. It appeared that she was telling the truth. From a personal standpoint, he hoped she was. But the criminologist in him was mistrustful. She was a damn good liar.

"Why didn't you leave me in the car to drown?" he asked. "You could have walked away. It might have been days before our bodies were discovered, miles downstream from where the accident occurred. It would have been even longer before we were identified. You could have completely disappeared in that amount of time, Kendall, and your trail would have grown stone cold. Why'd you pull me out?"

She licked at a tear that had rolled into the corner of her lips, although she no longer looked angry. These were tears of remorse. "You've slept with me, made love to me, and you have to ask me why I saved your life? *Any* life? Do you actually think I'm capable of walking away and letting an injured person die? Don't you know me better than that?"

He leaned over her. "I don't know you at all. You're a stranger to me, as much a stranger as when I walked into your front yard in Denver and saw you for the first time."

She shook her head, refuting everything he had said.

"You've told so many lies, Kendall, spun so many tales, I don't know what's truth and what's fiction."

"Kevin wants to nurse."

He jerked his head back. "What?"

The baby was gnawing at Kendall's breast and plucking at her blouse. It completely disarmed him. "Oh. Go ahead."

Short hours ago, he had made love to her. He had explored

her body with his hands and lips. But he couldn't watch now as she opened her blouse and offered the hungry infant her breast. He felt as guilty as a teenager getting an erection in the confessional as he recounted his carnal sin to the priest.

It was damn near impossible to maintain a professional posture while watching her nurse her baby. Fortunately, he didn't have to, because Kendall stunned him with a question of her own.

"Who is Lisa?"

"What do you know about her?"

"You talk in your sleep. More than once you've mumbled something about her. Who is she? Your wife? Are you married?"

Her concern struck him as funny, but his laughter was short-lived. "You've kidnapped a federal officer, but you're worried about committing adultery?"

"Are you?"

"No."

"Then who is Lisa?"

"She's just . . . this woman." Kendall continued to stare at him, compelling him to explain. He gave her a thumbnail account of his and Lisa's relationship. "She left like that," he said, snapping his fingers. "And it didn't even put a dent in my emotions. No more than when I met her."

"She was just a warm body to sleep with."

He immediately went on the defensive. "Exactly. It was as hassle-free as any sexual relationship can be. Besides, it made no difference to you. I talked about her in my sleep, but that didn't stop you from fucking me, did it?"

"You're as much to blame as I for . . . that."

"Hardly. I didn't ask to become involved in your life. In fact, I raised hell with Jim for turning you over to me. If I'd had my way, I would have washed my hands of you in Dallas. Why did you involve me, Kendall?"

"I had no choice, remember?" she shot back. "I tried sneaking out of the hospital, but you caught me and insisted on coming along."

"You had countless opportunities to ditch me before we got here. Every time I used the men's room, for instance. Why didn't you just drive away?"

"Because the more I thought about it, the more sense it made to keep you with us. Even though you were on crutches, you provided Kevin and me some protection."

"I wouldn't even touch him, wouldn't go near him."

"But I didn't realize that until we were here." She looked at him thoughtfully. "I've been curious about that. Why did you take such an instant dislike to Kevin?"

"Not to Kevin in particular. To all babies."

"Why?"

He gave a brusque shake of his head, indicating that the subject was off-limits. "Where are we, exactly? What's the name of that town?"

"Morton. We're in eastern Tennessee, near the North Carolina state line." She told him the history of the house. "No one except Grandmother and I ever came here. I knew this would be a good place to hide." She looked up at him and added earnestly, "John, I couldn't go back to South Carolina and testify against Gibb and Matt."

"The government needs your testimony to convict them."

She contradicted him with a strong shake of her head. "By now I'm sure Pepperdyne has found some files in my Denver apartment. I had a year to compile them. They're comprehensive. They contain a lot of incriminating information about key members of the Brotherhood. If the government can't convict them of murder, there are other felonies they can get them on. Just like when they nabbed Al Capone on tax evasion.

"I witnessed what they did, John, and there aren't words to describe the horror of it. Hours before he was executed, I spoke with Michael Li. He was a bright, gentle, mannerly

young man. When I think of the terror and agony they put
him through . . ."

She lowered her head and gazed sadly into near space.
Then she looked up at him again. "They've cost me everything, John. Thanks to them I became a fugitive, a criminal
in my own right. I can never practice law again. And I was
good," she stressed. Tears flowed from her eyes. "I believed
in what I was doing. I wanted to help people, wanted to make
a difference. They robbed me of the opportunity.

"Believe me, I want more than anyone to put these monsters
behind bars for the rest of their lives. I'm willing to do my
part as a good citizen, but I'm not willing to die for the cause."

She paused for emphasis and hugged her baby closer. "I
don't want Kevin to grow up an orphan as I did. And if I go
anywhere near Matt and Gibb, they'll find a way to kill me,
and it will be a brutal death."

John understood. Her responses were perfectly normal.
"They can't hurt you, Kendall," he said softly. "They're in
jail."

"Not any longer. They escaped three days ago."

John's first reaction was astonishment, then suspicion. Was
she lying? "How do you know?"

"Ricki Sue told me when I called her."

"When?"

"Today."

"That's why you were so upset when you got back from
town?"

She nodded. "I don't know any of the details because I
hung up right after she told me about their escape."

He plowed his fingers through his hair and took several
turns around the kitchen while trying to review the thousand
and one implications of the Burnwoods' being free. When he
came back around to Kendall, she was rebuttoning her blouse.
Kevin was asleep in the cradle of her arms.

"How far are we from your hometown? Sheridan, right?"

"About ninety miles."

"That close?"

"And they've been there." She told him about the FBI's aborted ambush in her grandmother's house. "The intruders weren't identified, but it was probably Matt and Gibb."

"No wonder you wanted to leave tonight. If I'd known they had escaped, I would have gotten us out of here days ago. As it is, there's—"

"Wait! What did you say?" Kendall slowly came to her feet. "You said that you would have gotten us out of here *days ago?*" Helplessly, he watched the changes in her expression as she assimilated the significance of his words.

"Then your memory . . . It didn't return just now. You've known . . ." She raised her hand to her mouth and caught a gasp. "You've known, and yet you . . . Damn you!" She struck him hard across the face. "How long have you known?"

He caught her wrist before she could hit him again. "Kendall, listen to me! We haven't got time to thrash this out now."

"Oh, I think we do, Dr. McGrath," she said with a sneer. "Why don't I lie down on the couch so you can practice a little more psychology on me? I'm a real case study, aren't I? You're just dying to open me up and find out what makes me tick. You're really into analysis, and you do your best work while I'm lying down!"

"To say nothing of how well *you* perform lying down!" he shouted.

"You bastard."

"Look, you're the one who wanted to play house with a man—a stranger—that you kidnapped. You're the one who made up the story that we were married. And, I might add, you were damn convincing. So don't blame me for responding like a husband."

He propped his crutch against the table, took her shoulders between his hands, and pulled her close, pressing Kevin between them. "All you can blame me for is acting out the role you wrote for me, Kendall."

"You played along to learn my secrets so you could use them against me. Tell your friend Pepperdyne about me. Discuss and analyze me. You manipulated me."

"No more than you manipulated me," he fired back.

"When did you get your memory back? Tell me. When?"

His fingers closed tighter around her arms. "Even now you don't realize how unsuitable I was to play the part of husband and daddy. But you were perfect in your role—the longsuffering wife, staying with her injured husband even though he had broken his marriage vows and cheated with another woman. You added just the right touch of martyrdom while holding out the promise of forgiveness and reconciliation.

"You were aloof but within reach. Modest but accessible. The sexy madonna no man can resist. Damn you, Kendall, you seduced me with the whole package, and you knew you were doing it. You made me want you. I wanted you to be mine. I wanted . . . wanted Kevin to be mine. It's the first time in my life that I've wanted that kind of oneness with anyone.

"See, I've never been any good at relationships. In fact, I've been lousy. I refused to let anyone get that close. But I think the amnesia changed me. Now that I know what it's like to need someone and to be needed, I don't want to go back to being the man I was."

His voice cracked, and, as though the speech had drained him, he rested his forehead against hers. "By sleeping with you I've violated God knows how many ordinances and rules and laws. When this is all over, they'll throw the book at me. I'll claim I was doing my duty the only way I saw fit under the circumstances, but I doubt they'll buy that."

He raised his head and looked deeply into her eyes. "I fooled you, yes, but no more than I tried fooling myself. Duty be damned. The only reason I made love to you every night was because I wanted to. No, I *had* to."

He doubted that she realized what a momentous statement that was. It was the closest he had ever come to professing his love to anyone.

Or maybe she did realize its import, because the fight had gone out of her, too. Gazing at him mistily, she reached up and touched his mouth. "I shamelessly manipulated you, yes. But I swear to you on Kevin's life that what happened between us was real."

They kissed, their mouths open and intimate. Even when they pulled apart, they continued to nuzzle. Against his lips, she murmured, "I love you, John, but I must protect Kevin. And you. And even though you'll never forgive me for this, that's still what I'm going to do."

Before he realized what was happening, she had whipped the pistol from his waistband and pushed him backward. He careened into the kitchen stove. Unbalanced, he slid to the floor, crying out in pain and outrage.

Kendall kicked the crutch out of his reach. "I'm sorry, John." She sobbed. "I'm sorry, but I can't let you take me back."

She fled through the screen door, which banged shut behind her.

The pain in his shin radiated up through his thigh and groin and belly and now seemed to be erupting out of the top of his head with volcanic impetus. He folded his arms around the injured leg and hugged it to his chest.

"Kendall," he called after her on a dry gasp of pain. Then louder, "Kendall!"

He didn't think for a minute that she would come running back. Therefore, he couldn't believe his ears when he heard the screen door creaking open.

He opened his eyes and blinked her into focus.

She had returned. But not alone. And not by choice.

Chapter Forty-four

ONE COULD SET HIS CLOCK BY ELMO CARNEY'S daily routine.

He got up every morning at 4:30, drank a cup of coffee, and then, rain or shine, sleet or heat, he went to the barn to milk his small herd of dairy cows. At 5:55 on the dot, he got into his pickup and drove the two miles into town to eat breakfast at the café, which opened at 6:00.

This had been Elmo's weekday routine since his wife's death. He resented Saturdays, when the café didn't open until seven, and Sundays, when, as soon as the milking was finished, he had to exchange his overalls for a jacket and tie and go to church. His stomach always growled during the service.

This morning began no differently from any other. He milked his cows, then struck out for town, having no premonition of what awaited him around the bend. He was lost in a daydream about soda biscuits and sausage gravy when the apparition materialized just beyond the grille of his truck.

Having emerged from the dusty bushes along the ditch, it planted itself dead center in the road and waved its arms high above its head.

Elmo practically stood up on the brake pedal and the

clutch. The tires grabbed for traction. The old brakes protested like arthritic joints. The truck skidded the final few yards and managed to stop only inches from the phantasm.

Elmo's heart was in his throat as he watched it run toward the passenger side of his pickup and open the door. "Thank God you came along, mister."

It climbed into the cab of his truck and slammed the door. "I've been waiting for hours," it complained. "Doesn't anybody live out here? And where the hell are we anyway? I've lived in Sheridan all my life, but I don't recall ever being out this way before. I sure as hell won't ever want to come back, that's for damn sure!"

It paused and looked at him, motioning toward the gear shift. "Well, what're you waiting on? Get the lead out, gramps. I've got to get to town p-r-o-n-t-o."

Stupefied, Elmo gawked, his hands frozen on the steering wheel. It walked, it talked. He could even smell it. But he still couldn't believe it was real.

"Great," it muttered in exasperation. "As if I haven't already been through enough, the person I flagged down turns out to be a dimwit. This has been a really shitty week."

It waved its hand in front of Elmo's glazed stare. "Yoo-hoo! Gramps? Anybody at home in there? Blink. Do something, for God's sake. What's with you? Haven't you ever seen a naked woman before? Or haven't you ever seen a natural redhead?"

Pepperdyne was awakened by a commotion in the squad room. An hour ago, he had finally surrendered to his exhaustion and lain down on the cot that the Sheridan PD had set up in the office for his use.

He hadn't thought he could fall asleep, and intended only to rest his eyes. But he must have slept soundly. Even though he had been abruptly awakened, he felt refreshed.

He sat up and swung his feet to the floor just as a policeman burst into the office. "Mr. Pepperdyne, you'd better come on out here."

"What's going on? Have they been found?"

"They" could have referred to any number of people, but Pepperdyne didn't specify as he followed the officer into the squad room where one cop was talking to a scrawny farmer in overalls and the others on duty were crowded around the windows that overlooked the front lawn of city hall.

"What the hell is going on?"

His angry roar captured everyone's attention, including that of the farmer, who approached him, obsequiously removing his dozer cap.

"You Mr. Pepperdyne?"

"That's right. Who're you?"

"Elmo Carney's the name. She told me to come in here and fetch Mr. Pepperdyne. Nobody else, she said. But I swear to you on my sainted wife's grave that I ain't did nothing improper or illegal.

"I's just on my way to have breakfast, and there she was, a-standing slap dab in the middle of the road, mother nekkid and a-waving her arms. Nearly gave me a heart attack. Climbed right into my truck, she did—"

"Excuse me. *Who?*"

"A redheaded lady. On the chubby side, she is. Said you'd—"

Pepperdyne didn't wait for more. He rushed toward the door. "Is she hurt?"

"Yes, sir, but like I said, *I* ain't did nothing to her."

"Somebody toss me a coat. A jacket. Something."

An officer rushed forward with a yellow rain slicker. Pepperdyne grabbed it and left the squad room at a run. He sprinted down the corridor, through the front door, and down the steps. He didn't stop until he reached the faded blue pickup parked at one of the parking meters.

"What took you so long?" Grumbling, Ricki Sue opened

the passenger door and yanked the slicker from his hand. "Those bozos have gotten themselves an eyeful." She shot a scornful glance up at the windows where several leering faces were still glued.

Pepperdyne followed the direction of her gaze. Under his baleful stare, the faces in the windows disappeared. Turning back to Ricki Sue, he couldn't much blame the men for gawking. Mother nekkid—as the farmer had said—she was a rather spectacular sight.

But once he got past the pure male reaction to seeing so much flesh on glorious display, his professionalism asserted itself. Simultaneously he noted several things. Her feet and legs were caked with mud. She had scratches and bruises all over her. Her pillar of hair had toppled. It now flowed over her bare shoulders and pendulous breasts, which were difficult to ignore even when scrutinizing them with professional detachment. The back of her head was matted with what appeared to be dried blood.

"You need a doctor," he said.

"It can wait. We've gotta talk."

"But you've been hurt."

"Pepperdyne, you're a freaking genius," she said sarcastically. She spread her arms wide, affording him another unrestricted view of her ample body. "I'm no raving beauty to start with. And I'm never at my best first thing in the morning. But I never look quite *this* bad. Of course I'm hurt, you jerk," she shouted. "They tried to kill me."

"The twins?"

"So your guys tattled."

"Yeah, my guys tattled."

"Does following people give you a hard-on, Pepperdyne? Is that your particular turn-on?"

"I had you followed for your own protection."

"Well, it didn't work, did it?"

"It would have if you hadn't picked up two strangers in a bar. In this day and age, how stupid can you get?"

"I didn't know . . ." Suddenly, her belligerence dissolved, her face crumpled, and she began to cry. "I didn't know they would hurt me."

He fumbled awkwardly in his pocket and produced a wrinkled handkerchief. She took it, asking, "Is this clean?"

"Your guess is as good as mine."

She didn't seem to care. She wiped her eyes and blew her nose. No longer crying, but still distraught, she pulled her lower lip through her teeth. Pepperdyne noticed that without the scarlet lipstick her mouth was much prettier.

"I could be dead," she said shakily. "They seriously tried to kill me."

"Who were they, Ricki Sue?"

"Henry and Luther. That's all I know." She told him about the motel, the liquor. "I came to as they were dragging me out of the car. I should have known then. . . . But I'd had so much to drink. Anyway, we waded into the creek. Next thing I know, Luther, I think, brings a club down on my head.

"I deflected the second blow, hooked my ankle around his and yanked him off his feet. They didn't expect me to fight back. And it was hard to do because my head was hurting like a son of a bitch. During the struggle, I almost blacked out several times. Anyway, I managed to keep myself from being brained."

"Where'd they go?"

"Go?" She gave a raucous laugh. "They didn't go anywhere. They're still out there. Or they were when I left. I knocked them both unconscious and tied them to trees with their own pants."

Pepperdyne began to laugh. It was inappropriate, he knew, but he couldn't help it. "Miss Robb, the Bureau could use a couple thousand of you."

She didn't share his mirth. Again she was gnawing her lip

in misery. "Not me, Pepperdyne. I'm afraid I didn't safeguard the secret any better than I did my virginity."

He sobered instantly. "What secret?"

"I think these look-alike assholes have something to do with the Burnwood matter."

"How so?"

"They were at my house asking for directions moments before I went in and discovered the break-in."

"And you didn't mention them to me?"

"I didn't link the two. And stop yelling at me. My head hurts."

"Last night, did they ask you about Mrs. Burnwood's whereabouts?"

"I'm still a little groggy, and the details are unclear, but I think they got me drunk so they could get information out of me. Maybe you should have tried that, Pepperdyne. Instead of relying strictly on your charm," she added caustically.

"Did they speak with anyone else? Make any phone calls?"

"No. Not that I saw, anyway."

"What did you tell them, Ricki Sue? I must know."

"Not so fast. If you find her, do you intend to put her in jail?"

"That won't be up to me."

Ricki Sue folded her arms over her midriff and assumed a stubborn posture. Pepperdyne gnawed on his inner cheek, thinking it over. "I'll do what I can for her."

"Not good enough, Pepperdyne. I don't want my friend locked away for trying to save her own skin."

"Okay, I'll do *everything* I can to strike a deal for her. That's all I can promise, and that's contingent on the condition John is in when we find him."

She assessed him for a moment, then said, "If she gets hurt, or the baby is harmed—"

"That's precisely what I'm trying to prevent. Their lives are my primary concern. Please. Talk to me, Ricki Sue."

"It'll cost you."

"Anything."

"Dinner and dancing?"

"You and me?"

"No, Fred and Ginger," she said, giving him a withering look.

He bobbed his head. "Agreed. Now talk."

Chapter Forty-five

*T*WO MEN USHERED KENDALL BACK INTO THE KIT-chen from which she had fled seconds earlier.

Matt snatched Kevin from her. Gibb gave the center of her back a hard shove that knocked her down. She practically fell on top of John.

"She's not going anywhere, Marshal McGrath. Y'all've got company." Gibb Burnwood smiled down at them pleasantly, as though this were another of those mornings when he dropped by uninvited to cook breakfast.

"Kendall, why don't you make some coffee? It's been a long, tedious night. I could certainly use some, and I'm sure Matt could, too."

He emanated a strong, evil aura. Had it always been there, and she just hadn't noticed it because she wasn't looking for it? Or had the corruption in his soul only recently manifested itself?

The light in his eyes was chilling. Remembering the nightmare of Michael Li's execution, she wanted to attack him, to scratch at those glacial eyes, but as long as Matt was holding Kevin, she couldn't risk taking that action. Indeed, she was powerless to do anything except exactly what she was told.

Fear had liquefied her muscles, but she pulled herself to her feet, and mechanically prepared a pot of coffee. While it was dripping into the carafe, Gibb sat in one of the kitchen chairs and laid a 30.06 deer rifle across his lap. He turned to John, who was still sitting on the floor.

"My name is Gibb Burnwood. We've never met, but there's been so much about you in the news lately, I feel like I know you. How do you do?"

John glared up at the older man. He couldn't have known that his silent refusal to acknowledge the polite introduction was to Gibb an insult of the highest caliber.

"I guess you're not too pleased to see us," her former father-in-law said tightly. "Although I can't understand why. In a very real sense, we've rescued you from my mentally unstable daughter-in-law. But it doesn't really matter whether you thank us or not. The more hostile you are, the easier it will be to kill you when the time comes."

He slapped his thighs as though a matter of importance had been satisfactorily settled. "Kendall, is the coffee ready?"

His conversational tone and friendly manner terrified her far more than if he had been ranting and drooling and tearing at his hair. Killers who exhibited the most self-control were usually those who killed without conscience or remorse.

Gibb appeared perfectly sane, but he had lost all connection to reality. Other members of the Brotherhood might have embraced the spiritual aspects of it only to salve their consciences for committing murder and hate crimes.

But Gibb believed in their creed, heart and soul. He had swallowed whole his own fanatic propaganda. He regarded himself as an entity apart from the rest of the human race.

He was deadly.

Kendall approached him with the steaming cup of coffee, wondering what would happen if she spilled it on him. He would react reflexively, leap from his chair. In the confusion, she could grab Kevin from Matt, and John could lunge at Gibb. She glanced at John. He was watching her. He knew what she was thinking.

But so did Gibb. Without even turning his head and looking at her, he said, "Kendall, I trust you not to do anything foolish." He turned and looked at her then. "You've been a disappointment in all respects save one—you're incredibly bright. Too bright, in fact. It would have been far better for you if you hadn't had a curious intellect. Don't disappoint me now by doing something stupid. Because if you do, I'll have to shoot your friend here."

"Go ahead and shoot him," she said, setting the cup of coffee on the table with a defiant thud. "He's no friend of mine. If I'd had a gun, I would have shot him myself."

She looked at John contemptuously. "He tricked me. He had amnesia following the car wreck, but he failed to tell me when he regained his memory. He's been trying to trip me up all this time."

John's crutch was still out of his reach, so he used a chair to pull himself off the floor.

"Dad?" Matt stepped forward, keeping a cautious eye on John.

Gibb held up his hand. "It's okay, son. He can't do anything."

John spoke for the first time. "That's right, Burnwood. I can't do anything. I haven't been able to do anything to defend myself since she kidnapped me," he said, sneering. "She brought me out here and pretended . . ."

He cut his eyes toward Matt and continued in an apologetic tone. "She pretended that I was her husband. I don't know why she did that when she could have ditched me here and kept running."

"She was waiting for the authorities to get tired of looking for her and turn their attention to something else," Gibb surmised.

"You're probably right," John conceded. "Anyway, I couldn't contradict anything she told me, because I had absolutely no memory. So I lived with her as her husband. In every sense of the word."

Angrily, Matt stepped forward, but again Gibb held up a restraining hand. "Marshal McGrath isn't to blame, Matthew. She is."

"That's right, Matt," John said. "I was only responding to the lies she told me. How was I to know we weren't married?"

"You knew," Kendall shouted. "You've known for a long time. You regained your memory, but—"

"But by then I was hooked," John said, interrupting her. He was still speaking directly to Matt. "I don't have to tell you, man, how good she is in bed. At least she was with me. Maybe motherhood got her juices flowing. Hormones or something, you know? But when I tell you she couldn't get enough—"

"You whoring tramp." Suddenly Matt turned and confronted Kendall. "Did you do your whoring in front of my son?"

"Most of the time he was in bed with us," John answered.

An angry sound boiled up from Matt's chest. Kendall had been following John's goading, wondering where it would lead, but neither she nor John was prepared for Matt's violent reaction.

He backhanded her hard across the face.

She hadn't seen it coming and took the full impact of the blow. Crying out, she fell forward, catching herself on the table. Matt raised his arm to hit her again, but John lunged for him, his hands going straight for Matt's throat.

"You maniac," he said with a snarl. "If you touch her again, I'll kill you."

John put all his strength into the fight, but it was no contest. Gibb picked up the crutch and swung it hard at John's back, whacking him in the kidneys. Kendall heard his groan of agony and watched his knees buckle. He landed on all fours, his head hanging between his shoulders.

Frightened by the commotion and loud voices, Kevin had begun to cry. Gibb took him from Matt and held him against his shoulder, talking baby talk to him as though this were a Sunday afternoon visit. But Kevin wasn't fooled by the sweet talk. He was screaming.

There was nothing Kendall could do for her child. Gibb wouldn't allow her to take him, so she knelt and placed her arms around John. "I'm sorry," she whispered directly into his ear. "I'm sorry."

If not for her and her lies, he wouldn't be here. He was going to die because of her. Gibb had promised as much. Their lives were going to end in this room, and they were helpless to do anything about it. But she wasn't going to let the Burnwoods see her cowed.

Blood was trickling down her chin as she raised her head and glared at Matt scornfully. She had called him her husband and carried his name, but he was much more a stranger to her than John was. Before she died, she wanted him to know how miserably he had failed as a husband and lover.

"During these past weeks I've known more fulfillment and love with this man than I ever knew while married to you."

"In the eyes of God, you're still my wife."

"You hypocrite." She sneered. "You divorced me."

"Because you deserted me."

"I ran away to protect myself and my baby."

"He's *my* baby."

"Some father you'd be, dividing your time between him, the Brotherhood, and your mistress!"

Matt's shoulders rose and fell on a harsh breath that sounded like a sob. "Lottie's dead."

To Kendall's speechless surprise, he covered his face with his hands and began to cry in racking sobs. Grimacing with pain, John managed to sit up and lean against a cupboard. He and Kendall exchanged glances. She could tell that he was as puzzled as she by Matt's emotional outburst.

"Son, stop that!" At first Matt didn't respond to Gibb's sharp command, so Gibb repeated it.

When Matt lowered his hands, his face was puffy and streaked with tears. "Why'd you have to kill her?"

Kendall gasped. Gibb had killed Lottie Lynam? When? Under what circumstances?

"You're bawling like a woman," Gibb said in rebuke. "It's unmanly and disgraceful. Stop it this instant."

"You didn't have to kill her."

"We talked about it, son, remember? She was the Devil's instrument. We did what we had to do. Service to God isn't accomplished without sacrifice."

"But I loved her." Matt's voice was raw from weeping. "She was . . . she was . . ."

"She was a cunt."

"Don't talk about her like that!" Matt shouted.

In the last few moments he had come apart emotionally and physically. His whole body was trembling. His skin had turned pasty and he sprayed spittle when he spoke. His eyes continued to stream with tears, and he seemed unaware that his nose was running. His disintegration was abhorrent to watch, but too fascinating to ignore.

"I loved her," he moaned miserably. "I did. I loved Lottie, and she loved me, and now she's gone. She was the only person who understood me."

"That's not true, son," Gibb said soothingly. "I understand you."

Then he swung the rifle toward Matt's chest and pulled the trigger.

The bullet exploded his heart; he was dead before his face could even register surprise. Gibb watched the body of his son drop to the floor, then calmly cradled the rifle in his arm again. Kevin lay screaming on his lap.

He addressed his horror-stricken spectators with perfect composure. "I did understand Matthew, you see. That woman had inflicted my son with a sickness. She had made him weak. Weakness cannot be tolerated, even in those we love." Devoid of emotion, he looked at Matt's corpse.

"In every other way, he was an ideal son. He was obedient.

A model member of the Brotherhood. He wrote what I told him to write, and he wrote it well. He had excellent hunting skills. He was a good fighter for the cause."

"Yeah, he was a prince," John said. "Very good at hitting a woman."

Gibb's icy eyes cut to him. "Don't waste your breath trying to provoke *me*, Marshal McGrath. Your taunts worked on my son, but they'll have no effect on me. Matthew couldn't tell when he was being manipulated. I can." He smiled. "But I admire you for trying."

Fixing his eyes on Kendall, he said, "Now, as for you, it doesn't matter a whit to me with whom you've set up housekeeping. All I'm interested in is this little fellow here."

He held Kevin up. He had been crying incessantly for the past several minutes, so loudly that they'd had to talk over the racket.

"He's a gutsy little cuss. The louder the cry, the stronger the boy. Look at those fists," Gibb said, chuckling with pride. "I'm going to make him into quite a man."

"Never," Kendall vowed.

Suddenly she was no longer afraid of him. Her courage was doomed to be short-lived. It sprang from her resignation to die. But she went with it because it was the only defense she had left against her nemesis.

There was even a smile on her lips when she said, "You won't have a chance to make Kevin into anything except an orphan. Because after you kill us, they'll find you, Gibb. An FBI agent named Jim Pepperdyne will hunt you down until he catches you.

"If you survive the capture, Kevin will be taken away from you, and you'll never see him again. I grieve that my son won't know me. But I thank God that he won't know you. You won't have an opportunity to indoctrinate him to your bigotry. You won't be around to twist his mind, steep him in hatred, and turn him into a cold-blooded monster like you.

"You failed with Matt, you know. Because in the end, he wasn't the heartless, mindless, obedient automaton you wanted him to be. He was a human being with all the frailties and emotions of the rest of us. He loved Lottie. Perhaps even more than he loved you. That's what you couldn't tolerate.

"And you'd fail with Kevin, too. Except you won't even have a chance with him. Kevin won't bear your name. Thank God he won't even know it."

"You sound exactly like my late wife," Gibb said. "Like you, Laurelann got curious about our expeditions into the woods at night and discovered the Brotherhood. Unfortunately, she wasn't blessed with the gift of understanding. She warned me about capture. She swore she would take Matthew away and that I'd never see him again, but her threats were as empty as yours." He nodded toward one of the chairs. "Sit down. My grandson needs his mother."

Torn between wanting desperately to take her son away from him, and wondering what sort of trap he was laying, Kendall hesitated. She was disinclined to move too far away from John, not knowing what Gibb's next move might be.

But maternal instinct won out. She came to her feet and took Kevin from Gibb. She clutched the baby to her chest and moved her hands over him, trying to touch as much of him as she could in the short time she had left. Kevin immediately stopped crying.

The change in the infant wasn't lost on Gibb. "I'm going to give you a choice, Kendall," he said. "Under the circumstances, I think I'm being much more generous than you deserve.

"It would only take a few days to wean the boy. At which time, you would be erased from his memory forever. He would become accustomed to me and would rely on me for everything. I could, and will, make him entirely mine.

"But unfortunately, at this stage in his development, he needs a mother. So you have a choice. You can either die now alongside your illicit lover, or you can come with me and tend to your child for a while longer.

"Either way, you'll pay with your life for your sins of treachery and fornication, but you'll have a little more time with the boy. I'm not making this offer because you deserve it, but because I want what's best for my grandson."

"Those are my choices?"

"I need your decision quickly. As clumsy as they are, it's possible that the FBI will also track you here."

"I'll go with you, Gibb, and I'll cooperate with you," she pledged. "I might even be an asset to you. As you know, I'm very good at disappearing. But let John live."

Gibb frowned. "I'm afraid his life isn't negotiable. He committed adultery with my son's wife. For that, he must die."

"I was no longer married to Matt. He had divorced me."

"Nevertheless. As Matt said, in the eyes of God—"

He aimed the rifle down at John.

"No, wait!" Kendall cried.

"Don't plead for my life with this son of a bitch," John said angrily. "I'd rather the bastard shoot me than have to beg."

"John didn't know I was married, or had been married. Remember, Gibb?" Kendall said urgently. "He had amnesia. I lied to him and told him he was my husband. It's my fault."

"But he recovered his memory," Gibb argued. "You said so yourself."

"I lied about that to defend myself against Matt. John didn't recover his memory until this morning."

"That's not true, Burnwood," John said. "I've known for more than a week who I was and who she was. I continued sleeping with her because I enjoyed it."

"He's lying, Gibb."

"Why would he lie?" Gibb asked her.

"To distract you in the hope of protecting Kevin and me. His sworn duty is to protect us. He'll do it, no matter what he has to say."

"You know what a liar she is, Burnwood," John said. "You'd be a fool to believe her."

"I'm not lying, Gibb. He woke up *this morning* with his memory restored. When he realized how I'd tricked him, he was furious. He intended to turn me over to the authorities for kidnapping him. I was running away when you arrived."

Her voice took on a pleading tone. "If you kill him, you'll be murdering an innocent man who was only carrying out his duty. You can relate to that, can't you? John abides by a code of honor similar to yours. He believes in what he does, and he doesn't let anything stop him from doing what he feels is right. Gibb, please. I swear I'm telling you the truth. He didn't know that in God's eyes I was still Matt's wife."

He pondered it, looking long and hard at John.

Finally he let out a heavy sigh. "Kendall, you're just no good at lying anymore. I don't believe a word of what you said. The man who made my son a cuckold must die."

He crooked his finger around the trigger, but a sudden and unexpected sound kept him from pulling it. If there was one sound Gibb recognized instantly, it was the click of a gun being cocked. He froze and cut his eyes toward Kendall.

"If you kill him, I'll pull this trigger." Kendall's voice was no longer thin and high with hysteria. It was low, level, and steely with resolve.

"My God," Gibb whispered. Some of the color drained from his ruddy face.

"That's right, Gibb. I'll protect Kevin from you, even if this is the only way I can do it. I'd rather see him dead than have him spend one minute in your company."

Kevin, exhausted from crying, had fallen asleep on the swell of her breast. His virtually translucent eyelids were closed, although a glistening tear still clung to his eyelashes. His lips were bowed and slightly parted.

The barrel of John's pistol rested against his temple.

When she had charged through the kitchen door, almost colliding with the Burnwoods, they had been as surprised as she. When they hustled her back inside, she had managed to slip the pistol into the pocket of her skirt, uncertain until this moment how she was going to use it.

Gibb had regained his composure. He was actually smiling over her theatrics. "You would never do it."

"Yes. I would."

"You love him too much, Kendall. Everything you've done so far—running to Denver, escaping the marshals, hiding here— has been to protect this baby."

"That's right. To protect him from *you*. If you shoot John—"

The blast startled her. She jumped out of her chair so quickly that it fell over backward and crashed to the floor.

"If I shoot John . . . what?" Gibb taunted.

Horrified, Kendall stumbled backward until she came up against the counter. She stared in disbelief at John's crumpled form. He had fallen on his side, his cheek against the floor. Blood was pooling beneath him.

"Well?" Gibb was standing and facing her now. He took a step forward. "Give me my grandson."

When she'd bolted from the chair, she had somehow managed to keep her hold on Kevin. Rudely awakened again, he was wailing. The pistol was now dead weight in her hand. It dangled lifelessly at the end of her arm at her side.

John hasn't moved. John's blood is all over the floor. John is dead. He killed John.

Gibb, with his keen hunter's instinct, smelled the imminent surrender of his prey. He closed in.

She raised her hand. It was trembling so violently, it appeared as though the pistol had a grip on her and she was trying to shake it off. "Don't make me do it, Gibb. Please."

"You would never kill your baby, Kendall."

"That's right. I would never kill my baby."

She turned the weapon on Gibb, and the small house echoed with a third gun blast.

Chapter Forty-six

"*JOHN!*"

Kendall leaped over Gibb's body and knelt beside John. "John? John?" She eased him onto his back.

"Is the son of a bitch dead?"

"Thank God you're alive." She bent down and hugged him close, squashing Kevin between them. "Thank God! I thought he had killed you."

"Is he *dead*?"

She glanced at the body. Gibbons Burnwood was unquestionably dead. "Yes."

"Good."

She could have laughed with relief that he was able to talk, except that she was crying too hard. "Oh, John, look at you. You're badly hurt."

"I'm okay." But he wasn't. Each word was spoken on a feeble hiss. "How's the baby? Is he okay? Was he hurt?"

Kevin was squalling louder than ever. "He's had a rough morning."

John smiled through his pain. "Haven't we all?"

By now the house was swarming with FBI agents. Pepperdyne, in full assault gear like the rest of them, stomped in. He took one look at John, swore lavishly, then poked his fingers in his mouth and whistled shrilly. "Get those paramedics in here. On the double."

"What took you so goddamn long?" John asked querulously as his friend crouched beside him. "I thought I would bleed to death before you struck. First, your approach was about as stealthy as a buffalo stampede, then you sat on your asses out there, scratching your balls, and let that bastard shoot me."

Pepperdyne pushed back his helmet and laughed. "No need to thank us, John. We know you're grateful."

Kendall was confused. "You knew they were out there, John?"

He nodded. "I saw motion through the screen and knew—hoped—what it meant. That's why I was doing everything I could to keep the Burnwoods occupied."

"You shouldn't have attacked Matt. They could have killed you right then."

"I didn't think about it. When he hit you . . . For a lot of reasons, I wish I'd killed him myself."

They exchanged a long, meaningful look that lasted until a paramedic slid an IV needle into his arm. "Ouch! Shit! That hurts."

"Which one of you is going to fill in the gaps for me?" Pepperdyne asked. "I want to know exactly what went down."

Kendall watched medical personnel futilely check Matt's body for vital signs. She couldn't feel grief over the death of her former husband, but she did feel sorrow for his misguided life. "Gibb shot Matt."

"We saw that," Pepperdyne said. "Was it because of Mrs. Lynam?"

"Yes. Matt said Gibb had killed her."

"She was found in a motel room with her throat cut," Pepperdyne told them.

"Matt really loved her," Kendall said sadly. "He never had a chance for a happy life. Not with Gibb as his father."

"One of our sharpshooters would have taken out the old man when he shot Matt," Pepperdyne explained, "except that he was holding the baby. It was too risky."

"You had him in your sights all that time?" Kendall asked.

"Yeah. Then when you sat down in that chair with the baby," he said, pointing, "you were in the line of fire. After he shot John—"

"No big deal," John muttered as the paramedics lifted him onto a stretcher.

Pepperdyne told him to stop his whining, but it was apparent to Kendall that the two old friends were glad to be exchanging insults and jibes.

Pepperdyne picked up his explanation. "After Burnwood shot John, you moved to the counter," he said to Kendall. "We hoped that holding that pistol to your baby's head was a bluff."

"Of course it was, and Gibb knew it. But I suddenly realized that after he shot John, he had laid the rifle on the table. He was no longer armed. I turned John's gun on him and would have shot him."

"Except that our guy got off a clean shot first. Straight through the head."

The sight of Gibb's head exploding was a horrible memory that would remain with Kendall for a long time. She shivered and held Kevin closer against her.

"How'd you get John's weapon?" Pepperdyne asked.

She glanced at John.

"I gave it to her," he lied.

"Yes," she agreed quickly. "He gave it to me for safe-keeping."

"Why'd you place your weapon into her safekeeping?" the agent wanted to know. "Come to think of it, you're supposed to have amnesia! In all the excitement, I forgot about that. No pun intended. When did you recover your memory?"

"Give us a break, Jim," John said, groaning. "Kendall can give you her statement later. Right now she needs to see to the baby, and I guess I'm due a few stitches."

Pepperdyne cleared a path for them and stood by while John was moved to one of the waiting ambulances. "Will you be all right?" Kendall asked anxiously.

"I'll be fine," he assured her. He patted Kevin on the bottom. "Will *he* be all right?"

"He won't remember it."

"I'll never forget it," he said softly. "None of it."

The paramedics folded up the legs of the gurney and placed it in the ambulance. She and John maintained eye contact even as the doors were closing, then she watched the ambulance until it turned off the lane onto the road.

"Mrs. Burnwood." Pepperdyne touched her arm. "My car's over here, waiting to take you back to town."

"Thank you."

He sat with her in the backseat while another agent drove. "John's tough. He'll make it."

She gave a little smile. "I know."

"You know that he's tough, or that he'll make it?"

"Both."

"Hmm. He seems to have taken a real shine to your baby." He nodded down at Kevin. "I never thought I'd see John so comfortable around a kid."

"Why?"

He told her what had happened in New Mexico. "He still blames himself."

"Yes. He would," she said, nodding wistfully. "He takes his responsibilities seriously."

"He ODs on responsibility. Daily. When he's had time to think about it, I'm sure he'll bear the guilt of Ruthie Fordham's death, too."

"I hope not. That would be awful for him."

Pepperdyne said nothing, although he was looking at her curiously. "I'm afraid it's my duty to remind you that you're still a material witness in the custody of the Department of Justice."

"I'll testify to what I saw that night in the woods outside Prosper, Mr. Pepperdyne."

"Those files you had in your place in Denver have already proved invaluable to us in preparing our cases."

"I'm glad. The Brotherhood must be exterminated with no more mercy than they showed their victims. I'll help in any way I can to see that all the members are brought to justice. No matter what it costs me personally."

He nodded, and gazed out the window for a moment. "Then there's this other matter of abducting a federal officer."

"That's right. I did."

"Hmm. Well, the government takes a dim view of that."

Looking him straight in the eye, she said, "I was desperately afraid of my ex-husband and father-in-law, and as we now know, my fear was justified.

"I thought the only way I could protect myself and Kevin was to disappear and remain hidden for the rest of our lives. I don't regret doing what I did. If necessary, I would do it again, except that I wouldn't involve John. I endangered his life, and I'll never forgive myself for that."

"He was performing his duty."

"Yes. His duty."

"Mrs. Burnwood, at what point did he recover his memory?"

"I wish I knew that myself, but I don't," she replied honestly.

"Mrs. Burnwood—"

"I hate that name. Please don't call me Mrs. Burnwood anymore."

Pepperdyne gave her a stern look. "Then what should I call you?"

* * *

"They're the Crooks."

"I'll say," Ricki Sue said. She was holding Kevin on her lap, letting him gnaw on her strand of purple beads. "Those bastards tried to kill me. Calling them crooks is putting it mildly."

"No, that's their name," Kendall explained.

She looked from the mug shots to Pepperdyne, who had asked her if she could identify the two men now residing in the Sheridan jail. They had been found where Ricki Sue had directed officers to look, bound to trees, naked, and lumpy with mosquito bites.

"Henry and Luther." She told them about the Billy Joe Crook fiasco. "His family held a grudge against me, so I guess they thought they would get in on the chase and try to find me before Matt and Gibb did."

"Thanks to me, they almost succeeded." Ricki Sue's eyes filled with tears. "Every time I think of what could have happened, all because I got drunk and blabbed my big mouth."

Kendall reached across Pepperdyne's littered desk and gave Ricki Sue's arm an affectionate squeeze.

"On the contrary. If it weren't for you, Agent Pepperdyne and his men wouldn't have arrived in time. Until they got there, John . . . Dr. McGrath played them perfectly," she finished huskily.

John, who had refused to stay longer than one night in the hospital, was standing propped on his crutch, ghostly pale, with the fresh scar on his temple, his broken right leg still in a cast, and his left arm in a sling. The bullet from Gibb's rifle had entered his shoulder and exited his back. It had missed a major artery by only a hair. Every time Kendall thought of how close he had come to dying, her throat constricted.

Pepperdyne cleared his throat noisily to break an emotionally wrought silence. "The government is willing to offer you immunity from any charges, in exchange for your testimony against the members of the Brotherhood."

"That's awfully generous," she remarked.

"Well, kidnapping would be a difficult charge to prove when the kidnap victim refuses to say at exactly what point he became a willing participant." Pepperdyne shot John a retiring glance.

"I don't remember," he said blandly.

"Very funny." Pepperdyne closed the folder and stood to conclude the meeting. "Thank you, Miss Robb, for your assistance."

"Don't think you can kiss me off so easily, Pepperdyne," Ricki Sue said. "You'll be in South Carolina for the trials, won't you?"

"In and out."

"I'll be around, too." She flashed him a grin. "I've been invited to go along and help take care of Kevin while Kendall's in court."

"I see."

"Well, you don't have to look so glum about it. And anyway, don't forget you owe me a night out."

"How could I possibly forget when you remind me of it every fifteen minutes?"

Suddenly the office door was flung open and a young man barged in.

Kendall blanched.

Ricki Sue groaned. "Oh, no. Now the shit's really gonna hit the fan."

The young man looked from one of the women to the other. "Hey, y'all."

"Hi."

"Hi."

"How're y'all?"

"Fine."

"Fine."

"Who's this guy?" John asked.

"Who's in charge?" the newcomer asked.

Pepperdyne stepped forward. "I am."

"What the hell is going on? I don't get it. Why am I here? I thought I was off the hook."

"Calm down," Pepperdyne said to him.

"Calm down, my ass! There I am minding my own business, having a plate of pasta in my apartment in sunny Roma, and these two goons show up and identify themselves as U.S. marshals. Next thing I know, I'm on an airplane, bound for the States, compliments of Uncle Sam."

Showing his indignation, he planted his hands on his hips and demanded of the group at large, "What gives?"

"I believe everyone here knows everyone else, except for John." Turning toward his friend, Pepperdyne said, "Dr. John McGrath, meet Kendall Deaton."

Chapter Forty-seven

"*I*T'S RATHER DIFFICULT TO EXPLAIN."

"Try."

She and John were alone in the office. Ricki Sue had taken the real Kendall Deaton by the hand and dragged him from the office. He was still sputtering demands for a full explanation, which she promised to give him if only he'd shut his trap and let her get a word in edgewise. Pepperdyne and the two marshals had followed them out.

"Kendall was a lawyer at Bristol and Mathers," she began. "He got into trouble with the partners when the D.A.'s office accused him of tampering with evidence. The allegation was never substantiated, although it was generally believed that he was probably guilty of some malfeasance. No charges were filed, but he was dismissed from the firm.

"For months afterward, he sent out résumés, but no other firm was interested in hiring someone with a tainted record. Kendall became discouraged and decided to go to Europe for a while. He asked me to forward his mail.

"A few months after his departure, he received a letter from Prosper County, South Carolina. Because it looked like a response to his résumé, I forwarded the letter to him immediately. He called to thank me, said it was indeed a job offer, but that he wasn't interested in pursuing it. He was living a swinging bachelor's life in Rome, working as a consultant to a marketing firm, and loving it. That's when I decided to go for it."

She looked at him, hoping to see understanding in his expression, but he remained impassive. "I had graduated third in my class from law school, John. I was the most promising new lawyer at Bristol and Mathers, but I was given grunt work. I didn't feel a spark of interest, or challenged in any way, until the case I told you about, the woman with AIDS who was desperate for my help.

"That's when I knew that I didn't belong in a large, revenue-oriented firm. I wanted to help people. I wanted justice for the down-and-outers. So I began sending out queries to states that use the public defender system, but received no encouraging replies. When Kendall declined the opportunity in Prosper, it seemed like a . . . a sign.

"Grandmother and Ricki Sue thought I was crazy, of course, but I wrote back passing myself off as Kendall. It's incredibly easy to assume another name, although I now know why Prosper County hired Kendall Deaton without conducting a more thorough personnel check," she added wryly.

"They wanted a corruptible public defender," John said.

"Exactly. The blot on his record appealed to them. *He* was just what they were looking for. Their initial reaction to me as a woman was negative. But I suppose that after further consideration, they decided a female would be even more malleable. Or maybe more vulnerable."

After a reflective moment, she continued. "Maybe my motives for becoming a P.D. weren't as altruistic as I would like everyone to believe. As *I* would like to believe. Maybe my goody-two-shoes ambition was based on pride. I wanted to show off, show everybody how smart I was. I wanted to please my parents, which your insightful comments helped me to see is impossible.

"Anyway, maybe the opportunity was taken away from me because my motives weren't as selfless as I claimed. Grandmother warned me that nothing good could come from a lie, and she was right."

She sat down on the corner of Pepperdyne's desk. Kevin was sleeping in his infant carrier. She heard John approaching her in what was now a familiar tread, with the bump of the rubber stopper of his crutch preceding each footstep.

He moved up behind her, reached around, and gave the infant carrier a push so it would rock gently. He stroked Kevin's cheek. Her heart melted at the sight of his tan, masculine finger against the smoothness of the baby's skin, not only because it demonstrated his affection for Kevin, but because it meant that he had slain his own dragon.

He said, "You knew that when the authorities discovered your false identity, you wouldn't have any credibility with either them or a jury."

"Who would believe such a tall tale coming from someone who's life was a fabrication? I had no choice except to run and find a hiding place. First in Denver, then . . ." Glancing over her shoulder at him, she whispered, "With you."

He drew her up to stand facing him. He ran his fingers through her short, cropped hair. His eyes roved over her face. Then, with an almost violent motion, he pulled her against him and held her tightly.

"They could have killed you," he said fiercely. "I thought I was going to watch you die."

Wrapping her arms around him, she buried her face in his neck. "What if you had died because of me, John? What if you had died?"

For a long moment they clung to each other. Finally he set her away. "Don't blame yourself for what happened to me."

"If you won't blame yourself for Marshal Fordham's death."

He frowned. "That's tough. We'll work on it together."

"Together?"

"I think the three of us might have a shot at making this family thing work. What do you think?"

"I think Kevin and I need you. And you need us." She stroked his face, lightly touched the scar from which she had removed the stitches. "I have absolutely nothing to gain by lying, so you know this is the truth. I love you, John."

"I love you, too." Clearing his throat of unprecedented emotion, he said, "It would be nice to know your name."

"I'll tell you my name if you'll tell me at what point your memory came back."

Slowly, a smile stretched across his face. He lowered his mouth to hers for a deep, sexy kiss. She could easily have become lost in it, but she angled her head back and looked up at him.

"Well, John?"

Still smiling, he kissed her again.

**If you enjoyed *The Witness*, you'll love
Sandra Brown's suspenseful new thriller
with a feisty female at its heart**

Seeing Red

Now available from Hodder & Stoughton

Read on for the first chapter . . .

Chapter 1

Six days earlier

Trapper was in a virtual coma when the knocking started.

"Bloody hell," he mumbled into the throw pillow beneath his head. His face would bear the imprint of the upholstery when he got up. *If* he got up. Right now, he had no intention of moving, not even to open his eyes.

The knocking might have been part of a dream. Maybe a construction worker somewhere in the building was tapping the walls in search of studs. An urban woodpecker? Whatever. If he ignored the noise, maybe it would go away.

But after fifteen seconds of blessed silence, there came another *knock-knock*. Trapper croaked, "I'm closed. Come back later."

The next three knocks were insistent.

Swearing, he rolled onto his back, sailed the drool-damp pillow across the office, and laid his forearm over his eyes to block the daylight. The window blinds were only partially open, but those cheerful, skinny strips of sunshine made his eyeballs throb.

Keeping one eye closed, he eased his feet off the sofa and onto the floor. When he stood, he stumbled over his discarded boots. His big toe sent his cell phone sliding across the floor and underneath a chair. If he bent down that far, he doubted his ability to return upright, so he left his phone where it was.

It wasn't like it rang all that often anyway.

Holding the heel of his hand against his pounding temple, and with one eye remaining closed, he managed to reach the other side of his office without bumping into the bottom drawer of the metal file cabinet. For no reason he could remember, it was standing open.

Through the frosted glass upper half of the door, he made out a form just as it raised its fist to knock again. To prevent the further agony that would induce, Trapper flipped the lock and opened the door a crack.

He sized her up within two seconds. "You've got the wrong office. One flight up. First door to the right off the elevator."

He was about to shut the door when she said, "John Trapper?"

Shit. Had he forgotten an appointment? He scratched the top of his head, where his hair hurt down to the follicles. "What time is it?"

"Twelve fifteen."

"What day?"

She took a breath and let it out slowly. "Monday."

He looked her up and down and came back to her face. "Who are you?"

"Kerra Bailey."

The name didn't ring any bells, but it would be hard to hear them over the jackhammer inside his skull. "Look, if it's about the parking meter—"

"The one in front of the building? The one that's been flattened?"

"I'll pay to have it replaced. I'll cover any other damages. I would have left a note to that effect, but I didn't have anything on me to write—"

"I'm not here about the parking meter."

"Oh. Hmm. Did we have an appointment?"

"No."

"Well, now's not a good time for me, Ms...." He went blank.

"Bailey." She said that in the same impatient tone in which she'd said *Monday*.

"Right. Ms. Bailey. Call me, and we'll schedule—"

"It's important that I talk to you sooner rather than later. May I come in?" She gestured at the door, which Trapper had kept open only a few inches.

A woman who looked like her, he hated turning down for anything. But, hell. His head felt as dense as a bowling ball. His shirt was unbuttoned, the tail hanging loose. He hoped his fly was zipped, but in case it wasn't, he didn't risk calling attention to it by checking. His breath would stop a clock.

He glanced behind him at the disarray: suit jacket and tie slung over the back of a chair; boots in front of the sofa, one upright, the other lying on its side; one black sock draped over the armrest, the other sock God only knew where; an empty Dom bottle precariously close to rolling off the corner of his desk.

He needed a shower. He really needed to pee.

But he also really, *really* needed clients, and she had "money" written all over her. Her handbag, literally so. It was the size of a small suitcase and covered in designer initials. Even if she had been looking for the tax attorney on the next floor up, she would have been slumming.

Besides, when had he ever been known to say no to a lady in distress?

He stepped back and opened the door, motioning her toward the two straight chairs facing his desk. He kicked the file cabinet drawer shut with his heel and still got to his desk ahead of her in time to relocate an empty but smelly Chinese food carton and the latest issue of *Maxim*. He'd ranked the cover shot among his top ten faves, but she might take exception to that much areola.

She sat in one chair and placed her bag in the other. As he rounded the desk, he buttoned the middle button of his shirt and ran a hand across his mouth and chin to check for remaining drool.

As he dropped into his desk chair, he caught her looking at the gravity-defying champagne bottle. He rescued it from the corner of the desk and set it gently in the trash can to avoid a clatter. "Buddy of mine got married."

"Last night?"

"Saturday afternoon."

Her eyebrow arched. "It must have been some wedding."

He shrugged, then leaned back in his chair. "Who recommended me?"

"No one. I got the address off your website."

Trapper had forgotten he even had one. He'd paid a college kid seventy-five bucks to do whatever it was you do to get a website online. That was the last he'd thought of it. This was the first client it had yielded.

She looked like she could afford much better.

"I apologize for showing up without an appointment," she said. "I tried calling you several times this morning, but kept getting your voice mail."

Trapper shot a look toward the chair his phone had slid underneath. "I silenced my phone for the wedding. Guess I forgot to turn it back on." As discreetly as possible, he shifted in his chair in a vain attempt to give his bladder some breathing room.

"Well, it's sooner rather than later, Ms. Bailey. You said it was important, but not important enough for you to make an appointment. What can I do for you?"

"I'd like for you to intervene on my behalf and convince your father to grant me an interview."

He would have said *Come again?* or *Pardon?* or *I didn't quite catch that*, but she had articulated perfectly, so what he said was, "Is this a fucking joke?"

"No."

"Seriously, who put you up to this?"

"No one, Mr. Trapper."

"Just plain Trapper is fine, but it doesn't matter what you call me because we don't have anything else to say to each other." He stood up and headed for the door.

"You haven't even heard me out."

"Yeah. I have. Now if you'll excuse me, I gotta take a piss and then I've got a hangover to sleep off. Close the door on your way out. This neighborhood, I hope your car's still there when you get back to it."

He stalked out in bare feet and went down the drab hallway to the men's room. He used the urinal then went over to the sink and looked at himself in the cloudy, cracked mirror above it. A pile of dog shit had nothing on him.

He bent down and scooped tap water into his mouth until his thirst was no longer raging, then ducked his head under the faucet. He shook water from his hair and dried his face with paper towels. With one more nod toward respectability, he buttoned his shirt as he was walking back to his office.

She was still there. Which didn't come as that much of a surprise. She looked the type that didn't give up easily.

Before he could order her out, she said, "Why would you object to The Major giving an interview?"

"It's no skin off my nose, but he won't do it, and I think you already know that or you wouldn't have come to me, because I'm the last person on the planet who could convince him to do anything."

"Why is that?"

He recognized that cleverly laid trap for what it was and didn't step into it. "Let me guess. I'm your last resort?" Her expression was as good as an admission. "Before coming to me, how many times did you ask The Major yourself?"

"I've called him thirteen times."

"How many times did he hang up on you?"

"Thirteen."

"Rude bastard."

Under her breath, she said, "It must be a family trait."

Trapper only smiled. "It's the only one he and I have in common." He studied her for a moment. "You get points for tenacity. Most give up long before thirteen attempts. Who do you work for?"

"A network O and O—owned and operated—in Dallas."

"You're on TV? In Dallas?"

"I do feature stories. Human interest, things like that. Occasionally one makes it to the network's Sunday evening news show."

Trapper was familiar with the program, but he didn't remember ever having watched it.

He knew for certain that he'd never seen her, not even on the local station, or he would've remembered. She had straight, sleek light brown hair with blonder streaks close to her face. Brown eyes as large as a doe's. One inch below the outside corner of the left one was a beauty mark the same dark chocolate color as her irises. Her complexion was creamy, her lips plump and pink, and he was reluctant to pull his gaze away from them.

But he did. "Sorry, but you drove over here for nothing."

"Mr. Trapper—"

"You're wasting your time. The Major retired from public life years ago."

"Three to be exact. And he didn't merely retire. He went into seclusion. Why do you think he did that?"

"My guess is that he got sick of talking about it."

"What about you?"

"I was sick of it long before that."

"How old were you?"

"At the time of the bombing? Eleven. Fifth grade."

"Your father's sudden celebrity must have affected you."

"Not really."

She watched him for a moment, then said softly, "That's impossible. It had to have impacted your life as dramatically as it did his."

He squinted one eye. "You know what this sounds like? Leading questions, like you're trying to interview *me*. In which case, you're SOL because I'm not going to talk about The Major, or me, or my life. Ever. Not to anybody."

She reached into the oversize bag and took out an eight-by-ten reproduction of a photograph, laid it on the desk, and pushed it toward him.

Without even glancing down at it, he pushed it back. "I've seen it." For the second time, he stood up, went to the door and opened it, stood there with hands on hips, waiting.

She hesitated, then sighed with resignation, hiked the strap of her bag onto her shoulder, and joined him at the door. "I caught you at a bad time."

"No, this is about as good as I get."

"Would you consider meeting me later, after you've had time to..." She made a gesture that encompassed his sorry state. "To feel better. I could outline what I want to do. We could talk about it over dinner."

"Nothing to talk about."

"I'm paying."

He shook his head. "Thanks anyway."

She gnawed the inside of her cheek as though trying to determine which tactic to use to try to persuade him. He could offer some salacious suggestions, but she probably wouldn't go that far, and even if she did, afterward he'd still say no to her request.

She took a look around the office before coming back to him. With the tip of her index finger, she underlined the words stenciled on the frosted glass of the door. "Private Investigator."

"So it says."

"Your profession is to investigate things, solve mysteries."

He snuffled. That was his former profession. Nowadays, he was retained by tearful wives wanting him to confirm that their husbands were screwing around. If he managed to get pictures, it doubled his fee. Distraught parents paid him to track down runaway teens, whom he usually found exchanging alleyway blowjobs for heroin.

He wouldn't call the work he was doing mystery-solving. Or investigation, for that matter.

But to her, he said, "Fort Worth's own Sherlock Holmes."

"Are you state licensed?"

"Oh, yeah. I have a gun, bullets, everything."

"Do you have a magnifying glass?"

The question baffled him because she hadn't asked it in jest. She was serious. "What for?"

Those pouty pink lips fashioned an enigmatic smile, and she whispered, "Figure it out."

Keeping her eyes on his, she reached into an inside pocket of her bag and withdrew a business card. She didn't hand it to him, but stuck it in a crack between the frosted glass pane and the door frame, adjacent to the words that spelled out his job description.

"When you change your mind, my cell number is on the card."

Hell would freeze over first.

Trapper slammed the office door behind her, plucked the business card from the slit, and flipped it straight into the trash can.

Eager to go home and sleep off the remainder of his hangover in a more comfortable surrounding, he snatched up the sock on the armrest of the sofa and went in search of the other.

After several frustrating minutes and a litany of elaborate profanity, he found it inside one of his boots. He pulled on his socks but decided he needed an aspirin before he finished dressing. Padding over to his desk, he opened the lap drawer in the hope of discovering a forgotten bottle of analgesics.

That damned photograph was there in plain sight where he couldn't miss it.

But whether looking at it, or acknowledging it in any manner, or even denying its existence, he was never truly free of it. He had lied to Kerra Bailey. His life was never the same after that photograph went global twenty-five years ago.

Trapper plopped down into his desk chair and looked at the cursed thing. His head hurt, his eyes were scratchy, his throat and mouth were still parched. But even realizing that it was masochistic, he reached across the desk and slid the photo closer to him.

Everyone in the entire world had seen it at least once over the past quarter century. Among prize-winning, defining-moment editorial photographs, it ranked right up there with the raising of the flag on Iwo Jima, the sailor kissing the nurse in Times Square on V-E Day, the naked Vietnamese girl running from napalm, the twin towers of the World Trade center aflame and crumbling.

But before 9/11, there was the Pegasus Hotel bombing in downtown Dallas. It had rocked a city still trying to live down the Kennedy assassination, had destroyed a landmark building, had snuffed out the lives of 197 people. Half that number had been critically injured.

Major Franklin Trapper had led a handful of struggling survivors out of the smoldering rubble to safety.

A photographer who worked for one of Dallas's newspapers had been eating a Danish at his desk in the city room when the first bombs detonated. The blast deafened him. The concussion shook his building and created cracks in the aggregate floor beneath his desk. Windows shattered.

But like an old fire horse, he was conditioned to run toward a disaster. He snatched up his camera, bolted down three flights of fire stairs, and, upon exiting the newspaper building, dashed toward the source of the black plume of smoke that had already engulfed the skyline.

He reached the scene of terror and chaos ahead of emergency responders and began snapping pictures, including the one that became iconic: Franklin Trapper, recently retired from the U.S. Army, emerging from the smoking building leading a pathetic group of dazed, scorched, bleeding, choking people, one child cradled in his arms, a woman holding onto his coattail, a man whose tibia had a compound fracture using him as a crutch.

The photographer, now deceased, had won a Pulitzer for his picture. The act of heroism he had captured on film immediately earned him and the photo immortality.

And, as Trapper well knew, immortality lasted for fucking ever.

The story behind the photograph and the people in it wouldn't come to light until later, when those who were hospitalized were able to relate their individual accounts.

Though, by the time the tales were told, the Trappers' front yard in suburban Dallas had become an encampment for media. The Major—as he came to be known—had been ordained a national symbol of bravery and self-sacrifice. For years following that day in 1992, he was a sought-after public speaker. He was given every honor and award there was to be bestowed, and many were initiated and named for him. He was invited to the White House by every subsequent administration. At state dinners he was introduced to visiting foreign dignitaries who paid homage to his courage.

Over time, new disasters produced new heroes. The fireman carrying the toddler from the Oklahoma City bombing overshadowed The Major's celebrity for a time, but soon he was back on TV talk show guest lists and the after-dinner speaker's circuit. September eleventh gave him a new slant to address: his random act of heroism compared to those performed every day by unsung heroes. For more than two decades he kept his story timely and relevant.

Then three years ago, he stopped cold turkey.

He now lived very privately, avoiding the limelight and refusing requests for public appearances and interviews.

But his legend lived on. Which was why journalists, biographers, and movie producers emerged now and again, seeking time with him to make their particular pitch. He never granted them that time.

Until today none had ever sought out Trapper's help to gain access to his famous father.

Kerra Bailey's audacity was galling enough. But damn her for snagging his interest with that remark about the magnifying glass. What could he possibly see in that photograph that he hadn't seen ten thousand times?

He longed for a hot shower, an aspirin, his bed and soft pillow.

"Screw it." He opened his desk's lap drawer and, instead of reaching for the bottle of Bayer, searched all the way to the back of it and came up with the long-forgotten magnifying glass.

Four hours later, he was still in his desk chair, still reeking, head still aching, eyes still scratchy. But everything else had changed.

He set down the magnifier, pushed the fingers of both hands up through his hair, and held his head between his palms. "Son of a bitch."